DAVID GEE

Originally earmarked for the Methodist Mission Field, David Gee discovered that the 'missionary position' didn't suit him. He has worked in London and the Middle East in telecommunications and journalism. He now lives on his native Sussex South Downs with two rescue-centre dogs, a greyhound called George and a lurcher called Mildred.

He blogs at www.davidgeebooks.blogspot.com

THE DROPOUT

David Gee

Matador
9 Priory Business Park,
Wistow Road, Kibworth Beauchamp,
Leicestershire. LE8 0RX
Tel: (+44) 116 279 2299
Fax: (+44) 116 279 2277
Email: books@troubador.co.uk
Web: www.troubador.co.uk/matador

ISBN 978 1780883 090

British Library Cataloguing in Publication Data.
A catalogue record for this book is available from the British Library.

Matador is an imprint of Troubador Publishing Ltd

For P.S.H. and J.R.

'Sunt lacrimae rerum'

('Life's a bitch')

Virgil

Contents

Part One

1. Campus life – and death   11
2. The single-parent diet   18
3. Home is the sailor   31
4. 30k per annum   41
5. Production line   50
6. Knickerbocker glory   61
7. Pinky and perky   72
8. On the road   81
9. *Les sofa-beds*   89
10. Shock and Awe   98
11. Football and porno   114
12. Family life – and death   122

Part Two

13. The Dropout's Mother's Tale   125
14. The Leather Merchant's Tale   139
15. The Wife of Boredom's Tale   164
16. The Mistress's Tale   206
17. The Factotum's Tale   254

Part Three

18. Clinic   291
19. Bayswater   298

Part One

1. Campus life – and death

Meredith dumped me at about 9.15 p.m. on a brutally cold Thursday towards the end of February. She said a lot of things, but what it boiled down to was she was fed up with me trying to get into her panties. It was true. I'd tried for four months. And on Thursday, for a couple of seconds, I got there.

Neil fell from Founder's Tower in a hard sleety rain at noon on Friday. I was twenty metres from where he landed. It's possible *he* was fed up with me not letting him into *my* pants. On Wednesday he'd surprised me with a kiss. Another guy might have knocked him down for that. I'm not sure why I didn't.

By Monday morning I knew that whatever it was I was looking for (a shag mostly, though not a gay one) it wasn't Higher Education. I skipped a tutorial and became the faculty's tenth dropout of the year. As a sabbatical student Meredith wouldn't count; neither did Neil, who'd dropped out in a more literal way than either of us. Abandoning textbooks and the posters of *Silence of the Lambs* and the Hale-Bopp comet which supposedly infused my spartan room in Hall with the aura of a cosmic and dangerous intelligence, I packed only my clothes, my laptop and CDs. There was no one left that I needed to say goodbye to. A taxi took me to the mainline station where I caught a late-afternoon train to London.

At no time in my life would I again possess so much pure knowledge nor, it seemed, know so little. My erudition, such as it was, was in the fields of English Literature and military history from Kaiser Bill to Osama bin Laden. Recent events in the Middle East and elsewhere suggest that my parents' and grandparents' generations scorn the lessons of Gallipoli and Monte Cassino. It was also clear that reading Jane Austen and D.H. Lawrence had endowed *me* with neither sense nor sensitivity.

But then Philosophy, Politics and Economics hadn't been much help to Neil in *his* long dark night, and Meredith's Gender Studies had failed to give her a handle on me.

My escape from the Midlands was masterminded by Virgin. Very droll. The view, leaving the city, was of made-over terraced houses with garden decks and conservatories and Veluxed lofts; then the tortured metal roofs of streamlined warehouses; finally farmland, flat and fertile, cold and wet. Rattling over points, the wheels seemed to grind an echo of Meredith's valediction: *'you're an asshole...you're a jerk-off.'*

My mind projected onto the rain-streaked window a screen-in-screen replay of her in my room, shuddering and crying as she pulled her sweater back on.

Another replay: Neil lying on the puddled asphalt, buckled and broken, blood and other gunk seeping from a fearful crack in his head.

My reflection was ghosted against the passing land-scape. I'd honestly thought Meredith was just playing hard to get. She wasn't religious, so I didn't take the Silver Ring stuff too seriously. In 2003 virginity was, like the dollar and the pound sterling, a debased currency. How long would it take her to get over me, forget me?

Asshole...jerk-off, sang the wheels beneath me.

'She's going to Paris for a few days and then home to Florida,' Neil had told me on Friday morning. Meredith had called him earlier, from the airport. She'd taken some Prozac but was still spitting tacks in my direction. 'You're lucky she didn't press charges.'

'I only tried to get my hand down her jeans. We've been dating since October, for Christ's sake.'

'It looks like attempted rape, Paul. *Date rape*. You could end up in jail.'

'I only wanted to touch her pussy,' I said, still on the

12

defensive. 'I wasn't planning to fuck her. It's not like I spiked her drink or jumped her in some bushes.'

His quiet sigh across the airwaves did not hint at absolution or acquittal. 'She was fucked-up before she came here,' I said.

'Well, you may not have fucked *her* but you've fucked her sabbatical.'

My turn to sigh. Contrition in one breath. After a moment I said, 'Shall we meet for lunch?'

'You haven't lost your appetite, then?'

'Give me a break.'

'I need to go to the Library. I'll see you under the Tower at twelve.'

But he wouldn't have. The Tower's rooftop balcony overlooks the quadrangle, not the footpath from the residential buildings. Why did he go up? Was it a spur-of-the-moment thing, or had he been planning it for weeks? Was it something I said? Or didn't say? Perhaps I had nothing to do with it.

The police sergeant who came to interview me on Saturday said they had found no note in Neil's room, so an accidental fall could not be ruled out. Two other students had seen him jump from the quadrangle side, so I was unlikely to be called to the inquest.

'You were his friend?'

'He was friends with me and my girlfriend,' I said.

'That's the young woman from –' he consulted his notepad – 'Florida?'

'Yes.'

'Doing a – "sabbatical", it's called?'

'That's right.'

'She's gone back to America?'

'Yes.'

'She finished her course?'

'She wasn't happy here,' I said.

'Did she break up with you?'

'Yes.'

'But you and she were friends with –'

'We met Neil through the drama group. We drank together, went clubbing and – you know - the usual student stuff.'

'You knew he was – gay?'

'Yes.'

13

'Did he have a – boyfriend?'

'If he did, we never met him.'

'We've spoken to the students he shared his house with. One of them thought he might be having problems with his studies.'

'No,' I said emphatically. 'He loved his courses. He had an assignment – a project - for this year, which he was really into.'

'Someone suggested he might be doing drugs.'

I hesitated and then said, 'Nothing heavy. No more than - most of us.'

'And you can't think of any reason why…?'

'No,' I said. It was the truth.

Surely he didn't do it just because he couldn't have *me*? Was he afraid that somebody was going to fuck *his* education, his life? Was it so hard to be gay? Same-sex marriages were legal now on the Continent. In London, Manchester and Brighton there were gay churches, gay lawyers, even gay greengrocers. Could I have saved him? Could anyone? I would never know.

A moan had passed through the small crowd of bystanders as the final spasm of a dying nerve twitched Neil's crumpled right arm. The uncrushed third of his face retained the fatalistic look of a cornered animal that had so often characterized it. 'He's kind-of like a fawn,' Meredith had said of him last term. '*Fucking sex-maniac!*' she'd called me on Thursday, her mouth twisted with anger or contempt. 'Meredith's very much an earth-goddess,' Neil had said last year.

Self-justification crept into the frame. I was nineteen, not ignorant but lacking in experience. Meredith was twenty. Alison, my one semi-serious girlfriend at high school, a home-grown blonde duller in every sense than Meredith, was likewise saving herself for Prince Charming and his-and-hers High Street wedding rings. 21st-century Britain and the US were well-populated with girls who were hot-to-trot; so how did I manage to find two consecutive prick-teasers who clung to their virginity like it was still something precious in an age that valued nothing?

Between high school and uni there had been a little real action. Tracey from the deli counter at Sainsbury's, with scarified red hair, who wanked me and let me finger her slit. Two nameless German bimbos in a hotel in Torre-molinos who took turns at blowing me. And one other sun-sand-and-sex *turista*, probably also German, not only nameless but faceless, whom I think I fucked although I cannot be sure: we were both totally smashed from Bacardi-Cokes. My deflowering. My 'awakening'. Last summer. Aged eighteen.

That's it. My entire Don Juan history.

Where Neil and his world were concerned, I had even less to draw on. A half-dozen thirteen-year-olds in the changing room comparing stiffies (mixed feelings at finding myself in silver medal position!). A year later: seeing a classmate force-feeding one of the more shameless junior benders in the showers after a soccer game that we'd won. Some gay porno videos that two friends and I watched one evening, feeling more furtive than when it was straight sex and making louder-than-usual comments: 'Yuck', 'Gross' and 'Owww'.

And that's the sum total of my homosexual experience before accidentally befriending one in my first term at uni. Whom I genuinely liked. Now that he was dead, I thought that I might have loved him to some degree – the first time I had felt this towards a male friend. Or perhaps I was only responding to the intensity of his feelings and now to his death.

In my head I replayed the history of these two ill-omened friendships in a series of brief flashes like the catch-up opening to a TV drama series: "Previously on *Campus Life* ..."

The pneumatic sabbatical blonde from Daytona downs her Guinness like one of the boys. 'I like to think I'll make some high-flying tycoon or politico an interesting and ornamental wife.'

The slim dark-haired second-year student from Bristol sips his sherry with elaborate delicacy. 'I see myself on a TV talk show knocking them dead with my brilliant one-liners.'

Meredith crosses her legs neatly on the high stool. She says, 'It isn't only Mormons and Muslim women who prac-tise the new chastity.'

Neil lies back full-length on my unmade bed. He says,

15

'Cerebral affinity wouldn't be enough. Socrates wasn't a puritan.'

Her laugh is hollow. 'Men are such animals. Why can't you love my mind and respect my innocent body?'

He gives a wry smile. 'I'm not cruising you. I'm in love with you.'

Meredith tugs my hand out from inside her sweater. She says, 'You don't love me. You're just trying to get your rocks off.'

Neil touches my face with the tips of his fingers. He says, 'It doesn't have to be sexual. Couldn't we just lie down and hold each other?'

She reaches into my pants and gingerly takes hold of the good friend I like to call Major Wood. (Meredith has only limited acquaintance with his alter ego Corporal Slack.) Her hand trembles and a shiver runs the entire length of her body.

He leans over my chair and kisses me softly, briefly, on the mouth. Amazingly, I let him, before pushing him away with some muddled words of repudiation. His eyes bore into mine. Then he silently picks up his coat and lets himself out of the room

On the very edge of creaming my jockeys I force one hand under her belted jeans and get two fingers – just – on the hem of her panties. I feel skin, trembling to my touch; I feel a curl of hair. With a surge like a tsunami Meredith throws me off her and catapults herself from the bed.

The phallic Victorian-Gothic symbolism of the clock tower brings a smile to my lips. Then, against the arc of sky that's visible through its base, a body flails to a gruesome impact on the opposite side and somehow I know - instantly - that Neil, with his flair for ironical over-statement, is keeping our assignation in the courtyard.

Meredith drowns my stammered apology with a litany of curses as uninflected as a shopping list.

My stomach heaves as I run through the arch towards the sprawled shape on the other side of the tower.

The train slumped through dejected suburbs into Euston. I took the Underground to Victoria to find I had just missed a train to the South Coast town that Neil had renamed *Boredom-on-Sea*. The next train was in thirty minutes. I

16

sat in a noisy bar whose flotsamed floor suggested a parcel bomb. Two pints of lager later I still wasn't ready to face my father. The death of a close friend (I wouldn't mention my new life as a cherry-chaser) would not excuse ditching my university career halfway through the second term of my first year. The script for this confrontation, which I now decided to postpone till tomorrow, was predictable:

'The money I've spent on you ...' Which had entailed no sacrifice.

'...squandering your education...' True, but only when compared to such alternatives as inputting an office PC or stacking shelves.

'...the opportunities you've wasted...' Yeah, like teaching History and English to the next generation of slags and headbangers.

'...breaking your mother's heart...' God – and Margaret Thatcher – had broken my mother's heart in 1982. To my father's horror, my mother voted Labour in the 1983 General Election (a wasted vote in Boredom-on-Sea); it was as close as she could come to voting against God. My birth, six months after the election, helped patch up her relations with God – and, eventually, the Tory Party – but I provided at best a flimsy Band-Aid for her broken heart.

London too was cold and wet. Behind the station were streets of Third-World hotels that might have been brothels. Some of them plainly were. The one I chose was run by an East European whose English sounded like Klingon. It was cheap and looked cheerful until I smelled the stairs and inspected the sheets.

It was 7.45, the time I might be taking Meredith into the city centre for a meal or a movie or, if she was studying, meet Neil for a drink in the Union Bar ('the *Puke and Firkin*,' he called it). University – and all it had promised – was more than 100 miles away and belonged to another me, the me I might have been.

Without undressing I lay down on a bedcover grey with the disappointments of a thousand other travellers. Ghosts and demons and the sibyls of all my unpromising tomorrows watched over me as I slipped into undeserved oblivion.

2. The single-parent diet

By four a.m. I was awake and communing with the dead and the sexually disabled. Today I dredged up memories of the zanier times we had shared before my libido and Neil's obsession went critical.

Pre-panty-raid dates with Meredith: dinners, movies and concerts (Coldplay, The Darkness). Clubbing nights. Meredith's inhibitions and her refusal to do E's made her a rogue elephant among all the sweating ravers whose feet barely touched the dance floor. Trips on trains, coaches, buses. She had 'done' London, Bath and Edinburgh, now she must do Shakespeare Country and Robin Hood. We re-enacted *A Midsummer Night's Dream* on the midwinter banks of the Avon and played Maid Marion games (non-PG rated) in Nottinghamshire.

She was into drama, so we joined the other aspiring Jude Laws and Samantha Mortons. Against type Meredith got herself cast as Lady Macbeth and Violet Venables, but Shaftesbury Avenue and Pinewood did not beckon. Neil's near-elfin size limited him to bit parts; there were no plans to put on *Peter Pan*. Despite my alleged and only slight resemblance to Ewan McGregor I had no theatrical skills or aspirations. Painting and shifting scenery proved to be my forte, although I bravely bore a broom-handle halberd at Dunsinane. I was only there for Meredith; Neil was an un-sought bonus.

He taught us bridge. Meredith couldn't grasp the finer points of bidding and we never found a permanent fourth. Between rubbers we fine-tuned our scenario for a Braver

18

Greener new world in which George Dubya and Tony Blair joined Bush Sr and John Major in the wilderness. Booze fuelled our debates: wines from Chile and Romania and, when someone's bank balance had received its monthly parental boost, supermarket rum or vodka. And, most days, Neil and I (not Meredith) smoked a little dope, bought on- or off-campus.

The drama group provided a circle of B-list friends and many highs, not all of them lime-lit or drug-crazed. Pub-crawls where we talked and shouted and finally sang until the regulars either joined in or kicked us out. A weekend just before we split up for Christmas we piled into a bor-rowed 4x4 with three fellow thespians and dashed to the Welsh coast; here we argued ourselves from agnosticism into atheism and anarchy; Meredith and I slept in each other's arms (only this once) on a sofa in the living-room of someone's aunt with Neil rolled up – 'like Cleopatra,' he said – in a rug on the floor beside us.

The first time I kissed Meredith she turned her head so that it landed on her cheek. Laughing she kissed me on both cheeks. 'Au revoir,' she said and hurried into her dorm. After two more maiden-aunt kisses I seized her head and forced my mouth onto hers. A moment of un-yielding stiffness and then her lips parted under mine, but she always erected her tongue as a barricade just behind her cosmetically perfected teeth. Very slowly I gained access to her killer breasts: through clothing, inside clothing, then bra-less and (this term) topless. Her nipples responded to my kissing and caressing but her panty-line was a Berlin Wall with no Checkpoint Charlie. As was mine, all last term. This term (she called it a 'semester') Major Wood crossed the Handjob frontier. Precisely twice; on Valentine's Day (cards exchanged plus chocolates and flowers from Major Wood) and again (with much cajoling) a week later. Meredith kissed with her eyes open, but for this she closed them. Reciprocity was not required, and I had to clearly understand that crotches were *not* on the verge of Reunification.

Her grandmother had grown up in the Fifties when, Meredith said, there had been similar stand-offs between boys and girls on dates. Her parents had come of age during the Seventies when How Far to Go was a challenge rather than a stricture, but Meredith was a throwback. My

19

parents' values were even more Victorian than Mrs Thatcher's; I couldn't see my mother in a clinging top, still less visualize my father trying to get into it. I doubt my father ever carried, as I did (more in hope than expectation), condoms in his wallet.

And so to last Thursday. I truly don't think my mind was set on anything more threatening than some fingerwork – or perhaps a dry hump. Last resort: handjob number three.

I had got her topless on my duvet. Going to the loo along the corridor gave her an excuse to put her sweater back on. Her absence gave me the chance to remove my sweatshirt and jeans. 'Uh-oh,' she said on her return, re-removing nothing. The two previous handjobs had begun equally unpromisingly.

I patted the bedcover. 'Come over here.' Beguilingly roguish.

'Not while you're in that condition,' said Meredith, unbeguiled. The waistband of my Calvins, well clear of my lower abs, shamelessly billboarded my 'condition'.

'You could do something about that if you came over here.'

'Paul, if you love me, don't do this.'

'If *you* loved *me*, you'd be over here by now.' My heart – and my balls – ached. My balls, in the Midlands, ached for days at a time.

'I'm leaving, Paul.' She took her sweater off and started to put her bra back on. I stood up and went towards her, my hands reaching for her centrefold breasts. She pushed me away, not roughly but gently - as I, after his kiss, had pushed Neil away the night before. The memory of this was almost as vivid as his grisly suicide.

'Lie on the bed,' he'd said. 'I won't try anything.'

'I can't, Neil. I'm just not – comfortable with - you know – gay stuff.'

'You let me kiss you.'

'It won't happen again,' I said.

If anyone in my hometown had attempted what Neil had done I would have beaten him to a pulp, so perhaps the grey grimy Midlands had opened up my soft underbelly. But 24 hours later, in reaction or perhaps retaliation, when Meredith pushed me away I threw her onto the bed, jumped on top of her and - who knows? - if she hadn't found the pro-wrestler strength to throw me off, maybe I would have tried to give her the fucking she (make that *I*) needed.

So much for exploring my feminine side.

My very own *Groundhog Day*. It kept coming back to this. It always would. Neil's kiss. Jumping Meredith. Neil quietly leaving. Meredith storming out. The Founder's Tower. Meredith (imagined) in a taxi to the airport.

Tears of guilt and self-pity in a crummy hotel bedroom in Victoria. The first day of the rest of my life.

In 40-watt light the shower looked clean. I changed my socks and underpants but wore the same sweatshirt and jeans. Faux Doc Martens. A fleece-lined coat that (like me, I suspect) was almost but not quite an anorak.

I might as well take advantage of being in London (and postpone the showdown with my father), but what to do with my suitcase? Al-Qa'eda had closed all mainline left luggage facilities. For £10 the night-clerk, another Moldovan or Klingon, offered to store it in a locked office stuffed with cases and backpacks. I tipped him two pounds and hoped this would deter him from levering the combination with a screwdriver.

Resisting the temptation of Death-by-Full-English-Breakfast in a Greasy Spoon, I settled for lower-calorie Starbuck's Danish and latte in Victoria Street. One of the Great Unwashed had thrust a free London tabloid at me as I passed the Underground. To Londoners the looming Gulf War Part Two was of less importance than council tax rises and the leadership of the Tory Party.

A five-minute walk took me into Hyde Park beside the Queen Mother's Gates – Art Nouveau meets Beatrix Potter. A fountain with a nude gladiator – Hercules or Achilles – with what Neil might consider 'an arse to die for'. Commuting pedestrians: the haggard night shift going home, apathetic day-workers. Grimacing joggers going for the burn. Horse-riders: just how rich did you have to be to keep a horse in Knightsbridge?

I trudged along the Bayswater Road. Meredith and I had checked out the open-air art gallery here one weekend in November. Amid the tourist tat a few works had as much impact as the best of what we'd seen in Tate

Modern. After an authentically ethnic dinner in Chinatown we ran the gauntlet of tired hookers between Kings Cross Underground and our hotel. Separate rooms, of course. No nookie for Paul, unless he went back onto the street (he didn't).

Into Queensway. The Arab Quarter. Black-shrouded women (some wearing Bat-masks) and men in robes. Even the men in jeans and black leather were swarthy, Levantine; I half expected to be pimped or mugged.

Another coffee bar, also Middle Eastern. Vile thick coffee exonerated by a sweet pastry. A bill the price of a cinema ticket.

Back to the park. Busier now, with schoolchildren and many more commuters. I found a Gents that was open. A city type in the urinal gave me the once-over, so I went into a cubicle to pee. Footsteps, then the door was gently tried. This had happened before – even Boredom-on-Sea had cottage queens; I held my cool and my breath. A sampler of the life Neil could have had, had indeed known: the kindness of strangers. Evidently it wasn't enough.

I walked a circuit of the Serpentine. Gulls and pigeons uttered desolate cries as they swooped over the grey water under a grey sky. Scotch mist, diesel-flavoured. Ten days ago a million people had marched from Parliament Square to Hyde Park, protesting against the wannabe war-mongers Bush and Blair. Today London felt post-nuclear. And yet the purposeful parents and commuters indicated that the world was continuing its business, and a part of me knew that *my* world too would go on. Even Meredith would get on with her life, finish her studies, meet and marry that promising politician. (Maybe she would tell him about the asshole Brit who'd tried to pip him to her cherry.)

Only Neil wouldn't get on with the rest of his life.

I stopped to watch a mother and child feeding the birds. Kamikaze gulls dived to beat the ducks to the chunks of bread the boy threw onto the water. Pigeons swarmed around his feet. He giggled at all this aggressive greed. His mother laughed with him. Swathed in a dowdy winter coat she looked no older than me. Auburn hair under a jazz headscarf framed a pale face. She smiled briefly when she saw me watching them.

As the boy showered the last crumbs onto the pigeons,

a gust of wind snatched the paper bag from his hands and blew it in my direction. I plucked it out of the air, inflated it and detonated it between my palms. 'Terrorist bomb in Hyde Park,' I announced the next day's headline.

The boy shot me with finger-guns: 'Pthaw-pthaw.' Clutching a hand to my chest I staggered to the nearest bench and died with a terrible groan.

'I killed the terror man, Mummy,' he boasted and ran over to prod me and make sure I was dead. I resurrected as a lurching zombie. Shrieks of fearful delight. His mother rescued him and made him take the discarded bag to a litter bin. A low-pitched unaccented voice and the mouth of Julia Roberts.

'Train them young,' I said tritely.

'Thanks for the entertainment. There's always an anti-climax when the bread runs out.'

'University dramatics. I'm usually just a stagehand.'

'I see a big future in pantomime,' she said, and we both laughed. The boy came back from the litter bin and ordered me to 'Make more bangs.'

'No more bags,' I said. 'No bags, no bangs.' This was a mega-hilarious joke at which he laughed loudly.

'Do some running, Simon,' his mother said. 'We don't want to get fat like Oliver and Kyle the Vile, do we? Over-weight boys at his playschool,' she explained as she sat down beside me. Simon duly ran, clapping his hands to scare the birds he had just fed.

'The junkfood generation. Like ours.'

'How come you're so lean?' A compliment - or a euphemism for scrawny? I yearned for the physique of Enrique Iglesias, as in his own way had Neil.

'I run and do workouts,' I told her. 'What's your secret?' Embarrassing if there was a fat girl hidden inside the heavy coat.

'I'm on the single-parent diet. By the time I've fed him and paid the bills and playschool, I can't always afford to eat.' A shocking disclosure. In the Oxfam coat she looked poor, but not destitute.

'And I thought student life was harsh.'

'We get by. He doesn't get many treats, but I try not to show him up in front of the other kids.'

'Kyle the Vile.'

She smiled. 'Most of the time he's Simon's best friend

at playschool.'

'Where are you when he's in school? Uni?'

She shook her head. 'I was in art school, but I had to drop out to have Simon. I'll try and go back when he starts primary school next year. For now I'm a teaching assistant at a primary in Kilburn two days a week. And I do some freelance artwork for a couple of advertising agencies. Not many fulltime jobs around.'

'Tell me about it. You're not the only dropout. This time tomorrow I'll be signing on.' Exaggerating my situation out of solidarity for hers, but it was the first implied admission that Life Would Go On. Clearly she didn't have affluent parents to fall back on.

'Why did you leave? I'm guessing you weren't pregnant.'

'Perhaps I'd better get a test kit from Boots.'

We shared a laugh as the boy, Simon, ran back to us.

'I'm cold, Mummy.'

'Let me buy you a coffee,' I said. She protested but the boy was already sold. We walked back to Bayswater and found a McDonald's: McMuffin and Diet Coke for him and what Meredith called Muck-coffee for us grown-ups. Simon was happy to watch cars and passers-by while I talked with his mother.

Her name was Rachel. Inside the shrugged-off coat she wore a jazz-themed sweater that matched her scarf. Designer items also from, I guessed, a charity shop. She wasn't fat. Her breasts weren't as sensational as Meredith's (not many were) but her hair, freed from the headscarf, was stunning. It fell in gleaming copper waves to her shoulders. Her features were almost butch: narrow nose, close-set brown eyes, a broad chin beneath the wide mouth. She wore no make-up, but the sheen of the hair cast a glow on her pale skin and turned her into a Da Vinci Magdalene. A crowning glory, would be my mother's verdict on the hair. A cliché a minute, my mother.

I told her about university without mentioning Meredith and Neil, allowing her to infer that I had quit out of indifference to my subjects. Indifference, my natural state, wasn't hard to feign. She, in contrast, enthused about art school, her courses, campus life. I hyped up the drama society and bridge and slipped in a reference to an American girl and a gay from Bristol.

24

I must have made it clear I was in no hurry to head for home. She invited me to lunch with them. Outside McDonald's Simon took my hand as well as his mother's; we swung him the first block.

She said there was food at home but I went into an off-licence and bought two decent bottles of wine and some sweets for Simon. Rachel made a show of annoyance at my extravagance. 'I'm one of your better-off students,' I told her. 'Monthly cheques from my dad.'

'How will he take your dropping out of uni?'

'There'll be blood on the lounge carpet,' I predicted. 'But my mum will have the stains out within the hour.'

Two blocks from Queensway, her building was a terraced Victorian mansion, handsome outside, the entrance hall shabby thanks to a parked bicycle and the marks it had made on the walls. Rachel was on the third floor: two small rooms plus kitchen and bath. Bright plain walls, large abstract prints in bright plain frames, second-hand furniture enlivened with throws and bright plain cushions. An art student's flat, and yet suburban couples paid good money to have their predecessors' chintzy decor replaced with this TV-makeover look.

I opened the first bottle of wine and sat at a pint-sized kitchen table while Rachel washed potatoes and boiled water in a saucepan.

'I get the feeling you're not close to your parents,' she said.

'Are you close to yours?'

'They were supportive when I decided to have Simon rather than – you know. But I've got two younger brothers still in school and my dad can't do much since he did his back in with too much lifting. He helps out in a pub. My mum's on a Tesco checkout. But we are close. They love Simon.'

'We don't do "close" in my family,' I told her. 'Not since my brother died. In the Falklands.'

She rinsed an iceberg lettuce. 'Before you were born.'

I nodded. 'I'm the replacement. A big disappointment.'

'And now you're a dropout.' The saucepan lid rattled; she reduced the heat.

'Yeah. "*Home is the sailor, home from the sea*." My mum embroidered a picture of my brother with that text underneath it for the dining-room wall. She puts fresh flowers on the mantelpiece twice a week. Trevor was a soldier, but he sailed in Mrs Thatcher's Task Force. He's buried in Port Stanley, but his spare uniform came back to them and that's hanging in my wardrobe. It reminds me of everything he was that I'm not.' Hearing the self-pity in my voice, I stopped.

'You won't be able to stay with them,' she said, slicing tomatoes plainly. My mother, schooled by the W.I., cut them into shark's teeth.

'No. But with a bit of luck I'll find some sort of job, get my own place. If you can do it, so can I.'

'Your rent won't be like London's,' she said. 'But neither will your wages.'

'How do you manage? Apart from not eating?'

She put the salad bowl, white china, on the table. 'This flat's owned by a housing association. Controlled rent. Richard – Simon's dad – moved in when his mother was dying of ovarian cancer. I lived with him for a year before he got me pregnant, and the association let me stay on when he took off.'

'He dumped you?'

'Said he wasn't ready to be a parent.' She opened a pack of ham that bore a reduced-price sticker.

'But you had to be.'

'Well - there was the other option. But I didn't go down that road. And now I've got this little treasure.' She gave the boy a look of 24-carat love. He was playing with Corgi cars on the living-room carpet. I'd never loved anyone with the intensity of that look. I envied her. I envied Simon.

'Does he see his father?'

She shook her head. 'Richard's never seen him. He went to the States. Last time I heard from him he was working as a janitor in Los Angeles. Hoping to get a Green Card or be discovered by Hollywood. Whichever happens first. Richard was a drama student.' She smiled her own movie-star smile. 'See, you're not my first brush with next year's superstars.'

'That's not what I want to be,' I said emphatically.

'But you could. You know who you look like?'

'Yes.' I steered away from my famous look-alike with a confession: 'I only joined the drama group because of this American girl.'

'Was she your girlfriend?'

'Yes.'

'Have you dropped out of college because of a broken heart?'

'It was hers that got broken, not mine.' I revised my earlier version of dropping out and told her the full saga of Meredith and Neil. She sat on the other side of the small table and heard me out without interrupting. The boy played with his cars. Waiting for the potatoes to cook, we finished the first bottle of New Zealand Chardonnay. Thursday night, in the retelling, sounded like the story of your everyday randy nineteen-year-old coming on a bit too strong. Rachel was not fooled.

'I've let a predator into my home,' she said. Unable to read her expression, I half stood up.

'I'll leave now if you want me to.'

'You may as well stay. I've done taters for three.'

'Saved by a boiled potato,' I quipped. Rachel smiled.

'A girl at art school was into that Silver Ring stuff,' she said. 'But Bush and Blair could blow the world up while she's waiting for her white wedding. She wore five or six of those rings.'

'Meredith just wears one on her thumb,' I said.

'I couldn't wait to lose my virginity,' Rachel told me. 'I was thirteen. He was a year older. Captain of the junior football team. He shagged half the girls in his year and mine. Doug Slade. I wonder where he is now. I've had better shags since. Including Richard.'

'But you've never been – made to go further than you wanted to?'

She took the second bottle out of the fridge and handed it over. 'There were a couple of times in college when I woke up with someone I wished I hadn't gone to bed with. Sex is a lot like dancing: it's hard to stop once your feet get the rhythm.' She misinterpreted my envious look. 'I'm not a slag,' she said. 'Well, no more than most girls. Just having fun. You grow out of sleeping around. Having Simon's made a big difference.'

'I'm still waiting to grow *into* sleeping around,' I said glumly. 'I wish *you*'d been at my uni.' She grinned.

'Maybe I do too,' she said and got up to empty the potatoes into a colander. I asked if she'd been on the anti-war march. 'Yes,' she said. 'And Simon.'

27

The march had clashed with the last night of *Suddenly, Last Summer*; otherwise we would have joined 300 of our fellow students on the streets of London. An uncle of Meredith's had died in Vietnam; my parents lost Trevor in the Falklands; Neil was a peacenik on principle.

A Yankee at the court of King Tony, Meredith took some flak in the British Midlands. In Florida she'd campaigned for Al Gore. She believed the next Democrat in the White House would right all the wrongs of a Bush Administration, as Clinton had. My parents came of age in the Sixties expecting a thermonuclear holocaust. Today we live with different terrors: jet-planes morphed into flying bombs and silent gassing on the subway. I cling to a Darwinian faith in the survival of the species but Neil, like Rachel, anticipated the arrival of apocalyptic horsemen and, lo, for him it had come to pass.

There was no third chair. Simon ate his lunch sitting on the floor at a coffee table. Rachel let him watch cartoons on TV.

'We've both fallen foul of gay men,' she said as we began eating.

'Did yours kill himself?'

'No, he's gone to live in Los Angeles.'

'Simon's father is *gay*?'

'Technically he's *bi*. Richard says he's a straight man who likes a bit of gay action now and then, but I think he's a gay who likes women.'

'Tough on you, though – him going off. Tough on Simon.'

She shrugged. 'Oh well – better no father than a half-hearted one.'

'Did you know he was gay before he got you pregnant?'

'I should have done. He had gay friends and he could be quite camp, actors mostly are. But if a bloke's shagging you several times a week, you don't think he's a queen. Then one day he just told me he liked to cruise Hampstead Heath and the gay baths. Said he needed that as well as me.'

'He could have given you HIV.' Gay plus promiscuous equals double the risk: the equation Neil evidently could not live with.

'And the baby,' she said. 'But I had a test and I'm OK.'

28

She was silent for a moment. Then: 'I'm sorry about your friend. You don't expect anyone to have a problem with being gay nowadays. He must have been depressed over more than that.'

'I just think he'd still be alive if I'd let him do whatever he wanted to do. Have me.' It felt weird to be articulating this notion to somebody else.

'If your heart wasn't in it, it probably wouldn't have helped him anyway. You can't do what isn't in your nature. It ticked me off that I wasn't enough for Richard but I don't have any problem with gay men and – what they do. But the thought of doing stuff with another woman makes my skin crawl.'

In Spain last summer the two German girls had licked and munched each other as well as licking and chomping me. A total turn-on. Remembering it, my skin crawled in a different way to Rachel's. Something to keep to myself.

In the living room Simon was asleep in one of the mismatched armchairs. He'd barely touched his food. Rachel crept in and turned off the TV.

She tried to lighten our mood with stories of gays she'd known at art school and in Bayswater ('they're always looking to score the randy Arabs around here,' she said). My mind was elsewhere. I was thinking about the 14-year-old footballer (Meredith would call him a 'jock') who'd taken her cherry. I wanted to have been him. I wanted to be all the blokes who'd ever had her. I wanted to be Richard, Simon's father, only without the gay peripherals. Why couldn't Meredith have been like Rachel?

I laughed with her at her stories, but the predator she had identified was stirring. The predator wanted to lock the child in the bedroom and rip the mother's clothes off. He wanted to see what size her breasts were, lick them, bury his face in her pussy-hair – would it be ginger? I imagined gliding into her. She would be a hot shag, I was certain, taking as well as giving.

She didn't need to look under the table to see Major Wood. She could see him in my eyes. She shook her head.

'It isn't going to happen,' she said.

My mouth was dry. I swallowed. 'Please.' It wasn't the predator speaking.

'Not now. Not today.' Was there a minuscule crumb of comfort?

29

'Another time?' I said.

'I'd need to know you better. I told you, I'm not a sleep-around slag any more. And there's Simon.'

'If I stayed here a few days you'd get to know me.'

'You need to go home and sort yourself out, Paul. It's too soon after what you've just been through. It's possible you need therapy.'

'You're all the therapy I need.'

She grinned. 'What you're thinking is *sex* therapy, and I'm not ready to take that up yet.'

'I just need to shag somebody,' I blurted. Well, it was true.

'There must be hookers in – Boredom-on-Sea.' Experimenting with the name, she laughed.

'I don't want a hooker. I want you.' There was desperation in my voice. Corporal Slack was back in command. Really the predator was no more than a horny teenage insect, easily squashed.

'I'll make us a coffee. Then you'll have to go. Catch your train.' She ruffled my hair as she passed me. I turned and wrapped my arms around her and buried my face in her midriff, halfway between the two places I yearned to bury all of myself. Either she sensed that I was not a threat or she had a few self-defence tricks up her charity-shop sleeve: she patted my head some more before gently pulling free and taking the kettle to the sink.

Conversation was stilted over coffee: London, Sussex, the Midlands. Was it my confession or the grovelling which had blown my chances?

Rachel was twenty-one, older than I'd thought in the park. The boy was three and three months, a Scorpio like me. She had been fending for herself since she was seventeen. I was nineteen – and rudderless.

Simon awoke grouchy. My departure did not faze him. Rachel and I exchanged addresses and mobile numbers. Opening the door she hugged me and gave me a quick coffee-flavoured kiss on the mouth. Major Wood surged an instant response. Rachel looked down at my out-thrust Levis as she released me. She laughed.

'You won't make it to the Underground,' she said. 'Some cruising queen will eat you up.'

Corporal Slack and I headed glumly for the Circle Line.

3. Home is the sailor

'He's done what?'

'He's dropped up.' My mother, Mrs Malaprop.

'Dropped *out*,' I supplied the correct adverb.

'I think not,' my father said.

'I'm sorry, but I have.'

'Then I suggest you get on a train and drop back in.'

'No.' Did my 'no' sound decisive? Just saying it was a small triumph.

'Oh Paul.' My mother had uttered a lot of *Oh Paul's* in nineteen years.

'Why?' Unusually, my father met bluntness with bluntness. Prolixity, not brevity, was the soul of my father.

'I can't go back.'

'Can't or won't?'

'Won't, then. Sorry, Dad. I couldn't stand it any longer.'

'Couldn't stand what?'

'Everything. The course. The Midlands. The whole university thing.'

'So what happens to your teaching career?'

'I guess it's down the toilet.' Meredith should get a credit here.

'Oh Paul.'

'My God,' said Dad. '*My God*.'

'Oh William.'

'Nineteen years,' he said in a flat toneless voice. 'Nineteen years we devote to making something of him, giving him the best possible chance in life, and he can't even stick it out for two terms.' He often did this, referred to me in the third person as if I wasn't there. *Hello*, I wanted to

31

say. *Over here.*

'I'm sorry, Dad.' Too many apologies.

He let rip. Mostly it amplified his first statement, emphasizing the years of sacrifice, my ingratitude, the laughing-stock I would make of him, the effect on his position in the town, blah-blah-blah. In the oak-panelled hall we were a Strindberg tableau, my father red-faced just inside the front door, my mother wringing a tea-towel in the kitchen doorway, me at the foot of the stairs trying not to look shamefaced. He looked at her, she looked at me, I looked at him. No word of self-defence would ever reach him. Maybe if I screamed, *I hate you and everything you stand for*. But that would only get an *Oh Paul.*

I sometimes yearned for an *American Pie*-type Dad, but it would have been an altogether different talking-to if he'd caught Major Wood embedded in one of Mother's famous pineapple-upside-down cakes.

'What was the point of going up to university if you can't see it through?'

'Search me,' I said. Ask about the Weimar Republic or the Bisexual Subtext in Shakespeare's plays and I'll write you an essay, a thesis, but about the Things That Matter I know nothing. Mine is the generation that knows every-thing and nothing.

'Oh dear,' said Mother.

Meet the parents. William and Mary. (And me an aspir-ing historian.) They got engaged in 1960, married in '61, had Trevor in '62, but they'd been neither Mods nor Rockers. Flower Power, marijuana and Free Love all pass-ed them by. But the Thatcher years, her 'Victorian Values' and the Falklands War, had left an indelible footprint on their lives, and – even before I was born – on mine.

William Henry Barrett, FCA, FCCA, of *Barrett & Son, Chartered Accountants*. Accountancy and auditing were his world. Figures (including election returns) turned him on. 'We call them bean-counters,' Meredith had said.

Treasurer of the local Conservative Association, Dad also kept the books for St Agnes's, the Rotarians and the British Legion. Mother and I knew that he yearned to be Mayor or Chairman of something, but he'd never been asked. He had no gift for public speaking, was not really a public person. He settled for being a backstage man, like me at uni, a scene-shifter, a counter rather than a raiser

32

of funds. He was not – nor would I ever be – a Mover and Shaker.

Pushing 65, my father had all his teeth and most of his hair. His angular face had the handsomeness of some bygone film-star. He played no sport, only took modest weekend walks with Mother, but was still fit and trim. Employees probably saw him as 'firm'. Mother saw almost no wrong in him (many more *Yes dear*'s than *Oh William*'s). To me he was a tyrant, but a second-division one, Mussolini rather than Hitler, more Macmillan than Thatcher.

'So paying your course and enrolment fees was a complete waste of money,' the bean-counter said.

'Yeah, looks like it was.'

'Not to mention your accommodation and living expenses.'

'Not to mention.'

'All those textbooks.'

'Yup.'

'Oh dear.' My mother's anguished expression, one size fits all, covered anything from a family crisis to a Christian Aid sponge-cake that failed to rise.

My mother. Mary Jane Barrett, née Pemberton. She had the faded chirpiness of one of those yesteryear celebrities who turn up in daytime chat-shows and tribute documentaries. In Florida she would have sported a blue rinse; in Boredom-on-Sea she went no further than silver highlights to put a sparkle into dull grey. Forty-one when I replaced (or failed to replace) Trevor, she had turned sixty in the week I went up (she would say down) to uni.

She was a quiet doer of good works, taking pies, cakes and company to widowed, sick and old parishioners, Rotarians, Legionnaires. Her mindless conversation ought to have driven them the final mile to the cemetery but it seemed not to. She meant well; this will be carved on her headstone.

Too passive to be a committee wife, she made tea, sandwiches, quiches, scones. Her confections won prizes at the W.I. and church fêtes. Unforgettably, one of her pineapple-upside-down cakes had been knocked off the trestle table by the bishop's wife who was judging and became a pineapple-right-way-up cake on the grass inside the marquee on my uncle Jack Pemberton's lawn.

33

'And now we're expected to go on keeping you while you loll around listening to pop music.'

'I'll sign on at the Jobcentre tomorrow.'

'You will *not* sign on. I don't want people saying a Barrett is drawing benefit.'

'Just till I get a job.'

'Doing what exactly?'

'Whatever's going.' Had it been the season, I could have got work as a park cleaner, a deckchair attendant, an ice-cream vendor. Not exactly suitable employment for the scion of the VIP Barrett clan.

The 'Son' in *Barrett & Son* was Trevor, not me. But Trevor had chosen the army over bookkeeping, a major disappointment in our father's life that led to a greater calamity. Time was, Good Families sent first sons to the army and second sons to the church. Holy orders my father could have lived with; even teaching. But not dropping-out. The Barretts were not quitters. Until yesterday.

'I suppose you want me to find you something to do at the office.'

'No, I don't,' I said. However unresolved my aspirations, I had long made it plain that they would never lean towards the field of bean-counting.

If we were the Kennedys of Boredom-on-Sea (and we weren't), then Trevor was Joe Junior, the golden-boy first son lost in war. I was meant to be Jack or Bobby, the second- and third-string sons fulfilling their father's vision, but no: I was Teddy, the wayward prince, the let-down, the son who lost the prize before he could reach it.

My father's eyes narrowed. 'There's a *girl* in this story, isn't there?'

'Yes,' I said. And then, anticipating his next question: 'Yes and no. It's not something you'd understand.'

'What does that mean? Have you got her into trouble?' This 'Oh William' was accompanied by a gasp.

'No,' I said. 'No, she isn't. Why? Were you going to offer to pay for an abortion if I go back to uni?'

Mother's 'Oh dear' was feebler than normal. My father's chameleon face went white with outrage.

'How dare you say such a thing,' he said. 'You filthy little *sod*.' Six foot one – *little*? But my father never swore.

Mother burst into tears and ran back into the kitchen. Dad said – or started to say: 'I wish Trevor –' then he

34

hurried after Mother before I could supply an *Oh William* on her behalf. I took my coat from the hall closet and went out into the inhospitable air of uptown Boredom-on-Sea.

When I read about teenagers in America who killed their parents to accelerate their inheritance I almost envied them their *cojones*. I wasn't capable of such ruthlessness and I didn't – quite – dislike my parents enough to wish them dead but I knew that if they died tomorrow, say in a car smash, I would get over my grief very quickly.

We lived in a Conservation Area named after a 19th-century mayor, although our house was a 1970s semi. In contrast to next door's boxy additions, our porch was mock Tudor, our conservatory cod Victorian. Outside (beams, leaded windows) and in (panelling, 'antique' colours, repro-William Morris wallpapers) our half of the property aspired, like my parents, to be something grander.

Six hundred yards away the sea, at half-tide, growled onto the shingle, only a flash of surf visible from the promenade whose Edwardian-era lamp-posts, knotted with overpainted bulges of rust, cast puddles of light. Even in winter the daytime promenade bustled with the town's geriatrics taking their keep-fit walks and young mums with pushchairs, but at 6 p.m., punched by a westerly wind, it was almost deserted. A few dog-walkers whose hoods and hats and scarves gave them the anonymity of terrorists. One raw-faced spandexed biker and one anoraked roller-blader. The only sounds were the growling shingle and creaking breakwaters. Homeward-bound cars on the coast road.

Closed and dark, the pier looked dead, although its arcades and cafés stayed open until dusk in winter and there was a late-night disco at the far end on Friday and Saturday. Bleak as a page from Dostoyevsky, the seafront suited my mood. My future, on this elephant's-graveyard coast, did not look promising. Too young to die, I could nevertheless wither away here.

The cold began to bite through my fleece lining. I turned inland. A few more people, hunched against the wind. Some asylum-seekers, Kurdish or Balkan, coutured by the Salvation Army. *I* would seek asylum, sanctuary, in

London, with Rachel and Simon. Rachel would save me from the mess I had so far made of my life and the greater mess that otherwise lay ahead.

The shopping centre, dating like my home from the 1970s and wearing its age badly, was closed. Except for a few corner-shops and off-licences and the out-of-town supermarkets, Boredom-on-Sea knocked off at 5 or 5.30. In case my father stopped payments into my account I took the maximum £250 from an ATM.

A pizzeria I had patronised from childhood was open. In my parents' youth it had been the town's first ice-cream parlour, operated by the current owner's father, a Neapolitan POW who'd sent home for a mail-order bride, as had his son. Luigi and Luisa looked as tired and worn as the mall.

'*Ciao*, Signor Paolo!' They greeted me with enthusiasm. Not many of their customers made the effort to speak Italian. '*Com'é stai*?'

'*Non c'é male. E vos otros*? How's bizniz?' At school I'd studied Spanish and French. It was in this pizzeria that I had learned what little Italian I knew.

'*Invernale. Capisci*?' I worked it out from Spanish and nodded. '*E comé va l'università*?'

'*Finido. Chiavata.*' Luigi had taught me the Italian for 'fucked'. He laughed. Luisa's ham shock-horror face reminded me of Meredith's Mrs Venables.

We chatted in *GoodFellas* English and Hispanitalian while they made me a Hawaiian deep-pan, about as authentically Neapolitan as shepherd's pie. I ate it there. No other customers came in.

Kevin and Gavin, my closest friends from high school, were in separate university towns, as I was supposed to be. The sodality of the smarter kids. As a half-decent footballer and runner I was tolerated by the sporting fraternity, but we failed to gel socially. If I tracked them to one of their haunts - made-over pubs or the town's solitary and dilapidating pool hall - conversation would be limited: soccer, *Big Brother*, over-egged sexual conquests.

I had one relative my age. Cousin Jenny, who wasn't really a cousin but my uncle's stepdaughter, a pretty girl with a wild reputation and breasts that were almost in Meredith's league, but Jenny moved in her stepfather's country club and golf club set. My parents, financially but

36

not sociologically equipped for that circle, preferred the more sedate pace of the church hall and the Legion. My father didn't like the drinking that attached to golf and talked of taking up bowls when – if – he retired. Bowls: the game for people with one-and-a-half feet in the grave, i.e. the majority of Boredom-on-Sea's citizens.

Scarlet-haired Tracey from Sainsbury's, from whom I might have caught some mutual hand action, had got married at Christmas and was pregnant. Or had got pregnant and was married.

Which left Alison, my high-school sweetheart, Olivia Newton-John to my Travolta. But Boredom-on-Sea wasn't *Grease*, it was Glenn Miller tribute bands and Ivor Novello revivals.

'Paul!'

'Alison!' I mocked her surprise. 'Long time no see.' Only since January, in fact. I tried to kiss her, but she pushed me away.

'Paul!' The second scarlet face of the evening. 'People might be looking out their windows.' Alison's house (detached, a minor humiliation for my parents) was in another supposedly select part of town.

'Aren't you pleased to see me?' If she returned my question, the honest answer would be, er, no. Acne on her forehead below the blonde ponytailed hair: Rachel she was not. Modest bumps under her angora sweater: nor was she Meredith. Skinny legs below a knee-length skirt: she wasn't even Tracey. Why had I come here? Looking for a friendly face – even one with zits.

'Shouldn't you be in college?'

'Should I?'

'You know you should.'

'Well – I've chucked it in.'

'Chucked it in? Goodness me. What's happened?'

Conversations with Alison tended to sound like a really bad daytime soap, although her life lacked even the mediocre drama of afternoon television.

Last term we'd exchanged letters and phone calls; her long letters full of coastal updates; my brief phone calls giving minimal details of university life. I had moved on, Alison had not, except that she now worked for her father – on the secretarial side; she wasn't ready to face his

37

particular public. We'd gone out two or three times a week during the Christmas vacation. I hadn't wasted energy trying to obtain from Alison the foreplay privileges that Meredith was reluctantly granting. After Meredith (and Neil) conversations with Alison were more stultifying than ever. She still expected to marry me after I graduated. Our children were already named: Harry and Rebecca. But this term there had only been one letter – and no phone calls from me.

'Aren't you going to ask me in?'

'Well – all right. I was just going to wash my hair. Mummy's gone to Bingo. Daddy had a call-out.'

The Grim Reaper would have called her father out. Alison's life did not lack drama: the daily trauma of bereavement – other people's. My future in-laws were an undertaker and his Bingoholic wife. Not so much soap opera as sitcom.

An hour of banality passed. Newsflash: our former head-teacher's 90-year-old mother had died. The wife of a local pharmacist had left him for a younger woman, a vicar, no less. X from our high school had broken up with Y and was now dating Z. All zzzz's to me.

I had to lie in the witness box. You don't tell your future bride about the fellow-student who had to fight you off. I said I'd lost interest in my courses in the Midlands. I told her that a gay guy from my year had killed himself but didn't mention that he'd been infatuated with me.

'How did he do it?'

'Jumped from a hundred-foot tower.' Was it 100 feet? Give or take.

'Splat,' said Alison. 'Messy. No viewings for the family.' Bingo-calling might be a better career option than handling the bereaved.

I wasn't invited to witness the hair washing. Shampoos and sex were matrimonial privileges. Even in the privacy of their hall (bamboo wallpaper, very retro) she backed off when I leaned in for a goodbye kiss. It was too early for Mummy to come through the door, flush with her winnings. Perhaps Daddy might walk in, an *Addams Family* moment, flushed with embalming fluid.

There was something else. Walking back to the centre, I put the backing-off with other small details – the occasional glances at the phone, the decline in correspondence

– and the answer was obvious. There was *someone* else.

Who? He hadn't featured in tonight's news summary. A nerd or dork was more likely than a sports jock. Had he got any closer than I had to her B-cup bra or M&S knickers? Did I care? Was my heart broken?

It was another link to the past broken, not my cold cold heart. Rebecca and Harry would have a different father. There were no reasons to stay in this no-horse town. If Rachel had let me stay with her I wouldn't be here now.

We had exchanged numbers before I left Bayswater. Huddled in a shop doorway so that the wind wouldn't whistle down the line I called her. Voicemail: where could she be with a three-year-old son that she'd switched her phone off?

'Hi, Rachel,' I managed to sound breezy. 'It's Paul from – Boredom-on-Sea! I'm freezing my ass off at 7.45 in the town centre. My Dad's pretty pissed that I chucked university, but I'm going to start looking for work and a place of my own tomorrow.' I could not beg for sanctuary on voicemail. 'Hope you and Simon are having fun. Call me when you get this message. Bye. Thanks again for lunch. I'm – very glad we met.'

Now what? The rest of the evening yawned emptily – as did the rest of my life. I could cruise the town's pubs and coffee bars for a new bit of totty (thin on the ground) or old schoolfellows (not thin enough). I could go to a movie; I'd checked out the cinema: there was the choice of a horror sequel, a brainless US teen comedy or Nicole Kidman in *The Hours*. Cancel last Thursday and Friday and Meredith and Neil and I might be going to see the Kidman picture at this very moment, it was 'our' kind of movie. I wondered if Rachel would be up for Virginia Woolf and who would babysit Simon for us.

The pub I opted for had been rebranded last year by a Northern brewery. Tuesdays had a Happy Hour from 6 till 8.30. And look: here were Richie (ex-Boredom High centre forward, now commuting to a security job at Gatwick) and Scott (goalie turned gas fitter), both well bladdered at 7.50.

The college dropout got rapidly pissed; he allowed the piss to be taken. Cherry-chasing – even date-rape - would give me kudos here. I told them there had been an American girl at my uni – killer boobs, silky shaved pussy –

39

whom I'd been 'knobbing' since last term and had now dumped. My life in replay mode became a UK take on *American Pie*. Something stopped me from claiming Rachel as another trophy for our returning hero.

They were going on to a pub with Sky Sports on big-screen TV – soccer from South America. It was only nine. I lurched to the place called home. There was nowhere else to go.

The TV was on in the lounge. My mother was addicted to house or garden makeovers, plus *Emmerdale*, *Holby*, *Inspector Frost* (Inspector Anybody) and old-fashioned character-based sitcoms – not the anarchic modern ones. My dad would be reading the paper or a library book. He liked biographies, especially politicians'. But nobody was going to write his.

I filched a slice of lemon drizzle cake from the kitchen and took it to my room with a glass of milk. Uneasy churning with the beer already inside.

And so to bed.

Rachel didn't call, but there was a text message from her in the morning.

Paul, got in 2 late 2 return yr call. Went 2 c THE HOURS w girl upstairs. Vile kyle's mum had s for sleepover. Meryl streep fab as always. Nicole kidman nose (joke) a good script. Ed harris reminds me of s's dad – hope he hasnt caught anything in LA. Good luck 4 jobhunt. Glad 2 meet u 2. Forget bad things. Try 2 b happy. Keep warm. R

Rachel. Coincidence. THE HOURS on here 2 and i was wondering if u'd like 2 c it w me. Guess I'll have 2 go solo. I'd much prefer to look 4 work in LONDON. Any more affordable flats in yr area? Luv. Paul

So much more I wanted to ask her, but the seeds in my voicemail had fallen on stony ground. She needed time. I was not short of time. It was ideas, ambition, drive, that I lacked.

4. 30k per annum

'Jack could give Paul a job,' my mother said at breakfast. 'He's always taking on staff.'

'And laying them off.' Taking on: Tories in power. Lay-offs: Labour. That's not how it was, it's how my father saw it. 'Why should we to go cap-in-hand to your brother? And what use is Paul to him, anyway?' Thanks, Dad.

'I don't know. He speaks French, doesn't he?' Now she was doing it. *Hello. Il est par ici, celui qui parle Français.*

'Be more use if he spoke Bosnian.' Asylum seekers. Y-a-w-n. Uncle Jack did not employ migrants.

Jack Pemberton was one of the borough's Movers and Shakers. He owned a local furniture factory and a property development company. On their wedding day he gave his eldest daughter Joanna and her groom his-and-hers BMWs and a neo-Georgian townhouse. The most Alison and I could have expected from my parents was an espresso machine.

'I shall call Jack this morning.' A positive start to her day. Almost as fulfilling as loading the food processor. She glowed with satisfaction.

'It can't hurt to ask him,' my father conceded.

It was not the moment to tell them I was hoping to go to London and live with a girl I'd only met yesterday.

There had been no moment of reconciliation at the break-fast bar, but perhaps the fact that we were talking at all, discussing my future (if not exactly a three-way debate), implied that we had put last night's 'episode' behind us. He had. They had.

I only wanted out. Goodbye, Alison. Goodbye, Mum and Dad. But Fate – and my family – had other plans.

Nepotism. The fast track to success. Marrying the boss's daughter is another route, but let's not get ahead of ourselves.

3 p.m. An interview for a job that was already in the bag, at the offices of *Pemberton & Co*, an Edwardian townhouse with art-deco features. In Grandfather's day it had been *Pemberton & Son*, but Uncle Jack had no children. (His stepson-in-law got a management job at the factory – as well as the house and a BMW.)

A blonde receptionist approaching her sell-by date escorted me up to Uncle Jack's suite on the first floor where an older greyer secretary coolly took over and ushered me into the presence. Unlike ours, my uncle's panelled walls didn't come from B&Q, they were original walnut polished to a dark glossy sheen. A bit like his Caribbean tan – he took regular marlin-fishing holidays.

'Hello, Uncle Jack.'

'Paul.' He stood up and we shook hands across a leather-topped desk.

Blubbery lips gave my uncle a fishlike quality. He was a hefty man in his mid-fifties, bald, brown-skinned, rubber-mouthed. Smart or casual, he always dressed expensively, today wearing a gunmetal-grey suit that hadn't come from Next (my father's tailor). He was a fat grey carp, or perhaps a koi.

'Agnes was only saying the other day, we don't see enough of you.' We sat down in leather chairs either side of the desk. His secretary withdrew as silently as a receding glacier. 'Why weren't you at our Christmas party?'

'You clashed with the church carol concert.'

'You preferred that?'

'You think I had a choice?'

'You need to stand up to him more, Paul.'

'I'm starting to. Being here – one giant step.'

He smiled. 'And dropping out of college.'

'Yeah – two giant steps.'

'You didn't like our country's black heartland?' Dad would have warmed to this, a presumed reference to all those Midland Asians. Uncle Jack, I hope, was recalling the region's industrial heritage, celebrated in literature from Mrs Gaskell through Bennett and Lawrence (my favourite) to Alan Sillitoe.

'Actually I didn't, but that's not why I quit.'

'Girl trouble, your mother said.'

'She was part of it, yes.'

'Who was she?'

'She was from Florida, a couple of years older than me, doing a sabbatical year in – Social Science.' I steered away from sneer-worthy Gender Studies.

'She's broken your heart, or you've broken hers?'

'Bit of both, I guess.' It was becoming easier to be glib about the girl I had 'wronged', in Mrs Gaskell's parlance.

'My Jennifer's been seeing an American she met in New Mexico.' She wasn't *his* Jennifer, she was one of his wife's two daughters by her first husband, but Uncle Jack had taken them to his heart – and given them the keys to his kingdom. Why was she in New Mexico? 'Nice-looking boy in photos: designer teeth, designer muscles. Father's a State Congressman. Jenny could do a lot worse, but most likely nothing will come from it. She gets through boy-friends faster than I get through boatloads of timber.'

My mind flashed back to a family barbecue: my step-cousin and I, aged 10 or 11, sneaking into a garden shed for one of those 'You-show-me-yours-I'll-show-you-mine' exchanges. It was a first for me but not, I think, for her. What Jenny revealed was on a daintier scale than the air-brushed models I'd perused with pre-pubescent curiosity in *Hustler* and its ilk. She told me I was bigger than other boys and pressed a tentative finger onto – let's call him *Scout Cub* Wood - who was also becoming a tempting target for mosquitoes from a nearby pond. The insect attacks brought proceedings to a close and we never resumed what was clearly, even at 10 or 11, unfinished business. Jenny still gave me sideways looks at family get-togethers and I was sure she remembered the incident as much as I did, if perhaps less acutely.

'Yours must have been quite a girl, worth throwing your career over for.'

'I think I was heading up the wrong path, Uncle Jack. I still love books, I always will, but the thought of teaching literature – and history – I don't know where I was going with that. It was never what I wanted.' Odd that I was able to talk to him more frankly than I could to my father. And be heard.

'You don't have to teach. A degree opens many doors. It shows you've got sticking power.'

'You've done all right without one.'

He preened. He liked to be thought of as a self-made man, your northern mill-owner type – though he was as southern as I was and self-improved rather than self-made. He admitted as much:

'Yes, but my grandfather started this business, and my father diversified us into property. Both enterprises have prospered under my stewardship, but I often wish I'd had the time to acquire more education. My life's all business.' *Nowt but business* would have sounded more like your northern mill-owner, but we don't talk that way in Sussex.

'Apart from a bit of fishing.' The favoured nephew, I dared to tease him. Another smile that was almost a beam – or, in his case, a bream.

'You'll have to come fishing with me sometime.'

'I'd like that,' I fibbed tactfully.

'So,' he said, 'here's what I could do with you. Mary reminded me you speak French and Spanish.'

'I've got A-Level French, but I gave Spanish up after GCSE.'

'But you speak them enough to get by in?'

'Yes, I can get directions to the station and rent a beach umbrella.'

'Could you buy and sell – never mind buying: could you *sell* in French and Spanish? Sell *furniture*?' Crunch-time.

'Yes,' I said. 'I think I can sell your leather sofas, Uncle Jack.' *Cuir*: French for 'leather', but it was Neil that the word brought to mind. I didn't know the Spanish for it and I didn't know 'sofa' in either language.

'But you haven't got any sales experience?'

'Actually, I do. I worked as a salesman last summer.' Another of Dad's ultimatums. Do something useful or else come and count paperclips at *Barrett & Son*.

'What did you sell?'

'*Furniture!*' I crowed. 'At The Project.' A warehouse that sold second-hand furniture and household goods to the town's poor and dispossessed, including asylum seekers, Dad's favourites. It was like a gigantic boot sale, selling stuff people threw out, much of it junk and the unwanted

44

effects of the newly dead. I'd been a volunteer, unpaid – or subsidized by my parental allowance in the interest of Good (and Useful) Works.

My uncle laughed. 'You'll do,' he said. 'Welcome on-board.'

'When do I start?'

'You haven't asked how much I'm going to pay you.'

'Surprise me.' And he did.

'With commission – assuming you're any good in the field – you could be looking at upwards of 30k per annum. That sound okay?'

Momentarily speechless, I nodded.

'I can't remember if you drive.'

'Yes.' Dad's reward for my A-level grades: driving lessons. Had I stayed the course, a small 4x4 (used) would have been my graduation present.

'There'll be a company car.'

My turn to beam a grateful smile. 'That's great, Uncle Jack. You've really saved my ass – arse. When do I start?'

'How about tomorrow?' Just like that.

'France or Spain?'

'One step at a time, my boy. You need to learn a few ropes. You'll start at the works.'

For thirty grand I'd even put up with being 'my boy'. For that kind of money I would seriously consider being his bum-boy. Sorry, Neil.

She answered this time.

'Hello, Paul.' Voices in the background.

'Where are you?'

'In the park, with Simon. Near where we met, actually.'

'Thinking of me, I hope.'

'Of course.' But she laughed.

'I wish I was there with you.'

A beat, a long one. Crackles over the airwaves.

'I've got a job,' I broke the crusty silence.

'That was quick.'

I told her about my uncle.

'Nice one,' she said. 'Trips to France and Spain.'

'Yeah, trudging round trying to flog chairs and sofas.'

'But you'll be selling to buyers in warehouses and stores, won't you? Not like ringing doorbells and asking people to a Tupperware party.'

'Still, I'm not sure I really want to be a travelling sales-man.'

'Your problem is you don't know what you *do* want.'

'Yes, I do. I want *you*.'

I heard a child give an excited cry, Simon presumably. And I heard a sigh.

'Give it time, Paul.'

'I'm so fucking horny. I've got a hard-on now, just talking to you.'

She giggled. 'Hyde Park isn't the best place for phone sex. Where are you?'

'On a bench overlooking the beach.'

'You'd better calm down, then. Think pure thoughts.'

I laughed. 'I prefer the *impure* ones. I wish you were here. Or I was there. Can I come up at the weekend?'

'Maybe,' she said. 'Or we could come down to you. Is it cold there?'

'Only freezing.'

'Still, a day by the seaside would be nice for Simon.'

'A *night* would be even nicer. I could book us a hotel.'

Another beat. 'Take it slowly, Paul. A day trip.'

'Okay, then.'

'I can't really afford it. You'll have to pay our train fares.'

'I'll put a cheque in the post tonight.'

'That's all right. I'll use the housekeeping and you can pay me back. My bank manager's liable to hold a cheque against my overdraft.'

'How big is your overdraft?'

'None of your business.'

'Tell me and I'll send a cheque to pay it off.' A passing Turk in a blouson gave me a hungry look. Was he leching after me or my warm coat?

'Don't try and *buy* me, Paul.'

'I'm not trying to buy you, for fuck's sake. I'm trying to *help* you.'

'I think you're trying to help yourself.'

'That too,' I admitted with another grudging laugh.

'It's starting to rain. I'd better get Simon home. I'll text you later.'

'I'll check the train times online and call you back.'

'Okay. Bye for now.' And she was gone before I could end with something sloppy or cheeky – and premature. I

46

willed Major Wood into submission.

Our first family dinner since my return as the Prodigal Son. Shock/surprise: the tapestry of my uniformed brother no longer hung over the fireplace. When and where had he been removed? His replacement was our mother's latest masterpiece, a benign alpine landscape that only needed Julie Andrews in a cross-stitched dirndl to have dinner guests puking into their soup bowls.

'So how much is Jack going to pay you for selling his three-piece suites?'

'Thirty thou – with commission. And I get a car.' Triumph in my voice.

'Is that what salesmen earn these days?' Evidently none of his clients were salesmen. Perhaps salesmen do their own tax returns, more creatively. 'You'll be able to give your mother some housekeeping.'

'Actually I thought I might buy a flat of my own.'

'Oh Paul.'

'No one will give you a mortgage until you've been earning for a year or two.' Pissing on my good fortune. He loved being a wet blanket.

'I can *rent* in the meantime.'

'Oh Paul.' Was that a tear in her eye? Cue Mr DJ: *She's leaving home.*

'You've only just got here. There's no need to move out right away.'

'I think it'd be better if I did.'

He took an audible breath. 'Paul – I'm sorry I - said what I said last night.'

Was he? Anyway, who cares? I didn't want to live with him, with them. I wanted a place where I could do my own thing, get bladdered with my mates, as soon as I found some. Not the ex-high-school lager louts. Real friends, like Neil and Meredith had been till I fucked up. A place I could bring girls to. A place where Rachel and Simon would come and stay for more than a day. Perhaps Rachel would move down to the coast. Easy, Paul.

'I've got used to being – independent,' I said carefully. 'You know, being able to stay up late with mates – listen to music.'

'You'll be the tenant from hell,' he said, smiling to show that it was an attempt at humour. I chuckled. I could afford to be benevolent. My uncle had opened the escape hatch.

'You can't stay up drinking when you've got a job to go to.' Dad reverted to type. So did I.

'I know,' I said testily.

'Anyway, you can have your friends *here*, can't he, Mary?'

'Can he?' Not enthusiastic. Imagining projectile vomiting on the freebie suite from Pembertons, on her priceless tapestries.

'This girl of yours can come and stay with you.' Last night she was some nameless tart I might have knocked up in the Black Country. Tomorrow we could be shacked-up in my bedroom. Was he really feeling that guilty?

'Which girl is that, Dad?'

'The one from college.'

'She's history.' My own guilt trip was winding down. I imagined Meredith meeting my parents. Mother's dislike of American TV and movies, junk food, baseball caps, T-shirts, big hair, breast implants. Meredith's admiration of Naughty-Boy Bill (notwithstanding That Woman, Ms Lewinsky) versus my dad's worship at the shrine of the Blessed Margaret and the Holy Reagan Empire.

'Well, with your new job and your own car, the local girls will be fighting to get their hands on you.' Trying really hard to be jaunty. 'I expect we'll see a whole procession of girls through the front door.'

'He can go back to Alison,' said Mother, not keen on the procession.

'She's history too.' I was almost tempted to tell them about Rachel but this was not the time to introduce a single parent and her three-year-old son by a bisexual *desaparacido*.

'Well, please don't think of leaving home too soon. We're getting used to having you back. Obviously, it's a bit of a surprise for us, you giving up your higher education like this, but if you do well at Pembertons it may turn out for the best.'

Smiles all round. Peace, love and harmony in the Barrett household. And there was more:

'Who knows what opportunities might come your way. You could end up starting a business of your own.'

'Don't get carried away, Dad. It's just a job.'

'But you must dream of working for yourself.'

'I'm not like you,' I said. My turn to piss on his parade.

'You will be,' he predicted confidently. I shook my head.

'No way.'

But it was a kind of truce. I would stay on in my new role as paying guest or tenant. Home Sweet Home: it was carved in their hearts but, mercifully, not depicted in another of her tapestries. It was their home – and Trevor's, still – but to me it was just the place where I lived.

For now.

5. Production line

And so, almost seamlessly, the Mill of Industry came to supplant the Grove of Academe. At nine a.m. on Thursday morning I reported to the receptionist at my uncle's offices. A few hours from now it would be exactly a week since I had attacked Meredith and set this transition in motion.

'Welcome aboard, Paul,' the bimbo said, shaking my hand. 'I'm Christine Turner.' She held on to my hand. Wedding and engagement rings on her other hand. A silk or satin blouse wrapped around soap-star cleavage.

'I look forward to working with you, Mrs Turner.'

'Christine. Jack runs an informal ship.' Was everybody at Pembertons into sea fishing?

'Christine,' I said and she let go of my hand. She was quite doable, in a Stifler's Mom sort of way. She looked about 30, although I sensed she might be nearer 40. If the blonde hair wasn't natural it was expensively maintained and she had terrific teeth and tits.

'You don't look like a Pemberton,' she said. Who'd want to look like Jack? Thank God even my mother didn't.

'I'm supposed to take after my father.'

'Bill Barrett?' Nobody called my dad Bill, unless he had a secret life involving busty blondes. 'You're a lot cuter than he is.'

If she wanted to flirt I was up for it. I came back with: 'I expect you're quite a bit cuter than yours.' Her teeth flashed as she laughed.

'I should hope I am. He's been dead for ten years. So – you're to report to Cynthia upstairs. We call her the Ice

Princess.'

And up I went to the domain of the Ice Princess, Uncle Jack's secretary.

'Your uncle's meeting architects this morning,' she said. Cynthia was no spring chicken (she probably had a cat instead of a husband) but her lilac dress was chic and she wore high heels. Less glacial today, she outlined my schedule: a tour of the office ahead of six days at the works to familiarise myself with the product and the production process before I joined the sales team.

Cynthia did the office tour. Ground floor: accounts. First floor: my uncle and herself, plus a conference room. Second floor: Human Resources and wages. Third floor: sales. The accounts manager was an Asian with the accent of the city I'd just left. HR was managed by a power-dressed woman, fortyish, with the aura of an attorney on a US crime series. The sales manager, Michael, my uncle's son-in-law and my new boss, was a Hooray Henry in his mid-twenties with the flash already-going-off looks (and red hair) of James Hewitt, Diana's bonk-and-tell paramour. Cynthia left me in his office, a small room with a view of the block of flats behind the building. Equine prints on the walls, later than Stubbs but not modern. A photo of his wife on horseback. Joanna was prettier than the horse but barely. Only Jenny had inherited their mother's looks.

'Jack wants me to clue you in on the product,' Michael said.

'I'm all ears.' I tried to sound enthusiastic as he showed me brochures for Pemberton suites and sofa-beds and computer graphics comparing their share of domestic markets with their rivals'. *Our* share; *my* rivals: I was 'onboard'.

Pemberton suites and sofas, mostly but not entirely up-holstered in leather, were sold up and down the land, not so much in discount outlets as in family-owned furniture shops and high-end department stores up to and including Mohammed Al-Fayed's Knightsbridge emporium. Most of the furniture was made to order, Michael said. With the ever-present threat of recession stores did not carry large stocks. And our reach across the Channel was barely a blip on Michael's PC charts. A vast virgin market into which I must launch myself like Columbus or Magellan. Nautical similes: I *was* onboard.

Michael introduced me to his secretary, Angela, thirtyish and no beauty. If office adultery was in the air, it wasn't here. The rest of the sales team was out selling. There were four of them, plus Michael and now me.

'Let's get some lunch,' Michael said. He drove me in his Hades-red BMW to a country pub where he knocked back three gin-and-tonics to my two halves of lager. We ate rabbit stew, microwaved to a tough consistency. I asked Michael about his life before Pembertons.

'Three years in the army,' he summarized. 'Four years in the City.' He'd served in Bosnia, which he didn't want to talk about, and seen the dot.com collapse decimate the staff at his brokerage, which I didn't want to listen to. What really pushed his buttons were horses: riding, show-jumping, the local hunt, polo. Dogs got a mention, he and Joanna bred red setters, but he was so far into horses I half expected him to neigh or take a dump in the car park.

Next stop: the Peugeot dealership, where I was allowed to select a diesel 206 roadster in an electric shade of blue. A cashless transaction; the company would be billed and the car would be delivered tomorrow. How cool was that?

From there we went to the mill. It wasn't dark or satanic but neither did it look like the kind of place where a settee would be created that was destined for Clarence House. Aunt Agnes's 1998 Christmas newsletter had head-lined the Queen Mother buying a Pemberton chesterfield from Harrods. Did it now grace the arse of Camilla Parker-Bowles or had it gone to a royal garage sale?

My great-grandfather manufactured cricket bats in his garden shed, a hobby that became a modest business. He died in the Somme in 1916; his son, Jack the First, sur-vived action in the Second World War and then, during the years of austerity, took the firm into utility furniture. The factory, a defunct rope works, expanded onto the site of an adjacent brewery that had taken a direct hit from a German plane puttering home down Bomb Alley. In partnership with a local builder my granddad also went massively into property development during the first big boom in the 1950s: offices and shops, council and private housing. His son, Jack the Second, led the firm into more upmarket furniture in the '70s and was part of the consortium that built the shopping centre.

His property division operated out of a new building in the same street as my father's premises. This was where my uncle was today planning the next phase of town-houses at the marina or a block of flats on the site of a Victorian mansion. Another half-million on Joanna and Jennifer's inheritance. Presumably they would one day also inherit – and quickly sell – the cluster of buildings that was the furniture factory, where I now began the next phase of my induction.

We parked outside the despatch office, where sofas and chairs, shrink-wrapped in heavy-duty plastic, were being loaded off a ramp into a lorry. Two of the loaders had been at my high school. We exchanged nods; one gave me the finger – nepotism did not go hand-in-hand with deference. Their foreman, who turned out to be the lorry driver, was also familiar but older. He was smoking a roll-up. He had a Sussex yeoman build, barrel-chested, beer-bellied, and wore blue jeans and a Brighton & Hove Albion sweatshirt. Michael introduced me:

'Yo, Charlie, this is Paul, Jack's nephew. He's coming to work with me.'

'Christ, not another fuckin' Pemberton.' He also had the Sussex brogue.

'No,' I said. 'I'm a fucking Barrett.'

He chortled and we shook hands. 'Charlie Turner,' he said. It was his son I knew, Jim, a year older than me, one of the school bullies. Jim was fitter and slimmer, but they both had dirty-blonde hair and a squarish face with deep-set blue eyes and a wide mouth. Click. Turner. He was married to the receptionist, Christine. What a pair, the buxom wench and the local yokel. It wasn't easy to see any of her in Jim, but if he was her son she must be in her late thirties.

'Is your dad Bill Barrett the accountant?' Bill again: it sounded so weird.

'Yes.'

'I know Bill from the Legion. Good bloke. They ought to make him mayor.'

Music to Dad's ears. My parents were not snobs, but it wasn't easy to see them hobnobbing with the Turners. My impression of the British Legion was that it was the military wing of the Tory Party, but then I wasn't a member.

Outside of sports I'd never joined anything before the drama group at uni, which was part of my stalking of Meredith.

Charlie Turner squashed the end of his cigarette and tucked it behind his ear for later. I didn't know working men still did that in the 21st century. The business community did not do it at Pemberton cocktail parties.

'Good luck to you, Paul,' he said and went back to work.

Michael took me through the production line backwards: packing, assembly, upholstery, raw materials. Zigzags in the brickwork of the old brewery showed where bomb damage had been rebuilt. The odour wasn't beer, it was new-car leather. Familiar faces at every stage. Friendly waves, but I steeled myself for signs of resentment. A *fuckin' Pemberton* by blood if not by name.

A mostly male workforce, except in Upholstery, a partitioned area with a dozen women seated at industrial sewing machines. The only male, the eunuch in this harem, was a tall thin man in an apron who cut fabrics on a table like a butcher's block with a built-in electric blade. In Assembly I'd seen industrial nail guns and bandsaws. All these deadly machines; I wondered what the accident rate was.

'My wife calls this the Cat-house,' Michael said. 'Hold on to your weapon!'

A grey-haired matriarch in a smock approached us smiling. 'Hello, Michael. Who's this nice-looking young man?'

'Yo, Auntie Lil. This is Paul Barrett. He's Jack's nephew. Coming to work with me. Call her Auntie Lil, Paul. Everybody does. She's in charge of this bevy of beauties. Best job in the plant!'

'Hello, Auntie Lil.'

'Hello, Paul.' We shook hands.

'Look out,' Michael warned. 'Here comes Saffron.'

One of the women waddled towards us, a streaked blonde of about 20 with big boobs and fleshy thighs. Her lips were a vivid purple. She wore a nipple-rubbing pink tank-top, a red leather miniskirt that may have been a factory offcut, patterned black tights and lilac trainers. The clatter of sewing machines stopped abruptly as she boldly wrapped her arms around me, her breasts squishing against my chest. Drenching perfume.

'Kiss me, you handsome brute,' she commanded. The line echoed the old movies Meredith liked to watch in my aching arms on rainy afternoons.

'If it's all the same to you, gorgeous,' I improvised a line worthy of Meredith's beloved Humphrey Bogart, 'I'd rather be shot than poisoned.'

A gale of screeching laughter greeted my reply. The women banged on their tables, rattling the machines. Auntie Lil cackled appreciatively.

'Nice one, Paul,' Michael chortled. 'I can't wait to tell Joanna!'

Waddling back to her machine in the front row, Saffron furiously resumed work on a length of dark green brocade. Michael's 'bevy of beauties' comprised a dozen different styles of hair, wardrobe, make-up. Blondes, brunettes, redheads; wives, bimbos and bags, all thrown together in a multicolour blaze of Gap and BHS and Matalan. Saffron was the archetype, with her cheap clothes and duty-free perfume, her tawdry allure and promise of backseat titillation. I was a long way from high school and uni.

The next two rooms, unstaffed, were for the storage of fabrics and stuffings. Leather was stored separately in an unheated room; in bales the smell wasn't new-car, it was slaughterhouse.

'We get our leather from Morocco and South America,' Michael told me. 'Jack makes annual quality control trips to the suppliers. With your languages he might start taking you with him.'

Outside, a short concrete roadway led to a building that had been the pre-war rope works. Beside it, a new plastic roof sheltered a twenty-foot-high stack of timber roughly hewn into beams the size of floor joists.

'Where does the wood come from?' I asked.

'Canada,' Michael said. 'If you're worried about the environment, don't be. Jack only buys from sustainably managed forests. We don't want protesters picketing the yard here or the shops that sell our stuff.'

With a teacher he idolized Neil had squatted a woodland outside Bristol to save it from developers. Meredith's parents, in spite of losing one house to a hurricane, still drove SUVs, but after Neil's banging on about gas guzzling and climate change and Kyoto, Meredith would be taking ecological awareness back with her. Was she home by now? And Neil: was he home too? Perhaps his parents would give him a Green burial in a woodland like the one he'd (vainly) defended. A great wave of grief and guilt shook me for a moment.

The noise inside the rope works suggested a heavier industry than furniture manufacture. A series of saws reduced the timber I'd seen outside to the requisite lengths. Bench-mounted machines shaped these segments, hacked out mortises and shaved tenons. The most raucous machine was the larger of two ripsaws: two men winched the beams off a forklift onto a polished steel platform dull with wear; a traction mechanism pulled the wood into a three-foot-diameter blade and drew the two halves out the other side. Splinters the size of vampire stakes thudded into the metal safety-mesh shrouding the blade, which screamed as it tore through the timber.

And the operator of this infernal device was the Scourge of Boredom High, Charlie and Christine Turner's son Jim. He grinned as he punched a button to stop the saw and the traction, then lifted the safety cage before pulling out some of the fragments. The noise level dropped by fifty decibels.

'Hey, Paul. Thought you was in college.' His accent wasn't as strong as his dad's; his bold cheeky grin reminded me of his mother.

'No, my uncle's given me a job here.'

'Who's 'e then?'

'Jack Pemberton is my uncle.'

'Is 'e now?' A nod that said, *another Pemberton, another wanker*. 'You gonna be workin' in 'ere with us?'

'Just to see what it's like, then I'll be working with Michael.'

'On the road?'

'Yeah.' I gave a dismissive shrug and avoided mentioning that Europe was to be my manor. He wasn't the bully here, the factory had planed his rough edges, so I didn't need to show off – the A-Level swot, the 800-metre runner.

'*Jim.*' A shout from the foreman, another sturdy yeoman. 'We workin' or doin' a chat-show?'

'Okay, Morris. See you around, Paul.' Jim flashed me

his mother's grin again and punched the machine control.

'How many more times?' yelled the foreman. 'Close the fuckin' cage.'

'Okay, okay.' He pulled the safety cage down just as the saw whistled back into full spin and the traction re-started with a jerk.

I waved goodbye to Jim Turner. He nodded again.

Back near where we'd parked Michael's BMW was a large Portakabin that functioned as a canteen. The tea was Midlands strength, not the delicate brew my parents favoured, and my teacake was thickly buttered, none of your low-cholesterol spreads. We sat with Roger Dean, the Despatch Supervisor. Roger raced greyhounds and bored for Britain. Michael seemed to like him.

At another table Saffron sat with two other women from the sewing circle. I grinned at Saffron who stuck her tongue out in reply.

After tea we inspected Design and Marketing above the despatch office in the site's only modern building. Michael's title was Marketing Manager; he worked partly from here.

'The Sales team used to work out of here, but Jack likes them to report to him directly, so they moved to the town office. As you'll see, he's very hands-on regarding both production and sales – design too. Everything, really.'

There was a creative force of two behind Pemberton furniture; today they were at an exhibition in Rome, checking out the competition. I was introduced to Linda who designed our brochures. With wild red hair, zany clothes, speech larded with profanity, Linda was an unlikely individual to be writing paeans to sofa-beds and chesterfields. She asked what school I'd gone to. I told her.

'My poor-bastard husband just started there this year. He teaches art.' Subtext: don't waste your time flirting with me. I wasn't planning to.

'I didn't do art after primary school,' I told her.

'Tough shit.'

'Yeah.' I laughed, but it was another unnecessary reminder of Meredith.

Then it was down to Roger Dean on the floor below. His secretary, Alice, was an older Alison: angora and acne, an air of anxiety. I was shown invoices, despatch notes, delivery schedules. Like, wow. Seriously fascinating stuff.

Roger wore two hats: Despatch Supervisor and Production Manager. And now a third: Development.

'You report to Roger tomorrow morning,' Michael said. 'Nine a.m. He'll throw you in the deep end.'

'I might start him in the shallows,' said Roger, joviality personified.

Deep end or shallows, my heart began to sink.

'D'you want me to give you a lift in tomorrow?' asked Michael.

'It's okay. My dad can drop me off.'

We drove back to town. Cynthia had some forms for me to fill in. Motor insurance, National Insurance, Income Tax, BUPA (a company health scheme for office staff). Breaking me in gently, she sent me home at 4.30.

I went to the pizzeria for a latte and tiramisu. I thought about my new car, my new life, Roger Dean, the week ahead. And I thought, inevitably, about my old life, Meredith, Neil, the week behind.

'*Sei un po' serioso òggi*,' said Luisa. '*Perché*?' Why was I so serious today? I told her about my uncle's industrial empire: *la fabbrica di mio zio*. She said I was *molto fortunato* have *un nuovo lavoro* so soon. I asked her the Italian for 'boredom'.

'*Nòia.*'

'*Questa ciudad è Nòia-sul-Mare*,' I told her. She laughed.

'*Ma non è vero. È una carina città.*' *Città*: not *ciudad*. A darling little town. Luisa and I were from different planets. Finishing my coffee while she served another customer, I projected this providential new life further into the future. Touting Pembertons' wares at furniture stores in France and Spain. Touring tanneries in Morocco and South America with my uncle. Would it be glamour or drudgery?

There was always Plan B. London. Rachel. Simon.

A retro dinner menu: shepherd's pie and rhubarb crumble. Rhubarb from our garden, via the freezer. We ate early: British Legion night. I told them I'd met the Turners and that Charlie had mentioned the Legion.

'He's one of our staunchest members,' Dad said. 'Lost his father and two uncles in World War Two. Imagine how his mother must have felt.'

'Christine Turner only comes to dinners and dances,' Mother put in. 'She's not one for talks and committee meetings.'

'Their son works on the assembly line,' I said. 'Jim. He was a year ahead of me in school. Left at 16.'

'Jim's not hers,' Mother said. 'His mother was Charlie's first wife. Margaret. Died of bone cancer. Jim was nine or ten. I visited her. She was in awful pain, more than the drugs could control. She wasn't anything like Christine. Margaret was very active in the Legion and her church. They're Methodists. I don't know about Christine, I doubt she's much for churchgoing.' Judgemental gossip; Mother was in her element. Dad put the boot in a bit further:

'After Margaret you wonder what made Charlie marry her,' he said. 'Apart from the obvious.'

'I like her,' I said, to annoy them but omitting the observation that I thought Christine was doable. Mother moved us on to another topic.

After they left I called Rachel to check she'd got the train times I'd texted her last night. She told me which one they planned to catch. I summarized my first day at work, including my exchange with blowsy Saffron but not my uncle's shag-worthy receptionist or the new car – a surprise for Saturday.

'What do you want to do on Saturday?' I asked.

'It's your town. Surprise us.'

'Are you sure you want me to?'

She laughed. 'Well – surprise Simon, anyway.'

I held back from describing the kind of big surprise I'd like to give Rachel; it was getting bigger as we spoke. After the call I ran for thirty minutes on the cold wet streets to try to stave off masturbatory fantasies. But no.

The liberal regime of a BA curriculum hadn't entirely cured me of the homework habit. And, like my father, I was as happy with my nose in a book as in front of a television. I looked through my shelves for something that might lubricate my rusty French. Of my A-level texts Racine and Verlaine failed to push any buttons. Françoise Sagan? (Did I gain or lose marks for comparing *Bonjour, Tristesse* to *Less Than Zero* by Bret Easton Ellis, who wasn't born when Sagan started writing?) I settled for a low-rent read, the

French version of *Dr. No*, bought three years ago during a school trip to Paris.

At the exact moment of the one-week anniversary of my assault on Meredith, it wasn't her or Rachel I was thinking of, or Christine 'Mrs Stifler' Turner's satin cleavage or the soft breasts of purple-lipped Saffron. I was adrift in a fantasy of Ian Fleming's all-time sexiest heroine Honeychile Ryder, sublimely incarnated in the first-ever Bond film by Ursula Andress. Now there's teeth and tits!

The smooth sophisticated superspy in me (aka the predator) seethed to be unleashed.

6. Knickerbocker glory

'I have always depended,' Saffron confided in a stage whisper, 'on the kahndness of strangers.'

'I coulda been a contender,' I responded. She furrowed her brow theatrically. I supplied the link: '*On the Waterfront*. Marlon Brando. *Streetcar*. Marlon Brando.' Saffron followed the Vivien Leigh connection to Clark Gable:

'Frankly, my dear, I don't give-a-damn.'

'After all,' I allowed, 'tomorrow is another day.' (Meredith had forced me to watch *Gone with the Wind* on DVD. She adored it; I did not.) Saffron's workmates looked on uncomprehendingly. We were plainly off our heads.

I was fated to fall among actresses. Improbable as it seemed, ultravixen Saffron was a leading light (well, a lesser luminary) in one of the local amateur dramatic groups. Her name was Emma; she'd reinvented herself as Saffron.

It was day one of my apprenticeship to Roger Dean. And my role today, Friday, was to study orders and invoices and delivery notes with acne'd Alice (a thrill a minute) in between errands for Roger (four or five thrills an hour).

'Take this to Morris.' Morris Jones, Jim's foreman in the timber workshop. An order for our biggest chesterfield.

'Take this to Auntie Lil.' Who was of an age to be Roger's sister, not his aunt. A special order for a suite in one of our 'exclusive' shades of leather.

'Take this to Charlie.' A revised delivery schedule. Charlie was to make a drop-off in Cambridge on his way to Glasgow and Edinburgh.

The sewing room quickly became my favourite destination. A warm welcome from Auntie Lil and a wet one from Saffron and her gang. I sat with them at lunchtime (fish 'n' chips). Michael was at his office in town.

Saffron's gang consisted of a few dumb blondes and dumber brunettes. Their conversation veered between Sussex versions of *EastEnders* and *Buffy*, a mix of domestic whingeing and post-high-school boyfriend talk. Saffron, the blondest of them, was the least dumb. She mentioned her drama group, I told her about university dramatics and my American 'ex' (so heartless, so soon) and then about our gay friend who'd jumped to his death.

'My Dad killed himself two years ago,' Saffron said. 'His firm went bust. The only jobs on offer were way below his level – stacking shelves, that sort of thing – and he got more and more depressed and hung himself in the garage. My mum found him. She hasn't been right since.'

'God,' I said. Real life is harder than soap drama.

'His insurance paid off the mortgage. We're more comfortable financially than we've ever been. But I'd rather have my dad back.' She smiled through tears: the show must go on. 'Life's a bitch, innit?'

'And you wind up dead,' I tactlessly completed the line, a liberal rendering of a theme by Virgil, much quoted by Neil. *Lacrimae rerum*: it could be carved on his grave, if he has one. Getting the sense if not the source, Saffron sighed.

'Fuckin' 'ell,' said one of the brunettes, 'can't we talk about somefink a bit more fuckin' cheerful?'

But I'd started a game with Saffron. Every time I ran a Roger Dean errand to the sewing room she had new lines ready. Vivienne Leigh. Bette Davis (*'Fasten your seatbelts'*). Nicole Kidman. Anthony Hopkins (Hannibal).

'You plannin' on shaggin' Saffron?' Jim Turner asked in the timber workshop after lunch, grinning his stepmother's in-your-face grin. I grinned back.

'Think I should?'

'If you don't mind slurpy seconds. She's 'ad 'alf the blokes 'ere.'

'Including you?'

He shook his head. 'Nah, she's got too much form. I like a bird with a bit more class.' Sussex boy sounded like an Essex boy. I wondered what kind of 'bird' with a bit of class would go out with Jim Turner, who operated ripsaws and the machines that cut mortises and tenons. At Boredom High he and his mates had made some younger boys give them blowjobs. Not me: a medal-winning runner was safe from the homosexual sadism with which school bullies compensated their failure to pull girls. Most of them, I surmised, 'matured' into the kind of men who roughed up their wives and girlfriends once they had a few pints inside them.

I'd told Neil about Jim Turner's gang. Neil had been the victim of sexual bullying and had developed a major crush on one of his tormentors. Teenage sexuality is full of mystery. The bullies go from gay to straight, their victims from straight to gay. It can't be as simple as that, can it?

Jim Turner solved one mystery, not that it had been nagging at me.

'Didn't you use to go out with Alison – what's 'er name – Saunders?'

'Yeah. She dumped me after Christmas.'

'She's goin' out with Keith Cartright. 'E was in my gang at school. Works with 'is dad in that fish-'n'-chip shop opposite the Bingo.'

Keith Cartright. Blowjob bully turned girlfriend-stealer. The chippy's son and the undertaker's daughter. Another Jim, Jimmy Porter from Osborne's *Look Back in Anger* (Eng. Lit. Year One: 20th-Century Drama) made up one-liners along those lines. He was only a fishmonger's son, but she showed him her 'plaice' and said 'fillet'. She was only a mortician's daughter but...the smell of her soon had him 'coffin'!

'You up for some football?' Jim shouted over the noise of the ripsaw.

'Yeah, why not.' Football would keep me fit and I intuited that my uncle would be happy for me to fraternize with the workforce. 'Where do you play?'

'Jack levelled a field for us be'ind 'is place. Give us changin' rooms and everythin'. We play our matches evenin's or Sundays.' My uncle's 'place', The Grange, was a sometime baronial hall six or seven miles inland.

'Who d'you play?'

'Other firms, local league teams. We 'ave a practice game most Wednesdays. After tea.' Tea meaning dinner.

'I'll be there next Wednesday.'

A job, a car, now a football team. Provincial life was engulfing me.

Mid-afternoon the Peugeot dealership delivered my car.

'You jammy cunt,' said Jim, now driving a forklift. Jim's car was a 20-year-old MG BGT he and his dad (who also drove one) had restored. Charlie was now en route to Cambridge and Scotland.

'I'll swap it for your motor,' I said.

'Like fuck you will!'

'It's all right for some,' went Roger who drove a 1-year-old Audi Quattro and had no reason to be jealous. I didn't offer to swap cars with Roger, who sent me on an errand to the town office so that I could get behind the wheel of my pretty new motor.

'Look what the cat's dragged in,' said Christine Turner. I stuck my tongue out at her, Saffron-style, and imagined sticking it down her throat.

At our next encounter Saffron was *Titanic*'s DiCaprio, so I had to be Kate Winslet. A dozen more errands, thirty more forms – I had graduated to tapping keys on Alice's PC, closely monitored by The Spotty One – and it was time to clock off. (I didn't but the factory workers, digitally, did.) I took the Peugeot for a longer drive. Roads clogged with home-going commuters – I was now one of them – so no chance to put the pedal to the metal. But I felt as flash as a metallic-blue roadster myself. I couldn't forget the circumstances that had driven me from my university but I no longer felt the need to regret abandoning higher education and, for the first time since running away, I was facing the future in a mood that might, just, be optimism.

Fish and chips on the domestic menu as well on Fridays. We were Anglicans but almost Roman in some of our observances. Foil-baked salmon and homemade oven fries, none of your nasty takeaways from Keith Cartright who had pinched Alison from me and was welcome to her.

Television for Mother. Dad was reading John Major's autobiography, an act of symbolic self-flagellation in the Blair era. I went for a run on a full stomach, then took the car for a night-time spin. My book at bedtime was *James Bond contre Dr No*. Honey Ryder tied up *pour les crabes*. For the second night running she came between me and thoughts of Rachel.

'Mummy, can I have an ice-cream?'

'It's not really ice-cream weather, pumpkin.'

'Pretty please. Can I, Paul?'

'Well –' his mother and I began simultaneously and laughed.

Up in the Midlands it was snowing. Here on the South Coast we were basking in cold sleety rain. In the Midlands they had Florida-sized attractions – Alton Towers, Center-Parc. In Boredom-on-Sea we had Crazy Golf and a fibre-glass recreation of The Alamo, and both were closed in winter.

'You've landed on your feet,' Rachel said outside the station when she saw the car.

'It's yummy,' Simon says.

'Wait till you see my new penthouse.'

'You're kidding, right?'

'For now I am.'

I drove them to the pier, where Simon was more interested in the roll-a-coin slides than in *Batman-* and *Terminator*-themed video games. He lost £2 on the 10p slide and a slower pound's worth of 2p coins. 'That's enough,' said Rachel, but I found one last 10p in my pocket and with it he dislodged eight coins plus a £5-note which I'd always assumed was superglued to a fixed coin and only there as bait. Simon retrieved his winnings with glee.

'Give Paul the fiver.'

'Mummee –'

'It was *his* money.'

'No way,' I said. 'Winner takes all.'

'How many ten p's in five pounds, Paul?'

'Lots. Hundreds.'

'Give it to me, Simon. It can go in the piggybank. We're saving for a DVD player.'

'Let me buy him one today.'

'No, Paul. We have to save for things. I don't want him to be one of those kids who gets everything ten minutes after they say they want it. He has to learn the value of money.'

'Yes, Mummy,' I said. Simon giggled. I winked at him, resolving to buy a DVD player before I saw them again. He was permitted to lose the other eight coins before we drove inland for a pub lunch. Certain that her budget rarely ran to a roasting joint, I made Rachel share a shoulder of lamb. Simon wasn't allowed burgers but homemade chicken nuggets were an acceptable concession to junk food. After lunch we drove to Beachy Head. Rainswept, pounded by heavy seas in a receding tide, the lighthouse was at its bleakest.

'Imagine living there,' Rachel said.

'It's on autopilot. I don't think any of them are manned any more.'

'There's no romance left in the world.'

'Was running a lighthouse ever romantic?'

'Depends who you're running it with.'

I banished a promiscuous thought of Ursula Andress running up the stairs of *my* phallic lighthouse as we hurried back to the car to get in the dry. Driving half a mile further I parked in a lay-by that was barely 20 yards from the cliff edge. On the hill above us stood the old Belle Tout lighthouse. 'You can imagine living *there*,' I said. 'Somebody does.'

'Is that the one they moved back from the brink a few years ago?'

I nodded. 'At a cost of about 250k, and it's sure to go over eventually. Next time it comes on the market I'll buy it, so you can fulfil your fantasy.'

She smiled. 'I'll think of a better one before then!' She looked over into the back seat where Simon had dozed off. Reaching back Rachel unfastened his seatbelt. Without waking he murmured something and sprawled full-length. Heart-warming to see him snuggled in the rear of my car. I had a comforting sense of the upside of parenting. Rachel reached over and took my hand. I was wise enough not to say anything. Holding hands we too dozed off for perhaps half an hour, in the rain, on the brink of a 300-foot precipice.

I awoke with Major Wood. Rachel smirked and gave him a feel. It took a major effort of mind over matter not to cream my pants instantly.

'Oh, Grandma,' she whispered – Simon was still asleep – 'what a big whatsit you've got.'

'All the better to fill you up with, my dear.' But it was the horny teenager, not the predator, doing a big-bad-wolf-grandma voice. 'Do you think Simon would mind if I popped him in the boot for ten minutes?'

'Make it twenty,' she said in a seductive tone, still pressing my groin, keeping *me* on the brink. The predator kicked in, but when I stretched an explorative hand into her lap she grabbed it. 'No, Paul. Not with Simon in the back. Maybe next time.' She removed her hand and I retrieved mine.

'Promise?' I noticed tiny copper freckles in her brown eyes as she smiled.

'A rain-check, anyway.' So many Americanisms in English these days, so many reminders of Meredith. I gestured through the windscreen. Sleetier at this height above sea level, the rain clung briefly to the glass before dissolving.

'Good day for a rain-check.' Down, Major, down.

'It's a good day in every way, in spite of the weather. Thank you, Paul.' As she leaned towards me her hair flooded both our faces, a torrent of autumn colours like a leaf fall. We kissed, a comfortable, companionable, romantic kiss with some gentle tongue action that hinted at future passion. I lightly fingered her breasts through her sweater but resisted the yearning to delve underneath. I was – almost – at peace and certainly happy. The L-word was hovering in my mouth but common sense told me to let it hover for now.

A voice from the back said: 'Mummy, can I have an ice-cream?'

I took them to my regular haunt where Simon was much clucked over by both mama-hen and papa-hen. Luisa taught him his name in Italian – *See-moe-nay* – which he quickly mastered, along with *Pa-oh-low* and *Rah-kay-lay*. He consumed one of the specials, a 'Coppa Vesuvio' which in my parents' day, I recalled, had inexplicably been known as a 'Knickerbocker Glory'.

'Sounds rude,' Simon said with relish. 'What's a knickerboxer?'

'You hit the nail on the head,' said Rachel. 'They were old-fashioned kind of shorts. A bit like what runners and bikers wear these days. But not Lycra.'

'I'd like to show you *my* "Knickerbocker Glory",' I said. Rachel laughed.

'You pretty well have!' she said and didn't explain the reference to her son.

67

Time to run them to the station. She wouldn't stay for the evening – 'He's not such a bundle of joy when he gets overtired' – and she wouldn't stay overnight: 'I told you. Anyway, we bought day returns.'

'Which reminds me.' I gave her two £20 notes.

'One would do,' she protested.

'Put it in the DVD fund. I'm a working man now, remember.'

'With a mortgaged penthouse.'

'And a wife and six children.'

'Well – just a stepson for starters,' she said, re-warming my heart. I walked them to the train, hugged and kissed Simon, hugged and kissed Rachel.

'Next weekend?'

'You could come to us.' Movement from Corporal Slack. 'I should warn you: parking's a nightmare. And there's a lot of vandalism of cars.'

'I'll come on the train.' I could not recall the last time I felt so euphoric. More kisses. Sliding doors. Waving.

Walking back to my shiny blue car I was *Raindrops-on-roses* happy. I was falling in love, properly and at the right pace, at last. With a girl who was falling in love with me. The South Downs were alive with the sound of music.

But Fate had other plans.

For both of us.

Not wanting to spend another ultra-provincial evening with my parents and the Rotarian couple they were entertaining, I ran Poppeia (yes, I'd already given my car a classical-allusion name) up the A22 to Caterham. On the North Downs the sleet fell as snow, patches of white that faded to black as I passed them. Poppeia handled the wintry roads with a contented purr and my mood remained upbeat. A short stretch of M25 and then back to the coast on the M23/A23. I pushed the car briefly to 80 mph but didn't risk her or my new career on anything higher. Conservative blood runs in my anarchist veins.

Parking on Brighton seafront I snacked in The Lanes on tapas and a single glass of white rioja. The bar was popular with students and I chatted to one called Stephen. He was doing Economics and wanted to do me. I told him I'd dropped out but not why, and that I'd started a new job along the coast.

'I've got a studio flat in Hove,' he said. 'You can crash on my sofa if you don't feel like driving back in this weather.' Nothing too crass or pushy. Gays have it so much easier than the rest of us. Would I ever know why Neil couldn't hack it? I was sure Stephen would have liked him.

'I'd better get home,' I said. 'My folks will be worrying. You know, snow on the roads. And I'm in a new car.'

He gave me his mobile number for the next time I came to Brighton, which he hoped would be soon. He was a little crestfallen, as if he knew I would discard his number. I hadn't offered mine. But hey, this was the South's gay Mecca and the night was young.

I took the coast road home, the A259.

'Are you – you know – okay about what happened at uni?' Rachel had asked over lunch.

'I'm – trying to be,' I said, the brave hero reining in his emotions, the phoney, the cold-hearted bastard, the predator-in-waiting.

'Good,' she said and we let it go: Meredith, Neil, my guilt-trip, running for home.

'You didn't say your friend from London was a girl,' Mother said at breakfast, her tone mildly accusing. My father looked up from the *Sunday Telegraph*.

'Didn't I?' Never apologize, never explain.

'Marjorie saw you in the ice-cream parlour.' The Rotary wife. 'There was a small boy with you.'

'Her son. She's the sister of a guy I was at college with who committed suicide.' If you're going to lie, mix in a bit of truth to make the lie convincing.

'Does her child have a father?' My batty mother was sometimes quite quick on the draw.

'Of course he does, but he's working in the US.'

'Why did this girl want to see you?'

'She wanted to talk about her brother. To see if I knew why he – you know – killed himself.'

'And do you?'

'Not really. He seemed kind of confused about things.'

'What things?'

'Everything, really.'

'Was he gay?' *Very* quick. Not batty at all.

'I think he might have been.'

69

My father gave a homophobic harrumph.

'You're not – one of them – are you?' *One of them.* My Stone-Age mother.

'No, Mother. He was just a friend. From the drama group.'

'You never told us you'd joined a drama group.'

'I'm sure I did.'

At least I'd diverted them from Rachel. Why couldn't I simply tell them the truth? I would have to eventually. But lying to our parents is instinctive. We don't want them to know what we're up to. Even if the lies get us into deeper water than the truth.

As a penance I went to church with them, a routine I'd broken with somewhere between GCSE and A-levels when – truthful for once – I announced that I had landed, faith-wise, somewhere between scepticism and non-belief. Sur-prisingly, my father did not over-react. He stopped asking if I wanted to go to church with them and didn't make too big a show of pleasure when, like today, I did.

My grandmother used to say she couldn't forgive God for the Nazi Death Camps and hoped He would have an explanation when she met Him (did she? Did He?). A woman friend of my parents from the Legion said it wasn't Hitler or Stalin or Pol Pot, it was BSE that did it for her: all those cows and calves and sheep burning on their vast pyres, like something from the Dark Ages; how did this square with the Divine Plan? Search me. Saddam and Bin Laden, Bush and Blair, Islamic Fundamentalists and Amer-ican Evangelicals – between them they keep the flame of medievalism burning, like those cattle.

But today, love was all around us. *My song is love unknown.* Sometime choirboy treble, now an uncertain baritone, I joined in with gusto. *O love that wilt not let me go.* I love that 'wilt'. It's none of my business, clearly, but I do think Almighty God should be 'Thou' and not 'You'.

'Let us now,' the vicar intoned, 'offer up our own silent prayers in our own words, knowing that He is the God from Whom no secrets are hidden [shouldn't that be 'hid'?], Who knows all the secret desires of our hearts.'

Presumably, then, the Old Bugger knows I jumped Meredith and failed Neil in his Hour of Need. Of course, meeting Neil's particular need would have drawn me into a theological grey area. St Agnes's was High Anglican with all the neo-Catholic trappings. Father Martyn, as he liked to be known, was more priest than pastor, celibate, doctrinaire, a string-puller at the Town Hall. He was vehemently anti-women-priests but not anti-gay. Probably a bit of a poofter himself. He often reminded us of the 'many mansions' in God's house. Some of these mansions may possess *closets* for the likes of Martyn to lurk in.

Did the O.B. also know that I was, in the secret desire department, leching after – in ascending order – Rachel, Christine Turner, Saffron, and Ursula Andress (vintage 1962)?

Anyway, it's just possible that in a confused silent prayer I said Sorry for jumping Meredith and failing Neil and Thank-You for Rachel and Simon (and Ursula Andress!) and may have even promised to try and be a better boy.

The sermon was on the theme of making amends for our misdeeds. But the lingering aroma of incense brought back the other smells of the last ten days: sea and country, sawdust and leather at the factory, my mother in the kitchen, my father by a log fire, the polluted air of London and the Midlands, trains and stations, the differing perfumes of Rachel and Saffron and Christine, the small-boy smell of Simon, Neil's aftershave when he kissed me and the stench of death on his smashed body at the foot of the tower, and the more metaphysical odour of fear on Meredith as she threw me off her.

Death and debauch, sacrilege and retribution. Like an American Evangelical, I was more in tune with the Old Testament than with the Gospel of Jesus. An eye for an eye, judge not lest ye be judged, thou art weighed in the balance and found wanting.

And, wouldn't you know it, the Old Bugger (I some-times think He may really exist) was right on my wave-length, getting ready to give me another shafting.

7. Pinky and perky

By Tuesday I was well fed-up of filling and filing forms and running errands.

'Can't I do something on the production line?' I asked Roger Dean.

'Like what? Can you sew?'

'Hardly! But I could learn how to operate the saws or the mortise-cutter.'

'Jack will have my guts for garters if I let you near any of them machines. They can be deadly. Just last month Lil's son lost one of his fingers on the mortise-cutter.' I'd heard this story in the canteen. Roger was exaggerating. Lil's son had lost only a fingertip feeding timber into the mortise-cutter, the mishandling born of endless repetition. 'And two years back a man lost his hand on the crosscut saw.' This too I had heard: the gory folklore of the mill.

'I *am* supposed to get to know the product I'll be selling on the road.'

Roger thought for a moment. 'Tell you what. Young Jim's covering in frame assembly starting tomorrow. Bob Haffenden's having his hernia done. You can work with Jim. But be careful! And don't do anything you're not sure of. We're losing too much timber already through careless-ness.'

And so I became, for three days, an apprentice assembler, one of the proles. It was almost as boring as form-filling, but the company was better. The company of men – a bit like, I imagined, an army barracks.

Jim was a jack-of-all-trades, able to operate (and service) all of the production line's infernal machines, most of which truly could in a single careless moment cause hideous injuries and even death. Under orders from Roger he wouldn't let me do much more than fetch and carry and hold things while he glued or hammered or power-screwed them into place. Surprising at what speed a woodpile became a sofa, a chair-frame. The frame for a chesterfield costing over £2,000 (in one of our top 'exclusive' leathers) looked like a rabbit hutch made by a d-i-y novice; lucky that the customers did not see this early stage.

Factory work was all noise: bangings, power-bursts, an inordinate amount of cursing, shouted exchanges of dialogue relating to work (and pay), domestic dramas (and sex), the issues of the day (they relished the coming war but they did not cherish asylum-seekers), television – and football. A lot of football. And dirty jokes. Dozens, hundreds of jokes.

'- the guy says, "Come on, Sugar. Nobody pays a thousand bucks for a blowjob" –'

'- George Dubya should shove an Exocet right up Saddam's arse'ole, or get the Israelis to drop a few nukes on Baghdad –'

'- they'll be back in the Premier League next year, you mark my words –'

'- the hooker says, "I own a piece of that bar across the street because guys like you can't get too many of my incredible thousand-dollar blowjobs" –'

'- the Guvnor should give us at least another 50p an hour –'

'- wouldn't let me give 'er one, but she tossed me off in the car –'

'- and the guy says, "Jesus, I never had a blowjob like that in my entire life. How much would I have to pay for some *pussy* action?" –'

'- this fuckin' glue-gun's fucked again –'

'- I'd put these anti-war wankers in concentration camps –'

'- so the hooker takes him to the window and says, "See that new casino they're building over there?" –'

'– needs to get 'is nose out of the trough and 'is mind on the game –'

'- no fuckin' daughter of mine is gonna marry a fuckin' Albanian –'

'- the guy says, "You're not telling me you own a piece of that casino?" –'

'- my ten-year-old wants to audition for the next series of *Popstars* –'

'- doesn't have to be a strike, we could threaten him with a go-slow –'

'- and the hooker says, "No, but I would if I had a pussy!" –'

'- what Albion need to get onboard is a Russian fuckin' billionaire who could buy in some decent players –'

'- just like Maggie, God bless 'er, pissed all over the Argies –'

'- so these three nuns went into a pub in Dublin –'

Some of the workforce were semi-literate. They were foul-mouthed to a rare degree (okay, I was *literate* and foul-mouthed). They had no 'culture', no sophistication. But *their* votes had brought Thatcher and Major – and now Tony Blair – into office. Many of them bore testament to the success of Thatcher's 'mission' to create a home-owning democracy, a process New Labour was consoli-dating. Uncle Jack reckoned he paid them a fair wage; they didn't agree. Fairly paid or not, they were shackled to his production line by their mortgages and credit card debts, a bondage as secure as any Victorian mill-worker's. And yet they had the power – if they chose to exercise it (part of me wished they would) – to tear down all that belonged to my uncle. In the 21st century the Bastille could again be stormed.

Yes, they were coarse and crass but they were spon-taneous and genuine, they were warm and – to the people and principles they valued – loyal. They had no time for Michael, but (thanks to the sewing circle) I was okay, I was *in*.

And one of them became my new best friend.

'No football practice tonight,' he said.

'No?'

'Pitch is too waterlogged.'

'Oh well – I'll go for a run instead. Got to keep fit!'

'Where do you run?'

'From my house to the pier and back.'

'What time?'

'Soon as I get home.'

'I'll meet you at the pier and run back with you.'

On a cold rainy night he ran in a singlet and shorts. I wore a tracksuit which my mother laundered every morning. I invited him in when we got home, knowing that his muscular footballer's body in wet clinging clothes would unnerve my parents (Dad would bluff it out by blathering about Charlie's work for the Legion), but Jim said, 'Nah, I'll get 'ome.'

Thursday was dry and a couple of degrees warmer. Jim ran to my house and then invited me into his place, half a mile from the pier, a first-floor flat in a small newly-built block.

'You don't live with your dad and Christine?' I'd been looking forward to seeing Mrs Turner off-duty. Charlie, I knew, was away again this week; Scotland was proving prime territory for Dennis, the best of our sales team who was to be my 'mentor' next week.

'I used to when they lived in town, but when they moved to the country I said I wanted my own place.'

'It's good,' I pronounced, though it was basic and boxy: a small square lounge, a small square bedroom, a galley kitchen and a cramped bathroom. No Pemberton chesterfield here. MFI and Ikea had furnished Jim's little 'pad' which was tidier than I'd expected. 'What's the rent?'

'I'm *buyin'* it.' The 20-year-old former school bully was now a mortgagee. O brave new Blairite world!

He told me that a legacy from his grandmother and a loan from his dad had helped with the down-payment. And my uncle, whose company had built this block, gave him a discount on the purchase price.

'That's pretty decent of him,' I said.

'Well, 'e would, wouldn't 'e?'

'Would he? Why would he?'

'Seein' as 'e's shaggin' my stepmother.'

Uncle Jack was boffing the office receptionist. Low-rent TV drama: my own family!

'Don't tell anyone,' Jim said. 'Dad'd kill me for tellin' you.'

'But – people must know. At work. At the office.'

'You'd think so, but they don't. The Guvnor's very care-ful.' Maybe not careful enough: this might explain the Ice-Princess's attitude towards Christine. For a hot titbit like this about her naughty brother, my mother might advance *me* the down-payment on a flat. Mrs Turner, I realized, had just dropped off the bottom of my 'must-do' list.

'Charlie – your dad – does he know?'

'Dad's always known.'

'And he doesn't mind?'

''E likes the money comin' in.'

'She – shags Jack for money?' At 19 I was as naïve as a 12-year-old.

'You don't think she fucks a fat pig like 'im for the *thrill* of it, do you?'

I had to know more, everything. Jim knew about sixty percent of it. Uncle Jack's generosity had enabled the Turners to trade their former council house for a cottage with a large garden on the outskirts of one of the county's heritage villages. A legacy from Charlie's mother was the official explanation for their move although Jim said his grandmother's modest savings had been divided between him and two grandsons in Canada.

Jack usually called on Christine when her husband was off on a delivery run, but so complaisant was Charlie that he would go and potter in his workshop at the bottom of the garden while his wife serviced their boss in the marital bed. Before, when they were living in the house Charlie and Jim's mother had bought from the council, Jack met Christine in motel rooms, like the adulterers in movies, or in a small flat he'd bought in Brighton which he gave to Jenny when she started (but did not complete) a course at the Art College.

'Fuck me,' I said, a philosophical reaction learned at my new workplace.

Jim's pallid winter face reddened with anger. 'Fuck the *Guvnor*,' he said. 'Fuck *Christine*. Fuck my fuckin' *dad*.'

I ran home for dinner, itching to spill the beans about Uncle Jack. Somehow I managed to hold it in. After dinner I met Jim in a different pub from the one where I'd encountered my fellow Boredom High alumni. With revelations in the air, I told him about Meredith and the events of that Thursday evening, now exactly two weeks ago.

'It was the same with Alison Saunders,' I said. 'She wouldn't even let me feel her titties.'

'I don't know if Keith Cartwright's 'ad more luck than you. Me an' 'im's not mates any more.'

I hadn't mentioned Neil in my tales of college life and didn't intend to. Attitudes towards 'poofters' at Pembertons were pitched midway between homophobia and derision. Gay television presenters (Norton, Clary, Winton) were funny and unthreatening; a gay footballer was a disgrace to the game, to the nation. Had high school blow-jobs from younger boys made Jim Turner sympathetic to suicidal gays? I doubted it.

'You need to go out with a different kind of bird,' he said.

'Who do you go out with?'

'Foreign students. You know, the ones at the language schools.'

'Bit thin on the ground this time of year, aren't they?'

'Nah. Some of 'em still do courses in winter.'

'Where do you pick them up?'

'Pubs, coffee bars, down the disco. On the street. They all want to meet nice English boys.' He grinned the grin that must have the language-school students dropping like flies.

'And are you a nice English boy, Jim?' I teased. He chuckled.

'I'm a nasty one, but I can be nice when I want to get me leg over. Why don't you come out with me on Saturday? *College* boys – they're gaggin' to score the likes of you.'

'I'm going to London on Saturday,' I said. 'I've got a girl up there.'

'From college?' I shook my head.

'Someone I met in the park.'

'Is she – you know – puttin' out?'

'Not yet, but I think she might this weekend.'

'Oh well, good luck, mate.'

I felt guilty discussing Rachel with Jim at the 'putting-out' level. Rachel was different. She was special.

And she had some bad news for me.

'Paul, I'm sorry, but this weekend's off.'

'Is *See-moe-nay* sick?' We'd taken to using the Italian versions of our names.

'No, he's positively pinky and perky.'

I heard a 'Mummee' in the background, protesting her baby talk.

'Then why can't I come?'

'Richard's going to be here. His father.' I knew who Richard was.

'Isn't he a janitor in California?'

'Not any more. He's actually made it as an actor. Been in one of their grisly daytime soaps. It's on the Sky soap channel over here.'

'We haven't got Sky.' My father considered satellite television to be softening the nation's brains.

'Now he's got a part in a TV movie they're filming in London. A new take on Jack the Ripper. And he wants to stay with me. You know – have some "quality time" with Simon.' She forgot to say *See-moe-nay*.

'Hasn't he got a boyfriend he can stay with?'

'I think he's between boyfriends at the moment.'

'So you're letting him move back into your life? Just like that?'

'This *was* his flat. And he *is* Simon's father. He has a kind of claim on us.'

'But I don't?'

A loud sigh came down the line; it should have been from my end.

'I'm sorry, Paul, but I suppose I've got to put you – *us* – on hold for now.' At least there was an 'us'. Now I did sigh.

'Can I still call you – and text you?'

'Of course. I don't want us to lose touch. And I'll try and get down to – to – Nausea-*sur-Mare*?'

I laughed – not that I felt like laughing. 'Nearly. Actually, spot on – for tonight.'

So on Saturday, instead of going up to London to finally make love to the girl I was falling in love with, I shagged a complete stranger. Thanks to my new best friend – and procurer.

On Friday I told him about Rachel's call.

'*No problemo*,' he said. Saffron had been Arnold Schwarzenegger in the canteen yesterday. 'I'll fix you up.'

And he did.

Helga and Kirsten (it might have been Kristen). Germans again. I began to hope Uncle Jack would send me to Germany even though it wasn't one of my languages. Kraut girls were easy. From my father's Thatcherite

78

viewpoint I was consorting with the enemy (it could have been worse: at least they weren't Argentinians). Not that I bragged about it over Sunday breakfast.

Jim got Helga, a Wagnerian blonde, your perfect Aryan. I got brunette Kirsten/Kristen who was, armpit- and crotch-wise, more of a hairy 'un. We all got bladdered first, in a series of pubs. Then back to Jim's boxy flatlet, where a half-bottle of vodka loosened inhibitions and pantyhose. Ms K. and I took the bedroom, Jim and Helga made do with the sofa from Ikea.

The details are nearly as hazy as my Teutonic *partouze* in Torremolinos. I remember her hair, lots of it, and her breasts which Rachel might (or might not) have called pinky and perky. She chomped on the Major with as much lip-smacking zeal as if he'd been a tasty bratwurst – perhaps he was. I declined to reciprocate in the chomping department. She relieved me of the condom and applied it with SS efficiency. I fucked her, not – I hope – too amateurishly. She liked it doggy-fashion and also in the 'Ride of the Valkyrie' position. Her guttural English was faintly comic: 'Ah *ja*, zat iz *gut*.' I half expected her to say, 'Ve have vays of makink you *komm*.'

If this was date-rape, at least it was mutual. I felt cheapened if not exactly violated.

It was after midnight when we walked them back to the house where they were lodging *en famille*, not far from Alison and her embalmer father. Jim then insisted on walking me home. 'I'm not ready for bed yet,' he said, his speech still blurry with booze.

'That was all right, wasn't it?' he said next. He didn't sound exhilarated.

'Yeah. Thanks, Jim.'

'Don't thank me. *You're* the one they liked. I told you, that college-boy stuff really gets to 'em.'

'Does it?' We'd talked about Boredom-on-Sea, about their hometown of Duisburg, about movies, music, football, the Olympics. We hadn't discussed Goethe or Beethoven or the Third Reich, so I didn't see that my higher education counted for anything.

'Did you shag yours?' he asked.

'Twice!' I was the cocky king of the fuck-fest. 'Didn't you?'

'Nah. I got brewer's droop when she started puttin' the

condom on me, I often do. She 'ad to just give me a blow-job. Only 'er teeth were a bit sharp.'

'Did you – you know – go down on her?'

'Eat the sardine sandwich? Yuck, I could never do that. Could you?'

'With the right girl I could. Well, I think I could. Not this one. Her pussy-hair was like a pan-scourer!'

We shared a dirty laugh, but the cold air was sobering me up. *Post coitum tristia*. I wished I had gone to London, to Rachel. Kirsten/Kristen had been a fast-food fuck, like a Chinese takeaway. I wanted more. Not more sex. What I wanted was sex with more intensity, more purpose, more feeling.

God help me, I wanted love.

8. On the road

Week two of my new life. While Bush and Blair tried to sell their war plans to a reluctant UN and a sceptical Europe, I started to sell living-room furniture to recalcitrant store-owners.

My 'mentor', trailing clouds of glory from Scotland, was Dennis Dawes. Dennis could have sold vibrators to US Evangelicals or pork scratchings to Osama bin Laden. Forty-five, overweight, balding and flatulent, Dennis was into a second marriage, with kids and step-kids. He had also sold double-glazing, insurance and cars. A nineteen-year-old college dropout, what did I know? Hiroshima or Henry James were not the ideal preamble to pitching leather suites.

Our mission this week was to follow up promising (and unpromising) leads in the South from the other members of the sales team. Dennis's initial onslaught was all butter and treacle:

'Mr So-and-So, it's good to see you again. How's that lovely wife/daughter/baby of yours? Still filling your life with sunshine?'

He was equally saccharine with people he was meeting for the first time:

'Mr So-and-So, I'm very pleased to meet you. You certainly made a big impression on Tim/Peter/Rodney last week/month. He hasn't stopped talking about you.'

I had to be introduced:

'This is Paul Barrett, the newest member of my team. Jack Pemberton's his uncle, so he's probably only here to report on my incompetence!'

I learned to smile disarmingly as I shook hands with the buyer or store-owner and affected intense joy at making their acquaintance. Dennis soon got them talking about their spouses, their kids, their house, their town, football, television, the news. A more enthralling topic than Gulf War 2 was the trial of Major Charles Ingram, whose coughing accomplice had helped him to scoop the jackpot on *Who Wants to Be a Millionaire?*

After a few minutes of chitchat Dennis would ask them how business was, congratulate or commiserate and then begin his pitch: a top-range item for this store, a lower-priced model for that one. Out came photos, brochures, leather swatches. Dennis became pushier, he wheedled, he cajoled. Sometimes he sounded almost desperate. Salesmen trade in desperation.

The clients always took our publicity material – maybe binning it as soon as we'd left. Very rarely did one agree to take a sofa, a suite or a sofa-bed for display. Afterwards, in his Saab or over coffee or lunch, Dennis told me which owner or buyer his instinct said would be worth a follow-up and which was a dead loss. His career (and mine), my uncle's business, the lives of the workers and their families were at stake here. And yet I found it hard to work up a head of steam over selling an armchair.

On Monday we toured Kent: Ashford, Canterbury, Gravesend, Sevenoaks, Maidstone, Tunbridge Wells. Not one sale. Tuesday we went west and north: Brighton, Worthing, Horsham, Guildford, Chichester. Both nights we came home in time for a late dinner – a reheated one in my case.

On Wednesday we retraced our tracks to Chichester en route to Portsmouth, Southampton and Bournemouth. In Portsmouth I found I might have a future in this field. We called on Mrs Cohen, the pint-sized czarina of an over-decorated store in the new shopping centre. 'And who's this young gentleman?' she interrupted Dennis's initial goodwill gush to enquire.

'This is Paul Barrett. He's Jack's Pemberton's nephew. He's –'

'He's probably capable of speaking for himself.'

I shook the proffered hand. 'Pleased to meet you, Mrs Cohen. This is a very elegant shop you have here.' I was picking up the patter, but it seemed more natural to do a number on this old biddy with her fresh-from-the-salon hair and her tea-dance dress than some dejected middle-aged man with tired hair and a tireder suit who looked as likely to be selling coffins as furniture.

'Oy,' she said, suddenly very Mrs Cohen indeed, 'I can see this boy was born to schmooze. Now who is it you remind me of?'

I told her and she clapped her hands. 'It's true! Paul, you should have his career.' She sighed theatrically. 'I wish I had a son who looked like him instead of one who looks like Boris Karloff.'

Dennis stepped back and let Mrs Cohen lay her Yiddisher Momma routine on me while I struggled to work in a few plugs for the product. She took a pile of brochures and a sample of a new shade of leather we called 'Mohajar'. Mrs C. called it taupe and said her best customer, a Mrs Sidebottom (pronounced 'Siddy-b'tham'), would consider it to die for – 'she loves those colours so much she may just *kill* for it.' And within the week, an order was placed for a *four*-piece-suite in Mohajar that earned me my first commission. ('It was your sale,' Dennis generously allowed. 'Or yours and Ewan McGregor's!')

On the way back to the car he unleashed a barrage of accumulated farts. 'I can see you're going to go down well with the ladies.'

'If not *on* them!' I crowed, well pleased with my conquest of Mrs Cohen.

'Let's not get carried away.'

My next 'conquest', later the same day, in Basingstoke, was a buyer rather than owner: Ms Christmas. 'No Yuletide jokes,' Dennis cautioned. 'She's heard them all before.'

Brenda Christmas belonged in a US daytime soap with Rachel's Richard. Thirty-something, she power-dressed to run IBM rather than the furniture floor of a middle-class store in Hampshire: a suit the colour of old port, hair a copper helmet that would not have stirred in a typhoon, make-up that gave her the look of a toned-down Marilyn Manson. Her eyes were the eyes of a jungle cat and today I was the fawn trapped against the thorn bush.

'Call me Brenda,' she purred, not letting go of my hand as quickly as she had Dennis's. It was a hand I could have had her eating from. There were other parts of me Ms Christmas would happily have eaten. Loosen the hair and scrape off some of the make-up and I might let her.

Again Dennis left me to do my stuff. Weird to be discussing furniture and fabrics with this woman who only wanted my tongue down her throat or on the inside of her thighs. She took brochures and samples, but I'd have had to fuck her to get one of our sofas in the showroom. It would have been worth it.

'See you soon, Brenda,' I promised as we left.

'I look forward to that, Paul,' she said. Her tongue flickered across her lips and I got the message I was meant to.

'It might be just me next time,' Dennis said. Brenda did not want Ronnie Barker, she wanted Ewan McGregor. Her expression, for a moment, was Hannibal Lecter with the Italian policeman.

'Then I'll try to look forward to that, Mr Dawes.'

There was football practice that night, but I missed it, ruling myself out of Saturday's game against a team from Newhaven. Dennis and I spent the night in a chintzy Bournemouth B&B run by a maternal North Countrywoman with an equally motherly husband who cooked our dinner and checked that every mouthful was heaven to our taste buds. Three other salesmen were staying, whom Dennis knew from the profession's rodeo circuit; I left them at the bar and went for a run after dinner and then fell asleep watching TV in my room. Dennis's farts reverberated against the partition wall between us.

Next day, in Bristol, I found there was one kind of male buyer to whom I was as irresistible as I was to Mrs Cohen and Brenda not-so-merry Christmas. Lionel Davis – 'Call me Bette, dear. Everyone does!' His mincing feet barely seemed to touch the floor. His waving hands were busily arranging flowers that only he could see. It was *Are You Being Served?* and then some.

'Well, I don't need to tell you who you remind me of,' he cooed. 'I hope the resemblance goes all the way down!' All the way down, it was painfully clear, was where Lionel longed to go.

'That's for me to know and you to try and find out!' Where did I get that line from? Dennis took more than his usual one step back, clearly unprepared for the fact that I might actually flirt with this flamboyant queen. But business is business, as Mrs Cohen would surely remind us.

84

I wondered – and asked – if Lionel had known Neil. 'I don't think so, dear,' he said. 'College boys don't come my way very often, I'm sorry to say. Still, thank God for cottaging lorry-drivers! Now, what have you got to tempt the jaded palates of the Bristol glitterati with?'

Lionel Davis (I wasn't up for calling him Bette) moaned orgasmically when I produced samples of Mohajar and Marrakech (taupe and mulberry to Mrs Cohen and Mrs Sidebottom). He sniffed them and ran them over his face. 'Hmm, I do love the smell of leather in the morning!'

I nearly told him I preferred napalm, but instead, remembering Neil's talk of London leather bars, said: 'It's even nicer after dark – mixed with a strong whiff of amylnitrate.'

Lionel licked his lips, much as Brenda had done and probably with the same tasty tongue target in mind. I gave him a jaunty Jim Turner grin. He would try very hard to sell one of our suites and I might tell Roger to send him enough Mohajar to run up a waistcoat and jockstrap.

'Excuse me asking,' Dennis said on the way back to the car, 'but – you're not one of these AC/DC swingers, are you?'

I laughed and shook my head. 'No, but my gay friend at uni, the one I asked Lionel if he knew, taught me a bit of camp.'

'A bit! You could take over Graham Norton's show if he wants a break!'

'Hardly.' But I basked in the praise, if praise is what it was. And it was good to think of Neil with humour instead of guilt. I didn't tell Dennis he was dead.

Another B&B that night, on the outskirts of Cardiff, run by a pair of Welsh divorcees. The décor was rustic chic. Many of the paintings featured cockerels and porcelain cockerels were dotted around shelves and tabletops. 'I enjoy telling people we collect cocks,' the older woman said with a smile. Her voice was like water dancing over rocks.

'But you've never asked to see mine,' joked Dennis, all subtlety.

'We try not to get the same one twice,' she returned, smiling at me rather than at Dennis. Over a lamb stew with dumplings that melted like communion wafers he whispered that he reckoned they were lesbians.

'Lesbians collecting cocks?'

'That's probably just an in-joke.'

'Looks more like an out-joke to me.' Neil had said he found dykes mostly humourless. My lesbian experience was limited to the two Germans in Torremolinos who were presumably what Dennis would call AC/DC swingers.

On Friday we went to Weston-super-Mare, Exeter and Plymouth before heading for home with stops in Southampton and Brighton to see a couple of buyers who'd been unavailable earlier in the week. No women, no gays. No sales. If Dennis was our top man, just how badly did the others do? I was home in time for a fish-and-chip dinner with my parents.

When I'd called Jim's mobile on Wednesday to cry off football practice, he asked if I was up for cruising more birds on Saturday. I said I'd let him know when I got back from my sales tour, thinking I would make up an excuse involving some activity with my parents. They were in fact going to see *Annie*, an amateur production by a local school with an imaginative drama teacher. But I didn't need to sit through another reminder of Neil and Meredith.

And I was horny after a week on the road.

Jim was his usual chipper self on Saturday evening despite Pembertons having been thrashed 6-2 by Newhaven's Parker Pens. In the first bar we went to I picked up a Spanish girl my own age, as cute as Penelope Cruz with comically fractured English. In one of the thrift shops she favoured with her chucked-out clothes my mother had found an Isabel Allende novel in the original Spanish, which I'd been labouring over all week with the aid of a dictionary. The girl, whose name was a grimly Catholic Immaculada – 'you can call me Ima' – laughed at my accent. Tit for tat (she had tits *a morir*).

'*Mi amigo tiene un apartamento*,' I told her after some bilingual byplay. I warned Jim that I was trying to invite her to his flat.

'Yeah,' he said. 'Let's go for it.'

'*¿Quieres venir con nos otros?*'

'Yah,' Ima said. 'Let us go for it.'

'*¿Tienes un'amiga para mi amigo?*' A friend for my friend.

'I like your friend.'

'¿*Un'amiga para* mi?'

'I like you,' she said.

'I think she wants to do us both,' I told Jim.

'Are you up for that?'

'Are you?'

'I'm up for anythin' that's goin'. Let me see if I can score us a few tabs.' He went to the toilet and was back within minutes. 'We're on. Let's go.'

E always does my head in but I remember every detail of that night as lucidly as my assault on Meredith or Neil's plummeting onto the asphalt. If we'd had a camcorder we could have made the next hour into a porn movie and retired on the royalties. In Jim's pocket-sized living-room Ima did a rapid striptease and then undressed us. She had a teenager's slim hips and bum; her small pretty breasts were the colour of a Digestive biscuit. She licked our chests, our armpits, our crotches, to an accompaniment of words of admiration and encouragement that usefully enhanced my Spanish vocabulary.

Not since the school showers had I been naked in front of another naked male. There were often erections in the changing rooms – but not mine – and sometimes sexual activity, which I'd never joined in. Tonight was a first. Jim's penis wasn't small, but it was smaller than mine and had a Presidential bend.

Describe the sociological changes that took place in Spain as a result of the transition from republic to monarchy. One of the topics in my A-level exam on Modern European History. Ima was definitely – definitively – a product of the post-Franco era. I could have added a paragraph to my essay.

We were the shrines and Ima the supplicant. What I felt was not ecstasy – in fact without amphetamines the sight of Jim's curved penis pressing against my ramrod straight one in her face would have seemed disconcertingly, detumescingly, *gay* – but my blood was up (oh yes) and Jim was up for anything and everything. As, it seemed, was Ima, reciting lines from US (or maybe Spanish) porn-flicks: 'Give me your big hard prick.' 'Hard' began with the 'ch' sound in 'loch': '*Geeve me yorr beeg chard prreek.*' I smirked at Jim, who grinned back, but he was probably smiling at what we were doing rather than at any linguistic anomaly. He got vocally into the groove:

'Yeah, suck 'is cock.' 'Lick my balls.' She didn't need encouraging.

She blew me while he fucked her facedown on the sofa. Then we got her onto the floor. She tongued his balls (as ordered) while he held her legs in the air for me to fuck her. Her pussy was slick and juicy. She screamed as she came.

Jim tried to fuck her in the arse. 'You'll feel my dick against yours inside 'er,' he said. 'It's fuckin' amazin'.' Was it? And was I up for this?

The girl wasn't up for it. '*No lo tengo en culo*,' she said. So after a brief time-out Jim settled for fucking her pussy from behind again. Then I put on our fourth condom to fuck her in this position and came for the third time. She was screaming and creaming again. My knees ached. Ima had a carpet burn.

Jim, now out of it, staggered to his bed. I walked Ima back to her hostel on the sea front. I told her about the Allende novel I was reading. We talked about Marques, whom I'd only read in translation. Outside the hostel she kissed me. It could have been an ordinary date with a nice girl from Almeria. But there were no nice people in tonight's story. This wasn't *Annie*.

Dennis Dawes would call me a 'swinger'. Perhaps – two guys and one girl – one of his 'AC/DC' swingers.

The way I see it, I'd gone from wannabe date-rapist to gang-banger.

A kind of graduation, I guess.

9. *Les sofa-beds*

Week three. George W. Bush gave Saddam Hussein 48 hours to quit Baghdad or be blasted out. In a similar display of medieval kingship, Jack Pemberton gave me 24 hours to prepare for banishment to France.

I was everybody's fall-guy at Monday morning's meeting of the sales team. Even my uncle's mistress had a tease lined up as I came through Reception:

'Is that a trail of broken hearts I can see behind you? I shall have to watch out for mine!'

I grinned and admired her breasts in a cashmere sweater. Who had told her of my small successes with Mrs Cohen and Brenda Christmas and (please God, no) Lionel Davis? My uncle was a likelier suspect than her stepson.

'Can I interest you in a leather suite, madam?'

'In a leather skirt you might be able to.'

'I haven't really got the legs for a leather skirt.'

'Idiot! That's not what I meant.' She wasn't as quick at the thrust and parry of saucy dialogue as Saffron, whom I hadn't seen all last week.

Uncle Jack was seated at the conference table with papers strewn around him – had they been scattered during a pre-work warm-up with Mrs Turner? I was the first of the reps.

'Dennis tells me you went down well with some of the female buyers – and a gay one.' His rubbery mouth went into dolphin mode.

I decided against repeating my 'going down' joke for Uncle Jack. Were his lips naturally moist or had he just been doing some going down of his own?

'None of them actually ordered anything.'

'You made a good first impression. That's what counts.'

'Does it?'

'It certainly does.'

Michael came in with Dennis. Then the other three salesmen: Tim, Peter and Rodney. Peter and Rodney were younger versions of Dennis, losing their hair and piling on the pounds; both wore suits. Easy to visualise them propping up the bars in B&Bs up and down the land, grumbling about the lack of business. Tim Reynolds was in his thirties with a worked-out body and rakish good looks. Designer casuals; hair gelled into pop-star crags; a strong cologne. Tim would be a hit with Brenda and Lionel, but not with Mrs Cohen. I could see him preening at the gym, then cruising town centre pubs for a lonely singleton or perhaps a restless housewife. If I stuck at this trade I might become another Tim Reynolds; hopefully I wouldn't become a Rodney, a Peter or a Dennis.

'Are you still wearing your *Christmas stockings*?' Tim asked me. Rodney got in before I could:

'No, but he has got a *yarmulke* covering his bum!'

'Covering Lionel Davis's *teeth-marks*!' Dennis added.

Michael laughed up a storm. Jack beamed. I stitched a good-natured grin across my face and, for a moment, wished I was back at uni.

Angela, Michael's plain-looking secretary came in with a tray of cups and saucers which she took over to the burbling coffee-maker on a credenza. While she did her waitressing, the comedy patter expanded to include Michael and the other reps (but not Jack). Then Angela took her place at the table and poised over a notepad as my uncle called the meeting to order.

Michael reported on the week's sales. These were better than my road trip had seemed to promise. The salesmen reported in order of seniority. Dennis made our week sound more like a sell-out tour by Oasis than a Cilla Black tribute show in empty village halls. He didn't make too much of Ms Christmas and 'Ms' Davis, but included Mrs Cohen among our most promising leads. Fly-boy Tim had fared better than the others in terms of secure orders, or said he had.

I was the headliner in the next phase of the meeting: Strategic Planning. Via my laptop I had been exchanging emails with Michael and Angela all last week as we plotted our continental invasion. It wasn't quite virgin territory; Tim had made forays to Germany and Switzerland, where most shopkeepers spoke English, but results were not promising. Scandinavia was ruled out: Ikea and the Finns had stitched up both ends of the market. Italian designers were unbeatable. Eastern Europe was under the control of gangsters. The US had import restrictions. The Belgians and the Dutch had a limited taste for luxury goods, but might be worth a look later. That left France and Spain. Angela had researched furniture outlets in both countries: their reported sales figures, the range they carried, their customer base, their suppliers. Michael had pinpointed two stores in Lille and five in Paris as primary targets for *meubles en cuir à la Pemberton*. Follow-ups in Lille and Paris would be combined with second-wave attacks on France's other major cities. Then we would begin to carpet-bomb Spain. Tomorrow *La Manche*, soon *La Mancha* – the storm troopers of a new *LeatherWorld* order!

But who should go? Whom would I serve as our roving interpreter? Tim, thinking – as was I – foreign totty – was hot to trot. Peter and Rodney, family men, weren't keen to stray so far from home. Dennis could see himself being usurped from the number-one spot but also didn't relish such far-flung travels.

'I could go,' Michael surprisingly said. Were the Pemberton apron strings starting to chafe? The poor bastard was married, almost literally, to a horse.

'I think your role is more to co-ordinate things from here,' Jack said.

'Yes, but I wouldn't mind stretching my legs for a change.'

'Yeah – right across some hot French totty!' I had definitely got Tim's number. Angela, plain but not prudish, sniggered. My uncle glared.

'Let's not forget that Michael's married to my Joanna,' he reminded us. The adulterer was not about to condone adultery in his son-in-law.

'*Pardonnez-moi*, I'm sure,' said Tim, smirking at me as he showed off probably ten percent of his rival command of a foreign tongue. Now my uncle fired his surprise salvo across all our bows:

'I think Paul should go on his own.'

'Do you think he's ready for that?' Michael asked, disbelief written uppercase across his face. Tim's expression was a sneer.

'Yes, he is,' said Dennis. A second shot across my bows.

'That's settled, then,' said Jack. 'Let's move on.'

And, the next day, on I moved. Leaving my car at Ashford, I was teleported through the tunnel on Eurostar. First-class. They were spoiling me. Ashford to Lille: 59 minutes. 63, as it turned out.

The first store was more downmarket than their advert in the online *Pages Jaunes* had promised. *Le patron*, M. Picard, looked like a plain-clothes *flic* from a *film noir*. He chain-smoked.

On Sunday I had written out my lines (in French) and memorized them. Now I declaimed them for the benefit of M. Picard, who told me that *les sofa-beds* were becoming popular among apartment-dwellers without spare bedrooms. He took brochures and samples but I didn't get a positive 'vibe'. Still, my French had passed its first test.

The second store, on one of the quaintly paved streets, was almost too snazzy, with some Italian leather furniture whose design – and price – took my breath away. The buyer – 'Call me Pierre' – had fluent English and film-star looks. Was he gay? The Italians hadn't got Mohajar or Marrakech, and our prices had just become reasonable. I invited Pierre to lunch but he had a date with *une petite amie*. Not gay, then. Our acquaintance was too new for me to ask if his *petite amie* liked to party. He recommended a restaurant.

By mid-afternoon I was in Paris for only the second time in my life. Lille had been charming and dinky. Paris was grand – *grande;* Paris was *magnifique*. The air tasted different, although some of that taste was exhaust fumes.

Angela had booked me into a hotel near the station. Four stars. Imposing exterior but bland inside. It was a relief to shed my overnight bag which mostly contained more samples and brochures. Instead of my college-boy fleece-lined zip-up jacket I was wearing a black Burberry normally reserved for grandparental funerals and other church attendances. Paris was cold, almost freezing. I took a taxi to the first store, off Place Vendôme. Occupying one and a half floors of a Haussmann-era building, it was even more chic than *chez* Pierre and carried a small range of high-end furniture.

The *propriétaire* was a French Brenda Christmas – down to her name: Mme Noëlle. Early thirties, she was glamorous, glossy and glacial. I picked up a gay vibe, but having been wrong about Pierre I could be off-beam with *Madame*. Franglais was not spoken here either.

'We do not sell sofa-beds,' she said coldly.

'But people must need them. When guests come.'

'If they need them, they do not expect to buy them from me.' I felt as if Dennis was with me, farting in her fragrant presence. She thawed a degree or two when I produced our samples. Mohajar might yet save the day. But it was Marrakech that pushed her buttons.

'This is a superb colour. What do you call this shade in English?'

'Mulberry. *Mûrier*.' I'd looked it up. She frowned.

'Mulberry? I do not think so. And Marrakech is completely wrong. You must give it a *Russian* name. Romanov. Zhivago. Something like that. Can you leave me this sample?'

'I can leave you them all.' Plenty more in my bag at the hotel.

'Just this one. The others are quite ordinary.' Jack wouldn't like that. And I wasn't sure how he'd take to Zhivago. It was nearly closing time.

'Would you like to join me for dinner?' The temperature plummeted.

'Thank you for asking but I have to go home and feed my husband and my daughter.' Her English was 100%: she didn't say 'dough-tare'.

'A drink perhaps?'

'No.' Did she think I wanted to get into her *culottes?* Below zero in there. I was only being polite. And a bit pushy. It was almost warmer outside on the street.

Swathed in winter coats the Parisians didn't look *très élégants*. Some even sported anoraks, or perhaps these were tourists. My guidebook said the Marais was a good district for restaurants, but the one I chose for its steamed-up windows that promised warmth had un-exceptional food served by a haughty waiter who seemed to find my French ridiculous. I couldn't think of a cool put-down.

The Marais was also the gay heart of gay Paree but the streets were not, at 7.30 p.m., teeming with queens. Neil, I said, *tu dois venir beaucoup plus tard*. With his ghost at my side, I trudged up the Boulevard de Strasbourg to my hotel. Not to spare my uncle a taxi fare but to walk off a second heavy meal. The hotel had no gym and I wasn't about to jog unfamiliar cold streets.

Alone in my room in the City of Lovers. Over lunch yesterday Tim Reynolds had offered a few hints for travellers. Hotel concierges can always fix you up with a hooker; both require generous tips. The guidebook hinted at the centuries-old delights of Pigalle where, unlike Soho, video-booths and lap-dancing have not entirely supplanted *le striptease*. But what I craved was *l'amour*, not commercial sex. I hadn't come to Paris for a handjob.

On impulse I called Rachel but got her voicemail. I sent her a text:

I'm in PARIS on 1st solo sales trip. Wish I had some1 2 share it with. U 4 instance. Hugs 2 S. xxxx P.

For someone to talk to I almost called Jim. I'd be home tomorrow but not in time for football practice. I could have called Uncle Jack. 'Let me know how you get on,' he'd said yesterday. 'Call me at home if you need to.' Or I could call my own home. Even Dad would be eager to hear of my progress. But I wanted to hear somebody say 'I love you', and my mother wasn't given to such gushes of affection. And hers was not the love I craved.

It turned out I *had* come to Paris for a handjob.

On Wednesday, thanks to cellular telephone technology, love came calling.

Rachel had sent me a text while I slept:

Congrats on yr news. R took me to CHICAGO. Show not city. Hugs back frm S. xxx frm me.

One less *x* than I'd sent her. The law of diminishing returns was beginning to apply to my relationship with Rachel. The other *R* had boxed me in. Or out.

Three cold calls this cold morning. Another store in the centre and two in suburbs on opposite sides of the city. Owners/managers all male and unprepossessing. The shop in Clignancourt was the most suitable for our wares, but the owner seemed very dispirited; *maîtresse* problems, I deduced.

After a coffee-and-brioche lunch, back on the Metro to Neuilly and another manageress. I'd dreamt of meeting my *Amélie* on this trip, but what I got was Mme Defarge from *A Tale of Two Cities*. Severe black dress. Shoes like clogs. Hair wrenched into a masochist bun. No make-up. And no English.

But she was a pussycat in battleaxe drag.

'*C'est très élégant,*' she exclaimed at a picture of our most popular black-leather suite. A sofa in Prince-of-Wales brocade was *charmant*. When I pulled out my samples she entered into ecstasy. Mohajar was *exquise*. Marrakech was *à mourir* and *authentique Africaine*. So much for Mme Noëlle and *Zhivago*.

She promised to show the brochures to *Monsieur le Patron* and said she would urge him to order a sofa in Marrakech and perhaps *une grande chaise au Prince de Galles* for their mezzanine, where the quality stuff was displayed.

I gifted myself two hours in the Musée d'Orsay. It blew me away. Tate Modern looks very dour, very Bauhaus, in comparison to the d'Orsay which must have dreamt of becoming an art treasury all though its days as a train station. Standing in a room dedicated to Van Gogh, I finally got the point of Vincent. Those violent edgy streaks of colour and sometimes of darkness. His joys and torments fly off the canvas. It's as if he were attacking *you* with his palette knife. All the Impressionists are great, but Van Gogh belongs to some higher order of tortured visionaries. (Thanks to Meredith and Tate Britain, I have a similar passion for Turner, but Vincent is *visceral*.)

Back to the hotel for my shoulder-bag and then back on Eurostar. 36 hours parking at Ashford cost the price of a dinner in the Marais. Halfway home my mobile rang. An old flame. An old cold flame. *Alison*. I hadn't got round to editing her from my Contacts. I took the call and lurched to a halt in front of a village store still open at 8 p.m.

'Alison?'

'Hello, Paul. Your mum said you're in France. Whereabouts are you?'

'Somewhere near Rye. I'm on my way back.' I almost uttered an over-formal *To what do I owe the pleasure?* (if pleasure is what it was). I came to the point instead: 'I thought you were through with me.' Very Meredith. Very

American Pie.

Alison began crying.   'Paul, I've made a big mistake.'

'Is that mistake called Keith Cartwright?'

'He's – horrible.' She didn't elaborate. Had the blowjob bully from high-school tried to force Alison's head in a southerly direction?

'I seem to remember he was a bit of a roughneck at school,' I said in what I hoped was a sympathetic tone.

'He – *dumped* me,' she gulped. *Just like you dumped me*, I might have said but didn't. 'He's going out with some awful girl from Pembertons factory. He and his dad help out with the Players, making scenery and stuff. He says he met her there, but I've seen her and she looks more like a – *prostitute* than an actress.'

My strait-laced mother thought that actresses who marry over-frequently – she could name names – were little better than prostitutes. I took a not-too-wild guess: 'Is her name Saffron?'

'No, it's Leanne. Do you know her? Your mum said you've gone to work at Pembertons.'

'I spent my first week on the factory floor. I got to know most of the staff.' Leanne, the dumbest of the sewing room's brunettes, was another wannabe actress but without Saffron's improvisational skills. She wore low tops and short skirts and sported an array of steel facial piercings that could get her into a remake of *Hellraiser*. 'Sounds like Leanne's practising to become a husband-stealing Hollywood bitch.' I laughed, but Alison was in no mood for jokes.

'I don't know if I wanted to marry Keith,' she said.

'You didn't want to manage a fish-and-chip shop?' I risked a tease.

'All I really want is a nice house and two children. I thought I was going to marry a teacher or a lecturer.'

'Did you? Who *were* these two guys?'

Finally she managed a giggle. '*You*, silly.'

'Oh well, there's been a change of plan. I'm a furniture salesman now.'

A beat. Alison primed herself for the next question:

'Are you – *seeing* anybody, Paul?'

A picture from Saturday night came vividly into my mind: Ima, legs in the air, slavering at Jim's scrotum while I pumped at her slick pussy. Was I 'seeing' Ima? I no longer felt that I was seeing Rachel.

'Not really,' I said. 'There was a girl at uni I didn't tell you about.'

'I thought there must be somebody,' Alison said, sniffing again. 'You weren't very good at answering my letters.'

'Sorry about that. She was part of the reason why I chucked it in. She dumped me.' Putting it mildly. A cherry-chaser's cold heart still beat within the salesman's breast. 'Look – do you want to go out with me on Saturday? Or even tomorrow night?'

'Yes. And yes. Tomorrow *and* Saturday! Friday, too.' A tidal surge of happiness came down the line. What was I letting myself in for? *Auld lang syne*? This Saturday would not be a repeat of the last two. Jim had just drawn the short straw.

Or perhaps I had.

Presumably, at this moment, in the White House Situation Room and at the Pentagon and on battleships in the Persian Gulf, they were watching satellite feeds and digital images of land and sea manoeuvres ahead of tomorrow's 'Shock and Awe' on Saddam Hussein. Not much sleep in Washington and the Middle East tonight, although George W. Bush, a cowboy with unimaginable powers of destruction, would sleep the sleep of the truly self-righteous. Tony Blair might perhaps toss and turn, wrestling with demons and with only himself to blame.

I, going to bed early after one of Mother's reheated dinners, was neither righteous nor self-righteous. Was I, on this eve of what might turn out to be Armageddon, hatching my own invasion plans, plotting a course through Alison's zips and buttons, flexing my fingers and knees for the battles ahead?

No, I wasn't. My assault on Meredith hadn't been premeditated. I'm more your off-the-cuff, spur-of-the-moment kind of date-rapist.

10. Shock and awe

'What did you bring me from France?' Christine Turner asked.

'What were you expecting?'

'A bottle of wine? Some nice cheese?' I looked blank. 'Only teasing,' she said. 'You don't have to bring me anything.' Her munchable breasts were today sheathed in blush-red angora.

'I'm going again next week,' I told her. 'There will be cheese. There will be wine. If I take the car there will be a *case* of wine.' I made a mental note to bring her champagne or perfume, although my uncle probably kept her well stocked with top brands of both. She always smelt nice. Pressing a button on her console to take a call, she flashed me a wide-screen smile. Down, Major!

My debriefing in the conference room had an audience of only three: Uncle Jack, Michael and Angela. Dennis was laid low with flu, and the other three reps were on the road.

'Brilliant work,' my uncle said at the end of my report. Considering my only achievements had been the leaving of brochures and samples, I wondered whether he was trying to boost his own self-confidence or mine. 'You'll need to make some follow-up phone calls next week.'

'I can do them today.'

He shook his head. 'Too soon. Today would look pushy and might put them off. Next week it looks like a courtesy. More businesslike.'

The etiquette of salesmanship. A learning curve.

'However,' he went on, 'this is exactly the right time to

follow up the leads you and Dennis made last week. It's what he was doing when he went sick. You'll have to phone him and see which ones he did, and then you can do the rest this morning. I want you back on the road by lunchtime. You're covering for Dennis. Start by calling on Mrs Cohen in Portsmouth. She's given us a very nice order. You should drop in and thank her with a serious bunch of flowers – at least thirty quids' worth.'

Could I put champagne for his mistress on my expenses, I wondered.

'And then you can take another crack at that buyer in Basingstoke – Brenda Christmas. Pretend you're just passing. If you stay there tonight, try and soften her up with a nice dinner.'

A 'Christmas Dinner'! A crack at Brenda's crack? A warmer prospect than Alison, now relegated to the sub-stitutes' box. There was more to my itinerary:

'Dennis was supposed to follow up a couple of Rodney's calls in Oxford and Gloucester - you can do them tomor-row. And there's an old couple in Cheltenham with a very nice store we've never managed to get into. Maybe your boyish charm will work where Tim's smarm didn't do the trick.'

I doubted that in my first solo week, if ever, I could outsell Brylcreem Boy. Who was hotter with the fans, Ewan McGregor or Robbie Williams?

We reps used a spare desk in Angela's office on a first-come basis: 'hot-desking'. I sat at my hot desk and made cold calls to the shopkeepers and buyers we'd visited last week. Last week we had met with recalcitrance; today it felt like the Siege of Leningrad. Only Lionel Davis in Bristol showed any warmth: I could practically hear his under-pants rustling with excitement. He reminded me to call him Bette, but I managed not to call him anything.

Midmorning Jack called to ask how I was getting on.

'They've all gone cold. Is it the war, d'you think?'

'Getting rid of Saddam will be good for oil prices, good for the world economy, good for our sales in the long run.' Don't Mention the War – I needed to heed Basil Fawlty's ignored advice to himself. My parents had watched the breakfast news in stoical silence, remembering the price our family had paid for a previous gung-ho expedition. Uncle Jack, another ultramarine Tory, clearly favoured this blitzkrieg on the poor beleaguered Iraqis. I must learn to keep a lid on my peacenik student opinions.

'I hope the long run turns out to be a short one,' I said.

'We'll see. By the way, we're having a family lunch on Sunday. Agnes is ringing your mother. Joanna and Michael will be there. And we've got a surprise for you.'

Stepdaughter news, I easily guessed: either Joanna was pregnant – the patter of tiny neo-Pembertons – or Jennifer had got engaged in America to the Congressman's son. Either way, a step forward for our 'dynasty'. These family meals were thankfully rare. Jack and my father had only Rotary and local politics in common. Aunt Agnes and Mother could talk good works, Joanna horses and, perhaps now, babies. Michael and I could talk shop. Bor-r-ing.

When I left the building to set out for Hampshire, Charlie Turner was standing in Reception. He greeted me and shook my hand.

'Jim tells me you're his new best mate. I'm glad he's hanging out with a better class of person.'

Best mates already! I didn't tell him that his son and I were only fellow joggers, fellow gangbangers. Christine, at her desk, had a *glow* I'd not seen before. The glow was the love she felt for Charlie, who basked in its warmth. How could she – how could *he* – let my uncle near her when there was this great passion between husband and wife? I wanted someone to feel like this toward me, love and lust and adoration. Alison was not going to hack it.

But there are other kinds of warmth, like the welcome I received from Mrs Cohen in Portsmouth at 2.15. I could have been revisiting my favourite grandmother, Grandma Pemberton who'd died in the last week of the millennium.

'Oy,' cried Mrs C. 'Are all those flowers for me? Paul, you shouldn't have. Yes you should! I shall have to share them with Mrs Sidebottom. Paul, you should have been here when I showed her your swathe of taupe leather. It was like – what's her name, that lovely girl – *Meg Ryan* in *When Harry Met Sally*! I thought the roof was coming in!'

I was here to schmooze this old biddy, but she seemed happy to do the schmoozing. Don't Mention the War: Mrs Cohen would doubtless approve of Shock and Awe against one of Zion's unruly neighbours. I sat through two cups of coffee and the terminal phase of her husband's medical history. Finally a customer came in and I made my escape.

In Basingstoke Brenda Christmas was also incubating flu. Her face looked puffy, her hair had lost its sheen; even her suit was rumpled. Last week's maneater was this week's Grinch.

'I haven't had the chance to show your samples to anybody.'

'I'm only passing through,' I lied as instructed. 'But I might stay the night and move on to Oxford tomorrow. Are you free for dinner?'

'No, I'm not. And even if I was I wouldn't want to listen to you banging on about Moroccan leather and timber from eco-friendly forests in Indonesia.'

'Actually we don't –'

'See, you're doing it already. Go away. I've got a makeover to plan.'

'I could help you with that.'

'No, you couldn't. Piss off, will you. Come back in the spring.'

'It'll be Dennis next time.' We might fare better with Tim.

'Dennis, Schmennis.' Very Mrs Cohen. 'Who gives a shit.' More Meredith than Mrs Cohen. I beat a retreat and headed for Oxford.

Dennis had given me the name of another cosy B&B, but I was in no mood to share gloom (sales figures) and glee (Iraqi casualties) with fellow travellers. So I checked into an anonymous Travelodge. Sky News was on a balcony in Baghdad, tracking cruise missiles as they whooshed into military targets and government buildings and 'collaterally' brought roofs down on a few misplaced Iraqi women and children.

Oxford's dreaming spires overlooked a shopping mall that replicated those in Omaha and Oklahoma City. I made a point of boycotting McDonald's and KFC. Was Pizza Hut American-owned? To be on the safe side, I went Chinese.

Back in my featureless room George Dubya's missiles, those million-dollar babies, were still hammering central Baghdad.

Shock and awe.

Yes, indeedy.

The day of my second tryout for date-rape started with unsuccessful assaults on male store-managers in Oxford

101

and Gloucester. Singing from a familiar hymn-sheet, both claimed to be mired in recession. The couple in Cheltenham, like Mrs Cohen and Lionel Davis, belonged in a sitcom. They engulfed me in sweetness and the love of all things leather, but I left with the feeling that they were a pair of sugar-coated nuts who would bin my samples and brochures.

I'd phoned Alison yesterday to delay our re-engagement. Her dad was in the middle of a coffin pitch, so she couldn't talk. She returned my call three times, the first while I was driving to Portsmouth, then just as I was walking into Brenda's store and again in the middle of my Chinese. I called her from my room. The 24-hour postponement was heightening Alison's excitement. I forced myself to simulate a matching enthusiasm, but even muted Sky News was a major distraction, plus I hadn't forgotten the look on Christine Turner's face while Charlie and I were talking in Reception. What I wanted wasn't a dizzy teenage girl obsessed with wedding plans and our unconceived (ill-conceived) offspring. What I wanted was a *woman* eager to worship at the shrine of my masculinity while I dove deep into the overflowing well of her voluptuous womanliness. Driving westwards my mind had been on the steely Ms Christmas, but unfortunately her steel had turned into razor wire. Driving eastwards today I was thinking of Christine Turner, and since she was out of my league and beyond my reach, I was thinking of getting down and dirty with whoever her stepson and I could drag back to his pussy-parlour. An encore with Ima, for instance. Or another brace of Krauts. Just so long as it was a woman – or women.

But I must make do with a girl.

Which I tried to do.

She came flying down the front path while I was remote-locking the car.

'Oh Paul.' Arms flung round me, then the longest, wettest kiss I could remember from this quarter. The faintest hint of tongue action – a bonus from Keith Cartright? I enjoyed the kiss and almost got away with flexing my pecs against her small breasts.

'Oh Paul.' She drew back breathlessly. Had the kiss timed out or was she safeguarding her un-erected nipples?

'Hello, Alison.'

'Oh Paul.' I thought of my mother and her *Oh William*'s.

On the phone yesterday Dennis had told me how much my commission would be on Mrs Sidebottom's order. On the strength of this I'd booked a table in the town's top hotel, where I could flash the plastic and bring home to Alison that she was a long way from the Cartright chip shop. She whinged on about the wretched Keith. No hint of intemperate behaviour. His only misdemeanour seemed to be dumping her for a thespian seamstress.

'I helped with scenery and backstage stuff for the drama group at uni,' I told her. 'That's how I met Meredith.' This wasn't the whole truth, but it was better than admitting I'd stalked her.

'Who's he?'

'She. My American girlfriend. I told you about her.'

'No, you didn't. What's an American girl doing at an English university?'

'Social Science, in her case. It's called a sabbatical year. Meredith was researching a paper on Gender Studies.'

'Is that like – animal biology?'

'*Human* biology. Social and sexual behaviour.'

Wrinkling her nose, Alison drew my attention to a zit masked with make-up. 'I suppose she was a bit of a tart - like, what's her name, Leanne?' Alison was even more old-fashioned than my mother who'd taken onboard words like 'bimbo' and 'Valley Girl'.

'Quite the opposite, actually. Very respectable. In lots of ways she used to remind me of you.' Mr Smooth! The only similarity was their tightly clenched knees. But I may as well lay my line on Alison. It worked – up to a point.

'Oh Paul.'

Three courses and many more *Oh Paul*'s later we were back in the car. Where now? She wasn't the kind of girl you take to a bar. Too early for a disco. She wasn't the kind of girl you take to a lay-by on the Downs (plus, the night was cold). She wasn't the kind of girl you shag and then don't marry. She was, still, the kind of girl you *don't* shag and *do* marry. And I was the boy – even the *man* – of her dreams. But she wasn't, never had been, the girl of mine.

I drove her home, thinking that I would plead road lag

or a good old headache. Then back to the bars and look for Jim and some foreign totty.

'Come in and say hello to Mummy and Daddy,' she said outside her house.

'Can I take a rain-check?'

'It's not raining.' Americanisms were lost on Alison. A faked yawn metamorphosed into a real one.

'I'm a bit tired, Allie. Lot of driving the last two days.'

'Just for a minute. They'll think it rude if you don't. They thought Keith had bad manners.'

'Just for a minute, then.'

My future in-laws were in non-designer casuals tonight. Sweaters and slacks. Mrs Saunders looked more like a chip-shop wife, but even out of his workaday funereal black Mr S. was every inch an undertaker. I always felt his small dark eyes were measuring me in terms of coffin size and weight.

'Paul!' they chorused a greeting. A future Barrett/Pemberton son-in-law had always been a better prospect than the scion of a chip-shop. They congratulated me on my new career. 'It's good to see another generation joining the family business,' said Mr S., tactlessly forgetting that the Barrett family business was Accountancy. 'Allie's doing very well in ours.'

I didn't enquire if she'd graduated to processing the dear departed, dressing and undressing them, cosmetically masking hideous injuries and the rigours of transition. Spooky to think that, if I married her, the hands that fondled Major Wood would come fresh from handling corpses.

'You must show Paul your lovely new bedroom, Allie,' said Mrs S., who seemed to be forcing the pace a bit. Even Alison was surprised.

'Shall I?'

'Go on, dear,' her father urged. Was he about to ask if I had a condom? (I did, of course.)

So, up we went, un-chaperoned, to the Temple Mount of their daughter's chastity. I had previously glimpsed Alison's bedroom only from the doorway en route to the bathroom. Teddy-bear wallpaper and other fluffy juvenilia. Now done over – not to say overdone – in pink and a colour close to Marrakech, it was a womb with no view. Pink-striped paper with a satin sheen above a red-wine gloss dado above red-wine emulsion. Fluffiness remained in the dressing-table stool (pink) and bedside rug (Marrakech in colour and possibly in provenance). The salesman I had newly become found suitable words of admiration for this Revenge of the Makeover.

She flung herself on her back on the bed to demonstrate its bouncy newness and patted the (red-wine) bedspread. Flashback to Meredith in my room on campus: deep kissing, fondled breasts, a handjob. Had Keith Cartright bounced on this bed? I wasn't, really, expecting a treat as lavish as a handjob or even to get my hands on Alison's breasts, such as they were.

Carpe diem. I sat on the bed. She sat up and offered her face, eyes closed. A tender kiss appropriate to young lovers for whom wedding bells might soon ring out, tolling the end of my brief life as a gangbanger. Alison's mouth was closed initially, then her lips parted, but as I slid my tongue forward she ended the kiss and lay back.

'Oh Paul.' *Oh Paul* as in *I love you and want to walk down the aisle of St Agnes's with you*, not as in *Give me your big hard prick*. The only hardness in Alison's life was butter straight from the fridge and perhaps the frozen ground in mid-January when burial was more than usually the 'hard' option.

The Major rose and, with him, the date-rapist. A horizontal girl on a bed meant only one thing. He – I – stretched out beside her, leaned over her, kissed her again: harder. Hardness, not love, was all around.

For a few moments she gave herself up to the kiss. Thank you, Keith Cartright. Then I sensed the beginnings of resistance. Captive beneath the weight of my upper torso, she squirmed and wrenched her mouth free.

'Paul.' Not the tone of a Pixar princess, more like a maiden aunt catching her favourite nephew with his genitals on display. This hadn't quite happened.

The predator didn't reach for Alison's breasts, which were several years younger than the rest of her. He went for the plum – for the cherry. One arm supported the weight with which I had her pinioned to the bouncy new bed. My other hand probed beneath her short skirt (Gap? Next? BHS?), which had rucked up close to the drop zone. Her thighs were clamped as if bound with rope, but the predator knew that one slight thrust of the wrist would bring him to the prize, the portal. And, for a nanosecond, his index finger pressed a few millimetres of tights and panties, substantially thicker than a condom, into that crevice where the hand of man (especially, I knew with sudden certainty, the hand of chip-shop Cartright) had never ventured. For Alison, the primrose path to woman-hood had (including her unpunctured hymen) triple defences.

And, intriguingly, there was moisture.

I wasn't far enough in to have deflowered her. It could still be blood, of course, but surely then I would have encountered a tampon or some other seasonal device? Perhaps Alison had started to pee herself with appre-hension now that her cherry was so close to being pipped or popped.

There was one other possible secretion.

I'd never brought Meredith to anywhere near the brink of orgasm, but last summer and the last two Saturdays I had seen women come, *made* them come. Was Alison – against all the evidence – juicing up to be a fantastic hot fuck? It seemed extremely unlikely.

And I would never know.

'PAUL!'

Under dire threat women are supposedly able to summon amazing reserves of raw strength. Mothers lift cars off their trapped children. This must be the kind of energy Alison now found to push me off her, exactly like Meredith on that Thursday in February. She pushed so hard that I rolled off the bed and onto the fluffy Marrakech rug. The porn-flick foreplay morphed into *American Pie*. Alison leapt to her feet on the other side of the bed.

'What's happened to you? I thought I'd get a bit more – *respect* – from you.' She was right, of course. I'd 'respected' Rachel. But not Meredith.

'Allie –'

'I thought –' (she'd become very pensive since Christ-mas) – 'Keith was a typical local yobbo, but you're even more out of control than he is.'

'Allie, I'm sorry. I don't know what got into me.' But I did.

'You didn't use to be like this.'

Yes, I did. And yet I don't seem to be cut out to be a rapist: you need to be rougher, tougher, more determined.

'It must be that factory and the awful people you're

working with.'

No, Allie, it's just me. This is who I am.

'You think buying me dinner in a nice hotel means you can -'

Get real, I could have said. *It usually does.* She started to cry, screwing her face up like a hurt child.

'I'd better go,' I said.

'I never want to see you again.'

Let's agree on that. For a moment I felt like doing violence, not to Alison but to her crap new décor; I wanted to trash the fluffy pink stool or hurl it through a window. Frustration was pretty much my natural state and this had been a frustrating week. Lionel Davis panting at the sound of my voice or Mrs Cohen gushing over a bunch of flowers were scant compensation for an unopened order book, just as a half-centimetre of Alison's virgin twat, however tantalizingly moist, did not slake my thirst for the deeper darker waters of Mrs Turner or Brenda Christmas or Rachel (for whom I had barely spared a thought this week).

I walked out of the bedroom in a cold fury and ran down the stairs. Mrs Saunders stood in the living-room doorway in her brown slacks and reindeer-patterned sweater. Would Alison one day be sandbag-breasted and lard-arsed? Her expression radiated more curiosity than concern. Behind her Mr Saunders didn't look away from the sports channel.

'Was that Allie shouting?' asked Mrs S. with a cheerful smile. 'Don't tell me you two are rowing again already.'

Still internally raging I felt like telling her to shove her daughter into a nunnery or a home for retards, but before I could tell her anything there came a cry of *'Mummee'* and loud sobs from upstairs. It could have been Simon calling to Rachel on account of a banged limb or a broken toy, not a woman old enough to drive and vote and take out a mortgage. *'Mummee's'* expression switched from twinkling to castrating. Either her mood or Alison's cry communicated itself to Mr Saunders; he cast a glare in my direction that was more about cremating me alive than finding the right-sized coffin.

'What have you done to her?' Not a chorus this time: an antiphonal chant.

'Nothing to worry about,' I said. 'Her precious virginity is still intact.'

As my not-to-be mother-in-law ran frantically up the stairs, my never-to-be father-in-law rose threateningly from his leather recliner (it wasn't a Pemberton). A scared schoolboy usurped the space occupied by the rapist. I could stay, explain, apologize, grovel, try to make amends. Or I could scarper.

Not a tough choice. In less than ten seconds I was in my car.

What do you do after a row with your girlfriend? You get drunk is what you do.

I could have gone looking for Jim, but I parked on the seafront and went into a favourite pub from sixth-form days, near the repertory theatre. The theatre was dark this week, so the pub was almost dead. No one from school or Pembertons was there. A man nodded a greeting, perhaps a client of my father's or someone from church. I nodded back and concentrated on sinking a couple of pints of Stella. Not enough to take more than an edge off my temper and frustration, but on top of the wine at dinner (a bland House Chardonnay of which Alison had drunk no more than two glasses and I the rest) more than enough to lose me my licence and with it my new career if I drove home.

I drove home. Carefully. As careful as you can be on two pints of lager, a half-litre of white wine and the adrenaline rush of attempted rape.

Bad news travels faster than a diesel Peugeot, especially when the driver has stopped off for a drink or two.

'I should think you would try and sneak upstairs,' my father said. Standing in the lounge doorway in a brown cable-knit sweater (homemade, natch), corduroy trousers and Christmas-present slippers, he gave me a *déjà-vu* from the Saunders household as I paused on the stairs.

'What's up, Dad?'

'Come in here and I'll tell you what's up.'

My bladder was urging me on to the bathroom, but I descended and followed him into the lounge. Mother sat with her latest embroidery on her lap. Floral-frocked Mother at her needlework, Father at the mantelpiece, sports-jacketed Son in the doorway: behind my father's corduroy legs the Living Gas Fire hissed sardonic amusement at this Norman Rockwell tableau. But look closer, gentle viewer. The embroidery is slipping unnoticed from the mother's lap; her expression is apprehensive, frightened even. And Father taps anxious fingers on the mantelpiece (he needs a pipe to complete the picture but this father doesn't smoke, has never smoked); his expression is anger tempered by disappointment tempered by a bitter foreknowledge of the inevitability of Son's conduct. Not a Rockwell painting, this is another frozen scene from Strindberg.

'My son the rapist.'

'Oh William.'

'Oh Christ.'

'Oh Paul.'

'Nobody's been raped,' I said. 'If that's what her mum and dad are saying, they're exaggerating.'

'But you did – molest her.'

'*Oh*.' Getting ready to faint again.

'I put my hand up her skirt is all I did. In 2003 I don't think that constitutes a sexual assault.'

'Oh dear.' Mother clutched a hand to her chest. The Players could use her in their next melodrama, if Saffron or Leanne didn't ream her at the auditions. Even in winter, downland walks and gardening kept my mother fit and ruddy-faced, but tonight she'd been whitewashed by the shock of my reported misdeeds. Dad, who didn't sunbathe in summer and rarely found time for gardening or walking, was pale all year round, but the news from the Saunders household had rouged him up a few degrees. Forget Strindberg, this was – almost – Eugene O'Neill.

'It does if it wasn't – consensual.' Molest. Consensual. My father's dialogue was lifted from some yesteryear courtroom drama.

'I may have pushed her a little further than she was ready to go,' I conceded. About five millimetres further. 'Alison's a bit backward compared to other girls her age.'

'So there have been others, have there?'

'Christ, Dad, give me a break.'

'Give you a beating is what I should do.' And he took a step, half a step, towards me across the Turkish rug that was probably woven in Taiwan.

'Oh please, no.' Not me: Mother.

But he wouldn't. We didn't do beatings in the Barrett

109

household. If I was ever smacked as a child I have no recollection of it, and from primary school to the Sixth Form I was never struck by either a teacher or a parent; nor was it about to happen now. Dad didn't do beatings, he did sarcastic putdowns and comparisons with my oh-so-perfect brother who, being dead, couldn't confess to me that he'd been a hooligan, a tearaway. My conservative parents were in tune with today's liberal vision of parenting. And yet they had spawned a serial predator. It wasn't nurture. It couldn't be nature. I was raised on home-cooked food and my intake of canned chemical drinks was never excessive. Maybe you have to look to *The Omen* and *The Exorcist* for the answer.

I spread my hands in a pacifying gesture that was more likely borrowed from Dennis Dawes than from university drama.

'Dad, look, I'm sorry. I got a bit carried away with Alison. I *am* nineteen, for Christ's sake.'

'I wish you wouldn't blaspheme in front of your mother.'

'Don't mind me,' said Mother, inappropriately. Not that we did, really.

'But you didn't think of *me* before you got – carried away with Alison?'

'Er – no,' I said truthfully. 'Was I supposed to?'

'You didn't think how a court case might affect my position in this town – or your mother's? Or even your uncle's, now that you're working for him?'

'Court case? I put my *hand* up her skirt, for – God's sake.'

My ashen-faced mother opened her mouth again but no sound emerged.

'Well, it may surprise you to know, Mr Clever-Clogs University-Dropout, that what you did is more than enough for a rape charge. Attempted rape.'

Not a good time to have an overfull bladder. I clenched everything. And yet it was hard to believe that pushing Alison's tights into her cunt put me in the Yorkshire Ripper league.

'They want to *charge* me? You've got to be kidding. Any court would throw it out.'

'You're probably right, but we can't afford to let it come to that.'

'We can't?' Stupidly, I thought he meant money. The Barrett empire was crumbling. The cash cow that had funded my life thus far had dried up - just when we needed to hire a top QC (Cherie Blair?) to defend me.

'Of course we can't. You only have to be charged for it to make the local papers. Even, God forbid, the national tabloids.' Some evidence here of paranoia, I thought. Dad's face was now as red as an Indian from one of the old cowboy movies I'd loved as a child. 'There goes my reputation and your mother's. It could ruin my business – and Jack's. And just in the year when my Rotary colleagues are planning to put my name forward for mayor.'

A nugget of good news amid the shale of my manifold sins and wickedness. Hard to believe that a fingertip of tights and knickers could have such Dostoyevskyan consequences. Part of me was inclined to view this in terms of one of the *Carry-On* movies to which Neil had accorded iconic status. Dad on the verge of becoming mayor somehow enhanced the comparison.

'There must be something we can do to – nip things in the bud.' It looked as if I might have to go back to the Saunders's for some major grovelling.

'What *we* can do has already been done – by *me*. No thanks to you who created this whole bloody mess. Sorry, Mary.'

But Mary, the Paleface in the Indian war camp, was past worrying about a rare expletive within her embroidered walls.

'Hey – thanks, Dad. What exactly did you do?'

He took a deep breath. 'I reminded Ted Saunders that years ago, before you were even born, I found a significant anomaly in his bookkeeping. I don't need to go into details, it's water under the bridge now, but it was something he would have been heavily fined for if I'd reported it to the Inland Revenue. It would have put him out of business. Luckily for him, even back then it was possible to use some "creative accounting" to paper over the problem.'

Another deep breath. 'So tonight I reminded him of what I'd done. I let him infer that those "irregularities" could still get him into hot water if I were to dredge them up in front of the appropriate authorities. I'm not sure he believed me, I'm not even sure it's true, but it was a

111

timely reminder of what I'd done for him in the past.'

Tax fraud and now blackmail. Easy to picture Uncle Jack getting up to such dark deeds, but not my whiter-than-white father. His next deep breath was more like a sigh.

'Can you imagine how it sticks in my throat to have to *threaten* a valued customer – an old friend – like Ted Saunders? Thank you for making that happen, Paul. Thank you very much.'

It was my bursting bladder that I was most conscious of, but I did feel a genuine pang of remorse at this moment.

'Dad, I'm really sorry.'

'I'm afraid an apology just won't do this time. You're a working man now, Paul. You're clearly too old for me to "ground" you. I wish I could say you're *not* my son, but you are and I have to live with that. However, if this is the kind of man you've turned into, one who attacks vulnerable girls, I won't live with you under my roof. I want you to move out of here.'

'Oh William, no.' Mother found her voice. 'Please, no.'

'Stay out of this, Mary.' He barely glanced at her. It was me that he faced – now scarlet-faced – as he elaborated on the terms of my banishment.

'I wish you weren't working for Jack, then you could move to somewhere where what you get up to won't impact on my position in this community. But I know your mother would prefer to have you near her –' (an 'Oh, yes' from that quarter) – 'so I shall just have to count on you to learn a lesson from what's happened tonight.'

'I will, Dad.' At that moment I felt truly contrite. He hadn't finished:

'I'm not going to set you a deadline and if you want to *buy* your own place rather than rent, I'll lend you some money for the deposit. That's *lend*, not *give*. Under other circumstances it might have been a gift to help you start up on your own, but I'm not going to be seen to reward your degenerate behaviour. We'll draw up papers to make it a formal arrangement. I shan't expect you to pay me interest, but you *will* pay it back. I hope that's totally clear.'

'Yes, Dad. Thank you, Dad. I'm so sorry about tonight. Dad, Mum – excuse me, I really need to get to the loo.'

*

And, upstairs in my own en-suite, I didn't just pee, I puked.

The puke of repentance. And, perhaps, relief at being off the hook again.

The wannabe date-rapist unpardoned, but reprieved. Living to fight another day.

11. Football and porno

'Hey, Paul. Fancy some football?'

'Isn't it a match day?'

'That's what I mean, tosspot. We need an extra man today. We need *three* more men, but one's a start.' A gull's shriek crackled through the airwaves.

'I haven't been to any practice nights. You don't know if I'm any good.'

'You can get in the way of the ball, can't you?'

I laughed. 'Yeah, I guess I can manage that. Are we home or away?'

'It's an 'ome game. You can pick me up at my place. Have you still got boots from school?'

'I've still got a full kit.' Everything washed by Mother, even my boots cleaned and waterproofed.

'Bring your own shorts if you don't want somebody else's crotch-rot! We'll give you a shirt in Pembertons' colours.'

'Do you want to do a pub lunch?' More bird noises in my ear. He was probably on the seafront, although the gulls had invaded most of the town's rooftops.

'I don't eat till after the game, but I wouldn't mind a pint. Pick me up at twelve. Earlier if you want. I'll be 'ome in ten minutes.'

I looked at my watch. Nine forty-five. I was still in bed, lingering in my room to avoid a breakfast confrontation. When my mother knocked and asked if I wanted tea I'd pretended to be still asleep.

'I'll be over about eleven-thirty,' I told Jim. My cellphone signalled a low-power warning. I put it on the charger while I showered and shaved and dug out my football kit. No need to go jogging. Plenty of exercise on the pitch this afternoon.

I looked out the window when I heard a car start up. They were both going out in Dad's car. He often did paperwork on Saturday morning; not today, it seemed. Perhaps we were both playing the avoidance game.

The pitch, a not-quite-level field shielded from view of my uncle's mansion by a hedge of leylandii, was waterlogged from heavy rains earlier in the month, although today was dry and not too cold. Our opponents were the local police, fortified by two parking wardens and a park ranger. Ten of them to our nine, but most of our players were my age and Jim's (his dad was one of our older players) whereas only three of the away team were under 25.

Michael and Angela were among the small crowd of supporters, as were some of the players' wives and girl-friends. Michael's wife, my step-cousin, was probably on horseback somewhere. And Uncle Jack wasn't there although Jim said he usually watched home games. Was he availing himself of Charlie's absence to get his leg over Christine in the marital bed? Jim's dad had a recurring back problem and only played when they were desperate. They were desperate today: they had me.

I was theoretically a defender, although attack and defence weren't clearly defined. Both goalies scored, ours twice. I almost contributed an own-goal with a sloppy pass to our keeper but redeemed myself with one brilliant pass which Jim followed through. He scored two more goals and made the key passes to two others.

Local matches tend to be high-scoring games. 13-12 today. *We* won!

The changing rooms bestowed by my uncle were a pair of recycled Portakabins. Enough benches and clothing hooks, knocked up in the works, for a full team in each cabin but only four showers per cabin in a communal tiled corner, so either a gay grope-fest was on the cards or we would wash in relays.

'Let's shower at my place,' Jim said. Even his face and hair were streaked with mud. Mine too. You'd think we'd been playing rugby. He wasn't shy about gangbanging, surely he couldn't be shy about showering with his teammates?

'We can't get in the car like this.'

'Yeah, we can. I'll get some towels.'

We changed our boots for trainers but otherwise stayed wet and muddy. I worried about the Peugot's interior although the towels he swiped from the Portakabin protected the upholstery. At his flat I showered and shampooed while he made tea. The dressing gown he told me to use had a Nieman-Marcus label, either a holiday gift from his stepmother or something my uncle had donated to Charlie. I laughed when Jim appeared from the bathroom in a voluminous dragon-patterned kimono tied with a wide black sash.

'My dad found it in a motel wardrobe,' he explained, grinning. 'Must 'ave got left be'ind by a very fat businessman.'

'Or a sumo wrestler!'

We watched Premier football on Sky, drinking tea and eating microwaved teacakes flooded with butter. It was already agreed that we would go out on the pull later. Meanwhile the evening yawned ahead of us. I didn't want to go home and face my parents, Dad doubtless still in a thunderous mood, Mother more like a patchy wet fog. I had Sunday lunch chez Jack and Agnes to look forward to; my uncle's promise of a surprise.

With one eye on Man U, I told Jim about my date with Alison and its repercussions. 'Fuckin' 'ell,' he said. 'All that fuss for a finger of pussy.'

'Not even that.'

'Imagine if you'd actually given 'er one.'

'Her dad would have killed me.'

'Or yours.'

I didn't bother to explain my father's use of verbal weaponry. I did tell him I'd been sentenced to banishment from the family home.

'You was talkin' about getting' your own place anyway.'

'And he said he'd lend me the cash for the deposit.'

'Well, it's turned out all right then, ain't it?'

'I guess.'

'You can stay 'ere for a bit if you want. You know, while you're lookin'. If you don't mind kippin' on the sofa.'

'Thanks, Jim, but I'll be OK. Think I'll rent somewhere for the time being.'

'Suit yourself.'

'I will.'

'Fuck you, then.' The dragons seethed when he laughed.

'Fuck your stepmother.'

'You wish!'

Now there's a thought.

After tea we started on lagers and watched the replay of another game. He cooked dinner, surprising me with pan-fried sirloin steaks, oven chips and a supermarket salad. The dressings let him down: only salad cream and ketchup.

'I'll get us some wine,' I said, reaching for my jeans. 'Where's your nearest Happy Shopper?' I remembered buying bottles of wine for Rachel in Bayswater barely a month ago. That, like university, was in another life.

'I've got wine in,' he said. 'No need to get dressed till we go out.'

The wine was Piat d'Or, once the nation's favourite rouge but never mine or my father's. We drank two bottles, still in our gowns, eating off a coffee-table. Appropriately there was a kung-fu comedy on one of the movie channels which we sent up. Jim did a flying kick en route to the kitchen and fell over; the kimono was too long as well as too wide.

Dessert was a chocolate ice-cream cake from Lidl which we demolished with liberal glasses of Bailey's. Beer, wine and Bailey's on top of football, family drama and a week on the road: I dozed off before the movie ended and came to with the feeling that puking might be back on the agenda. Jim had put on a porno DVD. A hairy man with a beer gut was fucking, from behind, a big-breasted blonde who was also going down on another woman, a brunette with un-augmented boobs and a frayed-looking vagina. Not an appetising sight. Jim was stroking himself inside the kimono. He grinned at me and stopped stroking.

'Thought this might get us in the mood.'

'Black coffee might be a better idea if we're going to chase down some pussy of our own,' I said. At twelve and thirteen, dicks had been flashed in the changing room and the showers – mostly for statistical, comparative purposes – but Jim and I had graduated beyond jerk-off parties, hadn't we?

'Think you'll be okay to drive?'

'Pour some coffee down me and let's see.'

His hard-on tented the robe as he went to the kitchen. Onscreen the lardy guy lay down on a rumpled bed. The brunette straddled him, grunting as if his penis was too big for her cavernous cunt. The blonde sat on his face and moaned as he slurped; her thighs were crêped with cellulite. Jim had lowered the sound enough to make the dialogue indecipherable. The sloppy guy, the clapped-out brunette, the silicone/cellulite blonde – porn is so gross. I closed my eyes. Drifting into a half-awake half-asleep state I tried to translate the movie into a replay of last weekend's scene with Ima, her supple limbs and olive skin, her pert breasts and tight wet pussy – and Jim, egging me on. Perversely, what came into my booze-hazed mind was a fantasy of his stepmother, riding me. The expression on her face was the one she'd worn for Charlie in Reception on Thursday. Now she was wearing it for me.

I came awake to find my dressing gown open and myself on the receiving end of a blowjob. Not, obviously, from a big-breasted blonde.

From Jim.

The would-be rapist was being raped. Was this *date-rape*? Were Jim and I 'dating'? And if we were, did steak and gâteau and a bottle of Piat d'Or entitle him to a blowjob? Was I a cheap date?

Jim was gay.

Or bi.

But I was neither.

I squinted down through narrowed eyes, not wanting him to catch me watching him. His mind was fully on the job, the blowjob. One hand was on my groin, holding step-mother-inspired Major Wood up to his face; the other was inside the kimono which had slipped off his shoulders like a starlet's frock at a premiere. Well, this was a first. For me, if not for him.

There was a visible thinning of the hair on his crown. Jim would be bald before he was thirty. Charlie still had a good head of hair, as did my father. Wasn't there a good hair gene? Was I too destined for early baldness?

He grunted something. It might have been a pleasure noise, or it might have been porn-speak. 'Give me that big cock.' 'Hey, help yourself, Jimbo.'

If I wanted to make a joke of it – and let him know I was conscious – I could have said, 'Didn't your mum tell you not to talk with your mouth full?'

I didn't want to make a joke of it. I didn't want to make an anything of it. I tried a vague grunt of my own, as if surfacing from unconsciousness. This only prompted him to suck harder. Replace him with his stepmother – or Ima – and I'd say what he was doing was yummy.

Neil was suddenly in the room with us. Was this all it would have taken to keep him from climbing the steps inside the Founder's Tower? Closing my eyes for a blow-job? It wasn't such a big deal.

Except that it was. I liked Jim, we were – so his dad said – 'mates'. But I had – almost – *loved* Neil, we were more than friends. I'd endured him kissing me, once, briefly, but I wouldn't, I don't think, have allowed this.

I didn't want it but I wasn't sure how to end it. I could declare myself awake, say 'What the fuck you doing, Jim?', make a drama or (somehow) a joke of it, get dressed and walk out, go to the place called home. But I'd had enough of drama and this wasn't something I was ready to make a joke of.

Or I could just let this unsought scene play itself out. I'd always been brilliant at doing nothing. I closed my eyes and even made faint snoring noises.

Jim wasn't the only one going down. Major Wood was now Corporal Slack. Jim didn't seem to mind. He now had both my balls in his mouth. This too had the potential, under different circumstances, to be enjoyed. Another, longer grunt indicated that he had presumably shot his load inside the second-hand kimono.

After a few more slurpings he gave up. There was a plopping sound as my gear came out of his mouth. He pulled the two halves of the dressing gown back together, closing the curtains on Act One as it were. I hoped he wouldn't try to kiss me, especially after having my balls in his mouth. He didn't. He uttered a deep breath, a sigh perhaps, and left me, left the room. I quickly sprawled full-length, face towards the rear of the sofa with my hands protecting my crotch and the gown tucked inside my arms. Oh God, did my bum now look as if it was up for grabs? A few minutes later I heard the loo flush. When he came back into the room I was snoring again. He threw a blanket over me and gently tucked a pillow under my head. I murmured half-asleep noises, which I hoped would deter him from trying to screw me.

He didn't try to screw me. Nor did he kiss my face or tell me loved me. He said, 'Goodnight, Paul' and went to his bedroom. Perhaps he didn't love me. Perhaps it was just sex, like the student in Brighton who'd invited me to crash on his sofa: Stephen. If I'd gone home with Stephen I might have been better prepared for this evening. Or – this thought again – I could have closed my eyes two months ago and faked some snoring for Neil.

Would things have turned out any differently? Pointless line to pursue. *Lacrimae rerum.* Life's a bitch, and you wind up dead. Neil hit the nail with that.

I went genuinely to sleep. It was three a.m. when I awoke. I dressed and let myself out quietly. Three a.m. was too late for even the hardier clubbers of Boredom-on-Sea, which was turning out to be a lot less boring than before. I felt totally safe to drive home. Gay sex was more sobering than coffee.

Mother had left two letters on my bed. A handwritten envelope from London and a bulky printed one from the Midlands which I opened first, expecting in a sudden burst of fatalism that my other sin (commission rather than omission) was about to catch up with me. Meredith was pressing charges for attempted rape.

It was a letter from the bursar's office, enquiring about my intentions since mail to my Hall had gone unanswered. There was a form for me to fill in if I intended to drop out. The bursar warned me that tuition fees paid in advance would not be refunded and that I would be charged for my room up to the end of term unless another student took it over before then.

Off the hook, still. Meredith had probably gone home. I had her address in Daytona. We'd sent each other comic Christmas cards. I could, too late, write her an apology. I made myself – and her – a promise that I would.

I sniffed the letter from London before unfolding it, hoping for a trace of perfume or deodorant or even kiddie shampoo, but it only smelt of paper.

Dearest Paul,

A letter is more personal than a text. I hope things are all right in "Boredom-on-Sea". I often think about the really good day we had there, you and me and Simon. He sends hugs and kisses. As do I.

I don't know if you watch <u>EastEnders</u> but Richard's going into it next month – actually he won't be on TV until May. Things are O.K. so far. He thinks we should get married for Simon's sake. I haven't said yes yet, but I suppose I will. It isn't easy to put the past behind you, as I think you know at least as well as I do.

Anyway, I hope things are going okay with your new job, your new life. Can we <u>all</u> have happy endings to our stories? Wouldn't that be nice!

Be well. Be positive! Be happy.

Thinking of you, often.

Rachel.

'Dearest' was a promising intro, but by the end the only thought I could formulate – she had mentioned marriage and Neil was on my mind – was from the opening sequence of *Four Weddings and a Funeral*: Fuck-fuck-fuck-fuck-fuck.

Lacrimae rerum.

Yeah.

12. Family life – and death

'So, how's my big cousin Paul doing?'

'He's doing okay. How's his little cousin Jenny?'

'Not so little, as you can see.'

'You still look the same to me.'

'If you think you can sweet-talk your way into my pantyhose, you're doing fine so far.' She flashed me a provocative grin. She'd had her teeth bleached in the States; a top front one that slightly overlapped had been fixed or perhaps replaced with an implant.

And she'd picked up an American accent. 'Fine' was 'fahn' and 'little' had been almost 'Lidl', where my gay mate Jim shopped for gâteau and ketchup.

This was Jack's 'surprise', his wayward stepdaughter back from the US. And without an engagement ring.

Nothing else had been implanted that I could see. Her breasts looked the same as last year, about the size of Mrs Turner's but half their age and probably twice as firm. Her blonde hair was in a ponytail that suited her Cameron Diaz girl-next-door prettiness. She wore designer denims, a cowgirl plaid shirt, decorated leather boots. And she had put on weight: she wasn't Supersize but neither was she a size ten. Either a US diet or her own hormonal development had given her a Christine Turner kind of voluptuousness. At twenty, a few months older than me, Jenny wasn't a girl, she was a woman: a whole lot of woman.

We got along 'fahn' before and during lunch, largely ignoring the old folks and her sister and Michael. We talked about the States, about New Mexico where she'd been staying and which I only knew from reading *The Plumed*

Serpent and biographies of Lawrence. We talked about clothes and food and movies, typical teenage conversation really. No mention of the Albuquerque congressman's son.

'So is this just a flying visit?' I asked, tackling the subject from an angle. 'When are you going back?'

'I'm here to stay – till I think of somewhere else to go.'

'Lucky you, to have that freedom.'

'You've got it too. You just - reach out and grab it.'

'My dad's not in the same league as Uncle Jack.'

'I'd be doing it even if I didn't have an allowance. There are always jobs a girl can do. Guys too.'

'You know I dropped out of uni?'

'Yeah. You're working for Jack now. Is that, like, gonna be your career?'

I checked that my uncle wasn't listening. He was telling my father about the council withholding planning permission from some development project.

Dad's churchgoing suit did double duty for Saint Agnes and her namesake my aunt. Jack's sports jacket looked twice the price of Michael's - and twice the size. My brown leather blouson matched Jenny's boots but without the decals; my jeans, embarrassingly, were only Debenhams.

'I don't know,' I answered Jenny's 'career' question. 'I guess it's got me started.'

'How can you stand it here? This is a one-horse town.'

'Yes, and your sister's riding it!' That got a laugh. Everyone looked at us. We exchanged grins and concentrated on eating until they all resumed their conversations: horses, local politics, church fêtes.

On any but the coldest of winter days my aunt dressed for the British High Commission in Jaipur: today, a chiffon symphony in pale lavender. Agnes had been born, raised, schooled – and married to her first husband – in India, where her father was a blender of the finest teas. Her daughters had grown up amid the burning sands of Arabia which their father, a hydroponics engineer, was converting to fields of grain and prairie grasses. At her stepfather's table Joanna was another W.I. clone; her dress was less flowery than my mum's by about twenty percent.

'I've got my own name for it,' I said.

'For what?'

'This one-horse town. I call it Boredom-on-Sea.'

Jenny smiled. She hadn't flirted with me since her

123

earlier remark about getting into her pantyhose, but I was on the lookout for the next window of opportunity. I smiled back. My cousin wet her lips briefly with her tongue.

Fighting tumescence, I tuned in on the others. Michael and Joanna were talking about their next litter, presumably red setters not babies. Mother and Agnes were discussing car boot sales, which I wouldn't have thought either of them knew anything about. Jack was on his current hobbyhorse, our Continental breakthrough. Dad was listening intently, although I'm not sure leather did it for him. I'd noticed at breakfast, when we all acted as if last night had not happened, that his colour was still high. It was high now, Red Indian red.

'Of course, young Paul's already spearheading our whole campaign,' Jack said, going into northern mill-owner mode. 'He got off to a fine start in France this week.' He even pronounced France with the short northern 'a'. 'You can be right proud of that lad of yours.'

It could have been worse, it could have been a Lawrentian '*reet* proud of that lad of *yourn*' and '*yon* Paul' instead of 'young Paul.' But still I cringed.

Whether my father was ready to admit to pride in my achievements or preferred instead to denounce me as a rapist we were not to know. As I grimaced at my now statuesque cousin and wondered whether her stepfather's fulsome patronage was helping me further into her pantyhose or setting my cause back, a stable-lad in this one-horse town of ours, Dad introduced a note of drama into Sunday lunch by falling, red-faced but with his customary quiet discretion, across the table. Impeccable as ever, he managed not to knock anything over although the gravy boat rocked under the impact.

The paramedics arrived within twenty minutes, a tribute to New Labour's much-trumpeted improvements in the NHS or perhaps to the power of the Pemberton name.

But my father was beyond resuscitation and my mother in a state beyond hysteria, almost rending her floral garments like the black-robed mothers and widows in news footage from Baghdad.

I wasn't going to get into Cousin Jenny's pantyhose today.

Part Two

13. The Dropout's Mother's Tale

'He's done what?' demanded William in a tone Mary hadn't heard since – when was it? – Christmas?

'He's dropped up,' she said.

'Dropped *out*,' her son corrected her. Up, down, out, schmout, Mrs Hirschfeld, Daddy's housekeeper, might have said. Mrs Hirschfeld had had a number tattooed on her wrist. Daddy had been part of the army that liberated her from – one of those places where Jews had a number tattooed on their wrist. Mary re-tuned to the conversation between William and Paul.

'I suggest you get on a train and drop back in,' her husband was saying.

'No,' said their son.

'Oh Paul,' Mary said. Moments later, when Paul said his teaching career was down the lavatory, William said, 'My God.' Said it twice. Here we go, thought Mary. 'Oh William,' she said.

Off he went. Money wasted. The Barrett name shamed. Paul's prospects, or lack of them. A girl Paul said was not pregnant. In his fury and disappointment William swore at Paul. Mary fled to the kitchen in tears. William came in to comfort her and promised to apologize to Paul and did so 24 hours later when Paul spoke about moving to a flat of his own.

Actually it was nice to have him permanently home again after – however long he had been away at college. Mary even enjoyed washing his sports gear every night when he came back from the gym or whatever it was. If only William didn't argue with him all the time. Had he argued with Trevor?

She couldn't remember.

Mary always started her spring cleaning in the bleak mid-winter, after the Christmas decorations came down. This January, on impulse, she'd taken down her embroidery of her fallen firstborn son and put it in the attic. She also removed his spare uniform from Paul's wardrobe and put it in the Salvation Army clothing bank at the recycling zone in Tesco's car park. Perhaps some Afghan refugee was now keeping warm in Trevor's uniform. Or – had Mary done a reckless thing? – would terrorists use it in some frightful masquerade? She didn't tell William, who hadn't commented on the disappearance of the tapestry. Perhaps he too felt it was time, past time, to let Trevor go.

Trevor's death was now the only event Mary could remember from the 20 years of his life. She could not even recall the day he was born. Grief had somehow robbed him of shape and substance. Even the details of his death were hazy. She knew it had come in a phone call, which she had taken. When her mother's brother had been killed in the Second World War, the news came in a telegram. A telegram in those days meant only one thing. Grandmother screamed and fainted at the sight of the telegraph boy coming up the garden path. How weird that Mary remembered vivid details of an event she hadn't witnessed, which had happened when she was barely two years old!

'Mrs Barrett?' If she strained she could still call to mind the voice at the other end. He had introduced himself as the Commanding Officer of her son's squadron or platoon or something. Not one of those posh voices you heard in old war films. Not a common voice either, but *unrefined*. Clearly a different class of soldier made it to the top in Margaret Thatcher's armed forces.

'Mrs Barrett, I'm extremely sorry to have to tell you that your son, Private Trevor Raymond Barrett – '

'Will you wait a moment? I'll fetch my husband. He's mowing the lawn.'

More weirdness. She remembered that William had been mowing, but she couldn't remember the details of their son's death. Had he died a hero? Or – it wouldn't matter to Mary – a coward? Had he been the victim of one of those 'friendly fire' accidents, like Uncle Raymond who'd been run down by an American jeep speeding on a blacked-out German road in October 1944?

She did not have to strain to recall the bottomless well of loss she and William had fallen into. No funeral, no coffin: only a pitiless Memorial Service at St Agnes's. And she remembered that after a suitable interval they'd begun to make love with a fervour and frequency that eclipsed even their honeymoon. Mary came off the Pill, and soon enough there was Paul. Paul brought Mary up from the well of grief and loss, but she knew that William took longer to surface and still to this day dangled his feet in it. He had twice made the long and awful journey to the Falkland Islands to visit the grave. Mary took flowers to her mother's grave on her birthday and on Mother's Day (Agnes, who was Catholic, went on All Souls' Day on Jack's behalf), but she could not face the arduous trip to Port Stanley with such a bleak prospect at its end.

'Come to think of it,' Daddy used to say by way of introducing into the conversation something he was actually itching to announce. Jack, when they were small, used to imitate Daddy and sometimes got clouted for it.

Now, when Mary came to think of it, she usually came up against a blank wall. She could remember details of her own childhood, like Daddy saying 'Come to think of it' and Jack falling down the back door steps and cutting his knee on a shard of glass so badly he needed stitches. She remembered the horrid French teacher at her prep school, Mlle Deaulnieux, who used to hit pupils with a ruler when they misused tenses or changed the sex of nouns. Even William appeared faintly in her childhood memories of Sunday-School and fêtes and garden parties. And she remembered the recipes for almost everything she baked for W.I. meetings and church fêtes, although she sometimes got the quantities wrong or missed out a vital ingredient such as sugar or salt and had to feed a crumbled-up cake or quiche or a batch of buns to the birds.

But Mary couldn't remember the name of any teacher of Trevor's or Paul's. Paul must have been bright in school, for here he was dropping down from university, but had he been *good*? She had a feeling Trevor had been naughty but no evidence to back this feeling up. Why did he join the army? He'd lacked *accountant* potential, she was almost sure: she couldn't recall William banging on about it the way he still did in regard to Paul.

'Banging on'. She'd picked that up from television. There was also 'banged up', which meant imprisoned: 'I shan't rest till So-and-so is banged up.' There was another use, more American than English, which Mary knew from reading novels. 'Bang' could mean 'fuck', as in 'I banged his old lady', which didn't mean 'I fucked his elderly mother' but rather 'I fucked his wife'. (In today's weird parlance 'old lady' could actually be a teenage bride.)

In her head Mary sometimes used the F-word, although she had never, as far as she knew, used it out loud in her entire life; and neither, she was sure, had William. She liked the sound of it, its staccato bluntness, although books and television threw it around a little too freely. What couples got up to every five pages or five minutes in books and films and television drama would have had both Mary's mother and grandmother swooning with shock.

But if the dialogue in the Barrett marital bed had been restrained, the sex itself had not been. William wasn't as adventurous as some of the men in films and books, but he was passionate and considerate. Occasionally the women at the W.I. spoke about their intimate lives (among themselves, not the guest speakers). A lot of them looked on sex as an unpleasant chore; some ad-mitted to faking orgasms; a few were sure, even relieved, that their husbands had a girlfriend or went with prosti-tutes. If sex was a duty, to Mary it was a joyous one. She loved William as fiercely now as when they first married, loved every inch of his body, especially those inches (the W.I. had led her to suspect William had more of them than some husbands) that he still inserted into her at least once a week – and sometimes, on sultry summer holidays, daily. Mary didn't always reach orgasm but she never felt the need to pretend that she had. And one thing she knew for sure in a world of growing uncertainty: William had never cheated on her, nor had he ever visited a prostitute.

Because of the long and disturbing gaps Mary tended to avoid looking back on her life, but certain things – perhaps because of the gaps – stood out. The house she grew up in, which was grander than her present home but not as grand as The Grange where Jack now lived with –

what's her name – Agnes. William, more serious than the other boys, in his Sunday best. After one of the worrying gaps, William again, emerging from a hotel bathroom in a foreign city on the first night of their honeymoon, his – (she pictured it rather than give it a name or a crude literary euphemism) – poking out of his pyjamas ready to give her what she soon began to crave. Another gap before the phone call telling them that Trevor's short life had ended on the far side of the Earth in a cause that she hoped had been worth the sacrifice. More heady sex as they tried to suppress their shared grief. Another gap, encompassing the birth and early life of another son. Then rows between William, wanting a son who was a carbon copy of himself or the idealized firstborn, and Paul who failed to fit that bill as, Mary suspected but did not know for sure, had Trevor.

Childhood joy giving way to adult grief and disappointment.

And fucking. Lots and lots of lovely fucking.

A life – *her* life – in recollection.

Within what seemed to be bare days of his return from wherever he'd gone to college Paul was jetting off to foreign parts to sell those things that Jack made. Whoever's idea it was that Paul should work for Jack, it had been a good one.

But the day he came back from whichever foreign part it was there was the most frightful row. Paul was accused of attacking that flat-chested blonde girl whose father was the undertaker. Mary found it hard to believe her son was a rapist, but then she found it hard to believe his brother had been the hero he was to William.

Next day they all went to Jack and Agnes's for Sunday lunch. Agnes, in a flouncy dress of some flimsy material, looked as if she belonged in a stage play by Oscar Coward. There were two younger women as well, a horsy-looking one Mary vaguely remembered with a red-headed husband. Hadn't Jack given them a house when they got married? Mary couldn't remember what Jack's father, her father, had given her as a wedding present, but she was sure it hadn't been a house. The other young woman seemed to be Paul's girlfriend, not the one he was supposed to have raped, another one Mary couldn't recall having seen before who was busty and tarty and possibly American. She and Paul flirted across the table. They looked as if they might leave the table at any moment and go off to a bedroom. Jack was banging on to William about the shortcomings of the local council whose mayor William had always dreamed of being. William looked as if he'd caught the sun yesterday in their walk on Seaford Head, looking for but not picking wildflowers; it was illegal to pick wildflowers. The horsy woman was talking horses or it might be dogs with the ginger man. Mary was trying to hold up a longer conversation than she was used to with Agnes about buying stuff at car boot sales to donate to the charity shops. She had gone through life in her brother's shadow and then William's, saying relatively little in case she was thought stupid, and now she said even less in case people thought there might be something wrong with her.

Jack said to William, 'You can be right proud of that lad of yours.'

'No,' Mary thought of saying,' not proud at all. We think he's a rapist.' Not that she would have dared to say any such thing. William would be mortified. But looking at her son flirting with the American girl, Mary *did* feel proud of him: he was handsome and clever, girls fell at his feet and even Jack was pleased with him. Of course, if she spoke up to give their son an endorsement like a TV commercial for dishwasher tablets, William would still die of mortification.

But William didn't die of mortification. He died of a heart attack. Right on Jack's dinner table. Mortifying in itself. What's-her-name's lunch was completely ruined. Roast lamb.

'You've been in a fugue state,' the nice doctor was saying.

'Have I?' Mary said, her voice sounding weak in her own ears. Wasn't a fugue something to do with organ music? She seemed to recall turning the pages for her sister Lenore in church as she practised somebody's Ciabatta and Fugue in D. Where was Lenore? Mary couldn't recall the last time she'd seen her sister.

'Yes,' the doctor said. 'But I think you're coming out of it now.' He was as black as the coal in Daddy's cellar. And big: huge. A huge black man; Mary felt she should have

130

found him intimidating, but in fact there was something reassuring about him. He was a big protective wall between Mary and the bad place she had been. This place in the state called Fugue, although Mary couldn't recall that she'd ever been to America. An American girl came with Trevor on one of the times he visited her; was she from Fugue?

'How long was I away?'

'Quite a while. A few weeks.'

'What's the weather been like in England?'

'It's been fine, Mary. Warm and dry.'

'Oh dear. I hope William has found time to water the garden. He leads such a busy life.'

'Actually your *son* has been taking care of things. Your son Paul.'

'Not Trevor?'

'No, Mary. Not Trevor. Paul.'

'Paul.' She experimented with the name. Something as light as choux pastry floated into the space between Mary and her memories of what had gone before. 'Trevor died, didn't he?'

'Yes, Mary,' the doctor said gently. He had a soft voice for such a big man. And no accent. You'd never know he was a nig-nog.

'And William's dead too, isn't he?'

'Yes, Mary. Can you remember what happened?'

'His heart...Jack's table...she gave us lamb.' Fragments dripped into Mary's mind like dropping vanilla essence into milk for homemade custard. Shouldn't she be weeping as she remembered the day her husband died? She had the feeling that she had cried and cried for days and days, weeks even. Now she was 'All Cried Out'. That was a song title by – oh dear. 'Paul was there,' she remembered, 'with an American girl called Jenny.'

'Think about Jenny, Mary. What do you know about her?'

'Winston Churchill's mother was an American called Jenny. Jenny Jerome.'

'Is that a fact? I don't believe I knew that.' His smile was big and white, like the Seven Sisters, only he had more than seven teeth of course.

'My brother has a daughter called Jenny. No, she's his *step*daughter. Her mother's name is Agnes. And her father

131

was another William. He died in – in Arabia somewhere.' See, she didn't need to worry about her memory! There wasn't anything wrong with her, not really. What had he called it – a 'fluke' state?

'I think she should come and stay with us,' Agnes said. Jack's face fell.

'Oh God. For how long?'

'For as long as it takes for her to get better.'

'Will she get better?' their daughter asked. 'Isn't she, like, brain-dead?'

'That's terribly cruel, darling.'

'It's a fact, though,' Jack said. 'Let's face it: she's gone doolally.'

'Her psychiatrist calls it a "fugue state". Brought on by the shock. She could come out of it any time.'

'Or never,' Jenny said. 'It could be the start of Alzheimer's.'

'Oh, I think we'd have noticed if it was that. You know, repeating herself, forgetting things.'

'She's always had William to hide behind,' said Jack. 'Now we're seeing the real Mary. A few loose screws. Quite a few.'

'Well, we can't just shuffle her off to a sanatorium, can we? In any case the government's been closing them down for years.'

'I bet there are still some private ones for people who are prepared to pay. *I'm* prepared to pay. It's the least we can do.'

'She's your sister, Jack.' She looked at her husband who looked down at the floor. 'The *least we can do* is have her here, shelter her, take care of her.'

'Jesus,' Jenny said. 'Count me out. I'm not living in a private loony-bin.'

'Well, since you're going to live with Paul anyway...'

'Says who?' Jack demanded.

'Oh Jack.'

'Don't go all shocked, Jack. I did ask Mummy if it was all right.'

Jack cast a baleful glance at his wife. 'And you said it is?'

Agnes held up helpless hands. 'It's what they do nowadays, isn't it? We didn't stop her going to live with Baxter

132

in New Mexico. Paul's a nice enough boy. You're always saying what a good job he's doing.'

'That doesn't mean he can do a job on my daughter.'

'*Step*daughter, Daddy dear.'

Jack took on the hurt look he always had at these reminders.

Paul was relieved to have a painful decision taken out of his hands. In the three months since his father's death he'd been making increasingly long trips to France and Spain. When he was home he dutifully visited his mother in the psychiatric unit of the local hospital, where her brother's name and influence had secured one of the few private rooms. Done out in pacifying pastels, the unit was clean but deeply creepy. The patients' disorders ranged from minor breakdowns all the way up to psychosis. One young male had a Michael Jackson fixation: he'd attempted d-i-y plastic surgery with kitchen utensils and domestic bleach. A middle-aged woman in a shapeless smock was God, apparently a repeat offender. Several inmates dressed and looked normal, if somewhat dazed. Drugs zombified everyone, including Paul's mother.

After six weeks she stopped calling him Trevor, but it was clear she still confused elements of his life and his predecessor's. She'd finally accepted that she was a widow and that her brother had taken over decision-making but she worried about 'what William would say' to almost everything. The visits were a chore.

'Jack says you're going to stay with them for a while.'

'I don't know what your father would say. But it's very kind of Jack. And –' a moment's hesitation – 'Agnes. Will you be there?'

'I'm still at home.' Was it okay to use that word, reminding her that she had lost it – her home – along with the plot?

'I hope you're keeping it clean and tidy. Your father would want that.'

'Aunt Agnes's cleaning woman comes in two afternoons a week.'

'That's nice of her. Are you taking care of the garden?'

'Their gardener keeps things under control. Mowing the lawn and so on.'

'You can't find time to mow the lawn?'

'I'm away most of the time – you know, France and Spain. For Jack.'

'Of course you are, Paul. Your father would be so proud of you. Are my salvias out yet?'

Paul didn't know what a salvia was. 'They're lovely,' he assured her.

'Is it too early for the zinnias?'

'I'm not sure,' he confessed. He decided not to tell her Jenny had moved in when he came back from Madrid. They slept in his bed, and he'd given her the spare room as a dressing room. He wasn't ready to shag his step-cousin in his parents' bed.

'I think she's making good progress,' Agnes said at the end of the first week, dispensing too many ice cubes into a glass that contained an inadequate measure of gin by Jack's standards. Of course, it was only lunchtime.

'I wish she wouldn't keep rabbiting on about when we were kids. I don't remember half of what she does.'

'Oh, Jack. Maybe you're the one who's starting Alzheimer's!'

'Very funny.'

'I suppose those are happy memories for her. The recent ones all end with William being dead. And before that there was Trevor.'

'She could think about Paul. We got a nice order from El Corte Ingles in Madrid yesterday. I told Mary about it but it seemed to go in one ear and out the other.'

'I think she has trouble memorizing anything new. Losing William has cast a shadow over the present as well as the last two months.'

'Is that you or the shrink speaking?'

Agnes smiled. 'It's something he said which I've – "taken onboard".' She put audible quotation marks around the idiom.

'You're very good with her. It doesn't get on your nerves that she follows you everywhere like a little girl?'

'She *is* a little girl for now. It doesn't bother me. I've had little girls running after me before. Given time, I'm sure she'll "grow out of it" just as they did. What does bother me is that some of the time she thinks I'm Lenore.'

'She doesn't remember the accident?' Jack and Mary's ski-mad sister had been engulfed in an avalanche off-piste in Zermatt in 1967 at the age of 28.

'Obviously not. I keep reminding her that Lenore's been dead for decades but she keeps talking about things she and I are supposed to have done when we were girls.'

'The shrink doesn't think it might be the start of –' he couldn't bring himself to say it – 'what Jenny said?'

Neither it seemed could his wife, although she'd named it not two minutes ago. 'He says to wait and see. It may be just the grief working its way out.'

Jack sighed. 'Don't hold dinner for me tonight. I've got a late appointment this afternoon.' He was never sure how transparent these lies were.

'Very well, dear.'

Jack usually went to Morocco in spring to meet with his leather supplier, but the Continental expansion had kept him in Sussex this year. He went in July, taking Paul and Jenny with him.

On the night Jack was due back Agnes and Mary were watching the local news on TV. One extremely local item concerned the town's mayor whose gold chain of office had vanished from the Town Hall safe. The agitated mayor, a retired lieutenant colonel from Jack's golf club - his much younger wife was sporting Bollywood quantities of gold - said he hadn't worn it since the spring.

Agnes laughed. 'She probably had it melted down into those bracelets.'

'William always wanted to be mayor,' Mary said.

'I hope you would have shown better taste as lady mayoress,' Agnes said.

'I can't remember, has Jack been mayor?'

'They've asked him twice, but he turned them down. He's too busy and he hates all that ceremonial stuff.' She hesitated before confessing, 'I very much wanted to be lady mayoress.' This was a sore point with Agnes.

'Was Daddy mayor?'

'Yes, in 1960. The year you and William were married. He wore the chain to your wedding.' Agnes, in 1960, had not yet met her first husband, also William, the girls' father who whisked them off to Arabia. But she knew the Pemberton family history and had seen Mary's wedding photographs many times.

'I think I remember that,' Mary said although her tone

suggested that she didn't. 'You were my bridesmaid.'

'No, dear. Lenore was your bridesmaid.'

'Not you?'

'No, dear.'

'You're not –'

'No, Mary,' Agnes said patiently.

There was a new *Poirot* later on. Agnes kept her sister-in-law loosely in touch with the plot and the characters. They drank chocolate when it finished and then went to bed. Jack's flight must be running late, in which case he might stay at an airport hotel overnight. Agnes normally read for an hour, but tonight she was tired. She'd gardened all afternoon, while her gardener was over at Mary's house trimming hedges and mowing the lawn.

If she'd heard a car she would have guessed it to be Jack. Mary hadn't driven for a year or more, so if Agnes heard her own car start up, she would assume it was being stolen. Which, in a way, it was.

The telephone woke her at half past midnight. She expected it to be Jack, now several hours overdue, but it was the police. A well-spoken young man verified her identity and introduced himself. Her next thought was that something had happened to Jack, driving back from Heathrow. Or to Jennifer and Paul in Morocco. Terrorists. Her heartbeat quickened.

'Mrs Pemberton, you're the registered owner of a white Audi Quattro, licence plate number –'

'Yes, I am,' she interrupted. 'I forgot to garage it this afternoon. It's parked outside my house at the moment.'

'If you look out the window, you'll see that it isn't.'

Agnes didn't waste time checking. 'Perhaps you'd like to tell me where it is.' Which the well-spoken young man proceeded to do.

A police car had been sent to the cemetery following a report of suspicious activity. The constables found a woman in a nightdress digging up one of the graves. Mary had climbed over the cemetery wall. She'd taken a trowel rather than a spade, plus a flashlight and her sister-in-law's Audi. When the policemen arrived she was dirty and dishevelled and had scraped a hole about three feet deep in William's grave. Smiling in a fashion that reminded one of them of the Queen Mother and speaking incoherently of gold chains and 'my husband the mayor', she allowed the men to settle her into the back of their car. They recorded the number of the unlocked Audi abandoned outside the gates. At the station they served her tea and got her name out of her. Failing to get a reply from the Barrett house, they checked – and recognized – the Audi's owner.

At 12.35 Agnes dressed and called a taxi to take her to the police station.

By two thirty Mary was back in hospital. The psychiatric unit was full but a bed was found in the geriatric ward. Before Jack came home at lunchtime Agnes had moved her to a private nursing home specializing in dementia.

Paul was shocked. In just a week she'd shrunk, like Lily Tomlin in that movie.

'Hello, Mother.'

'Trevor! What a nice surprise.'

He didn't correct her. It didn't faze her that 'Trevor' had tales of Continental furniture sales trips and a visit to Morocco to regale her with. She claimed to remember some of the cities he told her about – Nice, Marseilles, Barcelona – although Paul wasn't sure his parents had visited any of them; they'd mostly holidayed in Wales and the Lake District. He didn't stay very long. There was a surprise when she hugged him goodbye; getting his name right was only half of it.

'You don't need to come every week, Paul. This is a fucking awful place.'

Paul laughed and gave her a bigger than intended return hug. It looked as if there might be a few laughs as his mother slid into the abyss.

This was a cloudier place than the last one – not that Mary remembered it – but less dark. There was no resident psychiatrist at the home, just a mystifying number of attendants, all but one of them female. Mary memorized none of their names, although one or two faces became familiar.

That woman from Arabia Jack was married to came to see her almost every day and, at least once each, Jack and Trevor. There were other visitors too, women mostly, who spoke about Rotary, the parish church, the W.I., the British Legion; Mary didn't recognize them or their affiliated organisations. She drifted in and out of a reverie that was part childhood reminiscence, part fairy tale. She talked – or thought she talked – to Daddy and Mummy and Lenore, but never William. She had no memory of going to the cemetery to exhume him.

The mayor's gold chain was found in a filing cabinet in the Town Hall. No one admitted putting it there. A spokeswoman from the publicity department was tight-lipped during an interview with Meridian TV.

14. The Leather Merchant's Tale

'So who are you sending to France with him?' Christine asked.

'Nobody. I'm going to let him sail his own ship,' Jack said.

'None of the others wanted to go? Dennis? Tim?'

'Dennis seems to think he'd be a fish out of water in France.' Having paraphrased one of his salesmen, Jack paraphrased another: 'Tim was keen, of course; he likes to cast a wider net.'

'Yes,' she laughed, 'women in fishnets are definitely Tim's big thing!' Ten minutes after the sales conference ended, Christine was ostensibly delivering a couriered letter from the agency that hounded bad debts.

'Even Michael volunteered.' Jack bit off another nautical analogy; he knew he used too many of them. 'I think he just saw it as a bit of a junket.'

'You've always said he's not much of a salesman.'

'Except when it comes to selling puppy litters. And that's more Joanna than him.' Jack had fast-tracked his son-in-law to head up Sales and Marketing and then moved the department to the town office where he himself could keep an eye on it. If you buy a dog you don't expect to have to do your own barking.

'So, is Paul ready to go solo, after just one week with Dennis?'

'Dennis reckons he is. This is the best way to find out.'

'Well, I'm glad you're giving him a chance, Jack. I like him.'

'You do?'

'He reminds me a bit of Charlie when I first knew him. He's not sure of where he's going, but he's in a hurry to get there.'

'You think?' New-age psychobabble, in Jack's opinion.

'And of course, he's young and sexy,' she added. Charlie Turner had once been young and sexy. Jack had lost his hair early. Old photos showed him as a strapping youth, before he put on weight, but he knew that he'd never been slim or handsome and certainly not sexy.

'You think so?' he said again.

'Look how the upholstery girls are falling over themselves to get at him.'

'Are they?'

'And what about Mrs Cohen in Portsmouth? And the Christmas woman in Basingstoke!' Christine, on Reception, was the hub of the office grapevine.

Her eulogizing of Paul began to annoy Jack. She was perched on the edge of his desk, close to him. He reached out and played with her breasts inside the cashmere sweater, reminding her where her obligation lay. Duly reminded, she immediately and perfunctorily lifted the sweater to her neck and made a move to unfasten her lacy pink brassiere.

'You are a naughty boy,' she said in the tone she affected for their intimate moments: part governess, part Hollywood siren. 'I'd better lock the door.'

Her matter-of-factness reduced their relationship to the level of a whore with her client. Which it was, of course. He caught at her hands. 'Not now. I'll come round after dinner. Where's Charlie this week?'

'Getting ready for a run to Scotland. He's got Scouts tonight.'

Her husband was scoutmaster. He was also a major force with the British Legion and made scenery and props for a local amateur drama group. Charlie Turner was an all-round good citizen. Who pimped his wife to his employer.

'You'd better get back to your desk,' he dismissed his receptionist/whore.

So Paul was a sexy young man in a hurry to get somewhere, was he? *Was he?*

Interviewing him three weeks ago Jack formed the

140

impression that his nephew was as aimless as his step-daughters. Joanna had dogs and horses; Jenny had boys and pop music; what did Paul have? He'd pissed away his college opportunity, apparently over some girl; he didn't want to work for his petty tyrant father; and now he – and his mother - expected Jack to give him a chance.

Looking at him, Jack saw a replica of his brother-in-law's vaguely matinee-idol looks. Hopefully he hadn't inherited anything from Mary, dithering doormat that she was. But had Paul got William's small-town mindset, or did he have some of his grandfather's energy and drive?

Next minute the little bugger was trying to butter him up, reminding Jack that he'd done well in life without a degree. He even worked in a fishing tease. Jack found himself warming to him. He had languages but did he have salesmanship skills? Doubtful. But he was family.

Give him a chance. Promise him £30k per annum. And a car.

At Paul's age, nineteen, in 1967, Jack had been his father's Production Manager on a salary of less than thirty pounds a week. He'd bought his own first car, a Renault Floride convertible – a 'pussy-wagon' in a town without pussy.

Then at its peak *Pemberton & Son*, with a workforce of over 100, was one of the biggest employers locally. Even before he branched out into property development Jack Senior used to say, not entirely self-mockingly, that he liked to think of the town as *'Pembertown'*.

Today, with its workforce shrunk to 60, Pembertons remained a leading employer, up there with the top super-markets and d-i-y stores. Although he'd turned down the mayoralty when it was offered, Jack, like his dad, thought of himself as the town's First Citizen. Christine said he was; she would, of course.

But Jack, who yearned to be seen as a Captain of Industry, knew that in the great navy of commerce he was only commanding the equivalent of a tugboat. He wanted to be a whale, or at least a barracuda, but he wasn't much bigger than a remora.

And the real sharks were circling.

Baiting his hook with a new salesman when the com-mercial ocean was in a continued state of turbulence was probably taking nepotism and philanthropy (and the

141

analogy) too far.

But it might come good. Dennis Dawes reported that Paul had the old Jewish biddy in Portsmouth eating out of his hand. And Brenda Christmas in Basingstoke and that ageing poof in Bristol had both been wetting their pants with excitement. While Paul was on his first trip to France Mrs Cohen phoned in a very nice order.

'I told you it would be a good idea to give Paul a chance,' Agnes said.

'Yes, dear,' Jack replied automatically, though it had been Mary's idea – the last good idea his sister would have. But Agnes liked to take the credit for anything in the family that turned out well, and usually he let her. She too had an announcement:

'Jenny called this afternoon. She's coming home on Friday!'

'Is what's-his-name coming with her – Baxter?'

'No, they broke up last week. She's gone to Los Angeles.'

'Who with?'

'She's staying in a hotel. On her own.' Jack wondered if this was true.

'Did she say what went wrong in New Mexico?'

'Only that it just didn't work out.' If her daughters discussed their relationship problems with Agnes, she had never shared their secrets with Jack. 'I think we should have a family lunch on Sunday,' she added.

'Yes, dear,' Jack said, trying to watch the news. 'Family' meant Joanna and Michael. Horse and dog chat.

'A proper one. I'll invite Mary and William.'

'That'll be nice,' Jack said, though it wouldn't. His sister was getting dafter every year and her husband could bore for Britain.

'Shall I ask Paul, or would he be bored?'

We both will be, Jack thought, but he said, 'Let me ask him at work. Make him think he's being invited in his own right, not just because of his parents.'

'Jenny wasn't here the last time we had him. I wonder if they'll get on.'

'Why wouldn't they?' Jack said. Just because today's generation seemed like aliens to him didn't mean they couldn't connect with each other.

A wife, stepchildren, a mistress, had all come relatively late in Jack's life. What he'd most wanted was a son. That hadn't happened. But his daffy sister and her twerp of a husband had had two sons. How fair was that?

In 1990, when his 81-year-old father had a fatal stroke, Jack had been managing both the factory and the property company for almost twenty years. At 42 he still lived with his dad. He saw no sense in living alone. When his wife died of cancer in 1966, Jack Senior had hired a housekeeper. Although he yearned for a grandson to carry the Pemberton name to another generation, he didn't nag his son into an unsuitable marriage. The right woman would come along sooner or later (it began to look like later).

However unappealing his appearance, the son of *Pemberton & Son* was a notable catch. But none of the local gold-diggers had stayed the course. Some dating, two broken engagements, a brief affair with the bored wife of a builder who worked for them – and prostitutes: that was the sum of 42 years.

You had to go no further than Brighton to find hookers' numbers pasted up in phone boxes, but Jack preferred the more upmarket women that were advertised in glossy magazines. An agency in Mayfair had stunning Scandinavians on its books. Call-girls in Paris and Miami were even more inventive, with a gloss and an arrogance that mocked their pretence of submission. The Americans – cantilevered breasts, overdone hair and repetitious erotic talk – were the Stepford Wives of the sex industry.

After his father died Jack sold the family house in town and bought The Grange. He moved his father's housekeeper and her husband (who worked at the factory) into the gatehouse. Rattling around in a big country mansion, he felt the need for a wife – and an heir – more keenly. But he didn't just want a brood mare. Living in an old manor house, he wanted a Lady of the Manor.

Agnes Dixon, born in Kashmir, late of Qatar, couldn't have been more perfect. Well, maybe she could.

Her husband was even more late of Qatar than Agnes. William Dixon was an engineer making giant strides in the field of hydroponics until the bite of a sea-snake stopped his heart in 1991. Agnes, thirty-two when the serpent widowed her, had the aura not so much of a tea-planter's daughter as of a maharani. In John Major's allegedly class-less Britain, Agnes evoked a stratified and more gracious era at the other end of the century. Her dresses (*never* trousers) were at least mid-calf length and invariably in pastel or autumnal shades. Her shoes were always dainty. Agnes was every inch, every foot, a lady. A Lady even.

Why did a man who was starved of love and hungry for sex marry a woman who was sexually and emotionally frigid? It was a mystery even to Jack.

If passion was in her nature, which he doubted, it had been expended on her first husband. Or the savage heat of Arabia had baked it out of her.

Struggling to school her daughters on a widow's pension, it was clear to Agnes that she needed to remarry, and quickly. Jack was not the wealthiest of her new suitors but he was the one whose position in the town came closest to the life she had lost. With her as his hostess, invitations to cocktail parties and dinners (even dances) at The Grange would become the most sought-after in 'Pembertown'.

But she wasn't looking for a love match.

She was upfront about it. He could not fault her on that score.

'Jack, I'd be honoured to be your wife, to have your protection and your help in raising my girls, but this can only be a marriage of – convenience. I shall always treat you with respect, and with time I'm sure I will feel affect-ion for you, but I cannot promise to love you.'

Even her speech belonged in a Merchant Ivory film. There was one more T to be crossed:

'I will not sleep with you, Jack. That part of my life is over. But you need have no fear that I will disgrace you. I shall not.'

There was no courtship sex. Her kisses were passion-less. But Jack had been hoping that, as well as companion-ship and a hostess for The Grange, she would give him the longed-for son and heir.

'But – what do you expect me to do?'

'Jack dear, you're forty-four. What have you been doing?'

Blushing did not improve his appearance. 'Well, you

know – women from – escort agencies. In London. Mayfair.' He hoped the mention of Mayfair gave his seedy exploits a bit of class.

'I suppose that's preferable to picking up street-girls under the railway arches in Kings Cross, but really, Jack, you'd do better to find yourself a mistress.' Suddenly Agnes seemed a lot less Edwardian.

'You want me to marry you and take a mistress?' This was like buying a cow and renting a goat.

'It's what my late husband did. He slept with a native woman, our cook. She was from Sri Lanka, from quite a good family – or so she insisted.'

On the South Coast a 'native woman' in Agnes's sense would be an Albanian or Ukrainian with a pimp who roughed her up. Not the level Jack cared to sink to.

He married her anyway. After a chaste honeymoon (Mustique: Agnes's elegantly shod feet were firmly planted on the shore, but the marlin made up for the enforced celibacy), he went back to his call-girls.

He thought of investing in one of those inflatable sex dolls modelled on a California porn-star to tide him over between trips to London or overseas. But how to hide it from his wife, his stepdaughters and the staff? He and Agnes had separate bedrooms, but she often went to his wardrobe to hang up a newly pressed suit or put his shirts in a drawer. Imagine if his pneumatic sex-partner lurched herself silently, psychotically, at his wife from the depths of a cupboard! Or if Agnes found his toy hanging, semi-deflated, from a coat-hook like some scrawny suicide.

He did one thing to punish her for their sexless, sonless, joyless union. Knowing how she yearned to be the town's First Lady (and had perhaps married him with this in prospect), he turned down the Council's offer of the mayoralty in 1993. In 1999, with the town planning major celebrations for the Millennium, he turned it down again.

Agnes needn't have worried about Paul and Jenny getting on at her lunch on Sunday. They talked to almost nobody except each other. Jack would have said William was boring him to death with his talk about Rotary and Council budget cuts, but in the event it wasn't Jack but his red-faced brother-in-law who dropped dead at the table.

145

Across it, in fact. Mary screamed like a banshee.

When Jack came back from calling 999 on the phone in the hall, Joanna was pumping William's chest and blowing into his mouth on the dining-room floor. Mary was also on her knees beside them; her screams had turned to gulped sobbing. Paul stood over her with Jennifer and Michael.

'Get her out of here,' Jack said to his wife. 'Take her to the library. Give her brandy.' After a moment of resistance Mary allowed her sister-in-law to pull her upright and usher her out of the room.

'I'm not getting a pulse,' Joanna pronounced.

'Is there anything else we can do?' Jack asked.

'Only this.'

'D'you want me to take over?' Michael offered.

'I'm probably the best person to do it.'

She was red-faced herself from the exertion when the paramedics arrived and took over with a defibrillator. Jack went to find his sister-in-law who was ashen-faced and now eerily silent. Agnes was her usual calm controlled self.

'I'll take her to the hospital,' Jack said.

'Have they said –?'

'No.'

On the way to the hospital Jack offered consoling remarks to his sister to keep her calm. She remained unresponsive until the A&E doctor confirmed what had been obvious but unstated at the house; now she went into full hysteria, screaming and sobbing and tearing at her clothes, at Jack, at the nurses. The doctor injected a dose of tranquillizer which knocked her out. Getting her admitted to the psychiatric unit took almost four hours. Jack felt drained by the time he got home.

When his parents died Jack had presented a stoical face to the world, but inwardly he'd felt the same grief and bitterness as his lachrymose sister. Paul's reaction to his father's death seemed not so much stoicism as indifference. He asked to be allowed to begin his second sales run to France the next day.

'I'd rather keep busy,' he said. 'If you don't mind taking care of – things – here.' Things: his father's funeral, his mother's breakdown. Jack's view of the insensitivity of contemporary youth was confirmed. Agnes invited Paul to stay the night, but he said he'd rather go home and pack for his trip.

'Bit of a cold fish, isn't he?' Jack said after his nephew left.

'I'm sure he's feeling it as much as we all are,' Agnes said. Jack didn't think he – or she – was feeling any more than token grief at his brother-in-law's passing. He went to phone the undertaker who had buried both Jack's parents. Even on a Sunday evening he was answered not by a machine, but by Ted Saunders personally. His manner was suitably, traditionally, solemn.

William died on Sunday March 23rd. His funeral was held at St Agnes's on Tuesday April 1st. If anyone other than Jack saw the irony of this date they kept it to themselves.

Mary, still under sedation, missed her husband's funeral. Also absent from the pews of local dignitaries were the Mayor and his wife, who were on a visit to the town in France with which 'Pembertown' was twinned. The Rotary Chairman delivered a eulogy Jack considered too fulsome by half, although this was usual with eulogies. Most of the congregation came on to The Grange for the funeral tea; only Jack and Jenny joined Paul and a handful of Barrett relations for the grim ceremony in the cemetery. Joanna was helping her mother with the catering. After the burial Jenny and Paul went off somewhere on their own, which was understandable but still not the proper thing to do.

'He's grieving in his own way,' Agnes said when Jack expressed his feelings later, after their guests had gone and their daughter returned. 'Isn't he, darling?' she asked Jenny who was looking, Jack thought, way too pleased with herself for a girl who'd just buried a relative.

'Hmm?' Jenny grunted, her eyes on the TV screen. 'Oh – yeah, he is.'

'It's awful that Mary couldn't be there,' Agnes said. 'She won't forgive herself when she comes out of this state she's in. You must go and see her, Jack.'

'I will,' he promised. 'Last week I was just too busy.' (Not too busy to visit Christine after work on Wednesday while Charlie was in Wales.)

'I went again yesterday,' Agnes said, repeating what she'd already told them the day before. She sighed. 'Poor Mary. I suppose it's the drugs, but she barely knew I was there. She's so – *lost*.'

147

'She's so lost the plot,' Jenny said. Evidently the TV wasn't getting her full attention.

In the week of the funeral a few furniture orders trickled in from Paris, Lille and Rouen. After the funeral Paul took his car to Lyon and the Riviera; then, the following week, up to Bordeaux and northern Spain. At home he made dutiful visits to his mother in the Psych Unit and he continued to go out with Jennifer.

'They're not – you know – *seeing* each other, are they?' Jack asked his wife. Phrasing the question more crudely would offend her delicate sensibility.

'I don't think so, Jack. She's just feeling sorry for him about William and poor Mary. I suppose it helps that they've both had their hearts broken.'

'Is he heartbroken about his dad? That's not the impression I get.'

'No, not William. That girl from Florida at his university.'

'He told you about her?'

'Jenny did. It's a coincidence that they've both had – disappointments – with Americans.' Only Agnes could still think of student screwing and shack-ups as 'disappointments'. Jennifer's Albuquerque boyfriend, the son of a rising politician, had faded out of the picture like his many predecessors. There'd been an Irish disc jockey in Brighton who came and went more than once. Jack did not want a DJ for a son-in-law. He'd also feared there might be drugs.

Easy come, easy go. This was the attitude of young people today: money, opportunities, lovers. They took for granted that there was more to be had.

Born in India and raised in Arabia, Agnes's daughters, aged nine and eleven in 1991, had arrived in England with imperious ways that Jack found intimidating when he started courting their mother; but they soon captured his heart. Joanna embraced country life, demanding a dog, a pony, a horse, a car, eventually a husband and a house of her own. Effuse in her gratitude, she craved both attention and affection. To this day she called him 'Daddy.'

Once, in his second year of fatherhood, dropping her home from riding school he heard Agnes call down from upstairs: 'Is that you, darling?'

'No,' Joanna said, 'it's only me.' She knew she wasn't her mother's darling. From then on Jack made a point of using every endearment in the book.

Jennifer called him 'Jack'. She was the cuter sister, with her long blonde hair. Made-up to the nines for a party or a disco, she had the glossy sheen of an airhostess or a hooker. But Jenny was a secretive child who distanced herself as much from her doting mother as from her step-father.

The brother of two pretty girls, Jack empathised with Joanna, the plain sibling who found it hard to attract – and keep – boyfriends. In Michael she seemed to have found a soulmate who shared her love of animals, but Jack expected that his son-in-law, a disappointment in the firm, would sooner or later betray her, break her heart.

No one was going to break Jennifer's. Like Lenore, his ill-fated firebrand eldest sister, Jenny was a 'wild child'. When boys began sniffing round she picked them up and dropped them as casually as she bought and discarded clothes. Her precociousness was a worry. Agnes didn't relish discussions in this area but she assured him that both girls had taken onboard the safe sex message.

Jenny might be an easy catch, but reeling her in would be a big challenge for any man who fished in her pond. She wasn't his daughter but they were cut from similar cloth. He sensed that Jennifer, like so many of today's kids, was only interested in sex. Maybe love would catch her unawares, as it had him.

In June he and Agnes celebrated their eleventh anniversary. Last year he'd given her a diamond necklace which she said was too extravagant. This year he bought her a prosaic new motor mower which gave her more pleasure than the diamonds had, although it would be the gardener who used it. He also promised to take her on his post-poned trip to Morocco in July, but by then his sister was living with them and couldn't be left. They swapped Mary, aged sixty-one with a dwindling supply of marbles, for their prodigal twenty-year-old daughter who went to live with Paul.

Jack argued with Agnes about this.

'It's practically incest, for God's sake. They're cousins.'

'No, they're not, Jack. They would be if she was your

child, but she isn't.'

'Well, it doesn't seem right.'

'Paul's much nicer than some of the boys she's been with. Baxter would have been quite a catch if he'd married her, but I couldn't bear it if she'd gone to live in America permanently. I didn't even like it when she was in Brighton.'

'I still wish she'd stayed the course.'

'Oh I don't mean when she was at the art college. I meant with Fintan.'

At least they could agree on disapproving of the disc jockey.

'We have to expect her to fly the nest for good one day,' Jack said, though he did not relish a future shared solely with Agnes and his wacky sister.

'Having her at Paul's is almost as good as having her with us,' Agnes said. She liked to have the last word. With her sister-in-law to care for, Agnes, that tireless doer of not too time-consuming good works, was donning her robes of piety and near-godliness. He'd once joked to Christine Turner that he often felt he was married to Mother Theresa or to *Saint* Agnes, whoever she had been.

'She's so fucking fragrant even her farts smell of lavender,' Jack, mounting the stairs to the Sales & Marketing offices, had overheard Michael say of his mother-in-law to Tim Reynolds a year ago. Son-in-law or not, Jack Senior would have sacked him for a remark like that – but Jack Junior had chuckled grimly, as he retreated to the floor below before making a noisier ascent.

Was Agnes happy? Was he? These were questions Jack preferred not to think about. He knew that no woman had ever loved him. To his wife, his stepdaughters, to Christine, he was just a meal ticket, a cash cow.

As he reached the midpoint between fifty and sixty Jack's desire for a son of his own had faded. He wasn't a sentimental man but he sometimes thought that the great love of his life was the factory. The workers were his 'children'. They'd called his father 'The Guvnor'. Jack Junior had been 'Mister Jack'. Now *he* was 'The Guvnor' or even plain egalitarian 'Jack'. He liked to imagine that the workforce thought of him as a benevolent despot. Christine said this was more or less how they thought of

150

him.

As for women, Jack knew that he had only ever *bought* them: would-be gold-diggers; call-girls; even Agnes (who often made him feel as if *she* owned *him*) and his step-daughters; Christine of course.

It was nine months into his marriage when Jack, as his wife had proposed, took a mistress.

Charlie Turner was already working for Pembertons in 1990 when his first wife died, in the same month Jack's father had his stroke. Two years later Charlie married Christine in June, the same month Jack married Agnes. When the office receptionist left in September to have a baby, Turner asked if his new wife, currently working for Saunders the undertaker, could have the job.

Her predecessor had been a glum twenty-one-year-old brunette. Christine was twenty-eight, blonde, curvy and flirtatious. She'd been a secretary in Bahrain and then head waitress in a London restaurant. Jack fancied her from day one. But he was not in the habit of screwing his employees, and Charlie was a member of the British Legion. His first wife had been another notable doer of good works.

Jack had refused the mayoralty but he'd accepted the presidency of the local branch of the Legion (Agnes liked being the President's wife, though Lady Mayoress would have suited her better). He and Charlie Turner had each lost a grandfather in World War One and an uncle in WW2. One autumn night Jack drove Charlie home from a Legion meeting when Charlie's car wouldn't start. This had hap-pened a few times before when Margaret was alive. Charlie invited him in, as he always did. The ex-council house had undergone something like a TV makeover: new furniture, curtains, carpet, fresh flowers in a crystal vase, some nicely-framed Impressionists. Agnes, who was snooty about the décor in other people's homes, would be impressed. Only the house itself was wrong. And Charlie. And Charlie's ten-year-old son, a hooligan in the making, who was shouting at some console game or TV programme in his bedroom.

Christine Turner served a passable Chardonnay in decent glasses. They made small talk. Charlie still called his employer 'Mister Jack'. Christine, like most of the office staff, called him 'Mr Pemberton.' He called her 'Mrs Turner.' Tonight she invited him to call her Christine. As he left their house she said, 'Goodnight, Jack.' It started a ball rolling. Soon he was 'Jack' to everyone at the office except Cynthia. Very John Major, very Bill Clinton.

Jack sensed the Turners were living beyond their means. Christine's money went mostly on clothes: every day a new dress, a new skirt, a new top, new shoes. The refinements in the house meant an overdraft or credit card debts. Chances were, Charlie cheated on his driving expenses, as Jack knew the sales reps did.

In the early nineties there was recession. As during other recessions Jack pumped some of the profits from the property arm into keeping his grandfather's business afloat. A bad time for the delivery lorry to need replacing. Jack opted to put deliveries out to tender, making Charlie Turner redundant. Some younger factory workers were being laid off, but Jack gave Turner a job in assembly. There was no overtime. And no Christmas bonuses this year.

There was always tension at the office, at the works, during a recession. Christine Turner wasn't the only worker to lose some of her previous vivacity. She now wore outfits Jack had seen before, refreshed with accessories, a scarf, costume jewellery. Towards the end of February '93 Jack thought the time might be right. Cynthia was off with flu. Michael's secretary was doing Jack's typing. Christine was handling his calls and appointments.

He called her up to his office. She brought his diary. She was wearing one of her angora sweaters, powder blue. With her upswept blonde hair and vivid lipstick it gave her a 1950s Lana Turner look that Jack thought might be overdue to make a comeback; he preferred old movies to the modern stuff. Opening a desk drawer he laid a small wad of notes on the blotter.

'I think this might come in handy,' he said, sounding more casual than he felt. His heart was pounding, as was a hefty erection below the desk line. He had never before propositioned one of his staff.

Her smile narrowed as she picked up the notes and counted them. This was a tad vulgar of her but it lifted Jack's hopes. There were ten notes. They were fifties. For £500, topped up to 5,000 Francs or $1,000, Jack could have had a prime girl in Paris or Miami for a whole after-noon or evening (all-night was considerably dearer). In Curzon Street a top girl cost as much as £5,000, if only because their largely Middle Eastern clientele had more money than sense or manners. Christine Turner laid the money back on the blotter.

'Jack,' she said. 'Jack, Jack, Jack. What have I done to deserve this?'

He cleared his throat before speaking. 'It's more what you *could* do,' he said.

Christine Turner's lipsticked mouth was now redolent of Bette Davis about to let rip. She said, 'Hmm.'

'I hope I haven't offended you,' Jack said, losing his nerve. A half-minute of silence followed. It seemed longer to Jack. They both looked at the money lying on his blotter.

She said, 'I've never bothered to look, but does your door *lock*?'

'Yes,' he said hoarsely.

Christine Turner locked the door. Then she came back and knelt beside his desk and fellated him almost as expertly as the whores did in Mayfair or Pigalle or South Miami. He had a few feels of her breasts through the sweater. Her bra was filmy; it was clear her breasts needed no support. She had big nipples. Jack liked big nipples. He wondered how much practice she'd had, apart from Charlie. He came sooner than he wanted to.

She got up and went to his cloakroom. Through the closed door he heard her hawk into the basin or the toilet. Never a pleasant sound, but one he was used to hearing. When she came back she tucked the £500 into his diary.

'I take it this wasn't just a one-off,' she said. Her tone was all business.

'I hope not,' said Jack, still throaty.

'Well –' she laughed – 'you know where to find me.'

'Yes,' he said. 'I guess I do.' They both laughed.

'If you're worried about Charlie, don't be. I'll handle Charlie.'

'Good,' Jack said, relieved but no longer laughing. He *was* worried about Charlie. In 1994, following the sale of an office block that had begun to look like a white elephant, Jack bought a new delivery truck and put Charlie back on the road.

He and Christine used motels for their 'trysts' until a near-miss at a Happy Eater with a couple from Agnes's bridge club brought home to Jack the risk he was taking. He bought a small flat in Hove, which came in handy when Jenny started a course at Brighton Art College. By then the Turners had moved to a picturesque cottage outside Alfriston which Agnes would say was too good for them. Charlie and his son restored derelict MGs for a hobby. If Jack wanted to drop by when they were home they retreated to their garage workshop at the end of the garden. When the boy quit school at sixteen Jack gave him a job at the works. Jim Turner became a sort of journeyman; his mechanical skills came in handy when machines broke down. School-leavers hired when business picked up were paid the minimum wage, but Jim was soon on parity with the old hands. He was also something of a star player on the Pembertons soccer team. He treated Jack and his stepmother with a kind of restrained insolence. After three years Jack gave him a discount on a small flat of his own. It was a relief to know the boy wasn't at the bottom of the garden any more. Jack also preferred to call when Charlie was on the road.

Like his wife, Charlie now called their employer 'Jack'. There was no outward show of surliness or disrespect, but if his latest renovated MG failed to start after a Legion meeting he no longer asked Jack for a lift home.

'Is Charlie, you know, okay about – things?' Jack frequently asked her early in their relationship.

'Don't worry about Charlie,' she continued to tell him. 'I've got everything under control.'

In Jack's opinion the morality of a complaisant cuckold was more questionable than the adulterer's. He pressed her on the situation at home. She was sure Charlie was faithful to her. 'He's crazy about me,' she said, but beyond this she divulged no details of her marital or premarital life.

Jack told her about Agnes, about the hookers, even about the girls he'd dated in his youth. Having started out at £500 Jack never dared offer her less. Some of the Miami call-girls came in at less than $200. But there were no more call-girls. Christine, once a week on average, took care of him. It was a kind of bigamy, running on a parallel track to his marriage to Agnes.

The sex was like the sex he'd had with the hookers, although she wasn't vocal. No kissing; another echo of the call-girls. He liked to come between her fantastic breasts. He also favoured the doggy position; he could play with her breasts and finger her vagina and clitoris while he did her. Her climaxes, if there were any, were also non-vocal. She sometimes shuddered. Was this an orgasm or some involuntary expression of revulsion? He didn't ask.

Agnes, as she promised when they got engaged, treated him with respect and a degree of affection. Their friends and acquaintances thought they were a perfect couple, but they plainly were not. Did she know that, as suggested, he had taken a mistress and who that mistress was? He didn't ask.

'Fragrant', the word Michael satirically employed to describe his mother-in-law was so exactly the word for Agnes. She was as fragrant as a rose, as Mary Archer or Norma Major. But as she approached and passed forty, the rose began to lose its bloom, whereas Christine in her thirties seemed to get riper, sexier.

In the week he gave his nephew a job, Jack and his mistress celebrated their tenth 'anniversary'. If she was aware of the milestone Christine let it pass unobserved. Whores probably didn't expect commemorative gifts. Ten years at £500 a week: he'd paid her a quarter of a million pounds for sex! But then he'd spent a great deal more on Agnes and his stepdaughters. The house he bought Joanna and Michael as one of their wedding gifts cost £380,000. He also gave them a brace of BMWs. And bridesmaid Jennifer had to have a new car too.

He took Paul and Jenny with him to Morocco. Paul worried about Arab hostility but the natives were as friendly – and as pestering – as always. A guide supplied by the Fez hotel kept most of the peddlers at bay. Paul's French came in handy with Latif, the leather supplier. He picked up a gay vibe from the merchant and after the first discussion of this year's prices renamed him 'La Thief'. Confronted with the stench of the curing and dyeing processes, Paul gagged but managed, just, not to puke. This year's newest shade from the dyers was the palest of yellows – *Sorrento* – which Paul said could be called 'Pissoir'.

Their hotel in the new town resembled – indeed, was –

an oasis. The old town, the Medina, was baking and foetid in the first week of July, the odour from the tanneries pervasive. Jenny stayed by the pool or shopped in the souk. It was the first time she'd shared a room with one of her paramours under the same roof as her stepfather; even though it was Paul she was with, Jack was glad that his room was on a different floor.

Lying with them on the poolside he was more than ever conscious of his age and gross size. Paul's lean physique seemed bony next to his; not that Jack yearned to be bony but it would be nice to buy off-the-peg shirts and sweaters that were L or even XL rather than XXL. Christine and Agnes both nagged him about his weight and lack of exercise. Jenny had dieted since her return from Albuquerque but, twitching on Paul's other side in tune with her iPod, she was still a voluptuous sight in a bikini. Her hair was ponytailed.

Paul was reading a paperback thriller. Jack had the second volume of Margaret Thatcher's memoirs open: hardback and a hard read. Agnes had queued in Harrods to get the book signed by the Lady herself. Revisionists were reappraising the Thatcher years and her legacy. No hint of self-doubt in her own version. Struggling to concentrate against noises from the pool Jack became aware of the cacophony leaking from Jenny's earphones.

'Who are you listening to?'

Lip-reading the question she lay half on top of Paul to pass the earphones to Jack. He put the phones to his ears and as quickly pulled them off.

'God, what group is that?'

'Limp Bizkit. You won't have heard of them.'

'It's not music. It's just noise.'

'Jack, don't start,' she warned him. Her voice rasped. She'd developed a sore throat, which she attributed to the dusty streets of the souk.

'I bet your parents said exactly the same thing about Cream,' Paul said, peacemaking. Jennifer coughed and lay back on her own lounger.

'If I remember Cream properly, they were right,' said Jack. He laughed. 'How does anyone of your generation know about Cream?'

'I had a friend at college with very retro tastes.'

'I did rather like Roxy Music,' Jack recalled. Paul

156

laughed.

'Uncle Jack, you're a fox! Are you by any chance a fan of Freddie Mercury as well as Brian Ferry?'

'Oh well, even Jenny likes to hear my Queen albums.' Jenny made a face that indicated her preference not to be linked to any taste of her stepfather's. 'Your mother liked Herman's Hermits,' Jack told Paul. 'You kids won't have heard of them.'

'Want to bet?' Jenny croaked. 'My DJ boyfriend in Brighton was locked into the Sixties. The Hermits were a bunch of squeaky-clean boys from Newcastle.'

'Manchester, actually,' Paul corrected her.

'Really?' Jack raised his eyebrows. 'I was going to say Liverpool. What was their lead singer's name? It wasn't Herman.'

'Peter Noone,' said Paul. Jack laughed again.

'Mary also liked Cilla Black,' he remembered. Jenny groaned.

'I shall never speak to her again,' said Paul. He smiled at the thought of his mother having to endure Haydn and Bach and Handel all those years whilst secretly yearning for the Mersey Beat.

'I had a crush on *Sandie Shaw*!' Jack confessed. 'Who sang in bare feet. I think she won Eurovision one year.'

'1967,' Paul supplied. His recall of pop trivia was awesome. '*Puppet on a String*. You must have liked *Dusty*, Uncle Jack.' Jennifer made another face and retreated into her earphones.

'Oh, yes. Dusty was wonderful.' Jack pictured Dusty Springfield who in his mind's eye shed her mascara and some of her bouffant hair and morphed into Christine Turner. 'I'd like to meet this friend of yours with the retro taste in music,' he told Paul, hoping to drive off rogue thoughts of his mistress.

'He's dead. He committed suicide.'

'God, how dreadful. Do you know why?'

'No, I don't.' Paul returned to his book and Jack reluctantly re-opened *The Downing Street Years*.

'I like your dad,' Paul told her in their room later. Jenny made a face.

'Stepfather,' she corrected him.

'Joanna calls him "Daddy".'

157

'Jo's his little pet, his treasure. I'm the slag from hell.' Paul laughed.

'He doesn't think that, does he?'

She thumped him with a cushion from the ottoman beside the bed. 'You're supposed to tell me I'm not a slag.'

'You're not a slag,' he recited. She threw another cushion.

'Put more feeling into it, *asshole*.'

Paul shivered at the reminder of the last user of that expletive.

'I love you just the way you are.'

'You "love" me, huh? That's fighting talk! It's *fucking* talk!'

He laughed again, thinking how different she was to her mother. What was the word for Aunt Agnes? *Fragrant!* No wonder Jack was bonking the raunchy Mrs Turner on the side.

After three days Jack flew home. Paul and Jenny took him to Rabat airport in the hired Mercedes and went on to La Mamounia in Marrakech for the weekend, a hotel Jack loved. He'd taken Agnes there a half-dozen times. Christine had declined to be taken even to Paris or Amsterdam.

He had a story prepared for Agnes. Leaving the car at Heathrow for Paul and Jenny, he took a taxi to a characterless new hotel in the shadow of the Tower. It was full of Japanese and a few Americans bravely venturing forth into a world at war. Christine had come up by train and was waiting for him. She'd signed in as Mrs Jack Pemberton.

Their encounters only rarely included spending the night together. She insisted on separate beds. Jack had never shared a bedroom with the real Mrs Pemberton. Even on holiday they had two rooms, or a suite. Agnes was relentless.

'You've started a tan,' Christine told him in the bar before dinner. 'So it wasn't all work and no play.'

'You should see Jenny. She only left the pool to go shopping.'

'Not much to shop for in Morocco, is there? Except leather.'

'I couldn't buy you anything with Paul in tow all the time. I figured you wouldn't want another handbag.'

'A handbaaag.' It was three years since the amateur

thespians put on *The Importance of Being Earnest* but Christine never missed a chance to do Lady Bracknell. She probably thought it made her cultivated. Married to Lady Bracknell, Jack didn't find these moments hilarious. But he forced a laugh. Their drinks arrived.

'So is it serious – Paul and Jenny?'

'For the moment it seems to be. I don't know how long it'll last.'

'She needs a *man* to tame her. Paul reminds me of Tim Henman. He's just a boy in a man's world.'

'I thought he reminds everyone of – what's his name? The Scottish actor.'

'McGregor. He's fairly boyish as well. I think Jenny needs somebody older. Like me with Charlie.' Charlie was forty-four, the same age as Agnes. Christine was now thirty-nine. Jack didn't like talk of how old the people around him were.

'That DJ in Brighton was older than her and that didn't work out.'

'What do you expect? She needs something a bit better than a DJ.' For a lorry-driver's wife she could be quite snooty. Jack grunted.

She admired his tan some more when they were getting ready for bed. He was a 'naughty brown boy.' Jack was unused to flattery and didn't entirely trust it. Once they were stripped off he went for her breasts. His sanctuary, his haven. No goodnight kiss. Christine in some ways was as unrelenting as Agnes.

Around four he woke up and watched her sleeping in the other bed. The intensity of his stare seemed to wake her. She got out of bed and came over to fellate him. He came quickly and went back to sleep while she was still in the bathroom. In the morning he again woke before she did and took a 50mg Viagra. When she was awake he got onto her bed and went at her hard, in his favourite position, doggy-style. His vigour shortened her breath and she grunted with relief when he finally came.

They ordered a room-service breakfast. Only juice, coffee and croissants. Like Agnes, she watched his diet. (Breakfasting unsupervised in Morocco, he'd pigged out.) She told him he snored, though not incessantly. That was something else Agnes didn't know.

'Chris,' he said.

159

'Yes, Jack?'

'Marry me.'

A piece of croissant came to a halt in front of her open mouth, like a hovering helicopter. He'd surprised himself almost as much as he had her. Where had *that* come from?

'What about Agnes?'

'Well, obviously I'll divorce her. She's a cold-hearted bitch.' There, he'd actually said it. He laughed with pure relief. 'And you'll divorce Charlie.'

'Oh, will I?' She smiled and put the piece of croissant back on her plate. 'Why now all of a sudden?'

'I've been thinking about my retirement. I don't want to work till I drop. I'll find someone to run the business. Maybe Michael will shape up or Jenny will stop screwing around and marry someone with a bit of savvy.'

It was hard to believe he was articulating all this. It *had* been floating around at the back of his mind. But did he really want to share his retirement with her? Pillars of the community don't marry their mistresses, do they? A lot of people reckoned Prince Charles was going to marry Camilla sooner or later, but Jack wouldn't bet on it.

'Jack,' she began gently. It would be nice if she put her hand tenderly over his, but tenderness – like kissing – wasn't in the rulebook. This wasn't courtly love. It was more like professional wrestling. 'Jack,' she started again, 'I can't marry you. I couldn't leave Charlie.'

She was trying, unsuccessfully, to go misty-eyed. 'But it's sweet of you to ask.'

Fuck sweet. And fuck her if she didn't want to marry him. Well, he would: fuck her, that is. And perhaps he'd better stay with Agnes, with that life. If he tired of Christine or she 'retired' from their relationship, he could find another mistress. Or go back to the brothels. Some juicy thing in her early twenties would willingly screw his brains out. Fuck Christine Turner.

'Say you'll think about it,' he said in complete contrast to where his thoughts were headed.

'Of course I will, Jack.'

And of course she would. But her answer would, he knew, continue to be no. Would she tell Charlie about this conversation? He almost brought himself to ask her. Perhaps they'd have a good laugh about it. The ugly fat

160

bastard actually thought she would divorce Charlie and marry him. Ha-ha-very-ha.

His rage, Viagra-fuelled, gave him another erection. Removing his robe, he put on a condom and lay down on the bed. 'Mr Insatiable,' she said with humour but not affection. She took off her own robe and rode him. More sound effects this time. Sweat ran down her face and dripped off the breasts Jack never tired of. It took him a longer time to come. She walked stiff-legged to the bathroom. He'd given her a sore cunt. Good. Serve her right.

For propriety's sake they would return on separate trains, but having taken a day off she wanted to do Knightsbridge and Oxford Street. Jack had taken dollars to Morocco; the Great Satan's currency was always more welcome than the Queen's, even in wartime. He gave her $1,500 to shop with. $1,500 and a sore cunt. All in a night's work.

Leaving Victoria he remembered he'd switched his mobile off last night. There were two voicemails from Agnes. The first told him his sister had tried to disinter her husband. The second said she was now in a care home. Agnes sounded quite calm. Jack felt relief, followed by guilt. He called her.

'Did you call Paul and Jennifer?' he asked.

'No, I didn't want to spoil their holiday.'

'I came back last night,' he said, in case Jenny accidentally divulged his schedule. 'I had dinner with that buyer from Fortnum's.'

'Somewhere nice?' Agnes knew better than to attempt shop talk.

'Adequate. Look, you'd better tell me where Mary is before the train starts going through tunnels.'

'Aren't you in the car?'

'I left it at Heathrow for the kids.'

'They're not kids, Jack.'

'You wouldn't say that if you'd just spent as much time with them as I have.' He jotted down the address of the care home across a picture of Tony Blair on the front of the *Telegraph*. He said he'd call Michael to meet him; they'd pay his sister a quick visit and be home for a late lunch.

*

161

'Hello, Daddy,' Mary greeted him. 'Lenore and I have had such fun while you and Jack were working.'

'Have you?' Guilt sloughed off him. Beyond doolally, his sister was now bonkers. Obviously, since she'd even tried to resurrect William.

'Do you want a lift into town? Agnes asked him over a healthy lunch of salad with smoked trout. She was getting posher by the day: 'town' was almost pronounced as a Sloane Ranger 'Tyne'. 'You stupid stuck-up woman,' Jack felt like telling her, 'we don't live on the *Tyne*, we live on the *Cuckmere*.'

'I can take the Landrover,' he said.

'It's just that I'm taking some of the things she won't be needing any more to the Alzheimer's shop.'

'Isn't it a bit premature?'

'I know these care homes. They mix everybody's clothes up in the laundry.'

'Then keep her stuff here.'

'It's only cluttering up Joanna's room.'

Looking at his wife, as ruthlessly cavalier now with Mary's belongings as she'd always been with his feelings, Jack wondered at what precise moment his great awe and respect for her had turned to hatred. Attractive as the thought was, he couldn't really afford to divorce her and marry Christine Turner. Agnes would take him to the cleaners. For an absurd moment he fantasized killing her and disposing of her body - and getting away with it.

Jenny and Paul were home on Sunday. Jenny phoned to tell her mother that they were engaged. She would go with Paul on his next trip to Madrid to shop for a ring.

Well, Jack thought when Agnes relayed the news, at least someone's getting a new wife. He thought about what Christine had said, that Paul might not be man enough to handle Jenny. His stepdaughter, especially since she came back from New Mexico, often reminded him of one of those ball-busting women you see in American soaps and movies. Before Christine Jack had screwed some of them.

Man or boy, Paul was shaping up in his new job. Jack felt that he wouldn't mind having him as a son-in-law. A definite improvement on Michael. Fond as he was of his stepdaughters and especially of Joanna, Jack began to consider changing his Will to leave Pembertons to his nephew.

The planned autumn wedding was another one that he wouldn't bet on.

Agnes reported that Mary persisted in mistaking her for her long-dead sister. Her language was inclined to be 'ripe'. Paul had told Jenny the same thing. Jack went to see her. A waste of time. She still thought he was their father. At least she didn't dare use F-words in front of 'Daddy'.

In mid-August Mary developed an unseasonal cold that turned, rapidly, into pneumonia. Ten days later she died in her sleep. Her last utterance was to one of the carers; if it was profane this went unreported. Paul was in Spain, without his fiancée. The doctor called in by the home said Mary had suffered a massive heart attack.

'I never know she had a weak heart,' said Jack.

'I don't think she did,' Agnes said. 'It was like a clock winding down.'

'She needed William to wind her up again.' The wormwood in his soul was making Jack more sensitive and thoughtful.

'Well, she's got him now,' said Agnes.

'I suppose she has.'

15. The Wife of Boredom's Tale

'So, how's my big cousin Paul doing?' she asked him.

'He's doing okay. How's his little cousin Jenny?'

'Not so little, as you can see.' All those New Mexico cook-outs had really piled on the pounds.

'You still look the same to me,' he said gallantly.

'If you think you can sweet-talk your way into my pantyhose, you're doing fine so far,' Jenny told him, borrowing the line – and an accent – from Baxter's older sister Mary-Lynn. Jenny always flirted with Paul. It didn't mean anything. He'd showed her his willy once when they were kids but she couldn't remember what it looked like; she'd seen quite a few since. Like her, he'd chosen to dress down for Sunday lunch; his leather jacket looked more BHS than Paul Smith.

They ignored the others: Jo and Michael, the parents. Mummy was talking to Aunt Mary, whose frocks all belonged to the Women's Institute, circa 1955. Mummy was her usual floaty flouncy self in a lilac chiffon number dating from 1970s India, pre-Daddy. After twelve English winters she still felt the cold but never dressed for it. It wasn't too cold a day but a vast log fire blazed in the inglenook fireplace, augmenting the central heating. Everyone else has to suffocate so that Mummy can wear summer dresses at the end of March.

Like their aunt, Joanna dressed for the W.I. cake stall. She'd always cared more for horses and dogs than clothes. The girls hadn't been close since Qatar and maybe not even there. Across the table Jo kept touching Michael's hand while they talked. He's all mine, the gesture said.

The sister who'd had less luck with boys was the first to hook a husband, but a stockbroker's son with the reddish-blonde hair and ruddy complexion of a local yokel wasn't on Jennifer's wish list. Stockbrokers, farm boys: been there, done that.

'I've got my own name for it,' Paul said.

Jenny wasn't concentrating. 'For what?' she asked, thinking he might be about to divulge some lurid pet name for his todger.

'This one-horse town. I call it Boredom-on-Sea.'

Jack's father famously had a vision of it as 'Pember-town'. Jenny smiled, not so much at what Paul had said as what he might have said. Her lips were dry in the over-heated room and she licked them, not thinking that Paul might see this as a come-on. Her labia minora were also dry; it was almost a month since anybody (Baxter LaGrange IV) had licked her crotch. Jennifer's vagina was tribulation territory.

It would get up Michael's nose that Jack was telling Uncle William he could be proud of Paul. Uncle William's face was very red today. He always dressed as if for a funeral. According to Mummy her brother-in-law obsessed over his first son who'd died in the Falklands. A useless layabout until he went in the army (Mummy again, quoting Jack), dead Trevor was a paragon. Paul, academically bright and a bronze-medal runner, had somehow disap-pointed his father as a replacement for the idolized hero. Who'd have thought Paul would hack it as a sales rep? Her step-cousin didn't look like a nerd, but neither did he have that other typical salesman look – Del-Boy – that Tim Reynolds had in abundance. Tim had flirted with her at an office Christmas party two years ago when she was 18 to his – what? – 35? As if.

Uncle William responded to Jack's plaudit by collapsing across the table. Aunt Mary began to shriek. Jack rushed out to the phone in the hall.

'Get him on his back,' said Joanna who'd done First Aid in school. Paul and Michael lifted Uncle William off the table and laid him on the tiger-skin in front of the fire. (The tiger bought – but not shot – by Grandpa Lloyd.) Jo knelt and applied CPR. When they first knew him Uncle William had a moustache and Jennifer, aged ten, had fantasized kissing him, but he shaved it off when it began

165

to go grey and at twenty the thought of doing mouth-to-mouth on a comatose man of sixty was beyond gross.

Mummy, who'd been through a similar scene when his Egyptian workers brought Daddy back from the beach after the sea-snake bit him in the neck, looked more inconvenienced than shocked. She took Aunt Mary to the library to administer brandy and compassion. Paul and Michael and Jennifer stood and watched Joanna do her *E.R.*/*Casualty* stuff on the dining-room floor.

Jo was having trouble getting pregnant. Perhaps they both suffered with problem vaginas. Maybe it was hereditary, although vaginas weren't something that was up for discussion with Mummy.

By the time the paramedics arrived, Uncle William's red colour was fading, as was he. It seemed he had dressed appropriately for a funeral. His own.

'Pulmonary embolism.' Joanna's diagnosis, after the ambulance left. Jack and Aunt Mary followed Uncle William to the hospital. Lunch was abandoned; the housekeeper started clearing the table. Jo and Michael headed for the stables. They kept their horses and riding gear at Jack's; their mock-Georgian townhouse was on an estate that encouraged 4x4's rather than horses.

'I'll look after Paul,' Jenny said. She walked him down to the gazebo overlooking the ha-ha. Charlie Turner had built the gazebo last summer; he did odd jobs for Jack. In an older-man/country-yokel sort of way, Turner was quite doable; his wife, the office receptionist, was a bimbo en route to the menopause.

Jennifer couldn't remember – if she'd ever known – how to deal with grief.

'I don't know what to say,' she said.

'No need to go overboard with the condolence stuff. It's a bit of a shock – the suddenness and all that – but I'm more sorry for Mum than for myself. We've done nothing but row since I dropped out of uni. He disapproved of any decision I made for myself. I could almost admit that I – hated him, really.' Paul was now wearing the 'Barrett red' but unlikely to require defibrillation. 'Today's probably not the day to be saying this.'

'I'm not going to rat you out. When my dad died in Qatar I got over it much quicker than Mummy and Jo did. Jo was much more Daddy's little girl than me.'

'My brother Trevor was "Daddy's little boy". I'm more "Mummy's boy".'

'Well, I've always been my mother's little golden girl, which isn't very fair to Jo.'

'Mother love's so claustrophobic, isn't it?'

'Tell me about it.' They grinned at each other, co-conspirators in peeing on maternal love as well as bereavement. Joanna and Michael came trotting across the field below them. They waved at the pair in the gazebo before galloping their mounts to jump a low point in one of the hedges. Paul gave an equine snort of his own.

'I was hoping to see Michael fall into the hedge.'

'Me too. Jo in my case!' They shared a laugh.

'Well now,' Jenny said, 'What can I do to help you get through this great calamity?'

'You could let me shag you,' he said.

'Paul!' She affected shock, perhaps *was* shocked. 'Your dad just died.'

'That was an hour ago. I think I'm ready to get on with my life.'

Jenny laughed some more. Paul was showing the kind of promise she relished. Fuck parents. Fuck the world.

'Well?' he said. 'Can I?'

'Can you what?'

'Can I – shag you?' He was all boyish intensity. Jenny was accustomed to men who took their chances of success for granted. 'I've always wanted to.'

'Have you now?'

'Haven't you at least thought about it?'

'Maybe I have,' she said. Was this true? Probably it wasn't, but it was what he needed to hear.

'Do you remember – years ago – we went in one of your sheds and had a "You-show-me-yours-and-I'll-show-you-mine" moment?'

'As I recall, there were mosquitoes.'

Paul grinned. 'These are not places you want to get bitten!'

Jennifer smiled. There was a brief, uncomfortable silence.

'Well then?' More urgent now. Definitely more boy than man. Was she ready to make a man of this not-quite-cousin of hers? Did she want to?

'How about I give you some head?' Now wasn't the

moment to introduce him to her chaotic vagina.

'Oh yes.' Even younger now: the kid with his hand nearly into the biscuit tin. He looked at her. She looked at him, enquiringly, challengingly. '*Here*?'

'Yes, Paul. Go for it.'

He went for it, racing to unbelt and unzip. His penis surged into view and carried on surging. It was longer and thicker than Baxter LaGrange IV's and (by a smaller margin) Fintan Whylie's. Baxter was circumcised. Fintan was 'uncut'. Cousin Paul was what Baxter (who seemed to have done some hopefully non-gay research) called 'half-cut'. Cut was usually cleaner, fresher. Fintan could be quite gamy. Paul's incised foreskin tautened to near-undetectability. His penis was a smooth column, helmeted but not hooded like Fintan's and not as lumpy as Baxter's which had almost the texture of a gnarled tree stump.

Jennifer went for it. It wasn't gamy. Nor did it smell of cologne (Baxter). Paul grunted as she expertly licked and laved. He had heavy balls which she hefted in one hand. 'Lick my nuts,' Baxter liked to command. Paul remained silent apart from the grunting but she obeyed the unspoken order. He grunted and then, as she worked her way up the column and onto the turgid helmet, he came in her mouth without warning. Baxter issued warnings.

Congressmen, Baxter said, were either hawks or doves, girls were hawks or swallows. To be Safe, most girls were hawks. It might be unseemly to spit on Paul's grief. Today Jenny would be a swallow. *What's pink and comes in buckets?* Yummy.

Paul had creamed the sponge cake. The icing on top would be if Jo and Michael had ridden back and caught them at it.

Men (she allowed that Paul was more man than boy) are so predictable. Sex is followed by confession, confession – sooner or later – by *pro*fession. By the time Jack came back for one of Mummy's colonial High Teas, Jennifer had been treated to the last hectic months of her cousin's life story. A girl from Florida he'd forced himself on at university who flew home in a hissy fit, one of those born-again virgins America was full of in the era of George W. Bush. (The LaGranges were Democrats but Baxter's kid sister Laurette had embraced the whole Silver Ring thing). A gay

168

from Bristol whose advances Paul had spurned, who'd jumped off a tower. A girl in London he was getting close to, whose bisexual ex had reclaimed her. A local under- taker's daughter he'd fingered through her pantyhose, out- raging her parents and his.

Jenny did not match his candour with confidences of her own. Paul was a Scorpio; Jenny was Cancer and liked to keep her cards close to her chest. 'The guy I was seeing in New Mexico turned out to be a total prat', she said, but she didn't tell him she'd considered marrying Baxter to avoid coming back to Sussex and her family. She said, 'I dated a guy like that in art school', in reference to the London girl's bisexual ex, but she didn't tell him that Fintan was the lover who'd come closest to breaking her heart.

'So I'm a date-rapist's third victim,' she said after the episode involving the undertaker's daughter's pantyhose.

Paul looked stricken. 'Oh God, you don't think that, do you?'

She grinned and said, 'Now who's being a prat?' He laughed his relief.

There was more. And the rest was lurid even by Jenny's standards. Some German girls and a Spanish slag he'd gangbanged with a factory hand whose dad was Charlie Turner. Paul thought the factory hand might be bi as well. Tell me about it. Fintan liked to reminisce about boys he'd shagged in high school in Cork. After confessing to two lesbian dalliances at boarding school Jenny had to resist his demand to introduce a second girl into their sex life. Men. Animals.

Jack brought them up to speed on the William-and-Mary medical soap opera over home-made scones and cucumber-and-watercress sandwiches (Jenny thought that Balmoral might be the only other house in which cucumber-and-cress sandwiches were still served in the 21st century). Iced sponge-cake. Paul kept catching her eye and smirking. He declined Mummy's offer to stay the night. He was going back on the road tomorrow: Rouen, Paris and Orleans.

'Thanks for – you know what,' he murmured to Jenny as he got into Uncle William's 10-year-old Ford Escort.

'You're welcome, I'm sure,' she said, mimicking the

tone of a McDonald's employee. 'Let's, you know, keep in touch.'

'I'll call you from France. Can we do dinner when I get back – or a movie?'

'Whatever,' she said. 'You're so right about this town. Boredom-on-Sea.'

'Not today, it isn't!' He grinned. Jenny smiled blithely back.

Not the first willy she'd seen, Paul's was the first she'd (briefly) touched. Really she ought to have remembered it better.

Only nine when the sea-snake bit Daddy and banished her and Joanna and Mummy to England, Jenny left the Middle East without seeing a single willy. UK girls claimed they'd seen – and touched - them at a much younger age.

Still today, a photo of Daddy graced a dining-room wall in The Grange. Not to remind his daughters (and their stepfather) of Daddy. It was there because of the women in the picture and to remind dinner guests at The Grange just who they were dealing with. One of the women was Mummy, of course. The other was the Queen. Mummy and Daddy had been invited to dinner on board the *Britannia* in Doha during the Queen's Arabian tour in 1979.

For Jenny the man in the photograph was a dead stranger. He was better looking than her stepfather, but then who wasn't? But he looked dull and dry, like Uncle William, who like Daddy was now dead and would soon be buried.

'What made you marry Daddy?' Jenny had once asked her mother, when she was about fourteen.

'He was the pick of the bunch, darling,' Mummy replied. Something in her tone implied a poor bunch. 'As was I,' she added. Nothing in her tone implied a poor bunch this time.

'I can't remember much about him,' Jenny confessed. 'He always seemed to be working.'

'He reminded me of James Mason,' Mummy said.

'Who's he?'

'A very handsome English actor – from Yorkshire, I think – who became a big star in Hollywood. He made films with Ava Gardner and Margaret Lockwood.' These names meant nothing to Jenny. 'Grandma used to say he

170

had the most beautiful voice of any man in the cinema. She said she'd like to hear that voice on the other side of the bed.' This, from Mummy, was daringly indecent. She had left her daughters' sexual education to their teachers and would be well shocked by some of what Jenny knew (and had already done).

'And Jack. Does he remind you of anybody?'

Her mother laughed. 'Maybe the *whale* in *Moby Dick*!' Jenny assumed this was not a sexual reference.

'Why did you marry him?'

'I married him for you, darling. For you and Jo. Not for myself. To provide you girls with security.'

'I wouldn't mind if you'd stayed a single mum.'

'Oh darling, I think you would.'

All Jenny knew of her mother's life before Qatar was that it had taken place in India's tea country: the weather always temperate, the hills always green. Grandpa Lloyd, a master blender, had held on to his job with one of the UK's brand-leaders until 1978, the year his only daughter married. Post-colonial India sounded much like pre-colonial India: a society based on deference and servility still with the odd maharajah to lend glamour and a whiff of history to the mix. In childhood dressing-up games Jenny and Joanna recreated the Raj in the lemon grove behind their house in dry dusty Doha.

In his native Norfolk Daddy had been an engineer with the water board. More precisely, he worked with sewage. Sewage was not a word Mummy cared to use or hear. In India Daddy's work was in much grander aspects of hydro-engineering: harvesting the Himalayan streams to feed the arid plains. British bachelors were thin on the ground in 1970s Darjeeling.

Only weeks into his engagement to Mummy, Daddy's company, a subsidiary of a multinational, sent him to the USA on a crash course in hydroponics and then posted him with his new bride to Qatar to make the desert bloom. Being contracted to a (junior) member of the ruling family compensated Mummy for the harshness of this new en-vironment. Expat society in the Gulf was more *Coronation Street* than *Jewel in the Crown*, but here as everywhere the cream floated to the top. Dinner and bridge invitations to the Dixons were much sought after – and much mocked by those who didn't make the grade.

Mummy insisted on coming back to England for her daughters' births. 'Home' in England was Grandma Lloyd's dinky cottage in Rye where Grandpa had died of pneumonia during his first winter away from India. Jenny was two months old and her sister two years when Mummy flew them back to Qatar. Home in Doha was a twenty-year-old rambling villa whose style evoked Darjeeling's colonial bungalows; it was owned by the junior royal who'd hired Daddy. The large walled garden contained date palms, a small lemon grove and a pool. At the age of three Jenny was swimming without armbands. Daddy had his work, Mummy had the British Club (not British enough) and the British Council (hardly British at all), Joanna had horses, Jenny had the pool and, best of all, the sea. The Persian Gulf waters ranged from emerald green to deep indigo. In the coolest two months of what passed for winter the sea was warmer than the English Channel in a good summer. In the hottest months you had to apply high-factor lotion and stay under beach umbrellas when you weren't in the water. Mummy hated the sun, hated sand, hated the sea. Daddy was only free on Fridays. Jenny was entrusted to the care of her schoolfriends' parents and other (British) families from the British Club.

She and Joanna attended an international school opened by the Queen during her Gulf tour. Sixty per cent of pupils were British, the rest mostly from mainland Europe, a handful of Americans, some high-caste Indians. Arab children attended Muslim schools to avoid contamination from infidel religions.

Jenny was smarter as well as prettier than Joanna, but she was lazy. One of her teachers told Mummy that Jenny, 'with just a little more effort, a bit more attention', would easily be in the top two or three in her class. As it was she mysteriously came fifth in almost everything, even swimming.

Then Daddy got bitten and it was all over.

The insurance money wasn't enough to buy a house at 1991 prices. Mummy's inheritance, the proceeds from the sale of the Rye cottage, had evaporated in the fees for the care home in which Grandma luxuriated until her death. Rents were lower than Rye's in the town Paul called 'Boredom-on-Sea', which Jenny and Joanna thought of as 'The Pits'; their address was 'Horrid House, 51 Vile Street, The Pits.' Their school, local, private but neither international nor exclusive, was 'Poo Prep'.

A widow's company pension did not support rent, school fees *and* a very high standard of living. Joanna kept up her riding on hired horses. Jennifer, missing the limpid waters of the Gulf, went on CenterParc weekends with schoolfriends. There were days out in London and holidays on the Norfolk Broads and Suffolk beaches. Mummy joined a bridge club and the W.I. and helped out in the Oxfam shop on two afternoons a week. She dragged her daughters to St Agnes's where Jenny malevolently regaled her Sunday-School teachers with the Koran's less liberal teachings, learnt in a Doha playground rather than a mosque and none too accurately remembered.

The snake fund shrank, and not slowly. Mummy spoke of lodgers. 'Naff!' shrieked the girls. Mummy spoke of getting a paid job. The girls peed with laughter; Mummy hadn't worked a day in her well-cushioned life.

They endured fifteen months of what seemed like but plainly wasn't penury. Mummy, the popular bridge partner, had a card up her sleeve: remarriage.

At ten Jenny was less of a child than her twelve-year-old sister. She did not develop a passion for juvenile soaps or fanzines or boy bands. Joanna yearned for Mark Owen and River Phoenix; Jenny got the hots for Tommy Lee and Richard Gere. Mummy read nothing racier than *Country Life* and *The Lady*; Jenny bought raunchier women's magazines or filched them from other homes.

Her reading gave her knowledge of the 'Facts of Life' way beyond what was tastefully revealed in lessons. Even before her periods started she was aware of the distant discomforts of the menopause. And she knew the theory of vaginal and clitoral orgasms. The other girls reckoned she was 'up for it' in various unspecified ways, but there was no one to be up for it with. Boys of any age weren't interested in ten-year-old girls.

'Whose was the first pussy you saw?' she asked him in bed, his bed. It was the day before his father's funeral.

He laughed. 'Yours!'

'That time in the shed? With the mosquitoes? You're kidding.'

'We *were* only about eleven or twelve. You don't get to see much pussy in primary school.'

'Speak for yourself!'

He laughed some more. 'Unlike you, we didn't get to see girls in the shower. I bet you hadn't seen many dicks before mine.'

Jenny grinned. She was looking at it now. 'More than *you* did, I bet.'

'I bet you didn't. How many before that time with me in the woodshed?' His eyes devoured her body, topless on the bed.

'I'd lost count by then. Dozens.' She pulled the sheet up over them, more to tease him than out of modesty. Over the weekend she'd given him two more blowjobs, in his car and in her bedroom at The Grange, and a handjob in the back row of Screen 2 at the multiplex. Watching *The Life of David Gale* it struck Jenny that Paul had a superficial resemblance to Kevin Spacey, pitching her into a juicy fantasy.

'I don't believe you,' he said now.

'The year Jack married Mummy he took us to Barbados for our summer holiday. I wandered off on my own and came across a beach with some nude sunbathers. Blacks as well as whites.'

Under the sheet he ran a possessive hand over her breasts and stomach. 'Is it true what they say about black men?'

'Yes!'

'Is that based on observation or experience?'

'Wouldn't you like to know!'

'I'm asking, aren't I?'

Jenny shrugged and tried to look like a Woman of the World. Which, after all, she pretty well was. He pulled her towards him and kissed her. This was, thus far, the thing he did best. His Kevin Spacey mouth was made for kissing. If the moisture he generated in her throat could be duplicated in her pussy, good times might be on the horizon. He wasn't as cute as Baxter (who was almost *too* cute) or as hunky as Fintan (hunkiness verging on chunkiness), but she liked his lean runner's build and the cleft in his chin that made a weak face strong. And he'd gone to the top of the todger chart.

She rolled on top of him, enjoying the feel of his erection pulsing against her tummy.

'So who was your first boy?' he asked.

'Who was yours?'

'I told you. My college friend who killed himself. I don't think he counts. We never did anything. Well – he kissed me once.'

'Was that nice?'

'I don't know how I felt about it. It didn't turn me on. I was embarrassed but maybe a bit touched as well.'

Paul seemed not to have a regressive gay streak like Fintan, although Fintan, the pervert, had only been trying to wind her up for a threesome.

On Sunday, in her room, Paul had made a gesture towards reciprocation with a bit of finger-work. He had the geography of the clitoris right but hadn't acquired a tech-nique for manipulating it. It didn't seem to occur to him that oral sex was a two-way street. Fintan once told her that Irish boys liked Sixty-Eight rather than *soixante-neuf*: 'You do me and I'll owe you one.' The week of his dad's funeral might not be the time to start schooling Paul in cunnilingus but that excuse would soon run out. Oral sex was what worked best for Jenny.

'Come on,' he urged her. 'I asked about yours. Was it on the beach in Barbados?'

'No!' She laughed. 'That was just perving. I was only ten. My school in Surrey arranged parties and dances with a boys' school down the road. You know, like prom nights in American schools.'

'Yeah, we had them at uni.'

'Both our heads thought they were really trendy and liberal, allowing us to "interact" and "develop social skills". The teachers hung around to make sure things didn't get out of hand, but if you weren't out of sight for too long you could sneak a boy off to a classroom or one of the labs.'

'And did things get out of hand?'

'*In hand* was what they mainly got!' She laughed again. 'How old were you before you got more than a handjob?'

'How old was I before I got even that! So, who was the first boy you did that to?'

'He was a Jason. Stockbroker's son.'

'How old?'

175

'He was fifteen. I was fourteen.' Would he believe her? She was thirteen. Jason *was* fifteen.

'God, the years I wasted through not going to your school' She laughed with him. 'I was *eighteen* when my first girl gave me a wank and let me touch her pussy,' he told her.

'Name her,' Jenny commanded, relieved to have got away with an edited version of her own early life.

'Tracey. Your Jason and my Tracey would make a perfect couple. We should introduce them!'

They'd asked Jack on Sunday to let her accompany Paul on his next sales trip, after the funeral. 'No,' he said firmly. 'I want Paul to stay focused on the clients, the contacts.'

'It's so boring here when he's away.'

'Get a job,' Jack said. This always closed the subject. Jobs didn't work out for Jenny. Some lasted barely a week. One she walked out of on the first day.

He repeated his no to her flying to Madrid with Paul when Mummy put a word in, she who must always be obeyed. 'She can come to Morocco with us in July,' he partially relented, 'when we go to see the leather people.'

'You can call me Uncle Jack,' he'd said in 1992, days before the wedding.

'Do I have to?' said Jenny. Jack frowned and Mummy laughed.

Jack was like Daddy had been: he was *there*, and not there. He paid for things, everything, but he left all decisions about his stepdaughters to Mummy. Within months Joanna was calling him 'Daddy'. Jennifer avoided calling him anything. She didn't dislike him, but she didn't feel the need to adopt a second father or an extra uncle. The girls wondered why their mother and stepfather had separate bedrooms but didn't dare raise the matter with Mummy. If his repulsiveness was the reason, why had she married him?

She took them out of Poo Prep and sent them to a boarding school near Godalming which aspired, vainly, to be as upscale as Benenden and Roedean. 'Crap College', aka 'the Gulag'. Dormitories had been abandoned in favour of three-to-a-room. Considered more desirable than coupling, tripling promoted bullying and did not entirely

176

discourage unnatural activities.

From their over-rhythmic breathing or little gasps that morphed into fake snores, Jenny knew when her room-mates' fingers were busy under their duvets after lights-out. They discussed vibrators but doubted that Ann Summers would sell them to ten-year-old schoolgirls. Certain varieties of fruit and vegetable came in handy shapes and a range of sizes, but were you supposed to *peel* a banana first? And imagine the embarrassment if you had to ask the school nurse to remove a broken carrot or a rogue pen-top from down there!

In novels women's juices flowed as copiously as a mon-soon. Vaginal dryness was a problem of middle age. Jenny seemed to be menopausal at ten. Was she too young to write to an agony aunt? She also wanted to know if that moment of tingly warmth was all an orgasm amounted to, or would there be more when you were Doing It For Real with a boy. Her periods started when she was twelve-and-a-half, as had Joanna's, but her vagina remained worry-ingly unlubricated. She wrote Tampons below Toothpaste on Mummy's shopping list, but her mother left it to Jenny to read the directions for herself.

Two weeks after her thirteenth birthday Jack took them to Mustique. Jo was on a riding holiday in the Pyrenees with her best friend from school. Mustique was more chic than Barbados, full of posers and celebrities, a minor Royal. Not so much fun. No nudity on or near the hotel beach.

'Any ideas about what you might want to do after you finish school?' her stepfather asked her by the pool one morning. Mummy, not a sun-worshipper, was inside play-ing gin rummy with some rich old folks from Florida. Jack had wrestled with his biggest-ever marlin the day before. The marlin lost but - a Pyrrhic victory - it did Jack's back in.

'Not a clue, really,' Jenny replied truthfully.

His stomach wobbled like a giant jelly as he rolled, wincingly, to face her. 'How was your report this year?'

'Mummy didn't show you?'

He shook his head. 'She never does. Joanna showed me hers.'

'Mine was about the same as last year's. You know: "*Could do better.*"'

177

'Could you?'

'Could I what?' It was weird to be having any kind of heart-to-heart with Jack. She knew he had them with Joanna, Step-daddy's little girl. Jenny wasn't jealous, she had no desire to be his favourite. In his daily business suit he was just about bearable to see and be seen with, but here, looking like a beached whale in Bermuda shorts, with his ghastly fish face, she felt so not cool in his company and tried not to look at him.

'Could you do better?'

'Well, I suppose I could if I wanted to.'

'But you don't want to?'

She shrugged. This was not a conversation she wanted to have.

'Agnes did say you're good at Art.'

'It's my favourite subject.' Mainly because there were fewer textbooks.

'Do you think you might take it up seriously?'

'Be a painter or sculptor, you mean?' The contemporary art world seemed to be full of phoneys. Rachel Whiteread was almost the only one whose work Jenny sometimes admired and envied.

'Or a commercial artist.'

'Like – in advertising?'

'A talent for art can be parlayed into draughtsmanship, architecture, interior design – lots of possibilities. You could design furniture for me!'

As if. 'I haven't really thought that far ahead,' she prevaricated.

'Well, you know I'll pay for you to do any kind of art school you want, serious or commercial.'

'Yeah – thanks, Jack.' She'd long thought of him as Jack but this was perhaps the first time she'd said it to his face. He didn't seem to be fazed.

'When I was your age I dreamt of becoming an architect,' he confessed.

'Well, you sort of are one.'

He shook his head. 'No, I'm just a builder and a furniture-maker, like my dad. There's a lot of competition but I like to think we make some of the best furniture in our part of Sussex and I'm certainly the biggest non-corporate developer.' More jelly-wobbles as he rolled carefully onto his back again. 'If you're good at something, you owe it to yourself to try and be the best at it in the place where you're doing it.'

Deep stuff. Jenny managed not to grimace. 'Well, you're fantastic at making money, Jack,' she teased him.

'Yeah, and you and your mother and Joanna are good at spending it!'

They shared a laugh. She found herself liking him a bit more than before.

But she'd told him the truth. She had no ideas about her future, didn't know what she wanted out of life, other than to be distracted, to keep boredom at bay. She rarely felt any connection to the things that obsessed her contemporaries: films, soaps, music, celebrity-watching. Other girls looked forward to careers, a husband (or husbands), children. Jenny didn't want any of these. Well, maybe a husband, eventually. The thing she enjoyed most, more than Art or music or books or even shopping, was reading/talking/thinking about *Sex*, so near but still so far. Jenny resolved to work at becoming a Great Shag, one that guys would remember and compare all their future lovers to.

And she put art school on the shortlist of options for her future. It was a very short list.

Recalling Paul at the age of eleven, it was *mosquitoes* that came to mind, rather than what must have been, even then, an outstanding willy - the first one she had actually, briefly, touched. When she remembered Jason, the first boy she brought, manually, to orgasm, it was his cologne that flooded her senses. If this was her first brush with the widely advertised 'Lynx Effect', she preferred to meet boys sporting the 'locker-room effect'.

Jason was handsome in a wet, Hugh Grant sort of way. Three months after her thirteenth birthday, they met at a start-of-term party at the Gulag; two days later Jenny gave him her first handjob, in some woods off the A25, their bikes leaning against one side of a tree, Jason quivering against the other. His cologne was so vile that she stopped seeing him after two more bucolic encounters, two more quivering handjobs.

More Jasons followed. Some were even called Jason. She went out with schoolfriends on the prowl, on the pull. As well as socializing with the neighbouring school, they

179

connected with boys in shops and cafés or simply on the street in Godalming and Guildford. At home during the Christmas and Easter holidays there were Sussex guys whose parents golfed with Jack or played bridge with Mummy. Her sister rode and played tennis; Jenny cruised. On their next Caribbean trip she pulled her first American teenagers; they found her Englishness both appealing and intimidating.

Unlike English boys, who could be strangers to hygiene, the Americans were clean enough to eat off. She wasn't up for that yet. One of them (his name was Marvin) put a finger on her and in her, but what they mostly wanted, expected, was what Jason had got from her. Some were bold enough to ask for a full-on shag or a blowjob, but even in the 1990s a boy would settle for what was on offer. A handjob from a one-night stand was better than going home for some d-i-y. Most of them were one-evening stands. Some of the Surrey and Sussex boys she dated for a couple of weeks, one for a couple of months. Jenny got bored before they did. Their conversation was crap. The handjob could be the highlight of her evening. Or not.

A year after Jason One, Jenny, now fourteen, responded to the overtures of a fellow boarder at the Gulag, a Chinese banker's daughter. They did nothing heavier than apply fingers to each other, sunbathing naked in a glade in the woods on the North Downs, five cycled miles from school. In the sun the Oriental's porcelain skin gleamed like ivory. Her touch was like being brushed by butterfly wings. Jenny decided, for a week or two, that lesbianism was the way to go.

'You got very nice pussy,' the girl said. The way she said it – *poossy* – sounded uncannily like Sean Connery in *Goldfinger*, Jenny's favourite of the early Bond movies.

'You have too,' she replied out of politeness. Not that it was untrue. This other vagina didn't gush but it was extremely moist.

'But you got a problem,' the girl said. Actually she said *ploplem*. 'You very dry.' *Velly dly*.

'Do you know if other girls have this problem?' Jenny asked fearfully.

'I only done it with two more girls,' her paramour said.

180

'They not got same ploplem. You should tell doctor.'

No way. Mummy's GP was an old fart whose wife was in the bridge set.

'Shall we try it again?' Jenny asked, thinking butterflies.

'Sure. You not like other girls. Other girls bit smelly. They not shaving poossy like you and me.'

Saying 'smelly', a word with which she had no difficulty, the Chinese girl sounded spookily like Mummy, to whom smells were anathema. *Marie Claire* had encouraged Jennifer to buy her first razor, although her pudendum thus far sprouted only a faint fluffiness.

She took her ploplem to the school nurse who said it would sort itself out as she went further into puberty. Wrong call. Jenny's breasts expanded at a promising pace but her vagina, meant to be an oasis, remained a desert. Her dismal dryness was one of the things that stopped her from Going All The Way, which a few of her contemporaries claimed to have already done at twelve or thirteen. She knew about condoms and lubricants (and sexually-transmitted diseases) but no magazine article had addressed the issue of drying up with a boy inside you. Would someone have to throw a bucket of water over them, like rutting dogs, or would they have to slither into hospital in an ultra-intimate lambada to be surgically separated?

The Chinese banker was transferred to his HQ in Hong Kong and took his family with him. Another classmate introduced Jenny to her first dildo. Hard plastic with an offset steeple top, resembling no penis she'd ever encountered, it buzzed and vaguely vibrated. Suzanne had brought KY but it gave a better result outside than in.

Suzanne was also a banker's daughter, a native of Surrey rather than the Orient. Destined to be a major-league dyke or at least bisexual, she was the first person to go down on Jenny. 'Hmm, yummy,' she said.

'You can say that again.' The familiar warm tingle was warmer and tinglier, but this wasn't the Full Monty - was it?

'Yummy, yummy, yummy.'

Jenny didn't seem to be expected to reciprocate and didn't care to. Suzanne's thicket of pubic hair was doused in a product that smelled, perhaps aptly, like drain cleaner. In the world of butch ladies a dry, shaven – and fragrant – pussy might be an asset.

At home that Christmas she got serious with a blonde sixteen-year-old called Craig who was staying with his grandparents while his parents went through a vindictive divorce. He had a rugby-player's physique and a bump from a broken nose. His willy was fully circumcised – and clean. Even his come smelled nicer than other boys', yeasty but not stale or fishy. Tempting.

Blowjobs weren't as Safe as handjobs. You mustn't let someone come in your mouth; if they did, you must spit it out. There were flavoured condoms. But Jenny didn't want to taste a latex banana, a rubberised strawberry, she wanted the taste and texture of flesh, of *cock*.

'God, that's fantastic,' he groaned. In porn-films women talked back incessantly, but Jenny had been taught not to speak with her mouth full.

What a mouthful it was too! Amazing how perfectly it fitted. It didn't taste or feel very different from licking his chin or his shoulder. Should she lick as well as suck? She licked and sucked. Were their balls supposed to get some of the attention? Bit icky, all that hair. She stayed where she was, tried to get a bit more in, gagged but held steadfast.

'God, I'm coming,' he said. No need to tell God about it, really. She lifted her head and studied an ejaculation up close and personal. Yuck.

He didn't return the oral favour – she knew men generally didn't – but he'd learned to use his hands efficiently. Two dates later Jenny armed herself with condoms and KY and let him fuck her. In fact she so much took the lead, putting the condom and lubricant on him and then lowering herself onto his now slightly silly-looking sheathed organ, that it was more like she was fucking him. It fitted her vagina even better than it fitted her mouth. No pain and no blood – she must have lost her virginity to a sex-toy. There had been other dildos, including one that replicated a famous US porn-star's equipment, but it was gratifying to settle onto one made of flesh that came attached to a whole body. He grunted with pleasure as she rode him. Jenny grunted in a lower key.

One that came attached to a sixteen-year-old body came all too quickly. 'God, I'm coming.' There hadn't been

time for the usual tingle to build up. All in all a disap-
pointing debut, except for the satisfaction of having Done
It. *I'm a woman now*, she told herself Adrian Moleishly at
the age of fourteen-and-a-half.

They fucked throughout Christmas and New Year, in
her room on Mummy's bridge afternoons or in his room
while his grandparents shopped and attended medical
appointments. They tried various positions but Jenny
favoured being on top, not from any need to dominate but
for the control it gave her over the speed of entry. Riding
his shaft against her clitoris the sensation became more,
much more, than a tingle. Finally, one afternoon, it happened. Her entire body seemed to pulse, centring on the
part of her that rode him until suddenly her vagina
seemed to drain all the energy from every other part of
her in a kind of incandescence, and she almost blacked
out.

'Jesus Christ,' she said with a reverence that was not
inappropriate.

'What happened?' Craig asked, gleaming with perspir-
ation under her, his organ, post-orgasmic, still rigid inside
her.

'I think I came,' she said.

'What does it feel like?'

'Divine,' she said.

He was silent for a moment. Then he said: 'I love you,
Jenny.'

But it wasn't love that she craved.

'Shag me some more,' she said, applying a squirt of KY
and rolling over so that he could be on top, his preferred
position. She didn't come this time, although Craig –
almost as quickly as the first time – did.

After burying Uncle William on Tuesday Jenny and Paul
went to the movies: *Confessions of a Dangerous Mind*.
Paul's verdict: 'Totally brilliant.' Jenny disagreed: 'Too far
up itself.' Italian dinner. No sex on the day of the funeral,
but on Wednesday she fucked him.

They were in her bedroom at The Grange. Mummy was
visiting Aunt Mary. Deep kissing. Some more *soixante-
huit*, with accompanying finger-play. For the first time they
got completely naked instead of fumbling through and
around clothing. Paul lay on the bed in the X position, his

183

hands clenched in the chrome bedhead. Jenny was cruciform, her arms wrapped round his thighs, her mouth clamped to his penis. Suddenly she knew she had to have him inside her. She scrabbled in the bedside drawer for condoms and lubricant.

'Did you buy those in the States?' he asked when he saw that the condom was a Trojan. He took it off her and did his own thing. His star rating rose. Baxter and Fintan both insisted on her performing this part of the service.

'Yes,' she said. 'And this.' She held up the tub of Crisco. His eyes widened.

'Do you want to – you know?' She guessed what he was trying not to say, had even done it a couple of times but was not an enthusiast.

'No,' she said. 'Big boy like you, a girl needs a bit of extra lubrication.'

She climbed on top and lowered herself onto him slowly, allowing the gel to fully slick her, then rode him hard and fast. It was important to make him come fairly quickly, before the lubricant absorbed and left her high and dry. She didn't want to have to explain her problem in any more detail, not yet. She enjoyed the feel of his hands on her breasts and the sight of his film-star face, filmed with sweat, hair mussed, his brows furrowed as if he was concentrating on an important project. Leaning forwards she tongued the inside of his mouth. There was a very faint tingling in her vagina, which might be incipient dryness or even the start of an episode of thrush, but just possibly heralded the hope of an orgasm. Not now, but next time or the time after that. Today Jenny wouldn't come, but she made noises to egg him on, still kissing him, and she savoured the ripple effect against the wall of her vagina as he filled the Trojan's reservoir.

'Jesus,' he gasped. Which she took to be a compliment.

'Yeah,' she said, rolling onto her back beside him just before her pussy completely dried out.

Sorry ive been out of touch. S lost phone, found down back of sofa! U ok? Xrx

Good 2 hear from u. I'm in Barcelona, sales biz. Aok with u guys? xxPxx

*

184

Yes all fine. Going to IBIZA 4 hols next wk. Have u seen R IN EASTENDERS?

Don't see much tv. Travel a lot. And bonking cousin Jenny! She's a rattlesnake. Just what I needed!

Isnt that illegal? K winslet was bonking her cousin in that DHLAWRENCE movie.

JUDE. Thomas Hardy, not Lawrence. Sex between cousins is ok now, but Jenny's not my cousin. My uncle's only her STEPfather.

That's ok then. Have fun! Xrx

1997 was the year Jenny's lack of lubrication acquired a clinical name and some treatment. But not a cure.

Back at school after the Christmas holiday she boasted of her Winter of Love, mildly exaggerating her orgasms and still not mentioning her dryness. Two thirds of her year now claimed to have Done It. At least half of them were probably lying.

Craig had gone home to whoever had gained custody. In March, in the Virgin store in Guildford, Jenny was cruised by another rugby hunk. This one was dark-haired. His nose wasn't broken. He had a Tom Cruise boy-next-door handsomeness, only English and six-foot-two. And eighteen. Kevin. After coffee with her girlfriends, a Pizza Hut lunch (*ciao*, girlfriends), a snog on a park bench (big mouth, big tongue), Jenny administered a blowob in his parked car (big everything – not circumcised but well scrubbed). Kevin threshed appreciatively and came without warning. Jenny gagged and spat. Onto his Levi 501s.

'Hey, watch it,' he said.

'Watch it yourself, man. A girl likes to know what's coming – and when.'

'Excuse me for having a hot dick.'

'I just might,' she said.

He didn't come so quickly when she rode him two days later, in his house (neo-Georgian semi, parents away). His bedroom had posters of rugby-players she couldn't name and Pamela Anderson whom she could. He didn't come quickly at all. Or quickly enough. Instead of a warm sensation there was a burning which got rapidly worse. She extracted herself and reached for the tube of KY in her tote-bag. Never a Girl Scout, but always prepared.

'Sorry about this,' she said. 'I have this tendency to go a bit dry.'

'No big,' he said. 'Let me get on top.'

But it happened again. He was in a different league from Craig. It should have been nice, a slow lazy screw, but it wasn't. The warm tingle seemed to be the build-up not to orgasm but a friction burn.

'Stop! I need more lubricant.'

'There's something wrong with you,' he said irritably.

Was there?

At half term Mummy greeted her with the news that their GP had retired. They were now all registered with a husband-and-wife practice in the Old Town. The woman doctor had the busy hair and directness of a TV presenter.

'It's your Bartholin's Glands,' she pronounced.

'My what?'

'They're named after a Danish anatomist. They secrete the fluid that lubricates you during intercourse. What some people call "love juice".'

Jenny went a deeper shade of red. 'Uh-huh,' she muttered.

'I need to refer you to a gynaecologist. Are your parents happy to pay for you to go private? It'll be faster.'

'I haven't told anybody. My mum's not very good with stuff like this.'

'And your dad?'

'He's my stepfather.'

'Jack, I need to see a gynaecologist.'

'Christ Almighty, don't tell me you're pregnant at fourteen.'

'No, I'm not. But I've got some kind of problem in – that department. The doctor wants me to see a gynaecologist. I totally can't tell Mummy, but – you won't mind getting the bills? I don't know what the treatment will be or how much it's going to cost.'

'You haven't – caught something, have you?'

Jenny went crimson for the second time that day. 'No, nothing like that. Something's not working properly in my

– you know, down there.'

'Well, obviously I don't mind paying for you to be put right. Anything.'

'And don't tell Mummy. Please.'

'Our secret.' He patted her hand. It wasn't too repulsive to be touched by him, as long as he didn't kiss her. Christmases and birthdays were tough.

And so it began. Jenny's calvary.

'I thought only gays had to use this stuff,' Paul said. This was their fourth full-on shag. He'd come back yesterday from follow-up visits to Toulouse, Sitges and Barcelona and had visited his mother in the hospital's loony-toons ward. Jenny was spending the night *chez* Paul. Mummy knew, but not Jack.

'No, us girls sometimes need it too. I told you –'

'Extra lubrication. Yeah, but I thought girls are supposed to, you know, self-lubricate.'

'I have a slight problem in that department.' Here we go, she thought. Another boyfriend gets the yuckies and takes a walk. But no.

'Is it something *I* could be helping along?' Five bonus points for asking.

'Well, as a matter of fact...' She tailed off. It was never easy. Some guys simply weren't up for it.

'Like this?' He was there already, snaking down her body from the boob-zone (Jenny liked nipple action as much as the next girl but they weren't a prime erogenous zone) to the pleasure-dome. And, just like that, his tongue was inside her and his fingers were on her. Make that *ten* Brownie points!

'There,' she instructed. 'Back a bit. Press harder. And faster. Ohh, yes.'

The earth didn't move, it almost never had, but the rippling warmth that she felt when a big penis was moving inside her was now generating itself with only his tongue barely flickering and she gave herself up to the warm ripples and the whirlpool contractions. And then there was that moment, lasting perhaps fifteen seconds, when her entire being, everything that she was, seemed to centre on her burning pussy and her throbbing clitoris; and then it was over.

'I owe you one,' she said as he wriggled back to lie

187

beside her.

'Madame's credit is good,' he said and kissed her. His thick tongue was now inside her mouth. I could learn to love this tongue, she was thinking and laughed through the kiss.

'What?' he said.

'Nothing, Paul.' She smiled into his face which began to seem more handsome by the day as well as more familiar. 'Why don't you - lube up.'

'Madame wishes Monsieur to shag her now?' He was going back to work tomorrow, another trip to the Riviera.

'*Mais oui.*'

'We may and we shall.'

Ibiza was great. Hot, v noisy, v gay. How was Barcelona? Rattlesnake lady ok?

She's hot too! But she has problem I don't like to ask about. She's v dry in the u-know-where.

It happens to us all sometimes. Girly hormones. Dont worry.

Too many hormones or too few?

Go w the flow. Yr lucky yr getting yr end away! Luv from s and from me.

No 'Luv' from Richard. Did he know of Paul's existence? Paul had told Jenny about meeting Rachel and Simon, whose dad was bisexual and on TV in *EastEnders*. Jenny said Richard was good-looking but no great shakes as an actor.

'Luv' was a nice bonus. Meredith had quoted (for Neil's benefit) a line from a Bette Davis movie: 'There are people here who love you.' What had Prince Charles said in his engagement interview: 'Whatever "in-love" means.' Diana had laughed; but not for long.

Were he and Jenny falling in love?

A few guys since Craig had fervently declared, 'I love you.' 'Yeah?' was Jenny's standard reply. She'd only once ever said 'I love you.' To Fintan. 'Me too,' he'd replied. Ambiguous at best. She hadn't laboured the point. But he *was* the one. Her Mr Darcy. Her Rupert Birkin. (*Women In Love*: A-level text.)

She met Fintan in Brighton midway through her second term at art school. She'd dated three guys during the first term and shagged them in the small flat Jack had bought some years earlier as an investment (Jenny suspected it might be his nookie pad). Student sex was as indifferent as high-school sex. With their pranks and crap music and their heavy-handed environmentalism, students were just overgrown sixth-formers. At the age of eighteen-and-a-half Jenny decided it was time to date some older guys.

Fintan Whylie was twenty-eight, deejaying at a club that attracted an older crowd. He played almost nothing later than Queen and Abba. No Oasis, no Robbie Williams. There was a lot of The Four Seasons and Boney M and and plink-plink hits from Sixties groups with long silly names like Goldie and the Gingerbreads. Carving a name for himself, Fintan deejayed odd nights at two gay clubs.

He looked like an Irish gypsy; in his heart this is what he was. He had a long face with a squared-off jaw, a dark complexion (some of it was dirt), dark demonic eyes. His designer stubble came from forgetting to shave for days on the trot. His hair was long and unkempt. He looked like someone who'd been twenty-eight in the Sixties. His Irish accent was so thick it sounded like a piss-take, but it was natural.

'Hello, darlin',' he said on Jenny's third visit when she drifted close to his console. 'You slummin' agin?'

'I like the stuff you play.'

'You wouldn't rather hear some Westlife, some Will Young?'

'No thanks! Why'd you play all this old stuff?'

'Sixties music is so much cleaner, less synthetic. And the lyrics are simple and pure. They really resonate.'

'Yeah. "*Um-um-um-um-um-um*"! That really blows me away.'

He laughed. 'I was thinking more of "*You've lost that lovin' feelin'*" or "*Bridge over troubled water*".'

'Yeah, they're really neat.'

'Neat? I suppose they are at that. Listen, darlin', I get a break in ten. Can I buy you a drink?'

'I'll buy you one.'

'Ooh, a rich kid, are you? I'm hooked already!'

'You soon will be,' she said coolly. Why was she coming on to a guy who must be at least thirty and needed a bath and a shave and some clean clothes?

Before dawn she'd got him back to her flat and out of his clothes and into the shower. He still needed a shave and his stubble sandpapered her thighs when he went down on her. 'Jeesus,' he said in awe, 'I've eaten off tables that weren't as clean as you are down here.'

'Don't talk,' she said. 'Do me.'

'If you do me I will.'

Even after the shower his big uncircumcised penis was quite gamy, but she came to relish his aroma – 'the smell o' the peat-bogs,' he called it. Everything he did to her other guys had done before, but he was gutsier and earthier and simply better than anybody else. She told him about her problem, crying as she described the humiliation of both the examinations and the treatments. He held her and stroked her and soothed her in his velvet Guinnessy brogue.

'Did you never think about taking yourself to Lourdes?' he suggested.

'Jesus, what for?'

'For the waters, of course. Lookin' for a miracle. I'd come with you.'

'No way.' Even to half-hearted Protestant Jenny it seemed impious and impudent to pray to a spinster saint to help her achieve a better orgasm.

Her need to re-lubricate didn't faze Fintan as it had other men, and somehow she needed it less with him. It wasn't – or was it? – that he had a bigger penis, but he touched a part of her that no one else had touched. Her orgasms lasted longer, he could leave her weak and trembling after sex.

His rented Hove bedsit (shared WC) was somewhere between crummy and gross, overflowing with CDs and old vinyl. He moved more or less permanently into her flat. Music was his life, his passion. He came back from his studio or gigs with armfuls of albums. Jenny endured Tamla days, Merseyside days, Country days, days when he played nothing but Dionne Warwick or Bob Dylan or the Eagles.

He took on her political re-education, speaking of the

Camelot age of the Kennedys or the student riots of Paris or the last days of Hanoi as if he had lived them. In his mind, in his heart, he'd marched with Martin Luther King, fished with Hemingway, drunk with Dylan Thomas, fucked with Errol Flynn. No more than a cursory Catholic, he blessed John Paul II. At the other extreme he reviled Margaret Thatcher who he said had done more harm to Britain than Adolf Hitler. Jenny thought of taking him home to meet her stepfather and Uncle William who considered Mrs T. a candidate for canonization.

Jenny fed him, bought him clothes and toiletries. He needed lessons in hygiene. She'd caught him turning his socks and underpants inside out to get a second day's wear out of them. 'You should meet my dad,' he said. 'He wears the same socks for a week and turns his knickers back-to-front and inside-out again to get even more days!' Jenny bought Fintan socks and jockeys.

She became a DJ groupie, spending most nights at the clubs he worked. Late nights soon led to cutting classes, neglected reading, projects rushed or handed in late. Fintan, who considered most of today's culture to be 'petrified and Pepsified', was dismissive of contemporary art. His contempt fuelled her dissatisfaction with her courses. Too much emphasis on the Modernists and Installation. She thought of quitting, even though this would close off the only avenue of employment that had any faint appeal.

The club scene was big on drugs, from amphetamines through to crystal meth. A girl in the year ahead of Jenny in Surrey had OD'd on heroin, scaring most of the school off drugs completely. Jenny had popped pills and snorted cocaine; yes, drugs were a plus on the dance floor but they could seriously screw up your sex life and hers was screwed-up enough already. Fintan was a major pot-head (more Sixties regression). Sex on pot was giggly and slow, working up to intense, hallucinatory orgasms.

Jenny liked the gays: they danced and flirted with her, patted her bum and her boobs and then went back to snogging their boyfriends. One of the gay clubs had a backroom where according to Fintan unprotected sex went on. Not all the gays haunted the backroom: the others were only there to dance or were looking for something more, for romance, for commitment. Was she?

Fintan had got more out of her – and into her – than

any other man. She told him she loved him. 'Me too,' he said.

A local radio station offered him their mid-evening slot, two hours of Easy Listening. He raced from the studio to the clubs, from the clubs to Jenny's flat. Jenny found it harder than ever to focus on her studies. Her tutor told her she would need to repeat the first year – 'if this is what you want to do.' Fintan was what Jenny wanted most, but she sensed that his focus too was slipping away.

Mummy and Jack were planning another trip to Mustique. 'If you've got a boyfriend or girlfriend you want to bring along, that's fine,' Jack offered.

'Sounds groovy,' Fintan said,' but I can't take off when I'm just starting to make a name for meself. You go. I'll still be here when you get back.'

But he wasn't. An offer to join a station in London was another major step up. Back from the Caribbean she found his crummy Hove flatlet recreated in Holloway, an area the gentrifiers had passed by. He called her 'my darlin' lovely piccaninny' and took her to bed for what turned out to be last knockings. When she offered to move to London and rent them a better flat he said:

'Sorry, Jen, but my career's in a really interestin' place right now. I need to be on me own.'

This hadn't happened to Ursula Brangwen. She argued, raged, cried, but he was implacable. Jenny drifted back to Brighton to await the resumption of her course. She went drinking, clubbing, shagged two more losers. A girl in one of the clubs commiserated. She'd been Fintan's girlfriend two years ago.

'He sees girls as kind of like a dry sponge,' she said. The simile was a cruel one to Jenny. 'It's his mission in life to pick us up and fill us with the water of his wonderful wisdom. But once we're super-saturated we're thrown out like an old loofah, and he goes shopping for a new sponge.'

Halfway through the repeated first term Jenny dropped out.

'It's not what I want to do,' she told Jack. Mummy, who'd sailed through life without higher education or work experience, had no counsel to offer.

'Do you want to come and work for me?'

'Sorry, Jack, it's not that I'm ungrateful, but leather

192

furniture just isn't where I'm at.'

'Where *are* you "at", exactly?'

'*I don't know*! I wish I did.'

'You need to find a husband,' Mummy uselessly contributed. Joanna had just got engaged to Michael, the brother of a boy from Rye Jenny had masturbated a few times a few years ago.

'No, I don't,' Jenny snapped, though she thought it might actually be true.

Lucinda, the other girl Fintan had dumped, found her a job in an art shop run by a family friend. Jack continued her allowance and paid all the bills for the flat. A year of temporary shop jobs and temporary liaisons followed. After two Ecstasy-related deaths in Sussex she decided not to do any more drugs, but she carried on drinking, clubbing and shagging deadbeats.

Then she read about a clinic in New Mexico that took a holistic approach to sexual dysfunction. She'd convinced herself that if her biology could only be put right, everything else would fall into place. The clinic was pricey but Jack was still willing to fund these futile quests for a miracle.

'Is there something a bit wrong with you?' Paul asked her the week before they were due to go to Morocco. After five weeks he was getting used to her and didn't come quite so fast. Which, as with Kevin and the twenty or so guys since Kevin, gave her a better chance of getting off. And of drying out.

'Yes,' she said, thinking, Here we go again. Hello, Paul. Goodbye, Paul. 'If you really want to know, I have a problem with my Bartholin's Glands.'

'Your what?'

'They're just inside your pussy.'

'Not inside mine, they're not!'

'Oh, hilarious. Prat. These glands produce the gunk that lubricates a woman when she's aroused.'

'Yeah, I've noticed. That Spanish girl Jim and I shagged produced buckets of it. And a German girl in Spain did too. Hers smelt really – strong. You don't produce *any*. Is that the problem?'

'Actually I do, but – not enough. I'm underdeveloped in that area.'

'Well –' he played with her breasts – 'you make up for it in other areas!'

'Yeah, and there's no silicone!' She pushed his hands off, not feeling as good-humoured as she sounded. Experience showed that this was the precise moment when their relationship might go – tits-up. Ha-very-ha.

'You've seen doctors about this?'

'Doctors, gynaecologists, therapists. I've even seen surgeons who do sex-changes in case they had tricks other specialists didn't, but the things they do in gender re-assignment wouldn't work on me.'

'There isn't an operation for – your problem?'

'If I had the opposite problem, like your Spanish bimbo – if the glands are over-productive, they get blocked in some women – they can operate to open them up. What I've got normally happens to menopausal women, their glands stop producing, only mine have never properly *started*.'

'So what do you do, apart from use lots of this American KY?'

'What don't I do? I've tried fifty kinds of moisturisers and a dozen kinds of hormone treatments. I've had oestrogen tablets you take orally and some you put in your pussy. *My* pussy,' she amended quickly as he smirked again. 'I've had oestrogen *rings* you put inside and creams you rub in outside –'

'I could help with that,' he said. Jenny would kill to erase that smirk.

'Yeah, I bet you could.'

'Is it safe taking all these hormones?'

'Well, I haven't grown balls or a moustache, as you may have noticed. There is an increased risk of cervical cancer but you have to weigh the risks against the benefits, and anyway the doses aren't too high. I don't take them all the time and I don't need to take the Pill.'

'What about, you know, alternative medicine? Natural supplements?'

'You name it, I've tried it. A moisturiser made from kiwi-fruit. Minerals. Jungle herbs from Madagascar and Indonesia. Some of them make your pee go scary colours and smell disgusting. Some are bad for your liver if you take them for too long. And none of them fucking *work*.' This was the one thing that could bring her close to tears.

A schmaltzy book or movie didn't do it, even being *dumped* didn't do it, but thinking and talking about her desiccated pussy could almost always do it.

'Have you tried acupuncture?'

'It didn't help.'

'That's a shame. One of my aunties had it for arthritis in her hands and it really did the business. And she said the needles don't hurt at all.'

'Tell her to try sticking them in her *cunt*,' Jenny said.

Far from leaving her Paul became solicitous, spent more time fingering and licking her clitoris. She let him apply her vaginal moisturiser, which was more fun than applying it herself and a lot less embarrassing than having it applied by therapists – male *and* female – at the clinic in New Mexico last winter.

Then he did leave. For his last sales trip – southwest France and back into Barcelona and Sitges – before they took off for Morocco with Jack.

It's a glandular thing. She's had years of treatment.
Nothing works.

Poor jenny. Treat her gently.

I do. All the time!

Lucky jenny!

The only good thing that came out of Jenny's winter in Albuquerque was Baxter LaGrange. A lot cleaner than Fintan. He was being treated for premature ejaculation and, boy, did he have a problem. He had only ever been able to penetrate a girl *after* shooting his wad. His therapy was yet more mortifying than Jenny's, ejaculating over the female therapists, wilting with the males (Baxter was defiantly straight). As he started to respond to a regime of diet and pills and yoga-type exercises, he began to luxuriate for ten, thirty, sixty seconds in the hands of the females and, fairly soon, Jenny's hands. Diet, pills, yoga didn't improve Jenny's situation, or no more than minimally. Baxter did.

The clinic encouraged their relationship, hoping they

would stimulate each other's 'Sexual Interactability'. American men, when they weren't being anal, were very oral. Baxter ate her pussy tirelessly, ejaculating two or three times in the process and then, in a final erectile fling, got briefly inside her before squirting a few spermatic laggards into the condom reservoir. Her orgasms during the oral phase saw Jenny through the second phase, which didn't do much for her beyond the pleasant sensation of his sizeable penis, briefly (*too* briefly, even for Jenny) filling her.

He took her home to 'Meet the Folks' at Christmas. Home was a small town he called 'Asswipe' deep in the Oregon pine forests. The lumber mill owned by three generations of LaGranges produced among other things the pulp for toilet paper manufacture. The clan provided the community with its police and fire chiefs, its mayor, several councillors and a state congressman (Baxter LaGrange II). Asswipe knew Baxter III as 'Junior'. His extensive family embraced Jenny with gushing warmth.

British TV viewers had seen the LaGranges in soaps from *Dallas* and *Dynasty* through to *The Simpsons*. US sport and US politics were the principal topics of conversation. The only countries outside the US they knew anything about were Cuba and Eye-raq. When Jenny mentioned Tony Blair, Grandma LaGrange, whom the townspeople called Miz Aurora, said: 'Has Margaret Thatcher gone? Nobody told me.'

Jenny amused herself by Americanizing her own family. 'Pembertown' became Arsewipe. Mummy was Miz Agnes, her stepfather Jack Pemberton II, aka The Senator. Joanna and her creep of a husband were Mr and Mrs Jerkoff. Uncle William and Aunt Mary were The Dweebs; Paul was Sonny Dweeb.

Had Baxter proposed, Jenny thought she might accept. Oregon was no duller than Sussex, and with political office in Baxter's future Jenny went so far as to fantasize becoming First Lady – a Hillary clone rather than a Laura. But Baxter didn't propose, and they returned to New Mexico. When the clinic discharged them at the end of January, Baxter resumed his college career at the state university. The curriculum centred on sport, beer and his jock friends; Jenny soon tired of all three and of his small ugly apartment which she was expected to clean. Albuquerque was an ugly arid city. She was putting on weight from a poor diet and too much sprawling in front of the TV.

It was over. It had been over before.

'I think I'd better head home,' she said in the middle of March.

'You reckon?'

'Yeah.'

'Okay. Well, I guess you gotta get your life back on track.'

'Yeah,' she said again, thinking, *What life, what track?*

Goodbye, Baxter. Goodbye, Albuquerque. A week in LA. Then: hello, Pembertown/Arsewipe. Hi there, cousin Paul. Another big boy, also clean and learning to be sexy and considerate. He wouldn't be another Rupert Birkin to her Ursula, but he just might be a Gerald Crich to her Gudrun.

'I love you, Jenny,' he said.

Confession: been there, done that. Time for *pro*fession.

They were lying under a faux-Moorish gazebo beside the pool at La Mamounia. The air was heady with the scent of plants Jenny couldn't name. Waiters dressed like extras from an Indiana Jones movie hovered in anticipation of any guest's next whim.

She didn't say: 'I love you too.' She said: 'That's good to hear.'

'Shall we get married?'

She said, almost without thinking: 'Yeah, why not.' A waiter darted forward as she raised a hand. Unusually tall for a Moroccan, hunky and handsome; his Ali Baba trousers gave nothing away. According to Brighton's disco queens almost every Arab had a Dick of Death. Jenny had never shagged what the LaGranges called an Ay-rab (and would hardly have dared tell them if she had).

'I'd like a margarita,' she said. Her mouth was raspingly dry; like Fez's, the Marrakech kasbah in July pulsated with dust.

'Yes, *madame*. Sir?'

'I'll have another beer,' Paul said. He'd stayed by the pool this morning while Jenny shopped; after Fez he was 'souked out'. The heat, the flies, the savage odours. Megadecibel bangings from the hole-in-the-wall shops where kitchen pans were manufactured as well as sold. The men in striped robes busy scratching their crotches; was it crabs or a male-insecurity thing?

'Are you still with me?' Paul asked.

'Yes,' she lied.

'I thought you'd dropped off. I know how exhausting shopping can be.'

La Mamounia's loungers weren't the kind where you could feel the bars through the thin mattress. Jenny rolled onto her side to face her newly designated fiancé. 'Spare me the sarcasm,' she said.

'I wasn't being sarcastic.'

'Yes, you were.'

'We're having a row and we haven't been engaged five minutes.'

'Who says we're engaged?'

'Aren't we?'

'I suppose we are. So - where's the ring? I want *diamonds*.'

'Shall we look for one here? In the souk?'

'They'll sell us glass as diamonds. Let's leave it till after your next trip and look in London. Or I could come with you to Paris next month.'

'Okay, whatever. I love you, by the way.'

'Yeah,' she said, consciously borrowing her answer, 'me too.'

She didn't love him. But she liked him, and that might be enough. Most of the time he was like a randy teenager – a throwback to Craig and Kevin. His lovemaking was still clumsy but he was always up for it – way up. She enjoyed his company in front of the TV, although he could be hard work when he got going on politics or the environment. Jenny found it hard to care about Iraq or Afghanistan. 'You'll care when the price of oil hits $100 a barrel and it's costing you eighty quid to fill your car,' Paul had said. 'No I won't,' she'd replied. 'It's only money.'

Their drinks arrived. As the waiter bent down to set them on the low table there was movement within the Ali Baba pants. Jenny wondered if he was in the league the Brighton size-queens dreamt of. As if he could read her mind he gave her a Wouldn't-you-like-to-know smile.

Paul slurped his beer. 'When shall we do it?'

'*Now* if you like.'

'Can we do that – get married in Marrakech?'

'Sorry, babes, I wasn't thinking about the wedding. I

was thinking about – honeymoon action.'

'You want some right now?' Just like that a stiffie tented his shorts.

'Yeah.' After this honeymoon the wedding was likely to be an anticlimax.

'Shall we finish our drinks first?'

'We can take them with us.'

Paul held his towel over his shorts as they hastened to their room. The tall waiter watched them leave; dark, hawk-like eyes. He wanted her. Good. She liked to feel wanted. Back at their room she went at Paul in a frenzy, using her hands and her mouth as if they were weapons. She knew he had a vision of himself as an almost-rapist, because of the girl he'd jumped at college and the undertaker's daughter whose pantyhose he'd pushed up her crack. Jenny tried to show him what rape was like. Of course fantasy rape totally turned him on. Jenny licked him from his neck to his ankles. She drew the line at toe-kissing, but not at licking the furry crack of his bum, something Baxter had egged her into doing. (She could never have done it with Fintan for whom fragrant, fore or aft, was not exactly the word.) No more Sixty-Eights: she came abruptly, briefly, with Paul's tongue on her clitoris and his cock deep in her throat.

After a cuddly snooze on the double lounger on their private terrace they shared a jacuzzi, cool in the sultry air of late afternoon. With only the water to ease the friction Jenny rode him slowly and vocally to one of the most intense orgasms of her life. Riding him she was riding Fintan again and Baxter and Kevin and Craig, all the boys and men she'd ever had and all those who would never have her (waiters, pool-boys, the masseur in the hotel spa, leering shopkeepers in the kasbah) - especially not now that she was going to become Mrs Paul Barrett, the sweet-as-candy little bride of Arsewipe, aka Boredom-on-Sea.

'Hello, Rachel.'

'Paul? Where are you? It sounds like a football stadium?'

'I'm in the departure lounge at Rabat Airport.'

'Where's that?'

'Morocco. It's where my uncle buys most of our

199

leather.'

'I bet you're even warmer than we are.'

'We've been baking by the hotel pool. Jenny's here too. Guess what. We just got engaged!'

'Did you now?...You don't think we're all too young to be buying into this whole middle-class and married culture?'

'Did you and Richard do it?'

'No, we've put it off till Christmas. He's coming out of *EastEnders* next month and going into a West End play.'

'Tell him "Break a leg" from me!'

'Yeah, right. And you ask your Jenny to invite me to her hen night!'

'Ask her yourself! She'll be back from Duty Free any minute. Another year's supply of perfume.'

'Paul, I've got to go. I'm at work, and they need me.'

'Where are you working?'

'A local kindergarten.'

'Isn't that what Diana was doing – pre Charles?'

'That's right. If young William comes calling, Richard will find he's been stood up! Must go. Listen – congratulations, and good luck with your Jenny.'

You too – with Richard. Give Simon a hug.'

Aunt Mary turned out to have upstaged their engagement by attempting to disinter Uncle William. Swearing like a *Big Brother* inmate, she was now incarcerated in a care home for geriatric loonies. Paul said, in front of Mummy and Jack, that he was pretty sure there wasn't a genetic factor in necrophilia. Jack found this grimly amusing. Mummy did not.

Jenny and Paul wanted a quiet registry-office wedding. Mummy did not. Having gone into overdrive in the run-up to Joanna's wedding, it was hyper-drive this time. *Tout* 'Pembertown' would have to be invited, from the Mayor and Lord and Lady Whatnot, the town's top citizens, down to Jack's handyman/lorry-driver and his receptionist wife. Paul didn't invite his father's relations or any of his high-school friends but he too wanted some folk from the factory; Mummy put her foot down when he nominated the receptionist's stepson as best man.

Jack, whose only role was to walk his stepdaughter down the aisle of St Agnes's and pay for everything, seemed subdued since Morocco. Was he upset about Aunt Mary, or was he worried about the cost of this second wedding? Jenny and Paul didn't need a house, especially not in some pseudo-Georgian Sussex version of a Florida condominium. She was trying to talk Paul into selling his parents' house and buying a penthouse in Brighton. Jack could sign his flat over to them to give their funds a boost. Paul needed a more upscale car than the Peugeot, and Jenny's BMW was two years old. Jack couldn't be less generous to his younger stepdaughter. He gave Jenny the deeds to his flat plus a cheque for £200,000. His and hers BMW sports models (Paul retained the Peugeot for his company driving). Jenny sensed that her fiancé, as nephew *and* son-in-law, would end up with career advantages over Michael.

Mummy expected her second daughter to tour the London fashion houses for a dress whose maker would be mentioned in the local papers and *Sussex Life* and *The Tatler*. Jenny went to Brighton where a girl she'd been at college with was making a name as a hot new designer. The dress she sketched for Jenny was off the shoulder and off-white, which Jenny felt was particularly apt for an off-virgin. Mummy hated it, which was the clincher.

Aunt Mary further sabotaged Mummy's plans by going into a decline and then selfishly dying at the end of August, ten days before the wedding which now took place in the same week, at the same church, as her funeral. Jenny wore a black number from Harvey Nicks to her not-to-be-mother-in-law's memorial service but didn't go to the second re-opening of Uncle William's grave. The Devon and Dorset Barretts had to be invited to Saturday's wedding.

Sussex Life duly photographed the slinky off-white number from Brighton; *The Tatler* declined to report the occasion, which otherwise went pretty well according to plan. The day was warm and dry. They'd hired the same marquee as at last year's tenth-anniversary bash and the same caterers. Jack's speech was too long, Paul's too short. The groom got drunk but not enough to misbehave. Jenny had to dance with him (two left feet when it came to ballroom) and with her stepfather and her brother-in-law, Mummy's nominee for best man. Jenny's best partner was Charlie Turner who was light on his feet and had a semi-erection of Arabian promise. Jack also danced with Mummy and Joanna; with his secretary who always reminded Jenny of Miss Marple; with Mrs Turner whose scarlet dress was runner-up in the foxy-frock stakes; and with a ghastly factory bimbo called Saffron (Paul also danced with her) who was dressed like a Cabbage-Patch doll. Jim Turner, ostensibly squiring this creature, got drunk enough to paw one of the bridesmaids (a Dixon niece); Cousin Lorna pushed him off the ha-ha and he and the bimbo were taken off by his father.

The new Mrs Barrett was flown to Rome for a three-day honeymoon. *Shopping and Fucking*! Italy was off-limits to British furniture-makers, but Paul was to take his pitch to Germany, Switzerland and the Benelux countries. From Rome he flew to Berlin. September and October were busy months for all salesmen, desperate to get their wares into shops ahead of the December feeding frenzy.

Jenny was used to his absences. She needed time and space to do her own thing – or do nothing. Hedonism could be repetitive – beauty treatments, the gym, swimming in Jack's pool – but she could escape boredom (and Boredom) by driving to Brighton or taking the train to London. No reason to look for a job now. Mummy did good works. Joanna had her horses and her dogs. Jenny shopped, read magazines, kept Blockbuster and Starbucks solvent.

Married life.

They'd been married less than a month when Jenny discovered there was another woman in his life.

Store buyers didn't want to meet reps at the weekend, so he always came home from Wherever on Friday evening. Jenny tended not to have a delicious meal waiting to be conjured out of the oven; they would fuck, order delivery pizza or Chinese, watch a movie, fuck some more. Saturdays: flat-hunting in Brighton, food shopping, a restaurant dinner, more bed action. Sundays they lunched at the Grange or at Joanna's, or the others might come to them for lunch. Jenny didn't enjoy cooking, but she could do an acceptable roast.

On the first Friday in October he came back in Mr Grumpy mode from a week in south-west France in which he'd taken no new orders and even had a previous one cancelled. His lovemaking that night was at less than the usual Cape Kennedy thrust, which Jenny attributed to his sour mood. She ended up faking it and had the feeling he might have too.

Next morning, while he was showering, the cellphone beeped on the dressing table. Jenny picked it up and opened the message. It wasn't her phone, it was Paul's. The message was from Rachel. Who was she?

No, havnt seen it. Sitter problems. How's the missis? Shopshopshop? xRx

Ah. Rachel was the single mum in Bayswater with the bisexual husband who was in *EastEnders*. Paul had obviously told her his 'missis' liked to shop. Jenny contemplated sending a reply. *Shove it, u sarky cow.*

She didn't send a reply. But she deleted the message.

'That girl's husband wasn't in *EastEnders* last night,' she said in his BMW en route to Brighton for another viewing. 'Have they written him out?'

'She told me he was leaving the show. He's rehearsing a new play.' What a pushover he was.

'You're still in touch with her then?'

'We send each other texts from time to time.' He looked at her for a moment. 'I'm not – seeing her or anything. She's just a friend.'

'Somebody you only met once.'

'Twice, actually.'

'But never shagged?'

'No. I wanted to but she wasn't – ready for it.' Honesty and candour personified. Not enough, Paul.

'But you still send each other texts. Even though she's got a husband.'

'Actually he isn't her husband. They're getting married at Christmas. When the play finishes he's going to take her and Simon to LA. Some US TV work.'

'But you'll still be in touch with her. Texting.'

'I don't know. Maybe.' Another quick glance at Jenny as he accelerated past a tractor pulling hay. 'There's no need to make a – thing out of this.'

'I'm not.' The way she saw it, it was texts today, *soixante-neuf* tomorrow.

203

'I told you, she's just a platonic friend. She's – on the outside of things.'

If they were home Jenny would have thrown something – a cushion – at this point. 'You need that?'

'It's good to have somebody to talk things over with. You know – like a guru. Or a therapist. *You've* had them.'

'Only for my pussy problem. Have you got a problem with your dick?'

'Not any more! Thanks to you, *ma chère*.' Jenny was tempted to borrow a favourite phrase from Baxter's big sister: *blow it out your ass*.

'So, what problems have you been discussing with this – "therapist"?'

'*No problemo*, baby.'

'Can the *Terminator* stuff, Paul.'

'Sorry. And I'm sorry you're upset about Rachel.'

You will be, she promised him. The tension between them hung over the viewing (good size, but overpriced and no view), over lunch, over the remake of *The Italian Job* in a cinema filled with chavs who cheered the dramatic high points as if they were goals. They went to the early evening showing and then dined in an Italian restaurant, also overpriced. Jenny only allowed herself one main meal a day; she ate a Caesar Salad while Paul, also supposedly dieting, demolished a hefty main-course pasta. More strained small-talk.

She went to bed before him, leaving him to watch a horror schlock on DVD. This had happened before. Usually he woke her with his tongue or a probing hard-on. Tonight he didn't.

Trouble in paradise.

On Monday he flew to Spain. Still thinking about the text, about his therapist, his 'guru', Jenny drove over to The Grange and dug a discarded cellphone out of a drawer in her bedroom. Removing the SIM-card, she inserted it in her current phone, paged through Contacts. And there he was. She wrote the number down and swapped SIM-cards again. Had he changed his number, as she had when she switched networks? She keyed and waited. The voice was familiar, painfully familiar.

'Who's this?'

'Jenny.'

'Jenny Who?' The pain intensified.

'Jenny Dixon.' Time to explain Jenny Barrett later – or not.

'From Brighton?'

'Near enough.'

'To what do I owe the etcetera?'

'I thought I'd see how you're getting on – you know, without me.'

He laughed. 'Oh, Jenny, my Jenny.' Something in her opened up, like a sunlit flower. Paul wasn't the only push-over. 'You should know there's been quite a lot of murky water under this ramshackle old bridge.'

'I kind of expected that. Are you married?' Cut to the chase.

'No I'm not, but lately I have taken to specializin' in married ladies. You might not think so, but there are a lot less complications with married ladies.'

'Fintan,' she said, 'this is going to be your lucky day.'

16. The Mistress's Tale

'You've got to stop doing this,' she told him. 'If Jack knew you were buying me champagne...' This didn't sound right. 'On your expenses,' she added.

'I'm not fiddling my expenses. This is out of my own funds.'

'You're supposed to spend your money on Jennifer. She doesn't come cheap, as I'm sure you already know.' The whole factory knew Paul had been dating Jennifer since his dad died. The upholsterers were making bets on how long it would last. Jack had indicated to Christine that he too had reservations.

'Well, I can still afford to buy bubbly for my favourite member of the staff,' Paul said.

Christine hoped she wasn't blushing. 'Oh, is that me?'

He pretended to think for a moment. 'I suppose it's a toss-up – too close to call – between you and *Saffron*!'

He laughed as she threatened to throw the bottle at him. A different brand from last time, another unheard-of producer. Jack always ordered Mumms or Moët & Chandon. But this wasn't just cheap sparkling, and a bottle of anything from a handsome young man was to be savoured. Sitting at her console she mimed a curtsey and he flourished an invisible hat in an elaborate bow before taking the stairs at a run.

Jack came to the house that night. Charlie was on the road. Christine poured wine, bought and chilled in Jack's honour. He glugged the first glass. He went at wine the same way he went at her, like an animal at a trough.

'Where'd you get this?'

206

'Sainsbury's. Sauvignon.' She didn't tell him it was on special offer, £6.99 down to £3.50. Jack rarely paid less than £10 for a bottle of wine, but Christine saw no need to re-invest what she considered hard-earned money in expensive wines for his benefit. She and Charlie happily drank plonk.

'Jennifer's coming to Morocco with me and Paul next week,' Jack said. Small talk before they got down to business.

'Not in the same league as Mustique, is it? Not many designer shops in the – what's it called - kasbah.'

'She'll find something. Or she can just stay by the pool. And I'm sending them on to the Mamounia for the week-end. It's out of this world.'

She knew he'd taken Agnes there. Some mistresses would grumble, *You don't take me*. Christine said nothing. She had no desire to spend any more time with him than was necessary to earn her 'other' salary. He now said:

'I thought you and I could spend a night in London before I come home.'

'That hotel in Bayswater?' Popular with Arabs, its corridors so thronged with hookers you needed lollipop ladies to control access to the lifts.

'I think the one by the Tower is nicer, don't you?'

American tourists, overweight and loud. But yes, a lesser evil. 'Much nicer,' she agreed.

He glugged a second glass. Getting down to business, Christine got down on her knees. He liked that. He also liked to do her from behind, doggy-style. Sometimes they did both. Tonight the kneeling session was enough, which was a relief. With his nephew still on her mind, she tried not to think how handsome Paul was and how repulsive his uncle. Jack's repulsiveness was neither here nor there.

Christine's mother would have loved Paul, loved his Cary Grant cleft chin. Christine was raised on Cary Grant movies. 'He's the only man I might leave your dad for,' Mum used to say, probably oftener than was strictly necessary. In the event the man she left Dad for was a lorry driver, the one who fell asleep on the A22 and so totally crushed her brown Mini that it took the firemen and paramedics several hours to remove all of her from the wreckage.

Before leaving Jack gave her the usual cheque. After

she closed the front door behind him Christine ran to the cloakroom and gargled the taste of him out of her throat.

Christine tried, not always successfully, to think of her subsidiary employment as adultery rather than prostitution. And if a whore was what she was, she hadn't set out to become one.

Like Jim, she'd been mostly raised by a stepmother. She was eight when her mother died, the same age at which Jim was to lose his. Both women died at 31 and both their husbands remarried two years later. The similarities ended there. Christine had come to love Linda, her stepmother, almost as quickly as Jim had come to despise his. Linda once said that calling Jim a 'rough diamond' was a bit rough on diamonds.

Raising a stepdaughter in the late 1970s, the transitional years between the age of permissiveness and the era of excess, Linda had been neither over- nor underprotective. She and Christine's dad had two more children. In her teens Christine liked it when people thought Linda was her big sister; Linda liked it too. She helped Christine get on the Pill, told her about condoms and sexual diseases, and about orgasms. Christine told Linda about her boyfriends, which one was a good kisser, which one tried to go a bit further and which one too far.

One who was a good kisser – and tried to go too far – was Charlie Turner. Christine was fifteen.

'He's too old for you,' Linda said.

'He's only twenty,' Christine protested.

'A van driver.'

'What's wrong with that? He's a mechanic as well. Self-taught.'

'If you're looking for a husband, you can do better than that.'

'And I'm sure I will.' She resisted the temptation to point out that Linda (a hairdresser specializing in perms for the elderly) had married a gas fitter.

'You should go out with boys your own age,' Linda said.

'What do you think I've been doing?' Christine retorted crossly.

'Older men only want one thing.'

'It's the same thing the young ones want.'

'He'll just do you and dump you.'

208

'Well, he hasn't done me yet,' said Christine tartly. Charlie was the first 'older man' in her young life and the first of any age who had money to spend and liked to spend it. Small-town boys of fifteen and sixteen are mostly reliant on pocket money and Saturday jobs. Christine's own Saturday job was sweeping up and shampooing in the salon that employed her stepmother.

Virginity, in 1979, was not a much-prized treasure, but Christine wasn't quite ready to let go of hers. Charlie dumped her. Before the week was out she saw him at the cinema with a girl from Pembertons. She knew the girl worked at Pembertons because Christine's date was one of the furniture factory's carpenters. Not such a big spender as Charlie and a clumsy kisser.

Leaving school at sixteen, she began an apprenticeship under Linda's boss, at a different salon from the one her stepmother now managed. One day a week Christine spent at the local technical college where the latest styles were examined and tested. But her heart wasn't in hair and neither, always, was her head. Doreen, her employer and mentor, who came from plain-speaking stock like Linda, warned her that she needed to focus a bit more on this morning's dye-job and a lot less on last night's blowjob. After a few months Doreen sacked her. The Job Centre sent her to be interviewed for a receptionist post at a small local factory that made surgical appliances. The least quailfied of five applicants, Christine was the youngest and the prettiest. She got the job. Again there was Day Release once a week so that she could learn to take dictation and use an electric typewriter.

At seventeen she dated her first married man and let her virginity go. Peter. He was thirty, manager of his own office-cleaning company. He told her he was married (she knew there were others who kept it under their hats), separated, waiting for his divorce. He told her loved her, would marry her when he was free. She fell for it, fell for him; let him have his way, have her. It wasn't unduly painful; it wasn't unduly nice. It got nicer after a couple of goes. Then Peter told her he was sorry, but his wife wanted *them* to give it one more go.

'I thought you loved me,' she said. Awful to find your-self talking like the people in soaps and magazine fiction.

'I do. I always will,' he replied in similar vein. 'But I

have to try and make things work for the sake of Scott and Kirsty.' His kids. This would become a familiar song as other Peters passed through her life.

'Why can't you steer clear of married men?' Linda scolded her.

'He seemed so nice.'

'They always do when they're after something. But once they get it, they start to take you for granted.'

'How do you know? Have you been having affairs?'

'No, Chrissie, but I do live with a married man. Your father. Talk about taking you for granted.'

'But you don't think Dad's been off having affairs?'

'No, your dad's cut from a different cloth than – what's his name? – Paul.'

'Peter.'

After Peter there was Matt, then Desmond, a driving instructor who gave her free lessons, then another Peter with kids called Scott and Delia. The names changed (not always) but not the scenario. A nice man showed her a nice time. They had sex in his car or (more rarely) in a hotel bedroom. He gave her a gift or two. Married men tried to be generous within the limitations imposed by their salary, mortgages, school extras, riding lessons, etc, etc. Then they got a guilty conscience and went back to their wives or traded you in for a new girlfriend. Painful, but it hurt a bit less every time. After Linda said 'I told you so' once too often, Christine stopped confiding in her.

She went to London on Saturday and shopped in Knightsbridge. A lot of people said Harrods was like an Egyptian bazaar these days, but she still liked it. She even liked the outlandish hieroglyphs on the escalators – Cleopatra would surely have had just such escalators in her palace had they been invented. The basement shrine to Diana and Dodi was perhaps a tad over-the-top, but people fell reverently silent as they approached it.

Nothing took her fancy on the fashion floor, so she walked up to Harvey Nicholls and almost immediately found a stunning red dress by a new designer they were launching. Micro-thin shoulder straps and a scooped skirt, it looked like something Michelle Pfeiffer, her favourite movie-star, might wear. £800 on the plastic, four times what Jack had given her on Monday. Hopefully he would be extra generous after the night in London. Not that she was looking forward to the occasion.

The last time she'd had a vivid red dress Nassim had paid for it in the Al-Whoever-it-was Mall, Bahrain's answer to Harrods. A scarlet dress for a Scarlet Woman. Did people still think in those terms? Linda didn't, but Christine had the feeling her mother would have.

Married Peter Number Three had a gay brother who was a flight attendant with Gulf Air in Bahrain. 'If you're ready for a change of job, Arabs are really hot for blondes,' Peter told her.

'Be a flying waitress? No way.'

'It's a nice life. Good money. Lots of travel. Meet interesting people.'

'I don't think so,' she said. But after Peter Number Three went down the well-trodden wife-beaten path of Numbers One and Two, she decided it might be time to broaden her horizons, spread her wings. She got Gulf Air's address from Directory Enquiries and took a day off to go to London. Their offices were off Piccadilly. The woman she was referred to in Recruitment was immodestly dressed for an Arab, a deep-blue dress with deep-brown cleavage.

Having left school without any GCSEs, Christine learned she was ineligible to become a flying waitress. 'I'm sorry,' the woman said. 'We have to make a high standard. There is much *theory* in training programme. For safety procedures the passing mark is 100 percent.'

'Oh well,' said Christine, who thought airhostesses were just bottle-blonde airheads (a description which she knew applied equally well to her), 'it looks like I'm meant to stay a receptionist.'

'You do word-processor?'

'Yes.' Almost true. She now used an electronic typewriter with spellcheck.

'My husband brother is from Saudi but he has import-export business in Bahrain.' She said 'Bahrain' with a kind of gasp in the middle: 'Bahh-rain'. 'He is looking for English receptionist. You like to try this position?'

Christine realized there was an element of risk to this. The woman might be recruiting her into the sex industry. Arabs had famously voracious appetites. Well, she was practically a sex worker already, subject to the whims of the married men she dated. Marriage, if she went down that road, would be another kind of sexual slavery.

'Yes,' she said with almost no hesitation.

'I will tell my husband brother. You can go to Bahrain for interview him?'

'Yes,' Christine said again. And she did, one week later. Linda told her she was mad, but her father was supportive: 'Go for it. Get out of this dead hole. Have a life. You'll meet more interesting people out there.'

'Sex-mad Ay-rabs,' said Linda. 'You'll come to a sticky end.'

'She can come to a sticky end here,' Dad pointed out. 'Marry some oik.'

Her interview was on Saturday, which was a working day in Arabia after their one-day weekend on Friday. She took Friday off and was booked to fly back on Sunday. But it would be a year before she returned.

Her future employer met her at Arrivals, holding a sheet of copy-paper with her name on it. His sister-in-law had sent her a photo of him in Arabic robes with two small boys in school uniform. Today he wore a dark-grey suit. He was in his late forties, light oak in colouring, with a full head of jet-black hair going grey at the sides. He was plump, neither tall nor handsome although he had a wide full-lipped mouth and beautiful teeth. She thought it would be nice to kiss him.

'Hello, Christine.'

'Hello, Mr al-'

'Please, you must call me Nassim.' Another gleaming smile. She knew that he fancied her; the job was hers, however dismal her word-processing skills.

Through the airlock doors the heat of early-evening Arabia hit her like a furnace blast. Early-morning Heathrow, in late May, had been cold and wet. His car was a Toyota Landcruiser, with arctic air-conditioning. He took her to a hotel more luxurious than anything she'd seen in Benidorm and Majorca. The atrium had a waterfall and what must be a million pounds worth of marble. Christine felt as if she was in Hollywood – or Bollywood.

Nassim waited in the bar while she followed a Filipino porter up to her room, showered and changed into a white Marilyn Monroe dress from Next with a pleated skirt and a plunging neckline that might be a bit daring for the Middle

East. No fears on that score. The hotel restaurant was full of under- and overdressed young Western women with Arab men, mostly Nassim's age or older.

Over dinner he told her he had 'many businesses' in Saudi Arabia and Bahrain but didn't say what these were. He was obviously very rich. He wore a watch with diamonds round the face and a ring crusted with diamonds; she'd never seen diamonds on a man. He didn't touch on her qualifications or lack of. He asked about her life in Sussex, and about her family. She told him about her dad and Linda and the car crash that had killed her mother. He wanted to hear about her stepbrothers who seemed like aliens to Christine, not yet teenagers and interested in weird boy stuff.

'I have sons,' he said.

'How many?'

'Many.' Many sons, many businesses. Why was he so vague? Then he gave her one specific: he had *three* wives in Saudi, all in a 'compound' in a town called Dammam.

'Don't they fight?'

'Fighting is forbidden. Each one has a house with her children.'

She couldn't imagine his life. 'Can you have more than three wives?' she asked.

'Four is permitted. With divorces, more than four.'

'You have divorced wives?'

He shook his head. 'No. Ex-wives are a big headache.' The teeth flashed. 'Are you married or divorced, Christine?'

'Give me a chance!' she said. 'I'm still single. I'm only nineteen.'

'My youngest wife is nineteen. She has four of my children. You don't want children?'

The truth was she didn't. 'There'll be time for that,' she said.

'You have a boyfriend?'

'Not right now.' Next moment she found herself telling him about the married men she'd dated.

'Why do you fuck married men?'

She blushed at his casual use of the f-word. 'It just sort of happened,' she said. 'They asked me, and I let them.'

'I will ask you also,' he said. No flashing of the teeth; he was serious. 'But not tonight. Tonight you are tired from your journey.'

Actually she wasn't. But there seemed to be no need to rush things. Walking her to the bank of lifts, which travelled outside the walls instead of inside, he pushed some money into her hand.

'In case you want to buy anything in the morning,' he said. 'I will come for you at nine and show you my office and the place where you will live.'

She couldn't imagine shopping before nine a.m. He bared the teeth again as the lift doors started to close. She waved down at his miniaturizing figure. In her room she opened the wad of money. Red notes with a palm tree and a picture of the Ruler's jowly head crowned with an elaborate headband. The currency was called dinars. She now had 500 of them: she discovered next day that he'd given her the equivalent of approximately £800 sterling.

Jack gave her a thousand pounds in dollars for the night in London on his way back from Morocco, where he'd left Paul and Jenny to go on to the fabulous hotel in Marrakech. She had to work for the money. Four sex sessions between checking-in and checking-out. He went at her like a newly released prisoner. Her jaw ached, and so did her thingy.

The hotel near the Tower was nice if not swank by Bahrain standards. The bar and restaurant overlooked Tower Bridge whose reflected lights danced on the river's black surface. Jack seemed to think Paul and Jenny were getting serious. Christine had no illusions about herself – a gold-digging adulteress (with a doting hunk of a husband) – and none about Jennifer: a premier-league maneater. The news had reached her stepmother who sometimes did Mary Barrett's hair. Linda said that Paul was too good for Jennifer; Christine agreed.

Jack was about to learn that he'd flown home to a bombshell: Mary, who was his sister and Paul's mother, had been found in the cemetery trying to dig up her husband's grave. Over breakfast he dropped a bombshell of his own.

'Marry me,' he said. Christine's heart briefly stopped.

'What about Agnes?' The obvious thing to ask. He said he would divorce her, that Agnes was a cold-hearted bitch (like mother, like daughter). He expected Christine to divorce Charlie. She said no to that but let him think she would think about it. She did think about it. Jack, she knew, could guarantee her a good life. Whatever happened to the furniture business (the feeling in the factory was that the competition would do for them sooner or later), his property developments had secured his old age and his stepdaughters' futures. It would be her rather than Agnes sharing his retirement dream between Sussex and the Caribbean.

But it could never happen. She didn't love him, didn't really even like him. He was only interested in money, his businesses. She had never let him kiss her, that horrible blubbery mouth of his, like an octopus. But he wasn't the only man she'd had sex with without kissing.

She couldn't leave Charlie. She loved Charlie. He loved her. Leave him and marry Jack! As if she could or would.

Still, it was nice to be asked.

She'd thought on seeing Nassim that it would be nice to kiss him. She never found out. Perhaps Arab men don't kiss their mistresses; only the other stuff.

And the other stuff wasn't good. Stripped of his London-tailored suits or his robes he was obscenely hairy, werewolf-hairy. And he finished too quickly. Even if he did her three or four times in succession, he finished as quickly on the last time as on the first. It might be just as well. His you-know-what was bigger than anybody's in Sussex and would have hurt her if it stayed in for any longer. There were probably women who liked men with big you-know-whats but Christine preferred one that was a bit more manageable.

Linked to Saudi Arabia by a brand-new twenty-mile causeway, Bahrain served the Holy Kingdom as a recreational resort. Sex and drinking were the main recreations. Christine had indeed been recruited to the sex industry. Nassim did her in the office as well as at the flat. In his own country he could be hanged for adultery and Christine deported or even (had she not been a westerner) stoned. It thrilled her to be living in an environment that was simultaneously medieval and modern.

A 'middle man' for everything from Kashmiri carpets to vacant shops in the city's malls and plots of land in the suburbs, Nassim only required Christine to be in the office when he had clients visiting. He sometimes brought letters

215

prepared by Indian secretaries in his office in Dammam and had her rewrite them in less Victorian English. Out went *I remain, Sir, Your humble and obedient servant* and in came *Yours sincerely*.

The office was in a brand-new high-rise in Manama's diplomatic quarter. The flat he gave her was in an area called Zinj, a 30-year-old 5-storey block whose render was cracked and stained, its aluminium window-frames caked with salt or limescale. The lift was often out-of-order. The flat was on the top floor, furnished with clumsy Egyptian copies of classic English designs.

Nassim had instructed her not to talk about him to anybody. After that first night he never again took her to a restaurant. The only friends she made were Karen and Phil, a stewardess-turned-travel agent and her husband who worked for a local English newspaper; they lived in Christine's building. She told them she was divorced and let them think she'd been abused, more mentally than physically; nursing her wounds, she wasn't ready yet for a new relationship. A Gulf Air captain, in the throes of his own divorce, flirted with her at a couple of Karen's parties. He had a rough-around-the-edges quality that reminded her of Charlie Turner, but she couldn't afford to jeopardize her meal ticket. Nassim was cheating on his wives but a mistress had a duty to be faithful, didn't she?

'Christine's a Woman of Mystery,' said Jeremy, a gay steward (not Peter's brother) who was a regular at Karen's parties. His intonation supplied capitals.

'Woman of mystery, my arse,' scoffed Tiffany, a stewardess from North London. 'She's shaggin' a rag'ead, same as you an' me is.' Hard to believe that Tiffany had achieved the necessary grades during recruitment and training. Christine assumed a theatrically mysterious expression which got a laugh from the other guests. She knew they talked about her behind her back.

Jeremy had been with the airline for eighteen months. He had a steady Bahraini boyfriend – 'and quite a few unsteady ones,' he admitted. Tiffany had come to Bahrain two months ago aiming to capitalize on its citizens' well-known weakness for Western nookie. Already boasting several Arab merchant 'escorts', she was saving for breast implants. She and Jeremy regaled Karen's guests with scandalous tales of the Shaikhs and their stewardess harems. Nassim was not amused when Christine tried to pass these stories on to him.

At the other end of the Gulf there was war between Iran and Iraq. People were dying, civilians as well as soldiers. Mines drifted all the way to Bahrain; ships were blown up, planes and helicopters shot down. But Saddam Hussein's military adventures had little impact on the daily life of the island's expats.

In the wilting heat of Arabia, where the beach blistered your feet, where adulterers faced the threat of barbaric punishments, Christine – a professional adulteress - felt more liberated than she had in Sussex. Her job paid twenty times better than the surgical appliance factory; she could shop till she dropped; she had an air-conditioned flat and a car of her own; she had a lover who plied her with gifts as well as money: bracelets, earrings, necklaces. She'd got used to his hairy back and the breakneck pace of his lovemaking; she'd even got used to his oversized you-know-what. Perhaps, like her horizons, her thingy was expanding. Sometimes she even managed to come off with him.

'My little concubine,' he called her. And: 'my English peasant girl.'

One day in December she ran into him in a shopping mall. A half-pace behind him was a woman swathed in black, her face hidden behind a mask like Batman's; presumably one of his wives. A narrowing of Nassim's eyes as she moved towards him told Christine he didn't wish to be acknowledged and she went into the nearest shop instead, his wife unmet, un-introduced.

A year – nearly to the day – after her arrival in Bahrain, he told her she must go back to Mrs Thatcher's now dis-United Kingdom. 'I was only allowed to take you on for three months, and after a year the Immigration Department won't give you another extension.'

'I thought you cared for me.' She still had no source of reference other than romantic fiction or TV drama for dealing with being dumped.

'I'm very fond of you, Christine,' he said. His command of English was infuriatingly good. 'But I have no influence over these matters.'

'I don't want to go home.' She began to cry.

'I'm sorry, but you have to.'

He'd just changed his car for another Landcruiser, bigger. Perhaps he would replace her with a girl with enhanced breasts; she hoped it wouldn't be Tiffany. He'd offered to pay for implants but Christine didn't fancy the surgery and was in any case happy being a 36C.

'I have found a job for you in London. With one of my friends.'

'I don't care,' she sobbed. Jeremy would have called her a 'drama queen'.

But she did care. He was passing her on like taking a discarded suit or an unwanted gift to the charity shop. At 20 she was being traded in.

She didn't tell Charlie about Jack's proposal at the Tower of London. Not to make a secret of it – or a big thing. He knew she had spent a night with their employer, but he'd never wanted to know the details.

Between his sister going doolally at the beginning of July and then dying in the middle of August, Jack made fewer calls than usual on Christine's sexual services. He didn't mention marriage again; it must have been a moment of impulse, an aberration.

Paul and Jennifer had come back from Marrakech engaged. In spite of this and his mother's disintegration Paul continued to bring Christine champagne whenever he took his car across the Channel.

'You really shouldn't be doing this,' she reminded him.

'I'm afraid I really have to,' he replied with one of his cheeky grins that reminded her of Charlie when he was younger, or even of his tearaway son.

Two weeks and two bottles later, when she thanked him for her wedding invitation, he said, 'Aunt Agnes did all the invites.'

'Why on earth would Agnes invite *me*?' Jack had wondered whether Agnes knew who his mistress was, but she wouldn't invite her to a family wedding – would she?

'Search me,' Paul said. 'I wanted your Jim to be my best man, but she knocked that on the head pretty smartly. I've got to have Michael instead. I did insist on Jim being invited though, and I made him ask *Saffron* – just to get my own back on Aunt Agnes!'

'Well, I'm still amazed to be asked.'

'Isn't it obvious? Jack invited you.'

'I hardly think so. I'm only the receptionist.'

'Yeah.' Paul laughed: a knowing, almost nasty laugh. Once again Christine experienced a sensation she could only compare to impending cardiac arrest.

'You *know*?' It was barely a question.

He nodded, switching off the laughter as if turning a tap. Christine felt her skin warm at the shame of her 'other' life being known to this handsome young man who regularly brought her ignoble brands of champagne from his travels.

'Who told you? Jim?'

He nodded again.

'Who else has he told?'

'Nobody, I'm pretty sure.'

'And who've you told?'

'Nobody. I swear, Chris.' His voice sounded hoarse. It also sounded as if it was important that she believe him, that it was true. She took a deep breath.

'He promised his dad to keep it under his hat. Why would he tell you? Was he drunk?'

'Yes, but I don't think that's why he told me.' He hesitated. 'He needed to – unburden himself, and I'm the first person he felt – close enough to.'

'You must think I'm pretty disgusting.'

'I don't think you're disgusting. I'm in no position to be judgemental. I've done some things that might shock *you*.'

'How old are you? Nineteen?' He nodded again. 'What can you possibly have done at nineteen that might shock *me*? All the usual teenage stuff.'

'Jim and I gangbanged some girls in the spring. Germans. And a Spanish one.'

'I can see what you meant about getting close,' she said grimly. 'But I've got a feeling that's what young guys do these days.'

Paul was silent a moment. Then he said: 'I almost raped a girl at University. She cut short her sabbatical and went home - because of me.'

He looked stricken as he told her his big dark secret. Christine wondered what a 'sabbatical' was.

'I'm sure she'll have got over it,' she said tritely. 'Girls do at that age. *I* had to get over things.'

'But, if she hadn't stopped me I would have - *raped* her.' His guilt made him insistent.

'I'm sure you didn't mean to,' she said. This was even more trite. *There-there, never mind, dear.* Like a mother. A rapist's mother.

Mr Khan came through the front door, back from the bank. Paul switched his expression to neutral, greeted the accounts manager and followed him to the stairs. He threw a casual 'See you later, Chris' over his shoulder, but halfway up he turned and gave her a quick intense look with a finger to his lips. She thought he was sending her a kiss, then realized it was a vow of silence. She saw his confession as another gift, like the champagne, a part-exchange for the secret her stepson had recklessly divulged.

Nassim's friend owned, among other enterprises, a restaurant on the Edgware Road in the heart of London's growing Arab quarter. A year ago Christine had baulked at the idea of applying to be a flying waitress; now she was a non-flying one, feet firmly, achingly, on the ground. Technically she was the maître d', but her duties included serving alcohol and coffee; she felt like a waitress.

Omar, her new boss, supplied her with a tiny studio flat in a square near Lancaster Gate, in a building his brother owned. The rent - £525 a month, very reasonable for W2 – was deducted from her wages. Most months she made this back in tips. She made a great deal more out of the cash 'gifts' from the men she went out with and was done by. Omar, happily married to a beautiful Palestinian in her twenties, never laid a hand on her but he made it clear that servicing some of his diners was an unwritten term in Christine's contract.

'A happy customer will eat here again – maybe many times,' he said. Hairdresser Doreen had had a similar homily, but Christine had never been expected to have lesbian sex with the blue-rinse dowagers of East Sussex.

She had to service one or two diners a week, Arabs from all over the Middle East; most were more than twice her age. As Jeremy had said in Bahrain, sex with Arabs was 'wham, bam, *shukran*, ma'am – and you don't always get a *shukran*.' There was often a battle to make them wear protection. Some were quicker and rougher than Nassim, but at least they were always clean; evidently for Muslims cleanliness was next to ungodliness. Belatedly

Christine found herself empathising with Tiffany.

She had never liked the haggling that was supposed to be part of the Arab way of life. If they gave her £50 she accepted it with good grace, but most gave her between £150 and £250. Easy come, easy go: she spent a huge amount on clothes, now buying from higher-end stores. The lack of closet space in her flat forced her to throw out clothes as fast she bought them. She passed some of the less extravagant outfits on to Linda, but she didn't want her stepmother to realize how well-paid she was and ask awkward questions.

There were questions anyway. 'When are we going to meet your boyfriend?' Linda asked on more than one of Christine's trips home.

'When there's one I feel serious about,' she prevaricated.

'Well, it's about time you got serious, Chrissie. Don't you want to settle down with a husband and children?'

Did she? 'When I find the right man I will.' Would she?

'Are you still going out with married men?'

'Not all the time,' Christine said. This was less shameful than the full truth.

It was easy to be lonely in London and surprisingly hard to make friends. The waitresses at the restaurant came and went, like the clients. Omar and his wife didn't offer hospitality outside work. It was OK going to movies on her own, but you needed company for a concert. She discovered she liked live theatre and saw some memorable productions: *La Cage Aux Folles*, Stephen Sondheim's *Follies*, *Phantom of the Opera* and *Les Miserables*. She liked *Les Mis* so much that she went back twice.

After a wretched fortnight in Lloret de Mar fighting off Spanish waiters and British lager-louts she took all her holidays in Sussex. Now in their mid-teens and girl-oriented, her stepbrothers were less alien and more likeable. Linda was good company when she wasn't nosing into her love life. Dad was on the waiting list for hip replacements.

From Linda and a few former schoolfriends she received updates on some of her ex-boyfriends. One had gone to Australia, one had jumped off the pier for a dare and nearly drowned, another had ended up in jail for stealing cars. One of the married Peters had died of a heart attack at his gym, aged twenty-five. Her driving instructor's wife had run off with a woman. Charlie Turner had married Margaret Wilkinson, who'd been a prefect at their high school; they had a son.

In the summer of 1990 she had a sexual health scare. A rash appeared around her right nipple. The private gynaecologist she consulted in Lancaster Gate, a woman, asked embarrassing questions:

'Has somebody been biting your breasts?'

Christine went red. 'Well – yes.'

'A regular partner or a casual one?'

Christine went redder. 'Casual,' she mumbled.

'Are you a sex worker?

'No, I work in a restaurant.'

'Well, this gentleman needs to improve his oral hygiene. His gums are infected.' Christine remembered an Egyptian with bad teeth. 'He might even have herpes. Did he kiss you or lick your vagina?'

Christine was now as red as a tourist on a Spanish sun-bed. 'No.'

'That's good. If he does have herpes you're not too likely to have caught it from a love bite. You're just a bit sore. I'll give you some cream and a course of antibiotics. Do you practice safe sex?'

'Always,' Christine said emphatically. 'Even for – you know – oral stuff.'

A dozen Arabs later, in August, the month Saddam Hussein invaded Kuwait, a test kit from Boots confirmed the implications of a missed period. So much for safe sex. A condom must have burst or leaked. In a panic she went back to the same doctor who took blood for an HIV test and sent her to a nearby clinic. The abortion cost half of what the twelve Arabs had given her (one of them had given her this frightening bonus). The HIV test came back negative; there was immense relief, but she thought long and hard about the life she was living. She took Layla, Omar's wife, into her confidence. Layla took Omar into *her* confidence. He summoned Christine into his office.

'You tell Layla you want to stop looking after the special customers because of abortion?'

She took a deep breath. 'Yes.'

'You got rid of baby. What's the problem now?'

'The problem is I got pregnant. I could have got Aids.'

222

'You need to take more careful, is all.'

'Taking careful is not enough,' she said, lapsing into his mangled English. 'I don't want to do this any more. It's – dangerous.'

'This now is a very good time for us. All these people running from Kuwait and other countries to London. They come here to eat and they are looking for – other business also. Already there is a lot of money in London.'

'Well, I don't want any of it.'

'If you don't want this business, you cannot work here.' His dark skin did not register anger and he spoke calmly, but she knew he was furious. She was trembling inside but she replied with an equal show of calm:

'Then I'll go. When do you want me to leave?'

'Today. This minute.'

'Okay.' She turned to go.

'And you cannot stay in flat.'

'I don't want to,' she said.

And, just like that, she walked away from her job (both of them) and her pint-sized studio. She took an over-flowing suitcase to the Oxfam shop, returned with it empty; those of her clothes that would be suitable for Sussex and a few mementos of Bahrain and London barely filled it. She took a taxi to Victoria and was at her child-hood home in time for tea, about the time she normally started to think about what dress to change into for the restaurant.

'You can't live here again,' her stepmother told her with a bluntness that rivalled Omar's. 'The boys don't mind sharing for a night or two but they like having their own rooms.'

'I'll get my own place,' Christine said. 'And a job.' Dad found her a job. Saunders the undertakers needed a receptionist. She took a holiday flat near the sea front; before Christmas she bought and furnished a new one-bedroom flat built by Jack Pemberton on the site of an old cinema, paying a twenty-five-percent deposit; mortgage payments were more affordable than rent, although not by much. Her nest egg, never an eagle's, was now a sparrow's. No more Harrods and Fenwick's; now she bought her clothes at Debenhams and Next.

Winter was high season for undertakers. As well as answering the phone and word-processing letters Christine helped out with the customers. Having helped men to feel alive, she was now dealing with them dead or widowed or (most awful) mourning their children.

Even in a funeral home her colleagues propositioned her; she wasn't drawn to men who handled corpses for a living. The bereaved could also be bold. One man asked her out within minutes of choosing his wife's coffin. After the abortion she was ready for a spell of abstinence. She enjoyed family get-togethers and meals with her employer and his wife and their teenage daughter who was love-struck over a boy in her class. Lunching in local cafés she made friends with other office and shop workers and had the occasional girls' night out. Most of all, she relished the sanctuary of her own home.

The local theatre featured a mix of touring professional productions with yesteryear stars and performances by local amateurs. In October Christine saw Shaw's *Pygmalion* put on by pupils and teachers from a school in one of the town's suburbs. The teacher who played Professor Higgins was a terrible ham but the girl and boy playing Eliza and Freddy were appealing and affecting. In the interval bar queue Christine found herself next to an ex-boyfriend who seemed an unlikely patron of serious theatre: Charlie Turner. She knew he'd been widowed earlier in the year, while she was still in London; Saunders had handled the funeral. Charlie was now thirty to her twenty-five. He'd put on some weight, his face was ruddier but still handsome in a farm-boy sort of way and he still had a good head of unruly hair the colour of straw. His teeth were almost as good as Nassim's.

'I heard you were back,' he said. She'd forgotten that he had the Sussex brogue even more than her dad.

'Yes – the bad penny.'

'You said it.' She hadn't forgotten how good he'd been at kissing when she was fifteen and had fewer comparisons.

'I'm sorry you lost Margaret,' she said. His smile faded and she saw a shadow of that raw grief she witnessed every day at work.

'Yeah. Thanks. It's been a hard time.'

'Hard for your boy too. How old is he?'

'Jim's eight. Yes, it's hard for a kid to lose his mother.' The barmaid spoke to him and he ordered two beers.

'What are you drinking?' he asked Christine.

'A spritzer.'

'What's that?'

'I know,' said the barmaid.

'Don't let me keep you from your friend,' Christine said when they had their drinks.

'What friend?'

She pointed. 'Two drinks.'

'Oh, they're both for me. They don't do draught in here.' As if to underline the point he drained most of the first lager in a single swig.

'So, is this drama group from your son's school?'

'No, my sister-in-law teaches there. I get roped in to help build the sets. Margaret made costumes and played the piano when they did musicals.'

'I wish this was a musical.'

'*My Fair Lady*, you mean? Me too. They did that a few years back, when you were in Bahrain.'

'Who told you I was in Bahrain?'

'One of the women at the factory. I work at Pembertons now, doing their deliveries. You were in London for – four years?'

'Nearly five.'

'Why'd you leave? London get too much for you?'

'Something like that.'

'And now you're working for Ted Saunders?'

'Yes.'

'Not a lot of laughs, I suppose.'

She laughed now. 'Hardly!' This dry humour, if that's what it was, was new.

'You seeing anyone?' He'd always been blunt, and forward.

'Not since London.'

'I'm off to Scotland tomorrow. Have dinner with me on Saturday.'

'I'd like that,' she said. She told him later that she already knew he was the man for her, the one she was destined to marry. He would redeem her.

She wore the new red dress to Paul and Jenny's wedding, the only woman there in red and one of the few without a hat. She hated hats. She danced with the groom after he'd done duty by his wife and the bridesmaids.

225

'Jenny's awarded you the prize for the foxiest frock,' he told her as they boogied to 'Night Fever' performed by a local band of ageing rockers. Paul did a college-kid impersonation of John Travolta, lots of arm action, clumsy footwork. Christine had a toned-down disco routine of her own from high school.

'That's a pretty sensational dress *she's* wearing,' she responded to the reported compliment from the bride. Christine still felt that Jennifer was wrong for Paul. 'You look very elegant too.'

He performed one of his cavalier/courtier bows. 'Madam is most kind.'

She boogied again with Michael, the best man, who did something that was a throwback to the Twist. Later she took to the floor with her husband and then with her employer, fox-trotting with Charlie who was very light on his feet for such a big man and waltzing with Jack who wasn't. Charlie's mum had taught him to dance. Alice Pemberton hadn't done the same for Jack. Having danced with his secretary, dancing with the receptionist would be seen as a show of classlessness and not suspicious.

'I owe you an apology,' he said as she tugged her left foot from under his, more worried about her Italian shoes than her British toes.

'You're getting there, Jack,' she said, although he wasn't.

'No, I mean, I've been a bit off lately.'

'That's all right. You've been busy – the wedding, and losing your sister.'

'It's not that. Either of them.'

'Oh?' She raised her right foot and, anticipating a reference to his proposal in London, her freshly plucked eyebrows.

'I've had a takeover offer.'

'Oh.' Her heart sank. 'Who from?'

He named one of his rivals, a company with their own outlets in retail parks from Hampshire to Scotland.

'Are you going to accept it?'

'I'm thinking about it. Don't tell Charlie. Don't tell anyone.'

'I won't,' she said, although this, far more than his ridiculous proposal, was something she would prefer to share with her husband.

On their first date in ten years she'd decided to tell Charlie some of her sordid past: the married men, Nassim. But she ended up telling him about London as well. She kept the numbers down and left out the abortion.

'I wouldn't want you to think I was just a – pro.' There, she'd said it!

'What you've been is a *courtesan*,' he told her.

'A what?'

'Those women in France, before the revolution, who used to be the king's ladyfriends. He even gave them titles. Like Madame Pompadour.'

There'd been a mention of the Pompadour at hair-dressing college but she didn't remember its history. 'How'd you know about this stuff?'

'We were gonna do a play called *Dangerous Liaisons* - about courtesans in France. Margaret and I watched the film version, with Glenn Close. In the end they decided it was too racy. Kings of England had courtesans: Nell Gwynn, Lily Langtry. Wallis Simpson started out as one and then became a duchess.'

History lessons with Charlie Turner, this was new. The main thing was her own history didn't scare him off. 'We've all got a past,' he said. 'I was quite a bit more than second-hand when I married Margaret.'

'I was nearly part of that, remember!' she said. They shared a laugh.

He didn't seriously kiss her until their second date. With that big mouth he was still a great kisser but when it came to sex (she'd made him wait ten years for this) he was as rough and clumsy as an Arab. But he was considerate in his rough and clumsy way. He used his hands to help her finish and could even make it happen by angling his you-know-what against her love-bump.

A few dates later he asked why she hadn't yet married.

'I've been waiting for the right man to come along,' she said, clearly still under the influence of Maeve Binchy, Danielle Steel et al.

'How'd you think you'll know?'

'I'll know. I know *now*.'

'That's good,' he said. And that seemed to be that. They were engaged. When her coffee-shop friends asked whether she'd asked him or he her, she wasn't sure what the truthful answer was.

Now Charlie confessed his own secret. He'd had an addiction to gambling in the years before and during his marriage, had run up massive debts which he was still paying off. If it weren't for a sympathetic bank manager and Margaret managing their finances, they'd never have been able to buy their council house which was still heavily mortgaged.

'I'll be able to help,' Christine said. 'If we sell the flat we can knock a chunk off your mortgage.' Already the flat was *theirs*, not hers.

'I don't deserve you,' he said.

'Yes you do.'

She tried hard to like his eight-year-old son who was always sullen with her. 'He'll get used to you,' Charlie said, but he didn't. They wouldn't have a child of their own. Margaret had had a narrow pelvis and a defective womb. After a traumatic delivery with Jim the doctors said another pregnancy would kill her. In the end it was bone cancer that killed her, but Charlie had a vasectomy in the year Jim was born. A vasectomy could be reversed but Charlie didn't like the odds of its success. Charlie always calculated the odds on anything, everything.

Children didn't seem important, especially if they might turn out like Jim. The important thing was that after all the married men and the sleazy years in London she now, at last, felt secure. Safe.

'I think Jenny's cheating on me with one of her old boy-friends,' Paul said.

'Already? It's – what? – six weeks? – since she married you.'

'There was an Irish voice on the answering machine.'

'I think I know who that might be.'

'You do?'

'Jack told me about him. A disc-jockey Jenny went with when she was at art school in Brighton. It fizzled out after he moved to London.'

'She's been going up to London quite a bit lately, so I guess it's fizzed up again. She got mad when she found I was getting texts from a girl I met last winter – also in London.'

'Were you cheating on her?'

'No, I wasn't. This girl was just a friend – somebody I could confide in. Like you.' He smiled the smile that reminded her of more than one film-star.

'But Jennifer's getting back at you by seeing one of her exes?'

'Looks like it. What are you doing for lunch today?'

'What I usually do. I meet up with some women who work round here.'

'Have lunch with me.'

'You want to take me out because your wife's cheating on you?'

'No. Because you're my friend – my confidante.' Were they friends? He knew her darkest secret and she knew his: that was all.

'Okay,' she said. 'It'll have to be at twelve-fifteen. That's when Lucy spells me down here. And it'll have to be a quick lunch. I only get an hour.'

He grinned his cheeky grin. 'That's all right. I'm always up for a quickie.'

She laughed. 'I bet you are.'

He took her to the town's top Italian restaurant, popular with businessmen and the ladies-who-lunch brigade. Paul had a starter and pasta. Charlie was at the works and would expect a proper dinner; Christine only ate a starter now. They drank a fiercely dry Sicilian white; she didn't usually drink at lunchtimes.

He told her about the girl in London, who sounded a lot more his type than Jennifer. She was going to marry her son's bisexual actor father in December. If Paul and Jenny broke up, would Jenny marry her Irish DJ? Probably not, but Christine rather hoped she would: it was sure to be a disaster.

She'd supposed that Paul was lunching with her just because he needed a sympathetic ear. She wasn't expecting to reciprocate with any confidences of her own. So it was a shock when he suddenly asked:

'How long were you married to Charlie before the thing with Jack started?'

She went, for the first time in years, beetroot red. 'My God, Paul! You have absolutely no right to ask me about that.'

'Don't forget I already know about it from Jim. I'd kind of like to hear your side of things.'

'Well, you're not going to. My God,' she said again.

'Go on, Chris. I've shown you mine. Now you have to show me yours!' He grinned again, taking the edge off his sauce. She granted him a small laugh. Let him flirt if he wanted to; she had no intention of playing Mrs Robinson to his Benjamin. Charlie had taken her to see the stage version of *The Graduate* in London, with the actress, now sixty-one, who'd played J.R. Ewing's luckless wife in *Dallas* as Mrs Robinson. Christine didn't think *she* would have the nerve to take her clothes off in front of an audience when she was sixty-one – or indeed ever.

To give Jim time to get used to her, she and Charlie were engaged for eighteen months. The boy joined them on outings, and she had meals but not premarital sex under his dad's roof. Even the wedding was low-key: Charlie's old mum and two of his pals from the factory, Christine's family, the Saunderses, two of her women friends; no bridesmaids; Jim, now ten, was a surly page-boy. He still resented her but she knew he resented everybody and was frequently in trouble at school, when he wasn't truanting.

She sold her flat and gave Charlie all but £5,000 of the proceeds. They spent £3,000 on a makeover; Charlie put in a new kitchen. Now it was her home rather than Margaret's. The last £2,000 was meant to be a holiday and emergency fund, but she dipped into it for clothes. Three months into married life Charlie got her a job as Jack Pemberton's receptionist. Better pay than the funeral home and she enjoyed the jauntier atmosphere. The salesmen flirted with her; she flirted back. Jack didn't flirt with her but she could tell that he wanted to. He came in for a glass of wine one night after a Legion meeting.

In October Jack sold the ageing delivery truck, put deliveries out to tender and moved Charlie onto the production line. Sales were poor, there was no overtime. The last of Christine's nest-egg went on Christmas. Worrying about his debts and the mortgage, Charlie became almost as moody as the boy. So when, in February, Jack offered her £500 in his office, she sank to her knees and serviced him with barely a second thought, as readily as she had with the Arabs in London. Not until too late did she realize she was doing him without a condom; married life had made her complacent. She rushed to his private cloakroom afterwards and on her lunch-break bought a powerful mouthwash. Jack had made it clear this wasn't going to be a one-off and in her head she'd already annualized the value of a £500 weekly cash bonus, what it would do to Charlie's debt mountain and their mortgage, the clothes she could buy, things for the boy. She had told Jack she would handle Charlie and that evening she did. Her stepson, as usual, bolted his food and rushed to the game console in his bedroom. She decided on a head-on approach.

'Charlie, Jack called me up to his office this morning and presented me with five hundred pounds.'

'Good God, what was that in aid of?'

'What d'you think it was in aid of?'

'Oh, yeah.' A short dry laugh, like a cough. 'So – what did you say?'

She faced him across the kitchen table where they had all their family meals. 'I didn't say much of anything. I let him have what he was after.'

'Did you, by God! What exactly – no, forget I asked. I don't want to know.'

'I hope you don't mind too much. We can really do with the money.'

'Yes, I reckon we do.' He looked down at his dessert plate and then raised his head to face her again. There was a part of her that wanted him to berate her, call her a slut, strike her even; Jungle Man proclaiming his territory. But he didn't. He said: 'What've you done with it?'

'I paid it into the bank in my lunch hour.'

'Did you, already?' Another hoarse laugh. 'Well, that's good. D'you think there's more where that came from?'

She laughed herself now. 'Yes, Charlie, I do. A lot more. But only if you're okay with it.' Again she half wanted protest, condemnation, aggression. Yes, it would be good to buy nice clothes again and break free of the strangling burden of debt, but more than this, more than anything and everything, she'd wanted to belong to just one man.

He replied quickly, almost too quickly. 'I suppose I am if you are.'

'It won't be too different from – how my life used to be in London.' That was what was wrong with this new scenario, this life-plan.

'Well, all right then.'

And that seemed to be that. He called Jim back downstairs and, in the last week of February, they worked on their latest MG restoration project in the garage, which was not only unheated but too cramped to give them good access to the chassis and wheel arches. Going out into the cold, like Captain Oates at the Antarctic: 'I may be some time.' But at least Charlie came back.

And so it began, her double life. Even to herself she couldn't pretend that she had a husband and a *lover*; love had nothing to do with what she did with Jack, in his office, in motels on the A22, in a flatlet he bought in Hove which Charlie called 'the knocking shop'. After they moved, thanks to their enhanced income, to the cottage outside Alfriston, Jack came to the house when Charlie was away and Jim sleeping over with schoolfriends. If he came over when Charlie was home, Charlie and Jim would retreat to the barn-sized garage-cum-workshop while she serviced Jack in the spare room. After these 'house-calls' Charlie wouldn't make love to her for several days, and sometimes even when he came back from his delivery runs it took him a day or two to be ready for her. She was always ready for him; his lovemaking *purged* her of what she'd done with their employer.

A pretentious woman author on breakfast television, nobody she'd ever read, pronounced that women could be divided into two groups, wives and mistresses, domestic goddesses or whores. *What about me?* Christine wanted to ask her. *Where do I fit in? Wife* and *mistress*. Jack probably saw her as his 'courtesan' or concubine, Lily Langtry to the uncrowned King of 'Pembertown', but what she felt like (the woman author hit the nail on the head) was his whore, Christine Keeler to his Profumo.

Really Jack was no more repulsive than many of the Arabs she'd served in London. Some of them had been as fat or fatter, and even Charlie's waist was expanding at an annual rate (and his hair was going grey). At one of Karen's parties in Bahrain, an oil-rigger had made a joke about ugly women: 'You don't look at the mantelpiece when you're poking the fire.' To which Jeremy added: 'And you can't even see the mantelpiece when you're sucking the poker!'

Jack liked to 'poke the fire' from behind, which had the

232

makings of another joke; a lot of men favoured this angle, like dogs. He played with her breasts before, during and after - not as roughly as some of the Arabs. He liked to do sex on her chest, which was disgusting, but a few Arabs, including Nassim, had done this and so had one of the Peters. And Jack liked to just *talk*: about his business and his loveless, sexless and maybe even talk-less marriage. She told him almost nothing about her life, let him think that pre-Charlie there'd been just a handful of failed relationships that didn't make it to the registry office.

Jack used a condom for what she thought of as 'inside work' but not for the oral stuff. He said the high-price hookers he'd bought in London, Paris and Miami didn't use them for oral sex. *Well, I did*, she could have told him – but didn't. Not daring to be seen at a Sexual Health Clinic close to home, she went back to the woman in London for blood tests every six months. She knew oral sex wasn't as dangerous as 'inside work', but there were other diseases to worry about besides Aids and most of those could be caught through the oral stuff. Jack told her he wasn't going with prostitutes any more, but could she take his word for it? He was paying her to live with an element of risk in her life, but these were risks that she – and Charlie – could die from. Charlie had had what he called his 'little snip' but remembering the accident in London she went back on the Pill; she didn't want to have to abort any junior Pembertons.

Life – her double life – went on, although she never expected it would go on for a decade. Jim grew from a surly boy into a foul-mouthed teenager and a bully. At sixteen he started work at the factory. Charlie swore him to secrecy on the business between his stepmother and the Guvnor, and out of respect for his dad (not for her) he seemed to have kept his word. No-one at the factory gave any sign of knowing their dirty secret, although Cynthia seemed to sense that the receptionist's frequent visits to their employer's office were more than just a breach of the pecking order. Jim still helped Charlie with the cars when he wasn't playing football or out drinking with his mates. He never brought a girl home; perhaps he didn't want his girlfriends to meet the stepmother from hell. At nineteen he moved into a flat Jack had built. She and Charlie helped with the down-payment; it was worth it to have him out of the house.

Christine didn't join her husband and Jack at British Legion meetings, but she followed Margaret into the school drama group. It started with costumes, although she wasn't much of a seamstress. Better cast than they knew, she played an East-End tart in *Blitz* and then was the maid in a translated French farce and a matron in a *Carry-On*-type comedy written by the history-teacher director. The children were given as many leading roles as they could be convincing in. Her finest hour was playing Lady Bracknell after the director's wife went down with shingles. Jack and Agnes (and even Cynthia) attended some of the shows, but never Jim. Rehearsals, especially the early ones, were more fun than performances. The on-stage drama, good clean fun even when they were doing a suggestive comedy, complemented the sordid drama of her adultery.

It was amazing that this twin-track life had gone on for ten years. How much longer could it last? Thanks to a healthy diet and a moderate amount of exercise the thirty-nine-year-old face and body that she saw in bathroom and bedroom mirrors were not so very different from the ones she had flown to Bahrain at nineteen when she took the first steps on the road to what she still, honest to a fault but a bit old-fashioned, thought of as *harlotry*.

Two days – two evenings – after the lunch with Paul, Jack came to the house. Charlie was away again. He wanted to do sex on her chest. She found it harder than usual to shut her mind off from thinking how repulsive this was, he was. Serving him discounted wine hardly matched him for perversity but it gave her some satisfaction.

'You had lunch with Paul the other day,' he said.

'You saw us?'

'Agnes saw you. She was shopping.'

And now the old cow was shopping her son-in-law. Or was she reporting on *her*? Candour was the best defence.

'He thinks Jenny's gone back to her DJ boyfriend.'

'Well – I'm sorry to hear that. And a bit surprised that it's happening so soon. But I don't see why he has to tell *you* about his problems.'

'He needed a woman to confide in. He hasn't got any women friends round here. His mother's dead. He could hardly go to Agnes, could he?'

'But he's got *you*? You're his "friend"?' Jack was jealous of Paul. Good.

'He seems to think so,' she said.

Changing the subject, he told her the takeover bid had been withdrawn. The word on the grapevine was that one of the major furniture retailers was on the verge of collapse. These were tough times in the trade, as much from the effects of too much competition as from the somewhat exaggerated talk of a new recession. Even when house sales slowed, TV makeover shows kept everyone on their toes, décor-wise. People were always buying new furniture. Unfortunately, not enough of it came from Pembertons' end of the market.

Jack didn't say but she wondered how much longer the firm would go on. He did say, 'A lot of people may be in for a lean Christmas and an unhappy new year.'

And he turned out to be right.

Lunches with Paul became a regular event. He was usually in town on Monday and sometimes back on Friday. After a month he reported that his wife had become more 'attentive', so perhaps the thing with the Irish disc jockey had fizzled out again. Jenny flew out to join Paul in Barcelona on his twentieth birthday. Christine bought him a designer tie at Debenhams.

He loved to drive her new car, actually a twenty-two-year-old BGT, her favourite of the original MG range. Charlie, who salvaged MGs the way other people saved abandoned dogs, hated that the sacred name had been sold on to prosaic Rover. His great joy was the rarer MGA. This latest BGT, an accident write-off, came from a crushing plant in Wales; Charlie heard about it in a pub, bought it within the hour and drove back with a borrowed hoist-truck to take possession. An achingly bright yellow (not a colour Christine would have chosen), it was a 'work in progress'; the engine was prone to stalling, the transmission creaked and groaned.

'Shall we take Yellow Peril for a spin?' Paul said after their lunches, and they would dash up onto the Downs for a brief walk and be back at the office more or less on time.

'I'm going to ask Charlie to rescue one of these for me,' Paul said.

After her initial embarrassment Christine found herself

opening up to his persistent questioning. She told him about her early lovers, the married men, and Nassim. She confessed that there had been other Arabs and more married men in London; she hoped he didn't deduce that she'd been on the game. She didn't tell him about the abortion, her deepest darkest secret, nor would she talk about Jack whom she thought of as the second most shameful thing in her life (after ten years it was beginning even to eclipse her abortion).

'You must think I'm a complete slag,' she said in late November as they walked up to the old Belle Tout lighthouse above Beachy Head, a favourite walk of Paul's. She'd felt self-pitying and tense the last few days. Autumn blues. Charlie had been preoccupied and a bit distant for much of this summer. She put it down to money worries. He had never actually told her just how bad his debts were or how much they'd knocked off them in eleven years. His debts *were* shrinking, weren't they – not growing? Or was he still secretly gambling? She felt, obscurely, that something bad was about to happen.

'You're not a slag,' Paul said. 'You've slept around a bit, is all. Everyone does. I wish I'd done more of it.'

'You probably will,' she said grimly. He took this as a good-news forecast and laughed.

'Yeah!'

He walked closer to the edge to look down on the red-and-white-striped lighthouse: marooned on its rocky island at low tide, it looked like a stick of rock or a barber's pole. Christine pulled him back from the unfenced cliff; it wasn't that she was afraid of heights, but autumn and spring tides were the ones that did the most damage, undermining the chalk and precipitating the landslips which, like suicides, were an annual feature of these cliffs.

'My stepmother's pretty broadminded but she called me a tart once – and she doesn't know about Jack.' She couldn't believe she'd mentioned Jack.

He grinned. 'Well, my mum would say you're a *Fallen Woman*.'

'My real mum would have said it too,' she admitted, then pointed at her pillar-box red poncho (from Fenwick's). 'Look at me: I'm a *Scarlet* Woman!' They laughed together. It was hard to be glum in his company. He took her hand as they descended the slope to the lay-by. The slope was slippery with mud from yesterday's rain. They wiped their shoes on tufts of grass before getting back into the 'Yellow Peril', Paul back in the driving seat.

Agnes had told Jack. It was inevitable someone would tell Charlie.

'You've been going out with the Barrett boy,' he said, one day back from his latest trip to Wales.

'Just some lunches,' she said. It wasn't as gratifying to make Charlie jealous as it was with Jack. 'Makes a change from my usual ladies.'

'And you let him drive your MG.'

'We go up on the Downs for ten minutes after lunch – you know – to get some fresh air.'

'People are talking about you. They think you're having him away.'

'Well, you can tell them I'm not. Paul's going through a bad patch with Jennifer. She's been cheating on him with one of her old boyfriends. He needs someone to talk to.'

'Hasn't he got any friends? I thought he and Jim were mates.'

'This needs a woman's touch.'

'You let him bring you champagne from his trips. Now it's lunches and driving your car. He'll be getting a crush on you.'

'Don't be daft! I'm old enough to be his mother.'

'He's about the right age to be your toy-boy.'

'Well, I'm not looking for any toy-boys, thank-you very much!'

It was easy to make a joke of it; she felt that it was true. Paul was just a lunch date, like her women friends: someone to walk and drive with, someone she could talk to, listen to. There wasn't any more to it than that – was there?

'Charlie says they're talking about us at the works,' she told him over their next lunch. 'They think you're my toy-boy!'

'What a busy woman that would make you!' She assumed there was a hidden reference to Jack in this remark, but let it pass.

'We'd better stop going out in my car,' she said.

'I don't see why we have to.'

237

'Paul, I can't afford to attract gossip. It's not fair on Charlie.' Neither was it fair on Jack, but she hadn't told Paul that Jack was on their case as well.

'Oh well. Why don't you get Charlie to bring you to the game tomorrow? We're at home.'

'Is Jenny coming?' Since he resumed playing last month Jenny had attended precisely one game and sat in her car for most of it.

'She's got some girly thing on in Brighton. Lunch *and* dinner.'

Christine wondered if the 'girly thing' was another boy thing. Perhaps Paul did too. She drove herself to the match on Saturday. Charlie had gone back to Wales: a delivery for one of the sub-contractors. She suspected he was moonlighting but didn't quiz him about it, so that she could honestly deny all knowledge if Jack said anything.

Jack wasn't at the match either. It was a cold grey day, dry but only just. The pitch was soggy. The game, against a team from Chichester, went badly. The West Sussex side had an ageing ex-professional centre-forward who scored a double hat-trick. Jim scored Pembertons' first goal but was red-carded before half-time for fighting a player after a flagrant foul. A clumsy pass from Paul to the goalie resulted in an own-goal in the second half.

By full time – 10-2, for God's sake! – it was beginning to drizzle. The 30-or-so spectators hurried to their cars. Christine's MG wouldn't start. Even Jim couldn't make the engine fire. It wasn't the plugs, he said after two minutes with the bonnet up. Mud had dried on Jim and his kit after his sending-off; the damp gave the mud a polish-like sheen. Paul, equally caked, shivered beside them. The other players had gone home or into the changing huts to shower.

'Your dad says the transmission still needs some work.'

'I remember. Let's get off now. I'll come back and look at it in the morning.' Perhaps because of Paul's presence he wasn't being surly with her, there was a rarely seen shyness about him today.

'I'll run you home,' Paul said.

'I can take her,' Jim said. His latest 'toy', another rehab project, was an old Mercedes sports model; he hadn't got round to replacing the missing tonneau.

'It'll be drier in mine,' Paul said. 'And warmer.'

'Dry and warm wins the day,' Christine said. She kissed her stepson's cheek. He managed not to flinch. 'Don't waste your Sunday out here if you've got better things to do. You can leave Yellow Peril till your dad comes back.'

'Yellow Peril?'

'That's Paul's name for her.'

'Nice one!' Jim grinned.

Paul swapped his filthy boots for trainers and drove swaddled in an old duvet that was grubby from previous use as post-match insulation. Inviting him, for the first time, into her house she directed him to the guest bathroom. While he showered she freshened up and fixed her windblown hair in her own en-suite and changed into slacks and a heavy cotton shirt of Charlie's that she liked to lounge in.

Back downstairs she put the kettle on and unwrapped a lemon-drizzle cake from Tesco's. Paul came down in jeans and a designer sweatshirt Jennifer had surely chosen. His hair gleamed from the shower. He gave a wave that took in the ceiling beams and the range-style stove in its fireplace alcove.

'A fine and poncey period property you've got here,' he said. She smiled.

'My mum took me to a house like this in Rye when I was a girl. I can't remember whose it was but I never dreamt I'd end up owning one like it.'

'Dreams do come true,' he said, clearly teasing her.

She held out a plate with a hefty slice of the cake. The way he wolfed it down reminded her of her stepson, never a dainty eater. She cut him another slice and led him into the lounge so that he could admire more ceiling beams and the inglenook fireplace. She sat at one end of the L-shaped sofa. Paul set the plate on the antique pine coffee table. It was, apparently, time for another of this year's surprises: he sat down beside her, treated her to one of his film-star smiles, then took her in his arms and kissed her.

It was a long time since anyone other than Charlie had kissed her. Jack knew better than to try. She pulled herself free with some reluctance.

'Paul, for goodness' sake. We can't do this. You're married. *I'm* married.'

'My wife cheats on me and you're already cheating on

239

Charlie.'

'I don't think of – that – as cheating,' she said. 'It's strictly business.'

'Well –' another saucy grin – 'I'll give you a couple of hundred quid if that'll improve my chances.'

She wanted to laugh at his sheer cheek. She also wanted to slap his face. Deciding on the latter she lifted her hand but he caught it in his and pulled her to him, kissed her again. He was a lovely kisser. Christine had a flashback to the age of fifteen and her first kiss with Charlie Turner who was twenty, the age Paul was now. Perhaps because of this or perhaps because Charlie had been so moody of late, she surrendered to the kiss and opened her mouth to let his thick tongue in. Deftly he un-buttoned Charlie's shirt and put his hands on her bra-less breasts. Then it was his mouth on her nipples, which tingled to his touch. She held his wet-haired head with both hands and arched her breasts into his face.

'Oh God,' he said. Christine added a mental *Amen*. Charlie at twenty was still in her mind. Paul was just as masterful but with none of Charlie's roughness and with a confident ease that must come from Jenny and she wondered who else. Now he had her on her back on the sofa and her slacks and her panties were down to her knees, to her ankles. His mouth dribbled from her breasts to her stomach and still lower.

'Oh God,' Christine said as the tingling sensation became a throbbing – almost a burning – in the place where his tongue was. Charlie never did this; nor did Jack. The last person, possibly the only person, to do this to her had been an Oriental man, a dealer in rare carpets – where was he from? Malaysia? Vietnam? – in her Edgware Road days. Charlie usually made her wet and even Jack, sometimes, but not like this: she could feel the moisture trickling out of her. Paul made gurgling noises but carried on. A part of Christine knew that this was wrong, sinful, wicked, but the rest of her was caught up in the tumult of sensations which reached a peak and didn't stop.

'*Do* me,' she said. 'Do me now.' She'd never actually said this to Jack and not very often to Charlie either. Of course, they did her anyway.

Now Paul did her. She didn't see him his getting out of his clothes but suddenly – lean and tanned – he was naked and on her and sliding into her. Christine grunted. His you-know-what was as big as Charlie's, as an Arab's; it filled her, pounding and pulsing deep inside her. The tingling-throbbing-burning built to a new crescendo. She almost blacked out. Every nerve in her seemed to join in this overwhelming orgasm, the most intense since the first few joyous times with Charlie after she came back from her sleaze years in London. She wanted to say *I love you* but that would be wrong. Beautiful as this was, it was wrong, and to say *I love you* would only make it worse.

Paul finished with a series of gasping groans.

'I love you, Christine,' he said.

She said, 'Yes...love me, Paul.'

She opened a bottle of his champagne and served him a thrown-together dinner of tinned soup and bacon-and-pesto pasta. They talked about the town they'd grown up in, its schools, its people (not Jack). There were a few coincidences, overlaps, in their pasts. They didn't talk about the future; was there one for them, for this? He kept smiling and grinning at her. How handsome he was and how much he reminded her of Charlie at the same age; only his hair was darker and Charlie didn't have the dent in his chin. After dinner he got her back out of her clothes, used his mouth on her and did her again. He wanted to stay the night. She wanted this too but forced herself to send him packing.

Now came the guilt, wave after wave of it like the pleasure waves he had set off in her. She didn't get this with Jack, not since the first few times. Jack was, as she'd told Paul, merely business. This was different. She always put Jack out of her mind after each encounter. There would be a next time, there always was and they needed the money, but she didn't think about it. Now she couldn't stop thinking about Paul.

He'd gone off to Brussels and Luxembourg. That was *his* business. But she ached for him. Her thingy ached from him and for him.

Then Charlie came home, again, from Wales, more incommunicative than ever, and everything – guilt, confusion, longing for her hot new toy-boy – went out the window.

*

Christine had seen long ago that Jim's moodiness came from his father, not from Margaret. But she was used to their moods, the father's and the son's. Jim, now that he lived on his own, wasn't her problem and with Charlie she'd learned to wait for his mood to pass. It could have been worse. Some men, including the husband of one of her friends, beat their wives. Charlie never laid a hand on her in anything other than tenderness or passion.

But this mood had lasted for weeks or even months. His distance was a coldness that shut her out. He couldn't know about Paul, so what was it?

'Charlie, something's wrong. What is it?'

He burst into tears, an event she'd never seen before. She took him in her arms. How much more substantial he was than Paul. Crying with him, she soothed his thinning grey-streaked hair and tried not to think of Paul's thicker darker hair. Crying, distant, cold – he was still the only man she'd loved.

'What's happened, Charlie? You've got to tell me.' She feared the worst. He'd gambled away a fortune. They would lose the house. Would Jack bail them out?

'She's dying,' he sobbed.

'Who's dying?'

'Glenys. Glenys will be dead in just a few weeks.'

Glenys? His mother's name was Ruth. Ruth had been dead for ten years. There wasn't anyone at the factory or the Legion or the school called Glenys, not that Christine could remember.

'Glenys Who?' she asked. 'I don't know any Glenys.'

'The mother of my children,' he said.

Christine released him from her consoling arms. She thought a stroke or heart-attack must begin with a feeling like this: everything stopping, freezing.

'Your children? What children?'

'My poor motherless children. She's dying of bone cancer, just like Margaret. Is it me? Do I give them cancer? Are you going to get it?'

Christine, at this moment, was not worried about dying from cancer. Even her guilt at cheating on him with Paul had left her.

'Tell me about these children of yours,' she demanded. 'And who is this Glenys person?'

'She's my wife,' he said. Christine leant her bottom

against the pine table as her world disintegrated.

'She can't be. I'm your wife.'

'I started seeing her, having kids, while Margaret was alive. I married her after Margaret died. But she wouldn't leave Wales and I didn't want to leave here. I couldn't get such a good job there.'

'Does *she* know about *me*?'

'Yes. She calls you my "Sussex wife", and she's my "Welsh wife".'

'How could you marry me if you were already married to her?'

'When we met again, when you came back from London, I knew I had to have you.'

'But you didn't divorce her?'

He looked her directly in the eyes and gave what she could see was an honest answer: 'I didn't want to lose my kids.' Honesty and directness were not enough. 'But I had to have *you*.'

'You can't have two wives, Charlie. It's not legal.'

'Well, I do. I'm sorry, Christine.'

A voice from the past, her mother's voice, echoed incongruously in Christine's ear: *Sorry won't butter any parsnips.*

'In the eyes of the law I'm not your wife, Charlie. I'm just your *mistress*. I've been Jack Pemberton's whore for ten years and yours for eleven.'

As of Saturday she was also *Paul's* mistress, but this might not be the best time to mention the fact.

'You're my *wife*, not my whore. Fuck what the law says, the rulebooks.'

'You could be done for bigamy.'

'Well, right now that's the least of my worries.'

She'd almost slapped Paul, had started to. Now she wanted to hit Charlie, hit him hard, hurt him. Another realization came to her:

'You're not a gambler, are you? You never were. This is where all your money's gone, all *my* money's gone.'

'Actually I did get into trouble with gambling in the early years with Margaret. It was Glenys and having all these kids cured me of it.'

She didn't want to hurt him, she wanted to kill him. 'I've been Jack Pemberton's bloody whore all these years so that you could bring up another woman's children.'

'I'm sorry,' he said.

'Stop saying you're sorry.' She was close to tears now, tears for herself, for the mirage that the last eleven years had been. 'It doesn't mean anything.'

'It means everything. You mean everything to me.' Christine almost said the F-word in response to this.

'You never let me have any kids. You lied about that. You said you had your – little snip – after Margaret had Jim.'

'I had it after Glenys had our second little girl, our fourth child. Enough was enough. I'm not sorry about that. You were never cut out to be a mother, Chrissie. Look how you couldn't get on with Jim.' Grief made him callous.

'That wasn't my fault,' she protested, knowing it was hopeless. 'He never gave me a chance – because I wasn't his real mother. Does he know he's got all these brothers and sisters?'

'No. But I shall have to tell him before I go back there. I need him to spell me on deliveries. It's going to break his heart.'

'It's broken mine,' she said.

Two days later he went back to Wales. He was – almost – his old self again, as if telling her had been some kind of catharsis; now he could concentrate on coping with his dying wife. He'd shown her pictures, kept in his lorry, of the Welshwoman and their children. Glenys was, Christine now knew, only two years older than her, but in the most recent photo, wearing a chain-store coat in a dreary tartan tweed, autumn leaves on a tree behind her, she looked much older, hair streaked with grey, her unmade-up face lined like the veins on an autumn leaf. The children were from eleven to seventeen. Three had Glenys's dark hair but the youngest girl was blonde and the image of her father, even more than Jim was. Her name was Megan – a Welsh tribute, Charlie said, to his first wife, to Margaret. Perhaps she had to be grateful that there wasn't a boy called Chris or a girl with some Welsh version of Christine.

She'd thought something bad was going to happen and now it had. Well, at least she could cheat on Charlie with a clear conscience. It served him right.

But not with Jack. After Paul it would be harder than ever to close her mind to the grossness of servicing her

244

employer. At the risk of losing her nine-to-five job she was minded to sever this other side of their relationship. She could live, if she had to, on her basic salary. She would not put another penny into the joint account which Charlie was using to fund this other family of his. The betrayal was so great it left no room for sympathy for the dying woman.

On Thursday Jack called her up to his office. She closed the door but didn't lock it. He was holding out a cheque. She ignored it initially.

'I thought you might like to have a little shopping spree in the run-up to Christmas,' he said. She was thinking how to respond to this when he added, 'Considering the circumstances.'

'What circumstances would those be?' she asked coldly. Jack's nutmeg skin turned a reddish-brown shade, the colour of an over-ripe mango.

'Charlie asked for some compassionate leave. He told me about Wales. That woman. Her kids.'

'*His* kids,' she said with all the venom she felt.

'I can see you're upset. I knew you would be.'

'Upset,' she echoed. 'Yes, you could say I'm upset.' She appraised him as if seeing him for the first time. Dressed in bulging black pinstripe with his bald brown rubber-lipped head, he was like some monstrous slug; the few white hairs at the back of his scalp might be salt sprinkled to try and kill the slug-creature. With Paul in her mind and memories of a younger Charlie that she was fighting to suppress it was beyond belief that she had spent ten years of her life sexually servicing this man.

'If you need someone to talk to about it...' He tailed off, as if he realized that the someone she might need to confide in it would not – never could be – him. This might be an appropriate time for him to renew his proposal – there only need be one divorce since her marriage was invalid – but he didn't. Was she relieved or (nice to be asked) disappointed?

'I'm all right,' she said, though she wasn't.

'Take this anyway.' Podgy fingers pushed the cheque across his desk.

'Thanks, Jack,' she said in lieu of something withering. Best, really, to keep her options open. A cheque without sex: was this the first instalment of her *pension*? She left his door open as she went out, ignoring the Ice Princess who, head down over a pile of correspondence, also ignored her.

When Paul came through the front door on Friday she felt a hot surge of desire for him. Teenagers should feel like this, not women approaching forty.

'Would you like to come to dinner this evening?' Even *she* could hear herself lowering her voice to a seductive tone!

'Where's Charlie?'

'Gone back to Wales.' She enjoyed dismissing him, the cheating bastard. 'Is Jenny around?'

'She's still in Brighton. Why, are you inviting her as well?'

'Do you think I should?' They shared a conspiratorial chuckle. 'I thought you were going to sell that flat.'

'So did I, but apparently we're not.' That evening he did her twice more, with his mouth and with his you-know-what before and after dinner. Dinner was a readymade fish pie (did serving it with champagne lessen the shame of this?) She didn't tell him about her bigamous marriage or her new-found stepchildren. He *was* her 'toy-boy', she liked him (part of her was falling in love with him, the part that had once – twice – fallen for Charlie), but she saw no need to confide in him any more than in Jack. Wherever this affair was going (is that what it was? an affair?), it wasn't in the direction of the registry office.

'Do me,' she said after dinner. As if he needed to be asked. Benevolent in the afterglow of orgasm she found herself wondering how Charlie was, how Glenys was.

On Saturday they parked her MG above Beachy Head and walked the Seven Sisters, to Cuckmere Haven and back. She wished it was summer. She would like Paul to do her on the downs, in the marshes, on a deserted beach; December was not a month for outdoor sex. On the spur of the moment she did him with her mouth in the lay-by, with two other cars parked but empty within feet of the MG. Paul brought her off with his fingers. She enjoyed feeling reckless, abandoned; it drove away the darker thoughts.

There was no problem starting the car; if Jim had told her what he'd done to it she'd forgotten already. The transmission still creaked and groaned; Jim said his dad would need to sort it out when he had the time. Jim was now out with the lorry doing pre-Christmas deliveries. His father must have told him what he *had* had time for these past eighteen or nineteen years. Was Jim's heart broken? Did he even have one?

Paul drove them to her house, the house that Jack had partly built and largely paid for. He did her again in the bed bought with Jack's money. Christine cooked a proper dinner, a venison casserole. He stayed the night and did her twice more. She came and came and came.

But she felt an emptiness deep inside, as if Charlie had killed some inner part of her, much as she had years ago killed her unborn half-breed child. Paul filled that void, literally, with his you-know-what, but the emptiness returned when she wasn't with him. Perhaps sex was – had always been – the one thing that sustained her. Did this make her a nymphomaniac? She'd always thought sex was something she put out, or put up with, to keep men happy and get them to give her nice things. The nice thing Paul gave her, like Charlie, was sex for its own sake. And perhaps some love, as well.

Paul couldn't believe his luck. Just as his wife drifted back to her teenage life, fate threw him a passionate mistress. Fucking lovely. And lovely fucking.

'Here's to you, Mrs Robinson,' he toasted and teased her in her kitchen. '*Stifler's Mom*' was also in his mind.

'How would Benjamin like a black eye?' she responded.

Okay, so Jennifer's breasts were fuller and firmer than Chris's, which were somehow more fragile; blue veins were faintly visible just below the surface, like the grain in a fine marble. Her vagina was a little, a very little, slacker than his wife's but oh so much slicker, a gushing canyon river compared to the dry gulch that was his wife. And this 'Mrs Robinson' had a generous heart and it was Jennifer, in the daughter's role, who was sharp-tongued, manipulative, mean-spirited. He didn't know (or care) what (or who) his wife was doing in Brighton (or wherever).

'I love you,' he told his glowing, gushing mistress, on her marital bed, believing it almost and wanting it to be true.

'Yes,' she said. 'Love me, Paul.'

He knew it would end, because of the disparity in their

ages. He hoped it wouldn't end badly.

Charlie phoned from Wales to tell his Sussex wife he'd taken his Welsh wife to a hospice. The end was approaching. The children were distraught.

'Are you okay?' she asked him.

'I have to be. If only for the kids. It's tearing them up.'

'Yes,' she said. 'It must be.' She didn't say, didn't need to, that it was tearing her up too.

With Christmas barely two weeks away Jack called the foremen and department heads to a meeting in the conference room. Only one item on the agenda: workforce cutbacks. Christine took notes; Cynthia was off with flu.

'I'm sorry to do this now,' Jack said, 'when it's supposed to be a time for goodwill and all that guff. But if we're not to go down with all hands, we need to trim our ropes a bit.' Trust Jack to begin with a nautical metaphor.

The trimming was not as drastic as it might have been, might yet have to be. Three apprentices would be terminated. Two imminent retirees (one was 'Aunty Lil') wouldn't be replaced. Linda in Design was moving with her husband to London; the other two designers would take on her workload. Dennis Dawes, who'd mentored Paul, had tired of the road and was going to work in a furniture showroom in Hove. 'Hopefully he'll talk them into buying some of our units,' Jack said; a faint hope - these warehouse outlets were Pembertons' worst domestic customers. And Tim Reynolds was setting up his own business with a squash partner, marketing IT packaging. 'Whatever that is,' Jack said.

No new salesmen would be hired. Son-in-law Michael was to take to the road, taking over Tim's area. Not good news for Joanna and the red setters, the horses. And junior son-in-law Paul was to take over Dennis's area, part of which he already knew from his brief apprenticeship.

'What about the overseas business?' asked Roger Dean, the Production Manager. Roger had lost a lot of weight this year; was he ill or dieting?

'Paul will carry on with that as well as cover Dennis's beat. But, let's face it, he hasn't produced much business for us in Euroland. There's only that one shop in Lille and the one outside Brussels that have generated any volume of orders. I'm not blaming the boy, I'm sure he's doing his best, we just can't seem to muscle in on our continental rivals. He can still follow up any leads over there and keep up with the contacts that have paid off, but I think we have to concentrate on the domestic market. If we can't improve our share of that catch, then we're looking at some very rough water indeed.'

'I don't see how it's going to help to cut back on the marketing force,' Michael ventured. His facial freckles were flushed with the indignity of their demotion from Marketing Manager to furniture rep. Paul would be hurt too.

'Your department costs more than it needs to,' Jack said. 'You're going to need to haul a lot more sails to see us through these doldrums.' The pun on 'sales' was probably unintended. Nobody smiled. It wasn't a day for smiling.

Jennifer flew to New York for a seasonal shopping spree. 'For all I know, she's hooked up with another old boy-friend,' Paul told his mistress on Saturday.

They lunched at the festively over-decorated Golden Galleon. While everyone around them talked Christmas, Paul was excited by the news from Iraq that American troops were honing in on Saddam Hussein.

'Of course, it won't make the scandal about the duff intelligence go away,' he pronounced. 'Regime change was always the real objective. And the US getting its hands on Iraq's oil.'

'And revenge for the Twin Towers,' his mistress added. Charlie was strong on this point. Despite having a New Labour supporter for a father and an Old Labour husband, Christine had never taken an interest in politics. The Bush-Blair 'War on Terror' wasn't having much effect on life in Sussex.

'I'm with the people who think 9/11 was just another excuse,' Paul said. 'I wish I'd gone on the march in February. This war isn't making us any friends, but it *is* making us a new lot of enemies. We're liable to see some scary stuff on the streets of London by way of reprisal.'

'I'd better do my clothes shopping in Brighton from now on,' she joked.

Paul's expression remained earnest. 'Don't count on being any safer down here. If terrorists ever manage to bomb the power station at Dungeness, all of Southeast England would become uninhabitable.'

Christine remembered a boring man at one of Jeremy's parties banging on about the Rulers of the kingdoms and emirates on the Gulf being just as brutal as Saddam or the medieval mullahs of Iran. Paul was close to boring her with his gloomy predictions. 'Well, at least we'll go out with a boom!' she retorted, defiantly light-hearted.

'We won't be in the blast zone here. We'll probably just die a slow death from radiation.' The girl arrived with their food.

Christine contemplated annihilation and baked salmon. 'I'm not sure I've got any appetite.' Paul laughed as he dug in to his steak-and-kidney pudding.

'Don't worry about it,' he said, mouth full. 'We're just as likely to live long enough to be flooded out of our sea-side homes by global warming.'

'Are all your generation this cheerful about the future?'

Paul laughed again. He seemed to count her lowered spirits as a personal triumph. They talked about Jack's job cuts instead. Paul was sanguine about becoming a domestic salesman. 'I'll be able to see more of you,' he said.

'Jack's going to work you even harder when there's fewer of you.'

'Michael will feel that more than I will. Joanna won't be happy. Good. Stuck-up cow.'

'That's no way to talk about your sister-in-law. *And* she's your cousin.'

'Step-cousin, technically. It was a big mistake, marrying within the family – like the Ay-rabs do. Next year I'm going to have to put that right.'

'You think?'

'Yes, I think,' he said seriously. He smiled one of his smiles that could lift her mood from anxiety to euphoria. 'If you divorce Charlie as well we could get married.'

She almost told him then. *I don't need to divorce Charlie. I'm not legally his wife.* Two proposals and bigamy. This was a year full of surprises.

'Paul,' she said, knowing that he would not marry her but enjoying the moment. 'Let's take it one day at a time.'

'Isn't that we are doing?'

'Yes. We are.'

As they drove off the other side of the bridge over the

Cuckmere an oncoming van hooted and Paul swerved to the left. 'Whoops! Thought for a minute I was still in France.'

'Your mind isn't on the road.'

'My mind's on *you*.'

'Well, keep it on the road for now.'

'For *now*,' he echoed with a grin. The MG grumbled and groaned as they climbed the steep hill to Friston and on to Beachy Head. He parked in the lay-by where she'd performed oral sex on him last weekend. An old couple were snoozing in their car; a family picnicked half in, half out of a 4x4. The oral sex would have to wait till they got home. An arctic wind ripped at their coats as they walked the sodden grass to where there was a view, not too near the cliff edge, of the lighthouse. White-flecked grey-green waves rippled to the far horizon beneath low billowing grey-white clouds. High tide; the sea erupted round the lighthouse's rocky base, squirting foam up the structure, which was stouter than it looked from above. Christine shivered, not just from the cold.

'Let's get going,' she said.

'Okay.' He grinned again. She knew he was thinking about them getting home, getting – what did people say today – 'down and dirty'!

'I'll drive,' she said when they were back at the car. 'I can only drive on the one side.'

'After a week like this it's a treat to be a passenger.' He had driven across Belgium to Luxembourg and Strasbourg, returning via Paris and Lille. The last such intensive trip he would have to make for now, he'd learned on his return, and a fruitless one; in December furniture shops had their sights on the sale season, nowadays more likely to be pre- than post-Christmas.

Inside the car he pulled her towards him and kissed her hungrily. His tongue probed her mouth. Christine sometimes thought she would be able to come just from holding his firm body and touching his taut skin. Reluctantly she freed her face from his. The elderly couple ten feet away, awake now, smiled at her; either they didn't see the age difference here or they weren't minded to make a judgement. She smiled back at them.

Yellow Peril gave a throat-clearing cough before starting. Engine noise and rattles and shakes were, to

Christine, the backbeat to this affair with her oversexed young lover. She was as impatient as he to be at home, in bed, *on* the bed, but instead of turning back towards the A259 she pointed the car down the winding road to the Belle Tout lighthouse and Birling Gap.

'Now it's you going the wrong way,' he said.

'No, I'm not. I like the scenic route. And so do you.' He'd told her how often he'd come here during his school-days, cycling up all of the four steep roads that led to this downland peak. He had even told her about bringing the girl from London and her child up here last winter. The girl – her name was Rachel – had stopped replying to his texts since mid-November. Perhaps her boyfriend (by now he might be her husband) had discovered their corres-pondence and demanded she end it. Rachel had also been kissed in a lay-by, not the one they'd just left but the one lower down which they were approaching now, the one that was scarily close to the cliff edge. She put her foot down as the road began to straighten.

Paul's mind was in tune with hers. He said, 'This is *our* place now.' Christine's heart filled, overflowed. She thought at that moment that she loved him, that this was more than just a sex thing.

There came a loud crack from beneath their feet and then the sound of something dragging along the road below them. Christine stamped on the brake pedal. Instantly and unbelievably Yellow Peril rose into the air as if lifted by a giant hand. Christine screamed and Paul gave a shout as the car crashed across the sloping grass verge bordering the lay-by and overturned. The ground angled up towards the cliff edge but the car's momentum kept it rolling along this slope. On the second turn the passenger door sprang open and tore off. Paul was half thrown out. It was his turn to scream as the rolling car whirled him round by his trapped right leg and then catapulted him onto the grass a few feet from the cliff edge. The driver-side door buckled but stayed shut. Christine was flung to and fro against the steering wheel, her head and shoulders thumping against the roof which also buckled with each revolution. She tried to protect herself with her arms and, hearing bones break, whimpered helplessly. After three turns the car came to rest, right way up, the bonnet inches from the drop to the sea. The roof, the bonnet, the door, the wings, every surface was crumpled like bacon foil. Her broken seat trapped Christine against the steering wheel. A trickle of blood ran from her mouth. Blurrily her eyes focused on the stumpy former lighthouse at the crest of the hill to her right. *Oh, Charlie*, she thought. *Paul. Charlie.*

Paul lay twisted twenty yards away. He'd passed out from the pain of his shattered leg.

A car that had followed them down the hill screeched into the lay-by and two young men, no older than Paul, leapt out. Before they could reach the MG there came a primeval creaking sound from below the cliff. A narrow ravine opened up behind the wrecked car and, with a deep rumbling roar, a ten-yard platform of grassy cliff started to drop towards the sea 350 feet below, falling like a freight lift. Yellow Peril, now crimped and streaked with gleaming patches of bare metal, lurched forward and rolled off the sliding crumbling mass of chalk and turf and flint. The car somersaulted as it fell. Limbs flailing, Christine toppled out and plummeted into the water yards from where the car smashed onto a submerged rock and broke in half.

Keeping back from the raw new edge, the two men looked over, expecting a cinematic explosion that did not materialize. The landslide slithered and splashed into the maelstrom between the wrecked car and the base of the cliff. The woman lay loosely in the heaving swell, her platinum hair eddied by the tide like flotsam or some exotic seaweed.

The men turned and ran past the wedge of exposed earth and chalk to where Paul lay unconscious.

Paul's leg was broken in three places: ankle, mid-calf and upper thigh. The local surgeons were still working on him at 5.30 p.m., 8.30 in Iraq, when US troops hauled a smelly bedraggled Saddam Hussein out of a hole in the ground ten miles from his home village of Tikrit. In New York Jennifer was 'brunching' with and on a commodity trader she had picked up in the hotel bar yesterday evening and taken to her room.

Shortly before midnight, watched by her husband and children, Glenys Turner slipped gently from coma to death in a hospice 10 miles from her home village in Wales.

17. The Factotum's Tale

'Hey, Paul. Fancy some football?'

'Isn't it a match day?'

'That's what I mean, tosspot. We need an extra man today. We need *three* more men, but one's a start.' A gull perched on one of the seafront street-lamps let out a fearful shriek. Jim moved his cellphone to the other ear.

'I haven't been to any practice nights,' Paul said. 'You don't know if I'm any good.'

'You can get in the way of the ball, can't you?' Jim said. He checked that Paul had got kit, and they agreed to meet for a pre-match pint. Jim resumed his run. There were more gulls than people on the promenade. Three weeks into March it felt more like winter than spring.

He and Paul were 'mates'. This was as big a surprise to Jim as to his dad and his other mates at the works. It just happened, on the strength of working together at the factory while Jim showed him the ropes and jogging together on two consecutive nights. That, and knobbing three slags!

Two weeks ago Roger Dean ('Nellie' Dean, to his co-workers) had asked Jim to give Paul what he called 'an induction' on the assembly line.

'You're going to be my *mentor*,' Paul said.

'Is that good or bad?'

Paul explained. Taking his role seriously, Jim let his protégé do some fetching and carrying. He showed off his mechanical skills changing blades on the dowelling machine and oiling the ripsaw when the feed mechanism starting to scream louder than the saw itself.

254

'You're a factotum,' Paul told him at some point. Jim had been called a lot of things but this was another new one. Paul explained: 'It's Latin for someone who does everything. A Jack-of-all-trades.'

'Say it again.'

Paul obliged. 'I reckon I'm more of a *fuck*-totum,' Jim said. Paul laughed.

After their second seafront jog Paul came back to Jim's flat for a brew. Out of the blue Jim found himself telling him about his stepmother's dealings with the Guvnor, which his dad put up with because of the money that came their way. From the moment Dad brought her home in 1991 Jim could see Christine was a bit of a scrubber compared to his lovely dead mum, but it had been a shock, four years later, to find out the slag actually *was* on the game with Jack Pemberton. To Jim, fourteen years old, this discovery doubled the betrayal of his mum, but he promised his dad to keep it under his hat and a promise to Dad was like one of those 'kill me if I talk' sacred oaths Mafia goons went in for. No matter how rat-arsed Jim got with his mates he'd never let the cat out of the bag, and now here he was blabbing to the Guvnor's poncey college-boy nephew after just two shifts of his company.

On Saturday, they went on the pull together, like mates do. A totty in London had let Paul down. They picked up a pair of German slags and after a few beers in a few bars took them back to Jim's for vodka and knobbing. Knobbing in separate rooms. Jim had trouble getting it up but Paul said he'd shagged his twice. Paul had got the idea Jim was some kind of super-stud, but the stuff that came in bottles often got in the way of coming in women.

Paul was on the road with Dennis Dawes all the next week, but on Saturday he met up with Jim in the evening after the latest in the Pembertons team's run of wipe-outs. In their first pub he told Jim about the women buyers and store managers who'd flirted with him.

'I had a gay one in Bristol,' he announced. 'Camp as a row of tents.'

'You *'ad* him?' He didn't ask what 'camp as a row of tents' meant.

'Well, I don't mean I had him away. He got very saucy and I sauced him back, to keep him in an order-book frame of mind.'

255

''Ave you ever done, you know, gay stuff?' He made this sound casual.

'No, never, though I've had offers before. Have *you*?'

'Course not,' Jim replied quickly.

'Thought you were the great *fuck*-totum.' He grinned.

'Yeah, but – there are limits.' Jim decided to close off this dicey topic. 'Do any runnin' while you was down west?' he asked.

Tonight Paul did the chatting up; a skinny Spanish girl. Jim followed a bloke he knew to the Gents and scored a half-dozen E's. The girl looked less of a slag than last Saturday's Germans but turned out to be more of one. Back at the flat she undressed them and licked their chests and armpits on the way down to the action zone. It was like being in a porn-film. Paul had a runner's lean body, he didn't work out like Jim, his pecs didn't fully cover his ribs, but he had an amazing cock; it was a big turn-on to watch the girl sucking him and then trying to get both their cocks in her mouth. Jim would have liked to give her one up the bum while Paul was in her twat (he'd seen this on DVD), but the girl wasn't up for it. They took turns shagging her. Vodka and E's finally did Jim's head in but when he went to bed he couldn't stop thinking about Paul's cock. Not for the first time he woke up worrying he might be gay and wondering if, in 2003, it was anything to worry about.

Jim didn't know camp, but he knew gay. He knew 'glad to be gay.' Jim wasn't glad to be gay. '*Bad* to be gay' was nearer the mark.

He spent a lot of time worrying. The only things that took his mind off sex, off worrying, were vodka, football and fixing up cars with his dad. At work the men (and the women) talked about sex all day long. TV programmes all had sex scenes, from *Coronation Street* to *Big Brother*; Anne Robinson even talked smutty on *The Weakest* fuckin' *Link*. After soccer the players' conversation got steamier than the showers; Jim went home dirty: better to be thought a bashful girl than get caught with a suspect hard-on and be labelled a poof.

His first gay experiences, if that's what they were, had been in school. He and two teenage mates bullied younger, weaker boys into wanking them off. (Paul Barrett, a year younger, escaped because he was a runner; athletes and soccer players were spared – or feared). Occasionally a boy was pushed into giving a blow-job. You didn't dare do this with girls: sexual bullying of girls amounted to rape; boys were too embarrassed to blab. Soon his mates were pulling totty and drifted into girlfriend relationships. Jim had had his first girl at four-teen and others since, but he didn't think it was such a big deal. He missed the sight of his mates getting wanked or sucked. When there was only him left he had to stop this kind of thing; only benders did one-on-one boy action.

In his last year at school there was a girl called Liz. She was more serious than Jim, but sex with her kept his mind off the stuff with boys. When he went to work at Pembertons (thanks to The Slag) Liz started a beautician course in Brighton and met someone else. Jim dated some more girls; nothing serious.

There were men in his life – men rather than boys – although he didn't let this get serious either. Once he got his first car he found there were out-of-the-way toilets and lay-byes and country parks where men (mostly older than him and grateful for some young blood) got together for brief urgent no-strings sex. The lack of strings was part of its appeal. Girls wanted a relationship, marriage, kids.

What he did with men wasn't all that gay. No kissing – not that many of them wanted this. Beyond stroking and wanking he wouldn't do anything in return for what they did. He liked getting sucked more than anything else. He tried fucking men but it was a mucky business. He wouldn't let anyone fuck him, though a few wanted to have a go. 'You've got the best arse in Sussex,' one man told him; as compliments go, Jim didn't think much to this.

Conversation was not what these men were looking for. 'What d'you like?' was the most that most of them said. A few wanted to tell him about their lives and know about his. Jim said his name was John, he lived in Brighton and worked in a garage. He didn't pretend to be married, though it surprised him how many married men did this stuff. Was it worse for a woman if her husband had women on the side or if he went with men? Would it be okay if down the line he got married and carried on doing this? Questions without answers.

Only once did he make the mistake of going home with someone. The bloke took this to mean Jim was up for

257

kissing and cuddling and other full-on gay stuff. When he bought his flat, with his inheritance from Gran, a loan from Dad (the Guvnor's money at two removes), a mortgage and a bit of discount (Christine's despised influence again), he had his mates round and the family, a girl now and then, but never one of his male sex partners.

TV documentaries introduced Jim to the notion of bisexuality. It seemed to be accepted in places like New York and California, but he didn't think it would go down too well at Pembertons. Like his stepmother's dirty doings, it was something best kept under his hat.

Jim reckoned that Paul's speed qualified him to be a winger but the captain (another alumnus of what Jim now thought of, courtesy of Paul, as Boredom High) put him on defence with Charlie, Jim's dad. Dad only played when they were desperate; years of lifting furniture for Jack fuckin' Pemberton had done his back in. They were desperate this weekend. Their regular goalkeeper was off with flu; his substitute, not much helped by Dad and Paul, let in twelve goals. This would have been a mighty thrashing if the police goalie hadn't let in thirteen, three of them Jim's.

'Well played, Jimbo,' the captain said at the end.

'Well played, Jim-lad,' said Dad. Jim basked. 'Jim-lad' was from the 1950s Goon Show, repeats and recordings of which Grandad had inflicted on Charlie, and Charlie on Jim. Prince Charles liked the Goons; there was hope for him in spite of Camilla.

Keen as he was to see Paul with his kit off again, he daren't risk exposing himself in the showers. Paul drove them back to Jim's flat. After cleaning up they lolled around in dressing gowns. Jim's second-hand kimono got a laugh from Paul. The plan was to go out on the pull later. Over tea and teacakes Paul told him about a soap-style family drama caused by him trying to finger Alison Saunders's twat last night.

'Bit of a dry one, wasn't it?' Jim asked with a leer.

'On the contrary, Watson. It was a deep well in the arid desert of my life. A well, anyway. I didn't get into the depths. Her tights were like a diving suit – an *anti*-diving suit.' Jim laughed although muff-diving Alison Saunders – or any other girl – was not somewhere he dreamt of going.

258

They sank some cans watching the day's highlights on Sky. Jim defrosted two steaks, enjoying having someone to cook for. They watched a kung-fu movie, drinking wine and then Bailey's with a chocolate pud. When Paul dozed off Jim put on a dirty DVD and played with himself inside the kimono, hoping Paul would wake up and do the same.

'This might get us in the mood,' he said when Paul finally stirred. But Paul, still minded to go out and chase down some live pussy, wanted coffee instead. When Jim returned from the kitchen he had drifted off again but the movie had worked its magic: his cock, seventy-five percent stiff, poked out of the robe.

Jim had lost count of the number of cocks he'd seen: close to a hundred, of which he'd touched perhaps forty or fifty. Paul's, even seventy-five percent stiff, was in the top five percent for both quantity and quality. Some had too much foreskin or veins like tree bark or were smelly or weirdly bent (Jim's had a bit of a bend but then so, it was said, did a certain former US president's). Paul's was a smooth column, long and thick, big-knobbed with the foreskin out of sight. Jim's mouth went dry.

The way Jim saw things, giving head crossed the line from being a bit bi to being an actual poofter. He had done it (here he knew the exact number) only twice. The first time was with a pretty-boy of eighteen or nineteen in the toilet of a Soho bar, two pints in the rarely experienced atmosphere of a real gay venue having loosened Jim's inhibitions. The second time was stone-cold sober in a wood outside Arundel with an assortment of other men: a group grope evolved into a wank-fest and then a blow-fest, each guy bent over the crotch of his neighbour in a makeshift circle. When it turned into a gangbang of two willing takers, Jim went back to his car, exhilarated and conscience-stricken in equal measure. A threshold had been crossed. This was last summer.

Aware now that he was taking an immense risk, he rucked up the kimono and knelt in front of the sofa on which Paul was sprawled. Parting the dressing gown a few inches more he took Paul's cock in his mouth. It got bigger and harder. Jim grunted as it filled his mouth, threatening to choke him. There must be a breathing technique he hadn't mastered; more experienced guys also had a smoother action. 'Watch your teeth,' the boy in Soho had said. Jim watched his teeth as a faint grunt suggested Paul might be waking up. Would he see what Jim was doing and get on his knees to return the favour? No, he wouldn't. This was the last moment to stop – and maybe get away with it.

But there was no way he could stop this, doing this, having this; he felt more excited than even last Saturday (and other times) on drugs. Paul was snoring now; his hard-on started to subside. Jim licked his balls, rolling them in his mouth as other men had done with his. He barely had to touch himself inside the kimono before he came, shuddering and moaning, indifferent now to whether Paul was asleep or awake, excited or shocked. He continued licking and sucking for another minute until an aching mouth and the uncomfortable dampness inside his kimono brought home to him the incredible recklessness of what he was doing. If Paul blabbed it would be worse than Christine's secret coming out, a scandal Jim could not live with: he'd have to leave Pembertons, move to another town, never see his dad again.

He removed his mouth from Paul's groin and pulled the dressing gown over him. He held his breath for a moment, then let it out heavily. He went to the bathroom to pee and clean himself. His entire future now depended on whether Paul had been sleeping or faking, on whether he blabbed, dropping Jim in the deepest shit, or kept mum, which he might out of embarrassment or even for friend-ship's sake.

It was important to act natural. He took a blanket and pillow from the drawer under his bed and returned to the living-room. Paul was lying on his stomach and snoring again. A part of Jim, a new part, ached to lie down beside Paul, go to sleep against him, wake up with him, make this a night of something more than just one-way sex. This line of thought was more dangerous than the blowjob. He dropped the blanket over Paul and tucked the pillow under his head. Paul murmured in his sleep. In case he was on the verge of waking, Jim said, 'Goodnight, Paul' in a natural, casual way and returned to his bedroom where he fell quickly asleep, the afternoon's exercise and the evening's drinking overtaking his guilt and anxiety.

In the morning Paul was gone. And by next weekend he was seeing Jenny Dixon, the Guvnor's youngest stepdaughter. Between this new romance and his dad suddenly dying and his trips to the Continent for the Guvnor, Paul was too busy for soccer; and with Jenny on the go he didn't need to go out on the pull. Jim had pulled on his own before and now he did it again, starting on the next Saturday. Another year's twat-toll began to build: local slags and foreign totty, tourists and language-students and waitresses. And, in lay-byes, woods, parks and toilets, the cock count continued to grow. None of them was of the calibre of Paul's and Jim resumed the role of the one knelt to, not the kneeler. He wasn't gay. Bi maybe.

Not gay.

Turning twenty-one in April Jim became eligible to drive heavy goods vehicles. Dad had already let him manoeuvre the delivery lorry around the works and the trading estate. Now Jack Pemberton paid for him to have lessons with an instructor.

'Thanks for the HGV course, Guvnor,' Jim said when Charlie brought their employer over to speak to him on one of his factory inspections.

'Don't thank me,' said Jack. 'I see this as an investment. You'll be able to cover Charlie when he's sick or on holiday. And, please God, one day we'll have enough work to need two drivers.'

'Well, anyway...'

'I wish we had more men like you, Jim. You're a real Jack-of-all-trades.'

'I'm a factotum,' Jim said.

Jack laughed. 'Where'd you pick up that word?'

'Off of Paul Barrett.' He didn't repeat his '*fuck*-totum' joke. It was never easy to be natural with the Guvnor, despite all he'd done for them. It was as if the Guvnor, not Dad, was betraying Mum, whose face was fading in Jim's memory but whose presence he sometimes sensed as vividly as if she were in the room, even in the rooms of his flat which she'd never seen, the flat he only occupied because the Guvnor was shagging her replacement.

He passed his HGV test first time at the end of May.

'Christine tells me Her Ladyship's daughter's moved in with your mate Paul,' Dad said at the end of June. They were working on a rust-bucket MG from a Welsh scrapyard. The

261

Guvnor's imperious wife and her spoilt-brat daughters were not held in high regard by the workforce.

'Good luck to 'im,' Jim said. He heard about Paul's engagement in July via the canteen grapevine while Dad was on one of his runs to Wales. 'Paul's bitten off more than he can chew,' Auntie Lil pronounced.

'He's welcome to chew me any time,' said Leanne whose tits were in Jordan's league. Jim had shagged Leanne in his first year at Pembertons.

'Sorry, babes,' said Saffron, famously sharp-tongued. 'You're a KFC kind of girl and Paul's eating steak *tartare* these days.' Jim had told Paul Saffron had been through half the male workforce. Not true: even her girlfriends didn't know who Saffron was seeing; a married man was rumoured to be in the frame.

Paul still found time to visit the works and sit with the lower ranks in the canteen. He and Saffron had a thing going to do with plays and films, but he also made time to speak to Jim, his friend if not quite his mate any more.

'How's it hanging, James?' he might ask.

'It's pretty limp at the moment,' Jim would reply.

'Try Viagra instead of E,' Paul was likely to say.

Jim was fairly sure Paul knew what he'd done that Saturday in the flat and was keeping it to himself. It worried Jim that someone knew his darkest secret but there'd always been the possibility of his car being spotted in a suspicious location or of running into somebody he knew at one of the cruising places. Risk was part of the excitement. Married men took an even bigger chance.

In July he ran into his high school sweetheart Liz in the shopping precinct. She was wheeling a double pushchair with two toddlers in it.

'I'm visiting me mum,' she told him. 'I live in Shoreham now.'

'These both yours?'

'Course they are. Brad and Jennifer. Their dad's a plumber. Well, he will be.' Unlike Jim, Liz pronounced her aitches. 'Damian. He's an apprentice. We're not married. We just, you know, live together. We're buying a council flat.' Women always gave you too much information. 'You married, Jimmy?'

No one, since school, called him Jimmy. 'Nah,' he said.

'Still fancy-free.'

'Make the most of it while you still can.'

'I do,' he said.

'Same old Jimmy.' Her smile evoked memories of a less complicated time.

'You work in one of them beauty parlours?' he asked.

'Part-time. It's not easy with small kids.'

'I s'pose it ain't,' he said. Liz wasn't a walking advert for the beauty business. At school she'd been blonde, a dye-job. Now she was a brassy red. The harsh colour made her look cheap. Her face – she too was only twenty-one – was careworn. Life had been hard, still was hard. This could have been *his* life; these kids – they were becoming tetchy – could be *his* kids. Wasn't it better to worry about if you were a poofter than worry about finding money for the next gas bill, the next pair of kiddie-trainers, the next toy, the next unplanned kiddie?

'Nice to see you, Liz,' he said gallantly.

'You too, Jimmy. Take care.'

Jim didn't know what it was he wanted for the future but he knew it wasn't this. He spent the next three weekends working on the yellow MG with his dad, a 'god' among mechanics. Jim could replace an exhaust and strip a gearbox but his main value to Charlie was muscle-power, hauling hoist chains, loosening clogged cogs and nuts that had rusted solid.

Workshop time kept him from worrying, kept him out of trouble.

On the doormat when he got home: an invitation to Paul's wedding. Thicker than a birthday card, it was embossed in gold and black, very flash. Saffron and Auntie Lil had also been invited. In the canteen amazement (not unmixed with envy) was expressed at 'Her Ladyship's' guest-list.

'You taking anyone?' Saffron asked him in front of his mates.

'Who would I take? Some scrubber?'

'You can take me then.'

'Some scrubber!' Harry Smallwood (the soccer captain) contributed quick as a flash. General laughter, and dagger looks from Saffron.

'Or you can take Lil if you'd rather, and Nellie Dean can be my escort.' Roger Dean's wife had left him for a

Spanish waiter in Majorca, where she now lived with mixed feelings, according to her ex.

'"Escort" is it?' said Leanne, sat behind Saffron. 'Fuck me.'

'Not without a condom,' Harry said, fast out of the stalls again.

'If we 'ave to go as couples,' Jim told Saffron, 'I shall be honoured to be your escort.' He thought 'honoured' was particularly fine. Saffron curtsied.

'The honour is all mine, Squire Turner.'

'Get Saffron,' said Leanne. 'She's off with the fairies.'

Christine said the suit he wore to Gran's funeral wouldn't do and offered to go shopping with him, but he insisted on making his own choice: an Italian-style number from Marks & Spencer. He hoped pale grey wasn't a woofter colour. Christine was impressed when he paraded in it for her benefit.

By the beginning of September, when the soccer season restarted, he and Dad had got the yellow BGT's engine running, noisily but more or less reliably. A bodyshop-owner pal of Charlie's patched up the bodywork at a knockdown price (Dad could do it himself but he preferred to concentrate on the mechanical side). They took Christine for a test drive, Jim scrunched in the back.

'Don't drive her too hard,' Charlie said. Cars, like boats, were always feminine. 'There's a problem with her transmission I haven't quite sorted out.'

'You know me. I'm not a speed merchant.' Christine was happy to part with her current car, another BGT in baby-poo green. But she wasn't sure about yellow. 'Can I have a white one next time?'

'You can have this one in white if you want,' Dad said.

'No, leave it as it is. Her.'

Jim's stepmother, in a vivid red dress, outshone the bridesmaids and all the other female guests. 'Christine's quite a babe for her age,' said Saffron who wore a red sash as a belt round the waist of a calf-length purple-and-black-striped dress made of some kind of velvet. Rarely seen out of leather, it was Saffron's proud boast that all her clothes came from charity shops, more for the sake of recycling than tight purse strings. Jim didn't think red with purple was a good idea but what did he know. Her lipstick matched the sash. Possibly emboldened by champagne she fazed him with a question during the feast:

'Who d'you think's the best-looking: bride or groom?'

'They're an 'andsome pair,' he said, playing for time.

'Yes, but if you had to choose, which one would it be?'

'Well, 'er, of course.' This wasn't untrue; neither was it the whole truth.

'So would I, but I think *you're* fibbing, Jim Turner.'

'Go on,' he said. 'I never 'ad you down for a pussy-muncher.' This wasn't exactly true either; he and his mates had speculated. But no wonder she'd told them to get lost every time one of them asked her out.

'Now you know. Keep it to yourself, though, won't you. You don't tell on me and I won't tell on you.'

'What's to tell, for fuck's sake?'

'That you fancy Paul.'

'I never said I did.'

'You never said you didn't. But I've got your number, Jim Turner, even if you didn't have mine. You sort of light up every time he comes near you.'

'You reckon?'

'I *know*. Go on, admit it.'

The champagne was clearly affecting both of them. Jim grinned and said, 'All right then. Yes.' His answer surprised him more than her question. In the mood of the moment he almost told her about the Saturday night in March.

There was some semi-formal dancing on a square of parquet which he wasn't up for. Saffron danced with Nellie Dean and with Paul and even with the Guvnor. Jim, swigging champagne as if it were beer, was fairly legless by the time the music picked up a disco beat. One of the bridesmaids, a cousin of Jenny's, dark-haired and disturbingly tall, asked him for a dance. He lurched onto the floor with her and laid out what he could remember of the moves Liz had taught him five years ago.

'I think you could do with some fresh air,' the girl said after five minutes. Her name was Lorna. She had a posh voice. They walked out of the marquee and down to where the lawn ended in an abrupt four-foot drop-off to a field where hoof marks could be seen.

'They ought to fence this,' he said. 'You could break a leg fallin' off that.'

265

'It's called a ha-ha.'

'Hee-hee,' replied Jim, witty more by accident than intention.

Glamour-wise Lorna wasn't in Jennifer's league but a tantalizing pair of pink-melon breasts oozed out of her lemon-yellow dress. Leaning in for a kiss that looked as if it might be welcome, Jim attempted to get a hand inside her cleavage. Not easy: the fabric was pulled taut. And not welcome. 'Cheeky,' she said with a not unduly hostile laugh and pushed him off the ha-ha. 'Ha-ha,' she said, calculatedly apposite. By way of overkill she added: 'Ho-ho.'

Jim landed on his back on a pile of manure that was mercifully not recent. 'Cow,' he said.

'I think you'll find it's horse,' she retorted. 'Have you broken anything?'

'I'll break your fuckin' neck.'

'Oh, I don't think so,' she said. She went back to the tent and sought out Saffron who was doing a creditable salsa with Turner Sr. Charlie jumped over the ha-ha and heaved his son back onto the lawn and then drove him home, dropping Saffron at her mother's on the way.

'It can't be easy, bein' a lesbo in this town.'

'You'd be surprised.' She looked butch today: black leather blouson over a tank-top, black leather miniskirt, purply-black lipstick.

'D'you know what Paul calls it?'

'What: "bein' a lesbo"?'

'No. This town. 'E calls it Boredom-on-Sea.'

She laughed. 'It has its moments.'

'You never think of leavin'?'

'I couldn't leave my mum, not after what happened, you know – my dad.'

'Course you couldn't.' Her dad's suicide, his mum's cancer: they had grief in common. 'So, 'ave you got, like, a regular – ladyfriend?'

'Mind your own business. Have you got a boyfriend on the go?'

'Course I ain't.'

'So what do you for a bit of action?'

'There are, you know – places.'

'Toilets? What do they call it – cottaging?'

'There's better than that.'

266

'Like what?'

'Never you mind. D'you want to come out with me on Saturday?'

'No. Why would I?'

'If you 'aven't got anythin' better to do.'

'I have, and I'd think you have too.'

Since he was usually with his mates and she with her sewing-room crowd, there were few opportunities to get Saffron on her own in the canteen. After two more refusals he stopped asking her out. He had a half-formed fantasy that they could provide a smokescreen for each other – he even envisaged a marriage in which they produced, like Liz and her Damian, the required number of children and still gave each other the freedom to do their own thing on the side – but she seemed not to need this or want this.

During October Paul started playing with the team on a regular basis. He couldn't make practice nights but on Saturdays he was glad to get out of shopping with Jennifer. Michael and Nick, the male half of the Design Department, joined the team. They now had a full team as often as not. Michael, a tad overweight, wasn't fast but he was nifty at tackling and soon became their top scorer. Nick was like Paul, more speed than accuracy; they were both put on the wing. Pembertons won five of their next six games. Third from the bottom of their league last season, they were now third from the top.

As at the factory, Paul was friendly with Jim in the changing cabin before the match and at half-time but afterwards he went to his own home to clean up, wrapped up in an old duvet to protect the interior of his Peugeot. The Guvnor had given him a BMW but he didn't parade it in front of the workers. Michael wasn't bashful about his; he also went home dirty. Nick, who Jim thought might be gay (he was over thirty and single), showered with the rest of the players. Paul's wife came to one game but spent most of it in her car on the mobile. Christine watched a game at the end of November. When Jim couldn't get her MG to start, Paul drove her home. Within minutes of their leaving Jim had found the problem: a cracked fuel line, which he replaced on Monday after raiding Dad's workshop. Harry drove him back to the field and helped him fix the new line.

'Is Paul Barrett shaggin' your stepmum?' Harry suddenly asked.

'Don't be daft. 'E's only just got married. An' she's twice as old as 'im.'

'Your dad's away a lot, ain't 'e? My mum said she saw 'em eatin' in that Eye-talian place near the office a couple of weeks back.'

'Well, I expect a lot of the office folk eat there.'

'They was on their own, my mum said.'

'Nah, I bet the Guvnor was with 'em or – what's 'er name – 'is secretary.'

'No, Mum said they was on their own.'

Jim guessed that the office crowd often lunched together. Even if Paul and Christine were on their own, it wouldn't mean anything. She might cheat on Dad, but she wouldn't cheat on the Guvnor, her meal-ticket. Would she?

Paul missed the next two matches, claiming a backlog of paperwork to catch up on. Charlie wasn't available to take his place. Since they got the yellow MG back on the road he'd begun staying away weekends, in Wales where the Guvnor allowed him to 'moonlight' doing deliveries for a firm that made packing materials. But when he was back in Sussex to pick up his next load at the beginning of December he invited himself over to the flat. He sounded funny on the phone and half-an-hour later he arrived at Jim's door in a state of distress such as Jim hadn't seen since Mum died.

'What's up, Dad?'

'Oh, Jim-lad, what a bastard I've been, to you and Christine. And for such a long time. I've been leading a double life and now it's all gone tits-up.'

In a few stumbled sentences he laid on Jim the news that he had another wife, a woman called Glenys – kids too – in a village outside Swansea. Glenys was dying of bone cancer, the same thing that killed Mum.

''Ow many kids?'

'Four. Two of each. The youngest is eleven. The oldest is seventeen.' The television was on in the background, sound muted: snooker from Sheffield. They both spoke to the TV, unable to look each other in the eye.

'Fuckin' 'ell, Dad. Mum was still alive when you 'ad these kids!'

'Three of them, yes. Not the youngest.'

268

''Ow could you do this with 'er bein' so sick an' every-thin'?'

'She wasn't sick when it started. The thing was, I always wanted a big family but your mum couldn't have any more. Glenys's mum was one of my landladies, she ran the B&B where I stayed in Swansea. I could see she fancied me, and your mum was –' he reddened – 'out of action for a long time after you were born, and it just sort of – started. The first boy was an accident but after him we – planned the others.'

'But you married 'er.' On-screen the white ball followed the last red into a corner pocket.

'After your mum died, I did. Months after. And I never stopped loving Margaret through all the time – before. Losing her was the worst thing that ever happened, and now I've got to go through it all again with Glenys.'

'Why didn't you bring 'em 'ere after you married 'er?'

'I wanted to, but Glenys said it would have unsettled the kids too much. You know, school and their friends, all that. I spend as much time there as I can – that packing delivery contract came in handy in lots of ways.'

'*We* could have moved to Wales.' How different his life might have been. A step-mum who was a proper mum. Brothers to play with, sisters to tease.

'I thought about that, but back then there wasn't any work going. And then Christine came back from London and – you know the rest.'

'But – marryin' 'er as well. That's – what do they call it? – "buggery".'

Charlie gave a short laugh. '*Bigamy* is what they call it, Jim-lad. Bigamy's what I've been getting away with for eleven years. Buggery is something else entirely. Lots of men get away with that these days.'

Jim felt gobsmacked. 'Did Christine know about this – Gladys?' he asked.

'Glenys. No, not till today. She's well pissed off, you can imagine. Thinks I let her, you know, do the business with the Guvnor just so I could support this other family. Well –' he was red again – 'I suppose I did. But I love her, Jim-lad. I love them both. And all my kids.' He flashed Jim a shy grin which Jim turned from the television to see. Then they both looked back at the set as one of the players potted a snookered blue with a rebound shot.

269

'Fuckin' 'ell, Dad,' Jim said again. 'I wish you'd told me before.'

'So do I, Jim. I should have. I'm sorry.'

'I'd like to meet these brothers and sisters.'

'You will now. I promise you.'

But it wasn't going to happen quickly. Dad had to go back to Wales where Jim's other stepmother was dying. Jim did his first solo delivery run: Portsmouth and Bristol. An old biddy at the store in Portsmouth wanted to take him home and feed him; she was more grandmotherly than his own late Gran. The furniture buyer in Bristol would also have liked to take him home, to feed *off* him rather than feed him: a first-division Nellie. This must be the one Paul had mentioned. Not content with making flirtatious remarks Mr Davis ('Call me Bette, dear. Everybody does.') also felt his biceps. 'Maybe later I'll check your inside leg,' he cooed. Did Dad have to put up with this sort of thing on the road?

From Bristol Jim took the M5 to Birmingham and Manchester. A van-driver in the woods at Arundel had told him there was a secret freemasonry of gay and bi lorry-drivers: they overnighted at certain motels or in notorious lay-byes. There was no hint of this in the motels and B&Bs on Dad's list. No deliveries were scheduled for Wales, and Jack hadn't sanctioned him to take over Charlie's moon-lighting for the packing material company.

While he was away the Guvnor announced a new swathe of job cuts. The mood in the factory was grim when he returned on Friday. Jack summoned him for a de-briefing and assured him that his position was secure.

'We could do with more men like you,' he said again. 'A – what did you call it?'

'Factotum,' Jim reminded him. The Guvnor chortled.

Pembertons were two men short on Saturday and lost an away match. Jim hadn't heard from Paul. After the game Jim brought Harry and two other players home for the evening. They stopped off at Tesco for beer kegs and again at a Chinese takeaway. They watched Sky Sports and then a porn-film, not the one he'd showed Paul. His mates provided a running commentary. Semi-stiffies were induced but no one untrousered. When Harry requested a blowjob, it was treated as the joke he meant it to be.

At eleven-thirty, with his rat-arsed friends sent to their homes by taxi, the phone rang. It was Dad calling from Wales, more distraught than ever.

'She's dead, Jim-lad. My lovely wife is dead.'

'I'm sorry, Dad, but – they've got better drugs nowadays, 'aven't they? She didn't suffer the way Mum did.'

'Not her. Not Glenys, though it won't be long now. She's been in a coma since Wednesday. No – *Christine*'s dead.'

'Fuckin' 'ell, Dad.'

Somehow Christine had driven the yellow MG over the cliff below Beachy Head. Paul was with her. He'd been thrown clear. He had a broken leg and arm. Christine went over with the car. The coastguards had used a helicopter to recover her body. The car was still down there. Dad would have to come home to identify her. There would be an autopsy and an inquest.

'Fuckin' 'ell, Dad.' He'd hated her but he hadn't wished her dead.

It had taken several hours to contact Dad. Paul's mobile was smashed and there was no reply from the home number on his business cards. The police finally contacted the Guvnor who was out to dinner with Her Ladyship. Dad didn't say how Jack was taking it; presumably losing your bit-of-fluff could hurt as much as losing your wife, especially when your wife was as stuck-up as Mrs Pemberton.

'Is Paul all right?'

'Jack said they were operating on his leg. You'll be able to visit him in a day or two. I knew he and Christine were – friendly, like. Having lunch and going up on the downs for walks. She told me there wasn't anything in it, but going out with him at the weekend – I don't know what to think.'

''E's missed the last three games. Said 'e 'ad paperwork to catch up on. When I see 'im I'll ask what they was up to.'

'I'm not sure I want to know. Not going to bring her back, is it?'

'Is there anythin' you want me to do?'

'No, lad. It'll all have to wait till I get there. I'll talk to the kids and try to get home tomorrow.' Funny that he still thought of Sussex as home, even though he had a wife and four kids in Wales.

He called again on Sunday morning. His Welsh wife had died as well, within minutes of him finishing the call to Jim. Poor Dad. He'd lost two wives. Three, in fact. It was a good thing he had all these kids. Jim knew that, much as loved his dad, he wouldn't be much use in the comfort department.

Charlie came home on Monday. After the formalities at the mortuary he went to the factory. Jim was helping to load the lorry. His father hugged him – a rare thing in itself – but there were no tears. The men shook his hand gravely, the women embraced him, fussed and cried. Jim offered to stay the night at the house but Dad said he was going back to Wales, the kids needed him – there were no grandparents or other relatives, only good neighbours.

'Bring the kids 'ere,' Jim said. 'I'll 'elp you look after 'em.'

'We'll see, Jim-lad. These things need a bit of sorting.'

On Tuesday Jim headed north on another run: Newcastle, Edinburgh, Glasgow. At a pit-stop on the A1 he got wanked off in the Gents by a Scottish van-driver whose accent made English sound like Russian. That evening Dad called him on his mobile and told him Glenys was to be cremated on Friday. It would be a few days before the coroner released Christine's body. Her funeral would not take place till after Christmas. The police had been in touch with him. The wrecked car had been retrieved by another helicopter. Tests on the car coupled with statements from Paul and two witnesses in another car suggested that the propshaft had collapsed and pitchforked the MG onto the cliff, where it rolled over a couple of times before landing on a weakened stretch that gave way under the impact. 'They're calling it a freak occurrence,' Charlie said.

'Christ, Dad, is it somethin' we did – or didn't do? I told you she was only fit for takin' parts.'

'Jim-lad, we've brought back worse cars than that. Maybe we missed something when we put her back together after bathing her in the rust gunk. We know the transmission needed some more work, but I don't think the coroner's going to put the blame on us. If it had happened anywhere else Christine could have come out of it without a scratch or at any rate no worse than Paul did.

Did you go and see him?'

'Not yet.'

He stopped at the same rest area on his return journey on Thursday but there was no action. On Friday afternoon, while his Welsh stepmother was being cremated, he visited Paul who had declined his uncle's offer to subsidize a move to a private hospital. The male NHS orthopaedic ward held a mixture of road accident victims and old geezers who'd fallen over in their homes. Paul's right leg was in plaster from his toes almost to his crotch. His left arm was in a plastic sheath inside a sling. A raw new scar ran across the right side of his forehead and under his hair. He shook Jim's hand warmly. Jim would have liked to hug him but didn't dare.

'I won't be playing any more soccer this season,' Paul said.

Jim grinned. 'We'll manage without you.' He told him about Saturday's losing game in Rye and passed on various messages from the factory.

'I'm sorry about Christine,' Paul suddenly said.

'It's *me* what should be sorry. Me and Dad. We was supposed to 'ave made that fuckin' car safe to drive.'

'It *was* running pretty well. You could hardly have expected something like that to go wrong.'

'You know what it was?'

'A – "universal joint"? – came apart at the head of the propeller shaft?'

'Yeah. I've 'eard of this but it's the first time I've seen it actually 'appen to a car what I've worked on.'

'You shouldn't blame yourself. Or your dad.'

'But look what it's done. Look at *you*. Are you gonna be all right?'

'My leg's held together with pins and plates in three places. I'll be setting off airport metal detectors from now on. But I'll mend. I'm mending already.'

'What about your arm?'

'It's only a fracture. Thank God it's not my wanking arm!'

Jim laughed. 'It's a good job you've got a wife to take care of you in that department.'

'When she's not too busy taking care of her old boy-friends. Possibly some new ones as well.'

Jim said, 'Oh, dear.' This would have been his mother's

response.

'We're drifting apart,' Paul elaborated. 'I think she only married me to get away from her mother, and I got carried away by having all that sex on tap.'

'I've been wonderin' if I shouldn't get married for the same thing,' Jim said. 'Most of me mates 'ave done it.'

'If you want my advice: don't.'

'Not all it's cracked up to be, is it? I've always 'ad me doubts.'

'*Lacrimae rerum*.'

'Beg pardon?'

'It's Latin for "life's a bitch".'

'Ain't that the truth. Paul –' he lowered his voice – 'did Christine tell you about me dad's other wife?'

'Your mum, you mean? I remember her. She was one of my Sunday-School teachers when I was small.'

'No, not me mum. The other one. The one in Wales.'

'He had another wife between your mum and Christine?'

'Not between. As well.' In a few whispered sentences he told Paul about his dad's revelation that he was a bigamist.

'Christine didn't know?'

'Not till two weeks ago. Just a couple of days before the – accident.'

'She must have been devastated. I can't believe she didn't tell me.'

'Paul, was you –' he hesitated – 'you know – shaggin' 'er?"

Paul blushed. 'James, I'm afraid I have to confess that I was.'

'But – she's old enough to be your mother. She was my step-mum, you fuckin' prat.'

'Well, I'm not going to apologize. Love means never having to say you're sorry.' Jim missed both the reference and the irony.

'*Love*? You reckon you *loved* 'er?'

'Reckon so, Jim.'

'Fuckin' 'ell.' One of the old geezers heard this and tut-tutted. Jim gave him a fuck-off look and the old geezer looked away.

Pembertons were three men short for Saturday's rematch

274

with the police. Their star forward Michael had gone to Prague for a pre-Christmas weekend break with his wife. The police won 9-2. Jim didn't score. A cold day and a colder evening. The pubs were quiet. Jim didn't score.

Charlie stayed on in Wales to spend Christmas with his children. Paul was discharged from hospital and went to stay at The Grange. Jim wouldn't visit him there; the combination of Her Ladyship and the housekeeper was too intimidating. Jim's pals all had families or girlfriends. Invited to an aunt's in Worthing and to Christine's step-mother's house, he chose to spend Christmas Day alone, ate an overcooked turkey ready-meal, drank, watched TV, felt sorry for himself.

On Boxing Day he ran into Leanne on the promenade. She'd had a row with her boyfriend Keith Cartwright, a former schoolmate of Jim's whose dick bent the opposite way to Jim's (must be very inconvenient for shagging). Leanne came back to Jim's flat for what felt, possibly to both of them, like a mercy-fuck. She suggested a get-together on New Year's Eve but Jim fibbed his way out of it. Leanne was a goer, good fun, but a bit clingy. He didn't want to be joined in holy matrimony, he just wanted to get his leg over.

Charlie came back on Saturday, the day after Boxing Day. No match this week. Instead of going out on the pull Jim went over to his dad's. Christine was to be cremated on Monday. She used a lot of air-fresheners and had cut flowers in every room; now the house already smelt stale and dusty. They drank beers and watched Sky Sports. Charlie said he'd phone for pizzas later. He didn't seem to want to talk about his dead wives.

'I'm probably gonna go and live in Wales,' he suddenly announced.

'Not bring your kids 'ere?'

'No. They don't want to change schools, lose their friends – you know.'

'I thought you said there wasn't any jobs there.'

'If I sell this place I can buy my own lorry and carry on working for the packing people, maybe find some other stuff to deliver. There's a bloke there who restores MGs. He says he can put some work my way.'

Jim had always thought of his father as a tower of strength, but he wasn't. These two women had dragged him by the balls, and now his kids were telling him what they wanted. He should be telling them. Jim would have liked to say, *What about me?* Dad guessed what he was thinking – some of it.

'You'll have to come and stay, Jim-lad, meet my kids, get to know them. You could always move there too if you want to – you know, still be near me.'

The way he put it, Jim would be a right big girl's blouse if he chose to follow Dad to wherever the fuck this was. But Dad had made a choice: he'd chosen his Welsh kids over Jim. OK, they were younger, they needed him more than Jim did. But he still felt as if the rug had been pulled from under him. He had his friends *here*, his job, football, cruising places he knew and more-or-less trusted. But having Dad nearby – even with Christine, that slag – was what made Sussex not just the place where he lived, but *home*.

Christine's stepmother Linda had made the funeral arrangements. A good turnout: over twenty people from the factory, including the Guvnor and Her Ladyship, both in formal black. Saffron also wore black (leather); Leanne wore red (leather). Nobody, apart from Paul, knew about Charlie's Welsh family, about the bigamy; Dad's other big secret – Christine and the Guvnor - had stayed secret for more than ten years. Paul didn't make his ladyfriend's funeral. Did anyone else know that he had been getting the Guvnor's sloppy seconds, Dad's sloppy *thirds*?

Running mascara gave Leanne the look of an extra from a zombie movie; her skirt creaked loudly when she stood up for the committal, a sound as startling as a fart. Linda and her children and grandchildren were also in tears. Auntie Eileen from Worthing sobbed audibly. Dad kept a stiff upper lip, as did the Guvnor; Her Ladyship's lips were starched shut. Any grief Jim felt was more to do with his dad relocating. After the curtains closed and the vicar gave a blessing, the filing-out music was 'Bridge Over Troubled Water'. Trying to think of something more apt, Jim grinned when he came up with 'It's Raining Men'.

The Pembertons' wreath was the most tasteful of the array outside the crematorium. Did Her Ladyship know Christine had been her husband's bit-of-fluff? The tribute from Linda and her kids spelled out CHRISTINE in white chrysanthemums. Jim hadn't sent flowers; Dad said a donation to charity would be money better spent. Jim had put a tenner in the Salvation Army tin in a pub last week: they specialized in 'fallen women', didn't they?

The Guvnor and his missus didn't come to the tea-party afterwards, but most of the factory people did, crowding the lounge of Linda's small terraced house. A big spread: sausage rolls and sandwiches, shop cakes, crisps and choccie-bars for the kids. Leanne repaired her make-up in front of everybody.

Dad announced that Christine's ashes would be scattered on the downs above Alfriston, the village she'd made her home. On one of the trading estates there was a street that functioned as a red light district, occasionally raided by the police; men kerb-crawled half-a-dozen prostitutes, said to be asylum-seekers from Eastern Europe. Jim hadn't availed himself of their services, but two of his mates had. Oral was £20, full sex only £30. If it had been up to Jim this is where he would have dumped his stepmother's rendered-down remains.

The focus of Dad's life had shifted. On Tuesday he put the house in the hands of an estate agent, packed some of his stuff and went back to Wales. Jim was now the fulltime driver. He did a London run on Wednesday, New Year's Eve, some old and spoiled items to go in the sales. Desperate times, and not only for Pembertons: before he left he told Leanne his plans with his dad had been cancelled. They joined his mates and their wives/girlfriends for a lager-lout evening in the Old Town: beer and vodka shots, curry, more beer and vodka, darts (one accidental stabbing), karaoke, a brawl, Auld Lang Syne at midnight.

'Are you an' Leanne gonna be an item?' Harry asked him as they waited for taxis at half past midnight.

'Search me,' said Jim, too far gone to make a judgement either way. When they got home, Leanne passed out on his bed; just as well: he could never have got it up. She gave him a blowjob at about eight a.m., as good a way as any other to start the new year. An item in the making? Nah.

The Guvnor brought Paul to watch Saturday's home game, the gardener struggling to push a wheelchair over the soggy field. Michael's wife came out as well, but there was no sign of Jenny. One of Jim's three goals was disallowed, but despite having one less player they beat a team from Shoreham 6-1.

No deliveries in the first week of January. Jim resumed his factotum role. The ripsaws were playing up; new blades were on order. Dad was settling into his new life in Wales. Paul phoned to say that he was now on crutches and just about able to wash and dress himself. He went to physiotherapy three times a week at a private hospital, paid for by the Guvnor. He'd moved back to his own house. One of Her Ladyship's cleaning women came in to do housework and cook his lunch. Jenny was living in Brighton; they'd agreed to split up.

'I'm fed up of TV and the internet. Is there a match on Saturday?'

'Yeah, in Seaford,' Jim told him. 'I'll pick you up if you want to come.'

'Thanks, Jim. Let's do a pub lunch.'

'Not before a game,' Jim reminded him. 'A pint maybe.'

Paul was nifty on his crutches but it wasn't easy getting him into Jim's cramped Mercedes roadster. He was wearing a smart overcoat, a designer sweater, a pair of jogging pants with one leg amputated to fit over his cast, one shoe and two football socks to keep his exposed toes warm. He looked more like an injured sportsman than a hapless lover who'd had a lucky escape. He was overdue for a haircut; Jim liked him with longer hair, he looked like a college kid again. They sank a pint each at the Flying Fish outside Newhaven. Jim updated Paul on Dad's move to Wales and his own new routine as a lorry-driver, omitting the detail of his luck in lay-byes. He bragged about seeing the New Year in with Leanne. Paul had consulted a divorce lawyer: he and Jenny would have to be separated for two years unless one of them agreed to be cited for adultery.

'I'll 'ave a word with Leanne,' Jim said with a laugh. 'I bet she'd be up for it – as long as you give 'er one. Or Saffron might!' He decided to keep Saffron's big secret, since she was keeping his. Paul didn't seem to relish Leanne or Saffron being linked to the undoing of his marriage. He said Jenny was investigating whether an American 'quickie' divorce was valid here.

The pitch in Seaford had a covered stand no bigger than a garage. Paul insisted on getting there on his own; he skidded twice but didn't fall. His football socks and the bottom of his coat were caked with mud. Open on three sides, the stand had some cold concrete benches which were too low for him. A chair was fetched from the changing hut. There were less than a dozen spectators under the roof with him and a few more out on the field. The day was dry, but a bitter wind blew in from the Channel.

It was Nick's turn to be off with the flu. Michael was playing today, but his wife and father-in-law hadn't come to watch. They missed a heroic performance: he scored four goals and contributed passes to three more. Jim had a poor day; the lunch had slowed him down. The Seaford team, a mixed bag of teachers and office-workers, played hard but lost 8-2.

Paul was frozen to the marrow. Luckily Jim had bought a second-hand tonneau from a local Mercedes dealer and the heater was in working order. Taking a leaf out of Paul's book, he swathed himself in a bedspread to protect the car from mud on the return journey.

'Are you comin' back to mine?' he asked.

'No, take me home. Too many stairs in your building.' Jim's disappointment eased when Paul invited him in. He allowed Jim to help him out of his overcoat and remove the muddy shoe and socks, then pointed him up to the parental bedroom's en-suite bathroom, which Jenny had de-chintzified in the weeks before their wedding. The bathroom, a future makeover project she would not now complete, had an avocado suite which even Jim knew was beyond the pale of fashion.

When he came downstairs in jeans and a sweatshirt Paul was toasting his feet in front of the log-effect gas fire. Jim was sent back upstairs for a clean pair of football socks to cover the peeping toes. Then he went to the kitchen and brewed tea. Her Ladyship's cleaning woman had made a jam sponge which he took back to the lounge.

'Do you want to go out on the pull tonight?'

'I'm not much use like this. Unless it makes me a sympathy shag!'

'D'you reckon I'd get some of the sympathy?' They shared a laugh.

Jenny had had satellite TV installed. She had also

stocked the wine rack with more upmarket bottles than Paul or his parents had ever bought. Paul produced a bottle of rioja which still wore its £11.99 price tag. He passed it to Jim with the opener.

'Twelve quid! Fuckin' 'ell, Paul. You won the lottery?'

'This is what my wife thinks of as plonk. I'll open a good one later.'

Mrs Whats'ername had also left a homemade steak-and-kidney pie, which they ate in the kitchen with French fries and peas from the freezer and a bottle of Chateau-something, unpriced. After the meal they opened another bottle of the rioja and watched US forensic dramas back-to-back. Paul said he was becoming an addict.

'Sorry I haven't got any porno for you.'

'That's all right. I got plenty at 'ome, as you know. Seen one, seen 'em all.' But secretly Jim wished they had a blue movie that might get something started. In his torn joggers and dazzlingly striped sweater Paul looked even more like an overgrown schoolboy, cute and – courtesy of the cast and sling – vulnerable. Jim watched him out of the corner of his eye and imagined tearing the clothes off him and licking him all over. This was considerably more than he'd done to any boy at school or indeed to anybody since, although he'd been on the receiving end of such frenzied adoration in the woods a couple of times. Paul caught his eye and Jim had the disconcerting feeling that he knew what he was thinking.

'I'd better get 'ome,' he said at the end of the second set of cunningly solved murders. His speech was slurred. Expensive wine was as lethal as vodka shots.

'You're in no state to drive. You may as well stay.' Paul didn't seem drunk at all. He was getting used to fine wines, the Pemberton high life. 'There's a bed made up in my old room.'

'I'll 'elp you upstairs.'

'You need more help than I do!'

He wouldn't let Jim assist him to get undressed, so the fantasy must remain a fantasy. Strong wine, football, frustration: within seconds of getting into Paul's boyhood bed and before he barely had time to savour his situation, Jim fell catatonically asleep.

He awoke around three with a birdcage mouth and went down to the kitchen for water. When he returned upstairs he saw that there was a light on in Paul's room, the door left open. He was trying to decide whether to check on the invalid when the invalid called out: 'Are you up and about?'

'Yeah.' He went in. Paul lay on his side under the duvet, an open paperback beside his pillow. His shoulders were bare. 'Can't you sleep?'

'I've been sleeping so much lately my cycle's totally fucked. I read a bit, sleep a bit, read some more, count the hours till breakfast.'

'Anythin' I can get you?'

Paul shook his head. 'This is one of the few times I miss Jenny. One of her blowjobs usually sends me back to sleep!'

'You don't need 'er for that. You've got me.' His boldness surprised Jim. Paul's expression – self-deprecating amusement as he made his previous confession – was now unreadable. He seemed to be weighing up Jim's offer. After a moment he let go of the book and stretched out a hand to turn off the lamp. A shadowy head-and-shoulders sculpture in the light from the landing, he rolled onto his back and closed his eyes.

Jim took two steps nearer and threw back the duvet. Paul was now a full-length sculpture, a naked statue padded in places as if it was being prepared for travel. The hairs on his body shivered in the dim glow, or perhaps *he* was shivering. The heating was off; the room was cool but not cold. Jim put one knee on the bed.

Paul said, 'Jim, I don't know about this.' There was a tremor in his voice.

Jim said, 'Relax, Paul. Go with the flow.' It sounded daft, but there, he'd said it. He touched Paul's cock which surged rapidly erect, as impressive as he remembered it from their session with the Spanish tart. He would have liked to touch more of him. He wished he could lie against him, under him or on top of him. He wanted to stroke Paul's hair, lick his chest, his stomach, his thighs. But he knew how uneasy he himself felt when other men tried to take him over the limit of what he was up for and he realized that taking care of Paul's most urgent need was as far as he could expect to go. He put his other knee on the bed and, using his mouth, took care of Paul's most urgent need. *Watch your teeth*; he remembered. He felt the other

281

body tense below him, but unlike the last time Paul didn't lose it. In less than a minute and without any warning he came in Jim's mouth.

There were rules about this. You were supposed to warn people and not come in their mouths, just as you weren't supposed to fuck them without a condom. If it happened it was important to spit, not swallow. In the woods and other places men had sometimes wanted Jim to come in them or over them. Mostly they spat, but a few had swallowed.

Now Jim, for the first time ever, swallowed, kept swallowing. A yeasty yoghurty taste. He almost came, without touching himself, from the sheer excitement of it. He wanted to say something but – what?

He got off the bed.

Paul said, 'Thanks, Jim.'

Jim wanted to say – another, more alarming, first – *I love you, Paul.* But what he said, ludicrously, was: 'You're welcome.' And then: 'Goodnight, Paul.'

'Goodnight, Jim.'

He went back to the bed that had been Paul's. He had no vocabulary for his emotions. He knew what he'd just done was wrong somehow, unmanly, but he also knew he would go back and do it again, right now, if Paul called for him. Their situation was fraught with complexity and almost certainly futureless, but he felt a deeper contentment than he could recall from any previous man-to-man encounter, even though he was more accustomed to being the beneficiary than the benefactor. He slept dreamlessly.

Paul could not sleep.

The near-rapist raped, again. Oral rape: was there such a crime? He'd laid himself open to it, almost literally, turning off the light and lying back on the bed. Even thanked him afterwards, for God's sake!

Jim's eyes had been on him all evening. He hadn't articulated his need as Neil had, but the look in his eyes said everything Neil had said and more. Film-stars must have this feeling – and people of exceptional beauty: the *hunger* in the eyes of the onlooker. Like being stalked. Great for the ego, but – scary.

Jim wanted him. He himself was horny, missing Jenny, her ministrations. It's true what they say, it's either

282

famine or feast. Jim wanted him. A rose is a rose. A blow-job is a blowjob. It hadn't hurt the last time when he'd pretended to be unconscious. So – turn off the light. Lie back. Close your eyes.

In a strange way it felt almost *more* exciting than when Jenny did it. The sensation was the same (well, he was more aware of Jim's teeth than he was of hers) but there was an added *frisson* of difference, of daring, of danger. What would he do if Jim suddenly demanded reciprocity? He wouldn't, he couldn't. Just because Jenny had taught him to nibble her clitoris didn't mean he was ready to fellate a friend. Could he even wank another guy? He never had. And don't even think about sodomy.

Then – he *was* horny – it was over. The noises as his cum was slurped reminded him that this wasn't Jenny, this was Jim. At Jenny's private school in Surrey they must have had lessons in the etiquette of noiseless fellatio. Then: relief as Jim got off the bed. It looked like he wasn't expected to do anything in return. Should he say something?

He said, 'Thanks, Jim.' What else was there to say?

Jim said, 'You're welcome.' And everything seemed to be all right.

Neil, again, came into his mind. Could he have saved him? Just lie back, close your eyes, slurp-slurp. Thanks, Neil. You're welcome.

Paul knew he would not get back to sleep.

Music from below woke Jim just after nine: classical, cater-wauling violins. He dressed and went downstairs. Paul was in the kitchen reading a section of yesterday's paper. He had breakfasted but not cleared up. He smiled.

'Hi. Sleep okay?'

'Uh-huh. You?'

'Off and on. Help yourself to cereals. Want some toast? Boiled egg?'

Jim shook his head. 'I'm not big on breakfast. Any coffee goin'?'

'In the cafetière.'

'The what?' Paul pointed. Jim poured. Everything seemed normal. Two mates over Sunday breakfast. Nothing to indicate that one of them had sucked the other's cock six hours ago.

'Jack's coming to fetch me for lunch. Shall I ask Aunt Agnes if I can bring you?'

'No, ta. I'll get 'ome.' Jim couldn't imagine lunching with Her Ladyship watching his every move. Suppose he used the wrong knife or ate his peas in an inappropriate manner. 'Anythin' you need me to do?'

'I'm okay,' Paul said quickly. Did he think Jim was offering another blowjob? Perhaps he was.

When he left Jim held out his hand, feeling suddenly awkward. Paul pulled Jim towards him and kissed him on the mouth.

Jim wasn't big on snogging. Even with girls it was a problem. Some had lippie that came off all over you, some kept their mouths tightly pursed and were disgusted if you tried any tongue action, some were wet and slobbery. He'd always backed off from men who tried to snog him, it didn't feel right, it was *too* gay. He didn't want to back off from Paul but he didn't know where to hold him, whether to open his mouth and use his tongue, and while he was still calculating his response it was over. Paul ended the kiss and stepped back. He was smiling, as if a kiss between them was no big deal. To Jim it was a bigger deal than the one-way sex.

'When are you back from your travels?'

'Not sure,' Jim stammered. 'I'm goin' to Wales this week, see me dad and 'is kids. They may want me to stay over the weekend.'

'Well – call me when you're back.'

'Okay. And – thanks, Paul.' What was he thanking him for: the kiss?

'Don't be daft. It's me who should be thanking you. The pub lunch, the football.' He didn't seem to be thanking Jim for the blowjob. Perhaps that was what the kiss was for.

To Wales on Tuesday. Deliveries in Cardiff and Swansea, then on to the place that had stolen his father. From the back-garden photos of his other stepmother and her brood he was expecting an ex-council house like the one he'd grown up in, but this was an architect-designed property on a middle-class estate with manicured overlapping front gardens. The whole village was more like the North Downs than the industrial Vale of Glamorgan: no dark Satanic mills, no black-faced miners. As in the photos, the back garden, frosty at dusk in the first week of January, was overgrown and untidy. Unlike Dad's other wives, Glenys had not been keen on horticulture.

'Jim-lad.' Dad still looked the same: grey-blonde hair in need of a cut, work-shirt and jeans stained with grease from labouring on and under cars. There was a dark-green MGA in the open garage with its guts strewn around it. The eldest son had a poser's car, a first-version RAV, parked on the drive.

This son had his mother's looks: dark hair, narrow features, a thin mouth that produced a grudging smile for his half-brother. More nerd than poser he quickly retreated to his room and his PC. The younger kids also had their X-Boxes and PlayStations. Only Megan, the youngest girl who had Dad's blonde hair and eyes even bluer than his, seemed pleased to meet her new brother. She wore a pretty blue dress with matching shoes. Her fourteen-year-old sister was dressed like the boys: sneakers, baggy jeans, a sloppy sweater. This look had been the fashion when Jim was at school (nowadays he favoured tight jeans and figure-hugging T-shirts to show off his pecs, his bum, his lunch).

Shy at first, Megan was soon fussing around him, taking on her mother's duties as hostess. At eleven she too had a PC of her own in her bedroom. The younger boy had (reluctantly) given his room to Jim and would bunk in with his brother. Five bedrooms, two bathrooms and a cloakroom, four computers. Motherless they might be and with an absentee father until recently; poor they were not. Christine had shagged the Guvnor for ten years to pay for all of this!

Jim had no common ground with these techno-geek kids except that they shared a father. Dinner was as much of an ordeal as going to The Grange would have been. Megan filled his plate and his glass, Dad spoke to him about Sussex and the factory and driving the lorry, but the other kids just listened or talked among themselves. He would never be a part of their lives, nor they of his. They now owned his dad in a way that he did not.

He was twenty-one, he should be able – he was able – to stand on his own feet. All the same, he felt like an orphan in this poncified house that was his dad's home but could never be his. It was a relief to be on the road again on Wednesday. The Guvnor, who knew where he was, had told him to go for as long as a week, but he told Dad he had to get back for another run.

'Stay, Jimmy, why don't you,' Megan said before she left for middle school, clean and smart in navy blue. The others wore grunge – yesterday's grunge – to senior school. From them the Welsh intonation was a monosyllabic grunt; from Megan it was like a choirgirl singing. She hugged him.

Dad shook his hand. 'Come back soon, Jim-lad.'

On his way back to Sussex he stopped in lay-byes only to pee or for refreshment and refuelling. No cruising.

He couldn't stop thinking about Paul. This was a new and disturbing sensation. He often looked forward to – and fantasized about – sex with men, but it wasn't focused on any particular male. He'd rarely done the same man twice. New people, male or female, were a turn-on. But now he couldn't wait to see Paul again, touch him again, give him what he wanted. Anything and everything. He would try and get into kissing.

Jim could see he was getting gayer. He wasn't sure he wanted to be a fulltime poofter; in fact he was pretty sure he didn't. Maybe he ought to forget about Paul, concentrate on Leanne; in the canteen she honed in on him like a fly on shit. Or he could go into Brighton after Saturday's game (a bigger pool of student totty there), get shagging again. But he didn't feel like pulling totty and he didn't want to forget about Paul.

When he phoned on Thursday to tell him that Saturday's opponents had cancelled the match because of flu, Paul didn't suggest lunch or anything else. Jim's nerve failed him. He only had to suggest a meal or a drive or going on the pull, but whatever he said would sound like he was asking for a date and angling to get his hands on the meat again, wouldn't it? Well, he was.

Paul said, 'See ya around, Jimbo.' It sounded friendly enough. Perhaps he was shy, like Megan. This gay stuff, bi stuff, was obviously new to him.

Jim said, 'Yeah' and hung up. He almost wished he'd stayed on in Wales, if only for Dad's sake and Megan's.

Flu had also depleted the workforce at Pembertons. Jim spent Friday filling in for various absentees. He restacked

286

some timber in the frozen yard and helped Ken Bishop, the sewing-room supervisor, unpack a leather delivery from Morocco. The leather smelt hot, exotic, spicy.

Another come-on from Leanne in the canteen. She boasted to her workmates that Jim was the first unmarried man she'd gone with who had a mortgage (some of the others saw more of the bailiffs than of their landlords).

After lunch he went on the large ripsaw, his favourite of the factory's heavy machinery. After last week's shudders and groans the new blade fairly sang through 30-foot tree trunks with a whistling cry. A few orders had trickled in from the salesmen's last runs of 2003 and from two of Paul's continental customers. So far there had never been a big enough load for a cross-Channel run by Charlie or his son; a local haulage company took them. It might be fun to try lay-byes in France; he'd heard good reports.

Mid-afternoon he looked up and there was Paul just inside the door to the assembly area with Morris the fore-man. He was wearing ripped-up jeans and a windcheater, using only one crutch today; his arm wasn't in the sling. He waved at Jim but carried on talking to Morris. Jim waved back. He guessed that Paul had been much clucked over by the hens in the sewing room. Were he and Saffron still playing their movie-dialogue game?

The saw gave a sudden scream and began to throw off sparks. Jim pushed the red stop-button before raising a section of the guard mesh to peer into the cut. Nothing visible but there must be a piece of metal – hunters' bullets were common in Canadian pine – embedded in the wood. He gave the log, one half of a tree trunk, a hefty kick to alter the cutting angle and lowered the guard before returning to the control panel. Splinters splattered into the mesh as the log rumbled on with no more sparks. Jim wiped his sweating forehead on his shirtsleeve. The heating was too high; no wonder people were getting flu. His throat was dry. Dust danced in the air with the pounding of the machines. As the now quartered segments emerged from the mesh tunnel, Harry Smallwood and another of the footballers heaved them across to the rollers of the smaller ripsaw which would slice them into usable planks.

Leaning heavily on the single crutch Paul was watching Morris do something to the dowelling machine. Harry and

Pete helped Jim manoeuvre the other half of the tree trunk against the saw-blade and then went back to the smaller saw. Jim was moving to the far end when the blade shrieked again as it bit into more metal. Paul, now heading his way, paused to speak to Harry and Pete: football talk, you can bet. Defying safety regulations Jim lifted the guard with the machine still running. The rollers growled while the saw spat out a stream of sparks like a firework. He gave the log another kick and as it resumed moving he stretched up to pull the guard down.

The splinter that flew under the raised guard was some fifteen inches long with an average width of half an inch. It caught Jim below the chest at an angle of forty-five degrees. Approximately four inches of unseasoned pine burst through his abdominal muscle with the force of an arrow, puncturing his stomach and entering his right lung. The guard fell as he let go, landing with a crash that reverberated through the warehouse.

He sank to his knees and toppled onto his side on the dusty floor, clutching the huge splinter where it entered him and drawing up his knees to reduce the hot fierce pain. He was conscious of running feet, of heads and hands and horrified voices, of the whistling of the saw as it relinquished the timber. Someone punched the button and the whistling faded. It seemed to Jim that something within him was receding with the noise of the saw-blade. Only the pain kept him in the here-and-now, lying in sawdust on cold concrete, surrounded by his workmates. There was a coppery taste in his mouth. Blood trickled between his lips as he exhaled.

'Don't let him pull on the splinter,' a voice said: Ken Bishop's voice. 'He'll drown in his own blood.' Ken was senior First Aider since Aunty Lil retired at Christmas. Saffron was being trained up by the St John's people. Harry Smallwood knelt down and folded a jacket into a pillow under Jim's head. He slid one hand under Jim's hands where they clasped the splinter against his body.

'Hang in there, Jim,' Harry said: a line from a hundred movies. From the faces looking down at him above Harry's Jim forced one into focus: the face he associated with the three-way party with the Spanish slag, the highlight of his sexual career, a fantasy thrillingly fulfilled. Fair hair but not as fair as his own, a wide sexy mouth that had kissed him only last weekend, a kiss that he would remember for the rest of his life – if he had one.

'Oh, Jimmy, what 'ave you gone an' done?' A female voice: Leanne. There were women in the throng around him now. Saffron, black leather, purple lippie, knelt beside him. Her hands replaced Harry's under Jim's hands where the splinter pierced him; it felt like hot metal inside his body.

'Take it easy, Jim,' Saffron said. Nothing against her or Harry, but he wished Paul was holding him. Paul wouldn't be able to kneel. He tried to find Paul again in the ceiling of faces above him. It must look like a scene out of *East-Enders* or *Corrie*, he thought; they always have a crowd round anybody who collapses in the street, in the market.

'Ambulance is on its way,' somebody said. 'Five or ten minutes.' This kicked off a babble of conversation. Out of the babble he fixed on one fragment – an older female voice, one of the sewing machinists, it couldn't be Aunty Lil but it sounded like her:

'...all 'is life in front of 'im...'

Jim seized on this fragment. He reviewed his short life and its highlights which seemed to be mostly sex: girls in bars and bedsits and beach-huts; boys behind the school bogs and men in woods and cars and toilets; the three-some with the Spanish tart; Paul passed out on the sofa, Paul naked on his bed in the light from the landing. What else was there? Mum and Dad and all Dad's MGs and now his sweet little girl Megan. He wished he'd stayed longer in Wales, made a friend of her, a real sister.

'Jim.' Somehow Paul had got down on one knee oppo-site Saffron. His face swam into focus. There were tears in his eyes. He took out a handkerchief and wiped the blood off Jim's mouth. Jim half wished Paul would kiss him again but of course it was impossible in front of all these people.

'Hey, Paul,' he croaked, spitting blood. He wanted to say Sorry, but he hadn't got the breath for it. Breathing was hard. Sorry for this stupid mess? Sorry for the two blowjobs? Whatever.

'Don't try to talk, Jim,' Saffron said. Her voice seemed to come from a distance.

All his life in front of him. What life? He'd lost Dad to dear little Megan who needed him more than Jim did, although it would be nice to see what kind of woman she grew up to be. He could marry Leanne and have kids of his own, although he had a pretty keen idea of what kind of woman she would turn into. Paul wouldn't be in his life for long: he would slip off and marry somebody else while Jim drifted into the life of the unhappily married men and the sad old poofs who came on to him in woods and toilets. Not much joy in any of these visions of the life that lay ahead, was there? Wrapping his fingers more tightly around the protruding length of pine, he tugged it out of his body, through Saffron's hands. 'No, Jim, don't,' she said; too late. The pain evaporated instantly and was replaced by a weird rushing sensation that was not un-pleasant. He gulped for air and tasted blood.

The splinter dropped to the floor. Jim seized Paul's hands, blood dripping from his hands onto Paul's denims. Paul leaned down as if he intended to kiss Jim in front of all these people. Jim started to say 'Don't' but what came out of his mouth was not speech but a thick bubble of blood. He felt himself racing into something that wasn't darkness or light but was somehow darkness *and* light.

Leanne screamed. Saffron continued to hold Jim's head in her lap. One of the women put a hand on her shoulder. Tears fell steadily from Paul's chin onto the face below him, mingling with the blood and the sawdust. No-one put a hand on his shoulder.

An electronic clock on the wall above the dowelling machine loudly chimed five times, indicating the end of shift for those workers, the majority, who had come in at 8.30. An eight-hour shift plus half-an-hour, unpaid, for lunch.

Part Three

18. Clinic

Christine went off a cliff at about 14.45 on a brutally cold Saturday in mid-December. Her death was a bizarre accident, but if it weren't for me she wouldn't have been in that place at that time, and this gives me an inescapable feeling that, however unintentionally, I killed her.

Jim died at my feet on a dusty factory floor at the stroke of five p.m. on the second Friday in January, pulling the stake that had impaled him through Saffron's fingers. Had he left it to be removed surgically he would be alive today, which presumably is not what he wanted.

By the beginning of April, after twelve weeks of drug therapy and psychoanalysis at a private clinic in Hove, I knew that whatever it was I needed to get back to (Higher Education was faintly calling) it wasn't my shopaholic slag of a wife or my uncle's overpriced sofa-beds. Sanctuary would not be found in Boredom-on-Sea. Abandoning a well-paid job that had been kept open for me, the car (cars) that went with it and all my worldly goods (stored at The Grange), I packed only the clothes and CDs I had with me at the clinic and said goodbye to my shrink and the nursing staff. A taxi took me to Hove station where I caught a mid-morning train to Victoria.

The sale of the house I grew up in, my father's offices and other inherited assets had endowed me with more money than I might ever have again. My soon-to-be-ex-wife was not claiming alimony but I gave her half the proceeds of selling the family home to unshackle her (if only for a year or two) from the step-parental purse-strings. Would she use this money to get her life on some sort of track or piss it away on shopping and foreign travel? (Did I care?) Between them she and the taxman relieved me of my brief millionaire status, leaving me still 'well-heeled' and 'fancy-free'. But I was motherless, fatherless, loveless and loverless. Only time would tell if I had learned any lessons from the lovers Fate had, within months of each other, thrown into my path and, within weeks of each other, removed – permanently – from my clutches.

But thirteen years of bigamy and adultery didn't seem to have given Christine many insights into the ways of men, and bisexuality had apparently brought Jim not the best but the worst of both worlds.

Southern rail franchises keep changing, so I'm not sure which company conveyed me out of Sussex. The view, leaving the bracketed city of Brighton & Hove, was of houses, flats and office blocks; then a tunnel through the South Downs, a glimpse of woodland, a motorway bridge; fields and farmland, grazing sheep.

The land of my birth and of my marriage, but not – narrowly – of my death.

Am I trying to draw a parallel between my leaving Sussex on a morning in April that held the promise of burgeoning spring and my leaving university on a Siberian afternoon two Februaries earlier? Thanks to the restorative powers of Class-A antidepressants, hours of analysis and time's trusty healing magic I was, if not purged of guilt (would I ever be? did I deserve to be?), at least able to make the decision to quit my home and my career in a rational frame of mind. (I claim no credit for ending my marriage; my wife pre-empted that decision.) Leaving uni, I'd been running away; this time I hoped I was running *to* something rather than *from* something. What I was running towards was as yet uncertain.

'Why do you feel responsible for Christine's death?' the shrink had repeatedly asked. And, 'How is it you blame yourself for Jim's accident?'

'Isn't it obvious?' I liked trying to beat him at his own game: answer a question with a question. Not that it ever worked.

'How is it obvious?'

And, like a police interrogation, back we would plod through the facts of the case. Cases; plural.

Caked in plaster and stuffed with painkillers in the days after my Diana-and-Dodi disaster at Beachy Head, I'd imagined that Charlie Turner had found out about his wife and me and had tampered – lethally - with the car. Jack he could tolerate, there was gold in that thar hill. Me he could not be doing with; Christine might leave him and terminate the lucrative arrangement with my uncle. Narcotized, delusional, I even wondered if *Jim* had loosened the propshaft, eliminating his stepmother to make me available, as indeed I soon was, for his own amorous advances. This theory was easily demolished: if Jim had heard the gossip about me and Christine he would know I'd been seen out in her car. If I hadn't been thrown through the broken door, I would still have been in the car when the cliff gave way and would have joined Christine in the sea and the rocks and the rubble. No, it wasn't Jim and it wasn't Charlie, but I had a harder time convincing myself – and the shrink – that it wasn't *my* fault.

Analysis is as redemptive as Calvary and treads a well-worn furrow.

'Your father was a bit of a martinet, you said?'

'Oh yes. He liked to see himself as standing shoulder-to-shoulder with Mrs Thatcher, but he was way off to her right side.'

'And your mother?'

'One of God's natural hand-wringers. I always wondered why she didn't take up bell-ringing at St Agnes's. She'd have been a natural.'

'They were both serious churchgoers?'

'Yes, C-of-E. Fairly high church, actually.'

'You had a religious upbringing?'

'Morning service, Sunday-School, grace before meals, the full Monty.'

'And how religious would you say you are now, on a scale of one to ten?'

I laugh. '*Minus nine*! You can't study history and believe in providence.'

'You can't?'

'Sorry, *Brother* Martin.' He smiles, allowing me the piss-take. Martin King, my shrink (his middle name isn't Luther), has told me he's a renegade monk. He reminds me of the smoking/drinking/*noir*-movie-addict Father Karras in *The Exorcist*. Martin gave up on theology and took up psychiatry – trading one load of mumbo-jumbo for another. 'Let's just say *I* can't.'

'You can't believe in God?'

'Can you?'

'Not all of it, but Him – yes, I still do.'

'I'm afraid those mysterious ways of His are too fucking mysterious for me,' I confess. 'Excuse my French. I suppose I could believe in the God of the Jews and the Muslims, a God who cuts your legs off at the knees if you step out of line. But the Christian concept of a loving, forgiving, redeeming God – no, He doesn't push my buttons any more, if He ever did. Do you know about the *Cathars*?'

I'm sure he does but he pretends not to. So off I go on a brief lecture about Albi and Carcassonne, the Manichean Heresy and the Crusade that extirpated it. The schoolmaster in me; is it Destiny calling? 'It's easier to see the Devil at work in the evil that men do than some accidental thwarting of God's plan,' I conclude.

'So you don't believe in God but you're okay with the Devil?'

'Yeah, and I still believe in magic lamps and the Tooth Fairy!' But I can see where he thinks I'm coming from. 'It's not God or Satan making me feel I'm responsible for what happened to Christine and Jim, it's just the plain fact that if they hadn't got involved with me they wouldn't be dead. I'm like some kind of Typhoid Mary or a dark-side King Midas: everyone who comes into contact with me gets to die or be seriously fucked up.'

This I do believe. I'm still having a hard time taking onboard the idea of life as a series of random events: the Shit-Happens theory. Shit sure does.

As the first twenty years of my life were autopsied in Martin King's cubbyhole consulting room, I had felt strangely numb, detached from these events, from the people I'd hurt or killed. Was it the drugs or was it me?

'What-if' moments. Life is full of them, I guess. What if I'd never asked Christine out to lunch, never kissed her, never fucked her, never licked her pussy that was so much juicier than my wife's. When Charlie had quit Sussex to go to his secret Welsh wife (why did I have to hear this from Jim and not Christine?), I like to think my uncle might have ditched Aunt Agnes (as desiccated as her daughter), sold the factory (which, two years from now, he will do anyway) and sailed off into a Caribbean sunset with Christine. (Aunt A. is going to get this HD 3D Plasma finale and I bet she hates it!)

I can't do a 'what-if' scenario for Jim. I don't know what constitutes a good outcome for bisexual men. I'm not one, although I may have pretended to be one for Jim because I felt bad that I hadn't done it for Neil. Do bi guys settle for one side or the other, or do they carry on playing for both teams - and how happy does that make them?

I'd thought for more than a year that I would never know what was in Neil's mind when he jumped off the Founder's Tower. As my train streaked through grey concrete Gatwick, I was only three hours away from discovering that there was an answer to this mystery, but I would never, never, know what was in Jim's mind when he pulled the vampire stake out of his chest and flooded his lungs with blood. Was the pain more than he could bear? Too simple, surely. Could he see (as I could not) the far horizon for a man like him and choose not to go there? Or, in the more immediate future, could he see that what I had allowed to start between us, horny as I was and fearful of the consequences if I rejected him, would inevitably – and soon – end? I wasn't gay. I wasn't even bi.

Neil and Jim. Meredith and Christine. I could throw my father into the pot as well, dying from an internal eruption as Uncle Jack sang my praises, the prodigal and despised second son. And my mother – I'd always thought her blind loyalty to Dad a sign that she was a bit demented, but she turned out to be more than a bit dementia'd. Charlie: losing two wives looked like carelessness! But one of them was entirely my fault. Uncle Jack, losing his mistress, condemned to his raddled stick of a wife. I hadn't set out to ruin Jack's life but ruin it I did.

Jennifer? I don't blame myself too much for Jenny; we were a match made in hell. Pembertons' little-league soccer team hardly stood comparison with Manchester United, but Jenny was clearly Boredom-on-Sea's version of a footballer's WAG: shopping and fucking were what she lived for. I had told her, several times, that I loved her but I'm not sure I even liked her. Had she loved me? I couldn't recall her ever saying it. Divorced from me I see her making other infernal matches, in America, anywhere. I think Jenny's problem was not so much that she *had* a dried-out cunt but that she *was* one.

I can't make sense of Jenny. I can't make sense of any of them: Christine, Jim, Uncle Jack, my parents. Could *they* understand *me*? I'm not sure I understand myself.

I can no longer recall the moment – or the mental state – that induced me to take a knife to my veins. Did I seriously want to execute myself in order to pay for my manifold sins and wickedness or was it a poor-me call for help? What was in Marilyn Monroe's mind or Kurt Cobain's when they reached for the pills, the shotgun?

Lacrimae rerum. This vale of fucking tears. Old Virgil was right: life's a bitch and you wind up dead. And somewhere in between everything goes tits-up. (I can't quite translate that last bit into Latin.)

It was time for the dropout to drop back in. But not in Sussex. I was dropping out of Sussex, like Lot leaving Sodom.

As the wheels clattered over the multiple points of Streatham and Balham and Clapham, those 'evocatively' named inner boroughs, a cacophony of ghostly voices may have been cursing my name:
'*Murderer.*'
'*Father/mother-killer.*'
'*Cunt-licker.*'
'*Cocksucker.*' (Not true, Your Honour! Not that.)
'*Life-wrecker.*'
But if they were, I couldn't hear them.

The train rattled across the Thames, as silvery today as the glistening pods on the Millennium Wheel, and into Victoria, unhappy blend of cathedral and mall. A wait in an ethnically diverse taxi queue and then the crawl towards Hyde Park Corner and Park Lane, where we speeded up. Beside us the park, ripening green. I'd told the driver to find me a hotel in Bayswater.

'You want five-stars, mate?' Was he a Cockney or just naturally insolent?

'Three will do.' My new wealth hadn't gone to my head.

Turning off the Bayswater Road he stopped outside something that wasn't quite *Fawlty Towers*, but the Edwardian façade and porticoed entrance could have been transported from the seafront of Boredom-on-Sea.

Plus ça change.

19. Bayswater

I hadn't come to Bayswater to look for Rachel. Rachel was gone. After Jenny found some texts from her on my mobile I let a few weeks go by before calling, but she didn't reply to my voicemails and texts. When I tried again in March, surfacing from my breakdown, I got an Unable-to-connect message. Had she changed her number? By now she had married Richard. Perhaps, after the West End play, he'd gone back to LA and taken her and Simon with him.

Emerging from my tranquillized twilight zone, I'd fixed on London as the place I would run to, not just passing through but starting over. I would apply to a new university, then start a new career in something (anything) that didn't require salesmanship. It didn't have to be London, just as long as it wasn't Boredom-on-Sea.

My inheritance wouldn't run to a flat in Hampstead or Chelsea, and anyway I didn't yearn to live among the glitterati and Hooray Henries. Nor could I see myself joining the Primrose Hill intelligentsia or Islington's disaffected New Labour missionaries. I wasn't Hugh Grant or Jude Law, but I thought I might be a Notting Hill kind of guy. According to the property papers, Notting Hill now embraces some formerly downmarket outlands; a flat in Ladbroke Grove or Shepherds Bush would leave enough of my capital to see me through college and able to afford a car and maybe a second wife. Even children. Finding someone to share it with was the most important aspect of this new life.

My room in the not-quite-Fawlty Towers hotel, like other rooms I'd occupied last year, combined hints of Post-

Modernism and 'retro-chic' with a few touches that were just plain naff. Laura Ashley upholstery, a flat-screen TV, a Vettriano print (the couple under a parasol on the beach). I hung up my anorak, left my case unpacked and went out onto the street in my college-boy leather jacket.

After Paris and Strasbourg and Madrid, restaurant prices have lost their power to shock me. A chicken salad wrap in a Lebanese café on Queensway was the price of a family meal in a Pizza Hut. I drank juice. This was only my third day off medication and I was wary of drinking alcohol. At least a dozen different languages were spoken around me in the time it took to eat my lunch. There were Jews as well as Arabs on the pavements. Détente in our time. Not in Iraq, of course: our missiles had won the war, but their loony mullahs and brainwashed kamikaze kids were an unstoppable obstacle to peace.

I hadn't come to Bayswater to look for Rachel, but half an hour later I was sitting on a bench in Hyde Park. It wasn't the same bench or even in the same part of the park. It wasn't the same time of day. It's possible that I carry the gene for mental instability (my mother had tried to dig up my father's body!) but what drew me to the park was not obsessive-compulsive disorder. Here a Samaritan had found me at a bad time in my life. Perhaps another would find me today at what was, I hoped, the beginning of better times.

I wasn't the same person who sat on a bench near here fifteen months ago. Or if I was, I felt as distant from him as from the person - another version of me - who climbed into a hot bath in my parents' house (my own brief marital home) three months ago and took a kitchen knife to his veins. Two things saved me: I didn't cut deeply enough (it was more a cry for help than a dash for the exit) and my borrowed housekeeper came back with some Pemberton leftovers. If the suicide lives on inside me, he is kept in check – as, I hope, is the predator who jumped on Meredith and Alison.

At my own instigation, towards the end of my time in Brother Martin's care I'd written a letter to Meredith, telling her how truly-deeply sorry I was for what I'd done to her, hoping she was okay now and would one day forgive me. *I know I don't deserve to be forgiven*, I wrote.

I'm not sure if I can forgive myself. (Oh Paul: crafty even when contrite!) The letter came back a week later marked *RTS – return to sender.* I couldn't tell if the writing was hers. In evangelical America there is apparently no redemption for the wannabe date-rapist. But writing the letter was an important part of my recovery, Martin said when I told him. I felt like the drunk who stands up at his first AA meeting and finally admits to his love of bottled oblivion. I didn't write to Alison or her dad, the undertaker (who had come close to sealing me into one of his medium-range coffins).

I was, I truly believed, an *ex*-predator, an ex-murderer, an ex-wrecker of people's lives. I had resolved to be a better man from now on.

So there I was, on a bench in Hyde Park (Kensington Gardens, to be precise), within sound of the Bayswater Road traffic and within sight of a toilet block outside of which two people had left their dogs tied to railings, yapping at each other. The sun shone weakly. A light breeze whipped a froth of pink blossom from the cherry trees. The fauna of the park flowed about me: chirruping birds and foraging squirrels, nannies and parents, workers and tourists, courting couples and solo cruisers, a few weirdos.

And, just like that, a voice said: 'Hello, Paul.'

I remembered him from the drama group, a nerdy freshman in glasses, an aspiring playwright whom we'd used as an ASM. Dave Something; doing French and German. Now the glasses were gone (contacts?) and in place of college-boy grunge he wore a dark suit.

'Dave. Hi. Shouldn't you be at a lecture?'

He smiled and sat down on the bench. His shoes were so highly polished that you could see to put your lenses in. A different kind of nerdiness.

'I've followed your example and chucked it in.'

Dave was another Sussex lad. His hometown was a few miles inland from Boredom-on-Sea. He'd dropped out in December, he told me, had found a crash pad with friends in London and a temporary job in Selfridges in the run-up to Christmas. Now they'd put him on a trainee management course.

'Bit of a waste of all that Molière and Goethe,' I said.

He grinned. 'Tell me about it. What have you been

300

doing since you left?'

'Selling leather furniture to shops on the continent. My uncle's firm.' I left out the bit about Jack also being my father-in-law. Jenny, my failed marriage; don't go there. 'Not much of a link to Will Shakespeare and Adolph Hitler,' I said, 'although I did get an order in Berlin. I think dropping out was a mistake. I'm going to try and get back to uni.'

'What, back to –'

'No way I'll try and get into one of the London colleges.'

'And then what?' A pair of young Arabs went by with two giggling English girls. Perhaps if instead of missiles and cluster bombs we sent in wave after wave of prime English pussy, we could win over hearts and minds in Iraq and Afghanistan.

'Teaching, I guess.' A spontaneous answer, but not quite an epiphany – the Bayswater Road leading suddenly to Damascus. During my months of hawking Uncle Jack's wares around Europe I had come to realize that the life plan I'd turned my back on when I fled the scene of my Midlands crimes - a plan that seemed to have been mapped out by others: my headmaster, my father - was in fact the logical progression of my intellectual development, my natural 'bent'. It was time to set my life back on this track. I would graduate from a different university and then I would teach English and History to new generations of chavs and middle-class slobs, a handful of whom would value my lessons and go on to make something of their lives – as, hopefully, would I.

As I vocalized this reinstated scenario, I imagined Mum and Dad cheering me on from their chalky resting-place; and Trevor from his granite one so far away, the brother who had cast such a huge shadow over my life. Trevor died at the age of twenty years and four months; I had now outlived him by a little over a month.

Dave updated me on the drama group and the productions they'd done last year. He'd written a stage play which several agents had read and rejected, and was now writing a television drama about a group of anti-war student demonstrators (*Yawn*). At uni I'd suspected he had a crush on Meredith but today I was picking up a gay vibe. Jim had fine-tuned my 'gaydar'. Dave didn't mention

Meredith, but then he did bring up a painful name.

'Do you ever think about Neil Fraser?'

I felt my throat tighten. 'Yes,' I said.

'It's a small world. Me running into you like this in my lunch break. One of my flatmates is from Bristol. Went to the same school as Neil. They weren't friends but they knew each other. His death was just terrible, wasn't it?'

'Yes,' I said again.

'I forgot, you were there – right where he fell.'

I almost said, *I was meant to be*, but I did not want to be having this conversation. 'Yes,' I said. A quartet of bearded Arabs went by, talking loudly and with a lot of gesticulation. No girls with them. Were they plotting a raid tonight on some bimbo-packed club or disco, or something deadlier?

'You didn't go the inquest?' Dave asked.

'No, I wasn't called.'

'Neither was I. But we may be the only people who know why he did it.'

'Are we?' I so wanted to get up and walk away, but my leg ached from the walking I'd already done. I would be limping when I stood up and I didn't want to have to tell Dave about the accident. Christine, Jim too; let's not go there either. We were already opening one can of worms.

He picked up on something in my tone. 'You don't know?'

'Are you so sure you do?'

'Well, I know you and he were close. He had a bit of a schoolgirl crush on you.' I wanted to smack him for that 'schoolgirl'. 'Surely he must have told you his "Big Secret"?' His fingers supplied quote marks. I shook my head. 'About his brother?'

'Neil had a brother? He told me he was an only child.'

'He had a brother called Adrian; a year older than him. We got bladdered in his room one night and he told me he and Adrian were - lovers.'

'His brother - seduced him?'

'Neil said he was the one who made the running. I don't think it was anything very heavy. Just some, you know, fooling around. His brother probably wasn't even gay. But Neil was very – what's the word? – *fixated* on him. He said you totally reminded him of this dead brother.'

'His brother *died*? How?'

'He was motorbike crazy. Neil loved to ride pillion with him. I suppose the, you know, *holding-on* was a turn-on. Anyway, in the summer before we all met at uni – Neil wasn't with him – Adrian came off his bike on a dangerous bend and went under a lorry. In the Cotswolds, I believe it was.'

'I can't think why he didn't tell me about this,' I said. 'If it's true.'

'Why wouldn't it be true?'

Because I didn't want it to be true. 'In any case,' I pointed out, 'it doesn't explain why he killed himself.'

'I think it does. Especially since he practically jumped on top of you off the Tower. He wanted you to replace his dead brother, but you weren't up for it. Neil couldn't live with that, so –' He pantomimed Neil's ghastly leap with his hands.

'If you're not kidding me, I think Neil was kidding you,' I said. A Mediterranean-looking guy in a grey cord jacket glanced at us as he walked by. Dave's eyes followed him. The man went into the Gents. One of the dogs was still tied up outside.

'I don't think you kid about something this big,' Dave said. 'Anyway, I have to get back to work.'

We said goodbye and he walked off. Not this year's Samaritan; more of an Ancient Mariner, with a tale to tell. I watched as he too went into the loo. I began flexing my leg, so that it wouldn't let me down when I stood up.

I didn't want to believe what he'd said. Gay incest. How could Neil open up to a near stranger about this sick secret when he had me to confide in? He'd wounded me from beyond the grave.

Neil's infatuation for me – and that final, fatal kiss in my room - had fuelled my last assault on Meredith and led to my dropping out to go home to Sussex and all that was waiting to happen there. Now his infatuation – and his death - had another, darker edge. He hadn't yearned for *me*, he'd yearned for me to be someone else, this dead brother he'd never told me about. I felt somehow *diminished*. I didn't want to believe Dave, but I did.

If I'd closed my eyes for Neil the way I had for Jim, would he still be alive today, perhaps getting over his 'schoolgirl crush', recovering from this ghoulish obsession with a dead sibling, getting on with his life? Don't go there, Paul. I wish I hadn't done it for Jim. There was no point wishing I *had* done it for Neil. His life, like mine, was over-shadowed by a dead brother. My father wanted me to be another Trevor. Neil wanted me to be another Adrian. I'd failed them both, but it wasn't my fault. You can't be somebody else; you can only be you.

Dave came out of the Gents with the guy in the cord jacket. Neil had said that gay partnerships often started from the most unpromising of pick-ups. Perhaps Dave had just met the love of his life.

It was time to look for mine.

Who am I kidding? I *had* come to Bayswater and Hyde Park for no other reason than to try and find Rachel. It was possible she hadn't married Richard. For her sake as much as for mine I hoped she hadn't. Married to a man she knew was bisexual, wondering about his occasional clumsily excused absences - and those nights when he turned away from her - how happy could she be?

Brother Martin had told me that in the US in 1948, way before Gay Lib hit the streets and pornography went main-stream, Dr Kinsey's researches had revealed that thirty-seven percent of adult men admitted to having had a homosexual experience up to orgasm. About ten percent were gay and (Martin's estimate rather than Kinsey's) a similar percentage bisexual, but the total of gays and bisexuals was matched by a similar number who'd at least given it a go. As, now, had I – with Jim. But I knew that what I'd allowed Jim to do didn't make me gay, and I don't think it made me bi. I hoped there would never be another Jim in my life, but if there was he'd have to sink or swim on his own. I didn't save Neil, who hadn't had his way with me, and I didn't save Jim, who had. Perhaps only gays and bi's can save each other, and perhaps they can't. Perhaps we all have to find our own reason to live – or not to.

There was a dull throbbing pain in my leg but I man-aged not to limp as I walked down to the Serpentine. A young mother was feeding the ducks near the Peter Pan statue and smiled at me as I passed; she had blonde-streaked hair and her child was still a toddler in a push-chair. On the other side of the tunnel under the road bridge I found the Diana Fountain. My first impression was that it looked grey and brutal in the thin sunlight. A dozen worshippers and tourists were photographing themselves at the shrine. If the rivulet was an obvious metaphor - the Circle of Life - it was naïvely inappropriate for Diana whose life, like mine, had been a series of zigzags, driven by the machinations and infatuations of others - as well as her own (*our* own) infatuations.

I struggled up the incline to the top where the water bubbled up as if from a spring. To one side a formal cascade, to the other rapids that tumbled over hollows and protuberances carved into the Cornish granite. The circle was two interlocked semicircles; did they symbolize the dichotomy of the Princess's life: royal protocol and her turbulent quest for love? Love versus duty; in my own way I too had been torn between other people's expectations and the need to find a self of my own to be true to.

Two pigeons waddled off the surround into the deceptively calm stretch between the spring and the waterfall. Caught in the current they flapped their wings and flew out, scattering water that fell in momentarily sparkling rainbow drops. *Make a wish*, my mother always said. I wished, fervently: let me find love, or let love find me. Nothing else mattered.

Get going, Paul. Move on.

It's a huge park. Even if they were here, we could miss each other by minutes or metres. And as I stumbled on towards Kensington Palace and the area that had been carpeted with flowers and teddy-bears during the weeks of the Great Grieving, Rachel and Simon might be having their morning walk in Griffith Park or another of LA's open spaces. Was I tormenting my broken leg – and my bruised heart – for nothing, for something that could never be?

Married or not, Rachel was as likely to be in Bayswater as in Beverly Hills or Brentwood. She could have lost her mobile, had it stolen or changed the number because of nuisance calls or spam texts.

No other Samaritan would do. Really limping now, I returned to Queensway and found her street, found her building. Next obstacle: I'd forgotten her flat number and I had never known her surname. If she'd moved someone might know where she had gone. I was trying to work out which of the sixteen buttons belonged to third-floor residents when a young voice called my name from twenty yards away; not in English:

'*Paolo*!'

Had his mother prompted him or had he remembered his lesson in the pizzeria? His pronunciation was as good as any *ragazzo* from Bologna or Brooklyn. I turned my head. They were coming from the other direction, from Notting Hill.

'*See-moan-ay*!'

I took a few painful steps towards them, then – pure agony - knelt and held out my arms. He threw himself at me. Tears filled my eyes as I hugged him fiercely. Shampoo had left a smell in his hair, the pure scent of boyhood just as crushed grass on a dog's paws is the quintessential odour of puppyhood. Rachel joined us, put down a hand and ruffled my hair. Her own hair had been cut to pageboy length, reminiscent of the young Lady Di, but it was still the colour of an autumnal New England maple.

'Why are you limping?'

'Broke my leg last December. Car smash.' I would tell her all about the accident, about Christine and Jim, two more deaths on my conscience, other lives wrecked. I would tell her that I'd come to see myself as a destructive force, like Shiva, that I ruined the life of everyone who came near me. Somehow Rachel would bring me absolution. She would tell me – what? – that you can't blame the flame for the moths who fly too close to it and get burned? Maybe she would remind me that shit happens and some of us survive it and some of us do not.

'But you're okay now?'

'Oh yes,' I said. I stood up, Simon still clinging to me, kissing me. I kissed him back. This boy needs a father; does he have one? I was now face-to-face with his mother. I liked her new look. Her clothes – black jeans, a snazzier brown leather jacket than mine – surely came from a designer shop, not from Oxfam. Among the detritus I'd abandoned in Uncle Jack's garage was the off-white linen suit from Paul Smith that I'd been married in, chosen by Jenny; it encapsulated the makeover she'd wrought on me. Richard, with the money from *EastEnders*, had revamped Rachel. *Where was Richard*?

'How's your marriage?' Rachel asked.

'It's over. Divorce pending.' Simon was heavy. I put him down. He ran towards their building and waved through the railings at someone in the basement. 'How's yours?' I reciprocated. She smiled, and was beautiful.

'Over before it happened. He got cold feet and a new boyfriend. Not necessarily in that order. He's gone to do a play in New York.'

'My wife's gone to New York. New boyfriend too, I guess. Perhaps they'll run into each other!'

'Yeah, and become the best of friends. And talk about us!' She laughed. I liked that 'us'. 'So, are you coming in?'

'Am I invited?'

'Provided you behave yourself.'

'I'm not sure about that. Am I allowed to kiss you when we get inside?'

'You don't need to wait till then,' she said and leaned in towards me. Her lips were moist and trembling slightly. I kept my tongue to myself; good behaviour. Our heads parted and we smiled into each other's eyes. A few hours from now, after the boy went to bed, I would unleash Major Wood, that sleeping beauty, from his four-month hibernation and fuck her. No – I would *make love* to her. It wouldn't be amazing, we might not set the Thames on fire – there could be some awkwardness, some clumsiness - but it would be *good*. And being good would make it – perfect. I hoped she would let me stay the night, not go back to the hotel. Tomorrow morning I'd wake to find her still quietly beside me, perhaps with Simon snuggled on her other side – or mine. While she fixed our breakfast Simon and I would play Happy Families on the kitchen table or run his cars around on the floor. After breakfast we might go to the park and feed the ducks.

Happy Families.

I know. It's not what I deserve. Life's a *bitch*.

SHAIKH-DOWN

David Gee

A sassy American airhostess and a gay British banker help their Arab boyfriends to kick-start a revolution on the imaginary island of Belaj in the Persian Gulf. An Arab princess's life takes surprising turns before and after the coup, as does her brother's, the Emir's Chief of Security.

David Gee's 'blueprint' (fairly blue and not PC) centres on the Emir's bedchamber and offers swifter, less brutal Regime Change than current events seem to predict for the region.

* * * * * * * * * * * * * * *

"*Witty, entertaining, raunchy and very well written.*"
Peter O'Donnell, creator of *Modesty Blaise*

"*Ribald and politically incorrect. Set in a fictitious but absolutely believable Arab state where sheikhs and their minions are locked in a life-and-death struggle to survive the relentless move towards democracy. Entertaining.*" **GAY TIMES**

"*Probably a Zionist plot masterminded by the CIA to undermine the good image of morally irreproachable Gulf Arabs.*" **GULF TIMES**

* * * * * * * * * * * *

Available from bookshops and from Amazon

and as an e-book from Smashwords

2012 is the 50th anniversary of the Cuba Crisis.

* * * * *

THE BEXHILL MISSILE CRISIS

David Gee

'If only, *Evelyn would think later: if only there hadn't been the bother in Cuba; if only she'd stayed in London or insisted on going to Amsterdam with her husband; if only she hadn't knocked the Horseman of the Apocalypse and his friend off their motorbike: the week might have turned out very differently.'*

* * * * *

to be published later this year